The Best Short Stories 2022

The Best
Short Stories
2022

The O. Henry Prize Winners

Guest Editor:
Valeria Luiselli

Series Editor:
Jenny Minton Quigley

Anchor Books
A Division of Penguin Random House LLC
New York

AN ANCHOR BOOKS ORIGINAL 2022

Anchor Books Trade Paperback ISBN: 978-0-593-46754-1
eBook ISBN: 978-0-593-46755-8

anchorbooks.com

Printed in the United States of America
10   9   8   7   6

*To my niece María—my ferocious reading companion
in these past pandemic years*

—Valeria Luiselli

Contents

Foreword

Terms of eligibility can be as revealing through those they exclude as through those they welcome. The first O. Henry Prize collection, published in 1919, ruled out all non-American writers. Yet in that very first edition, series editor Blanche Colton Williams called attention to several accomplished stories that she regretted were ineligible for consideration. Jacke Wilson, host of the *History of Literature* podcast, recently unearthed Williams's introduction to that 1919 O. Henry collection and found in it this admission: "According to the terms which omit foreign authors from possible participation in the prize, the work of Achmed Abdullah, Britten Austin, Elinor Mordaunt and others was in effect non-existent for the Committee." Williams goes on to describe at length the three missing stories by these authors, highlighting their unfortunate absence from the book and from the prize.

Over the next decades at least one expansion was made to the eligibility rules for the O. Henry Prize. It is not clear exactly when this happened, but in 1955 a student in Florida mentioned in her master's thesis on the O. Henry series that "foreign-born authors were eligible if they became U.S. citizens." In the 1990s the prize was further opened to Canadian writers. We can guess that the motivation for that may have been to allow consideration of stories by the widely acclaimed Canadian short story writer (and future Nobel laureate) Alice Munro. A further expansion came in 2003 under the ninth series editor, Laura Furman. The *Publishers Weekly* review of the 2003 edition noted, "A new, wider-ranging selection process (allowing the consideration of all English-language writers appearing in North American publications regardless of citizenship) makes this one of the strongest O. Henry collections in recent years, with stories by, among others, Chimamanda Ngozi Adichie."

Nineteen years later, the guest editor for the 2022 volume, Valeria Luiselli, has selected a brand-new story by Chimamanda Ngozi Adichie, along with ten remarkable stories in translation. This means that fully half of the winning stories this year are artistic collaborations with talented translators who enable readers of English to enjoy fiction originally crafted in Bengali, Greek, Hebrew, Norwegian, Polish, Russian, and Spanish. The subjects of this year's twenty winning stories are predictably varied, but many touch on the pandemic, love, and loss, though there is also humor, and their appeal is universally human.

A century ago, the writer O. Henry popularized stories about the downtrodden and humble during a time when fictional protagonists belonged mostly to high society. In 1906, he titled his second collection *The Four Million* in response to an op-ed written by Ward McAllister in *The New York Times* claiming that New York City had only four hundred people worth getting to know. O. Henry believed that the stories of all four million people then residing in New York City were worthwhile, and *The Four Million* includes his best-known story, "The Gift of the Magi," about poor newlyweds in the city who sacrifice their favorite belongings for love. Ward McAllister has recently resurfaced in a new television series, *The Gilded Age*. In the show created by Julian Fellowes and set in New York during the 1880s, McAllister—played by Nathan Lane—is the gatekeeper for the socialite Mrs. Astor, who famously could fit four hundred people in her ballroom. When O. Henry arrived in New York in 1902, bars more than ballrooms were his scene. As he labored under the conviction that elite writing need not be elitist, it seems apt and exciting that *The Best Short Stories 2022: The O. Henry Prize Winners* celebrates ordinary people, though now on a more global scale. One can imagine O. Henry would be pleased by the continual expansion of his namesake prize and that Blanche Colton Williams would see the series she helped launch—the oldest literary prize for short fiction in America—as moving in the right direction.

Readers of English have relied on translated stories at least since the Bible, and yet translations have long taken a backseat in our culture. If stories give us a window through which to momentarily enter the soul of another person, then translated stories magically transcend the limits of the language that has shaped our consciousness. What I learned from Valeria Luiselli this year is nothing short of how to read in a new way. I learned to dissolve my previous conception of "successful" (perhaps tidy) literary translation and open the borders of my thinking to the living, dynamic melding of languages undertaken by the translators here in a way that opens one's capacity to engage with literature and language generally. For every story is a work of translation, if only from thought to page and then into the reader's particular consciousness.

I am grateful that Valeria has led the O. Henry Prize toward the removal of geographical requirements for eligibility and congratulate the thirty O. Henry Prize–winning artists of 2022, both writers and translators. Valeria, I hope readers everywhere are inspired by your brilliant vision.

—Jenny Minton Quigley

Introduction

A little over a century ago, in 1919, the first O. Henry series editor, Blanche Colton Williams, explained in an introduction much like this one that the committee of the newly created O. Henry Prize had agreed upon these two seemingly simple rules: "the story must be the work of an American author, and must first appear in 1919 in an American publication." One hundred years later—one hundred and two, to be precise—during what seemed like an eternal second wave of the COVID pandemic, I was asked to guest-edit the following year's iteration of the O. Henry Prizes. One fundamental thing had changed about the prize over the years: the clause "American author" had been replaced by simply "author," and just last year the prize became open to work in translation. That alone was reason enough for me to accept.

What had seemed like a simple rule, "American author/American publication," had, over the years, accumulated a number of absurd consequences, such as the automatic exclusion of foreign-born authors who had been living, sometimes entire lifetimes, in the United States, or, simply, the exclusion of authors who were published and read widely in the United States and therefore formed part of the literary culture—except that they didn't have a

U.S. birth certificate. This exclusion of course persists, even today, in several national prizes.

The idea of a "national literature" as a monolithic, pure, uncontaminated collection of work by people who hold the same passport is ludicrous. Imposing upon literature rules written in some government office, in a nation's obscure and labyrinthine immigration system, is not only absurd but simply contrary to the very nature of literature. And part of that nature is to travel—across borders, despite borders. We write and read not in order to engage with an idea of nationhood but to engage with the human soul and human stories more generally. But somehow we continue to nod to the arbitrary consensus of "national literature," just as we forget that "American" means "from the continent named America" and not just from one country within the continent. (Perhaps, in the not-too-distant future, the *Best American* series will seize the opportunity their name contains and include work by authors from the entire American continent.) In any case, that the O. Henry decided to do away with its national clause is, I hope, part of a wider trend in understanding literature and the literary ecology as a complex, beautifully messy thing and not one that fits neatly in the pages of a passport. A movement in this direction is surely overdue and particularly needed after these past years of xenophobia, hate, and an asphyxiating nationalist discourse that certainly did not make America anything but more isolated and lonely.

I spent the second half of the year 2021 reading a selection of eighty stories, published in a wide array of journals. Of the eighty stories I was sent, twenty were translated from other languages. The ratio was not ideal, but it was not bad, considering that still today, only approximately 3 percent of the books published in the United States are in translation. (I imagine that in literary magazines, unless they are specifically devoted to seeking out translated work, the number is even lower.) Editors acquire far less material in foreign languages, either because most are still mono-lingual and cannot base their decisions on directly reading origi-nals, or because they believe that the niche for work in translation is smaller and less profitable, or because there are a number of unconscious biases at play—or a combination of all of the above. Of the twenty stories in foreign languages, ten made it to this anthology—a number I could be proud of, if only I had deliber-ately intervened in their favor, championing translation. When I realized I had chosen so many stories in translation, I asked myself seriously, cautiously—why? Was I biased somehow, or did they have qualities that set them aside? And here, dear reader, you will simply have to trust me. I was no less scrupulous while reading the translations, no less meticulous while pondering whether each should receive an O. Henry Prize. But as it happened, I didn't have to intervene in their favor. With some exceptions, their over-all literary quality was simply excellent.

What was it, specifically, in those ten stories that seemed so deeply appealing? Surely, whatever quality it was—if it indeed was one single thing—it was also present in the rest of the stories I'd chosen. The twenty stories included in this volume are of course widely varied and have distinct qualities of their own. Some of them have a wild and contagious sense of humor; others capture the desolation and difficult loneliness of these past couple of years; others—more timeless—reach into the depths of the absurd to show us how fragile our conventions around reality and normality actually are. However, all these stories do, in fact, share one com-mon quality.

Marcel Proust once wrote that "beautiful books are always written in a sort of foreign language." Indeed, all the stories pres-ent in this volume belong to that family of literary works that read as if they are written in some kind of foreign language. In other words, they straddle the familiar and the unfamiliar—a rare qual-ity that only good literature possesses. The world each of these stories contains immediately opens up to us, as if we already know or remember it. But at the same time, these stories present us with the unknowable, the unpredictable, and the strange.

The word "strange," which English shares with Romance languages—"*extraña*," "*étrange*," "*estranha*," "*strano*," "*straniu*"—comes from the Latin "*extraneus*," meaning "foreign, external, alien, unusual." And also, "curious, queer, and surprising." And that is precisely what good stories feel like: within the setting of complete familiarity, the flowering of the *extraneus*. Too many stories published today follow the most predictable paths possible. Dialogues, sensibilities, plots, and characters often feel no different from those in any of the myriad streamable series, all like each other, all packed neatly and ready for immediate consumption. Under banners such as "relatability," a significant part of the literary field has given in to streamlined, marketable prose. The dictum "write about what you know" has become the epitaph under which the "foreign, unusual, curious, queer, and surprising" is prematurely entombed.

If the currents of our present culture are driving fiction to its most predictable, most conventional paths, what are the undercurrents that can alter that path? The German writer Rudolf Pannwitz, known mostly via Walter Benjamin's essay on translation "The Translator's Task," criticized translators who "germanize Indic Greek English instead of indicizing, graecizing, anglicizing German." In other words, he thought of translation as a means to foreignize the language into which something was being translated, rather than a task that domesticized a foreign language, making it more palatable and digestible. His criticism continues: "They are far more awed by their own linguistic habits than by the spirit of the foreign work . . . the fundamental error of the translator is that he holds fast to the state in which his own language happens to be rather than allowing it to be put powerfully in movement by the foreign language . . . he must broaden and deepen his own language through the foreign one." Pannwitz is referring to translators when he writes this, but he may as well be referring to writers more generally, and even to readers. This idea of translation as a kind of fertile contamination, as a way of putting a language back in movement by allowing the currents of different languages, foreign to one another, to mix and blend is, deeper down, a theory of writing and reading. And it is, moreover, an approach to literature that motivates and animates this year's awards and anthology.

Perhaps no other genre encapsulates the general sensibility of a society in a particular moment in time as much as the short story. The short story is like a slice of the immediate present. Novels, because they are usually long-term commitments, may encapsulate the ethos of an era; the short story, the temperature of a moment. And this moment, as these twenty stories will hopefully show, is a moment in which we are beginning to open the doors and windows of this old locked-down house, letting new light and air come in to stir us powerfully into movement.

—Valeria Luiselli

The Best Short Stories 2022

Alejandro Zambra

Translated from the Spanish by Megan McDowell

Screen Time

Many times over his two years of life, the boy has heard laughter or cries coming from his parents' bedroom. It's hard to know how he would react if he ever found out what his parents really do while he's asleep: watch TV.

He's never watched TV or anyone watching TV, so his parents' television is vaguely mysterious to him: its screen is a sort of mirror, but the image it reflects is opaque, insufficient, and you can't draw on it in the steam, though sometimes a layer of dust allows for similar games.

Still, the boy wouldn't be surprised to learn that this screen reproduces images in movement. He is occasionally allowed to see other people on screens, most often people in his second country. Because the boy has two countries: his mother's, which is his main country, and his father's, which is his secondary country. His father doesn't live there, but his father's parents do, and they're the people the boy sees most often on-screen.

He has also seen his grandparents in person, because the boy has traveled twice to his second country. He doesn't remember the first trip, but by the second he could walk and talk himself blue in the face, and those weeks were unforgettable, though the most memorable event happened on the flight there, when a screen that seemed every bit as useless as his parents' TV lit up, and suddenly there was a friendly red monster who referred to himself in the third person. The monster and the boy were immediate friends, perhaps because back then the boy also talked about himself in the third person.

The meeting was fortuitous, really, because the boy's parents didn't plan to watch TV during the trip. The flight began with a couple of naps, and then his parents opened the little suitcase that held seven books and five zoomorphic puppets, and a long time was spent on the reading and immediate rereading of those books, punctuated by insolent comments from the puppets, who also gave their opinions on the shapes of the clouds and the quality of the snacks. Everything was going swimmingly until the boy asked for a toy that had chosen to travel—his parents explained—in the hold of the plane, and then he remembered several others that— who knows why—had decided to stay in his main country. Then, for the first time in six hours, the boy burst into tears that lasted a full minute, which isn't a long time, but, to a man in the seat behind them, seemed very long indeed.

"Make that kid shut up!" bellowed the man.

The boy's mother turned around and looked at him with serene contempt, and, after a well-executed pause, she lowered her gaze to stare fixedly between his legs and said, without the slightest trace of aggression:

"Must be really tiny."

The man apparently had no defense against such an accusation and didn't reply. The boy—who had stopped crying by then— moved to his mother's arms, and then it was the father's turn. He also knelt in his seat to stare at the man; he didn't insult him, but merely asked his name.

"Enrique Elizalde," said the man, with the little dignity he had left.

"Thanks."

"Why do you want to know?"

"I have my reasons."

"Who are you?"

"I don't want to tell you, but you'll find out. Soon you'll know full well who I am."

The father glared several more seconds at the now-remorseful or desperate Enrique Elizalde, and he would have kept it up except that a bout of turbulence forced him to refasten his seat belt.

"This jerk thinks I'm really powerful," he murmured then, in English, which was the language the parents used instinctively now to insult other people.

"We should at least name a character after him," said the mother.

"Good idea! I'll name all the bad guys in my books Enrique Elizalde."

"Me too! I guess we'll have to start writing books with bad guys," she said.

And that was when they turned on the screen in front of them and tuned in to the show of the happy, hairy red monster. The show lasted twenty minutes, and when the screen went dark, the boy protested, but his parents explained that the monster's presence wasn't repeatable, he wasn't like books, which could be read over and over.

During the three weeks they were in his secondary country, the boy asked about the monster daily, and his parents explained that he only lived on airplanes. The re-encounter finally came on the flight home, and it lasted another scant twenty minutes. Two months later, since the boy still spoke of the monster with a certain melancholy, they bought him a stuffed replica, which in his eyes was the original itself. Since then the two have been inseparable: in fact, right now, the boy has just fallen asleep hugging the red plush toy, while his parents have retired to the bedroom, and surely they will soon turn on the TV. There's a chance, if things go as they usually do, that this story will end with the two of them watching TV.

The boy's father grew up with the TV always on, and at his son's age he was possibly unaware that the television could even be turned off. His mother, on the other hand, had been kept away from TV for an astonishing ten years. Her mother's official version was that the TV signal didn't reach as far as their house on the outskirts of the city, so that the TV seemed to the girl a completely useless object. One day she invited a classmate over to play, and without asking anyone, the friend simply plugged in the TV and turned it on. There was no disillusionment or crisis: the girl thought the TV signal had only just reached the city's periphery. She ran to relay the good news to her mother, who, though she was an atheist, fell to her knees, raised her arms to the sky, and shouted histrionically, persuasively, "It's a MIRACLE!"

In spite of these very different backgrounds, the couple is in complete agreement that it's best to put off their son's exposure to screens as long as possible. They're not fanatics, in any case, they're not against TV by any means. When they first met, they often employed the hackneyed strategy of meeting up to watch movies as a pretext for sex. Later, in the period that could be considered the boy's prehistory, they succumbed to the spell of many excellent series. And they never watched as much TV as during the months leading up to the birth of their son, whose intrauterine life was set not to Mozart symphonies or lullabies but rather to the theme songs of series about bloody power struggles in an unspecified ancient time of zombies and dragons, or in the spacious government house of the self-designated "leader of the free world."

When the boy was born, the couple's TV experience changed radically. At the end of the day their physical and mental exhaustion allowed only thirty or forty minutes of waning concentration, so that almost without realizing it they lowered their standards and became habitual viewers of mediocre series. They still wanted to immerse themselves in unfathomable realms and live vicariously through challenging and complex experiences that forced them to seriously rethink their place in the world, but that's what the books they read during the day were for; at night they wanted easy laughter, funny dialogue, and scripts that granted the sad satisfaction of understanding without the slightest effort.

Someday, maybe in one or two years, they plan to spend Saturday or Sunday afternoons watching movies with the boy, and they even keep a list of the ones they want to watch as a family. But for now, the TV is relegated to that final hour of the day when the boy is asleep and the mother and father return, momentarily, to being simply she and he—she, in bed looking at her phone, and he, lying face up on the floor as if resting after a round of sit-ups. Suddenly he gets up and lies on the bed, too, and his hand reaches for the remote but changes course, picks up the nail clippers instead, and he starts to cut his fingernails. She looks at him and thinks that lately, he is always clipping his nails.

"We're going to be shut in for months. He's going to get bored," she says.

"They'll let people walk their dogs, but not their kids," he says bitterly.

"I'm sure he doesn't like this. Maybe he doesn't show it, but he must be having a horrible time. How much do you think he understands?"

"About as much as we do."

"And what do we understand?" she asks, in the tone of a student reviewing a lesson before a test. It's almost as if she has asked, "What is photosynthesis?"

"That we can't go out because there's a shitty virus. That's all."

"That what used to be allowed is now forbidden. And what used to be forbidden still is."

"He misses the park, the bookstore, museums. Same as we do."

"The zoo," she says. "He doesn't talk about it, but he complains more, gets mad more often. Not much, but more."

"But he doesn't miss preschool, not at all," he says.

"I hope it's just two or three months. What if it's more? A whole year?"

"I don't think so," he says. He'd like to sound more convinced.

"What if this is our world from now on? What if after this virus there's another and another?" She asks the question but it could just as well be him, with the same words and the same anxious intonation.

During the day they take turns: one of them watches their son while the other works. They are behind on everything, and although everyone is behind on everything, they feel sure that they're a little more behind than everyone else. They should argue, compete over which of them has the more urgent and better-paid job, but instead they both offer to watch the boy full-time, because that half day with him is an interval of true happiness, genuine laughter, purifying evasion—they would rather spend the whole day playing ball in the hallway or drawing unintentionally monstrous creatures on the small square of wall where drawing is allowed or strumming guitar while the boy turns the pegs until it's out of tune or reading stories that they now find perfect, much better than the books they themselves write, or try to. Even if they only had one of those children's stories, they would rather read it nonstop all day than sit in front of their computers, the awful news radio on in the background, to send reply e-mails full of apologies for their lateness and stare at the stupid map of real-time contagion and death—he looks, especially, at his son's secondary country, which of course is still his primary one, and he thinks of his parents and imagines that in the hours or days since he last talked to them they've gotten sick and he'll never see them again, and then he calls them and those calls leave him shattered, but he doesn't say anything, at least not to her, because she has spent weeks now in a slow and imperfect anxiety that makes her think she should learn to embroider, or at least stop reading the beautiful and hopeless novels she reads, and she also thinks that she should have become something other than a writer; they agree on that, they've talked about it many times, because so often—every time they try to write—they've felt the inescapable futility of each and every word.

"Let's let him watch movies," she says. "Why not? Only on Sundays."

"At least then we'd know if it's Monday or Thursday or Sunday," he says.

"What's today?"

"I think it's Tuesday."

"Let's decide tomorrow," she says.

He finishes cutting his nails and looks at his hands with uncertain satisfaction, or maybe as if he has just finished cutting someone else's nails, or as if he were looking at the nails of a person who just cut their own nails and is asking him, for some reason (maybe because he's become an expert), for his opinion or approval.

"They're growing faster," he says.

"Didn't you just cut them last night?"

"Exactly, they're growing faster." He says this very seriously. "Every night it seems like they've grown out during the day. Abnormally fast."

"I think it's good for nails to grow fast. Supposedly they grow faster at the beach," she says, sounding as if she's trying to remember something, maybe the feeling of waking up on the beach with the sun in her face.

"I think mine are a record."

"Mine are growing faster, too," she says, smiling. "Even faster than yours. By noon they're practically claws. And I cut them and they grow again."

"I think mine grow faster than yours."

"No way."

Then they put their hands together as if they could really see their fingernails growing, as if they could compare speeds, and what should be a quick scene lengthens out, because they let themselves get caught up in the absurd illusion of that silent competition, beautiful and useless, which lasts so long that even the most patient viewer would turn off the TV in indignation. But no one is watching them, though the TV screen is like a camera that records their bodies frozen in that strange and funny pose. A monitor amplifies the boy's breathing, and it's the only sound that accompanies the contest of their hands, their nails, a contest that lasts several minutes but not long enough for anyone to win, and that ends, finally, with the longed-for burst of warm, frank laughter that they were really needing.

Daniel Mason

The Wolves of Circassia

T HE OLD MAN LIVED IN A HOUSE with a wife he no longer knew was his wife, a son he no longer knew was his son, a little boy, and a woman named Seini, who told him each morning, when he asked where she was from, that she had been born in the island nation of Tonga. The old man, who once served as a physician on a battleship in the South Pacific, had been to Tonga and could recall, with clarity, an American nurse there named Rita—"like the movie star"—and when he told Seini this, his wife would stop and listen from a place he couldn't see. Almost every day, he told Seini about Rita—it was one of the many stories he told her. He had known this nurse only briefly, he said, and it was wartime, but often in the years that followed, he wondered what would happen if they met again.

"Who knows?" he'd say to Seini, and she'd laugh and answer that he must have been a flirt. Actually, the old man said, he had been a cardiologist.

The first time the old man had spoken about Rita, his wife had pulled Seini aside and explained that this story must be another confabulation. He had never served in the South Pacific, though he'd been stationed in Japan at the end of the Vietnam War. In fact, they'd lived there together. She didn't know where the story came from, or who this Rita was. To this, Seini listened with the same patience with which she listened to the old man. During the frequent moments when she was asked to take a side between truth and fantasy, she found she often chose the latter. She had been working with the old man and woman for only a year, but she had been a home health aide for patients with dementia since the week she had arrived from Tonga, and she knew with whom, on the deepest level, her allegiance lay.

The house was in Walnut Creek, in what the man had once called "Old Walnut Creek," to differentiate it from the subdivisions. It sat on a winding road lined with tall walnut trees, and had a small orchard of apricots and apples and a view of Mount Diablo. From the orchard, a path led down into a cool valley of oak and laurel, and from there to the boundary of a state park. Around them, the subdivisions had grown, but this valley remained. "I have the largest backyard in the world," the man liked to say. The last time he had climbed to the peak was twelve years prior, for his sixtieth birthday, but his physical vigor had long outlasted the functioning of memory, and he could still walk in the valley with his wife, or with Seini. It was thirteen miles to the top, he often told her, just as he told her that the Miwoks of the area had once thought the peak was the center of creation, and that because of the flatness of the surrounding landscape you could watch over everything, could see all the way to the Sierra Nevada, a view farther than from any other mountain in the world.

Later, the old man's wife must have felt it necessary to confirm this. Or at least to confirm that the old man wasn't the only person to say this about the view. It wasn't the height of the mountain, she told Seini, it was its loneliness. This was a funny description, Seini thought, and sensed that it was unintended, and that the old woman was embarrassed she had noticed. So she said nothing, and the old woman continued. She'd been there many times, she said. With her husband. Where they could see clear across the Central Valley, to the thin, white strip of distant mountains, like a tear between earth and sky.

The arrangements of the household had come together quickly, in the second week of the order to shelter in place. Seini had never met the old man's son or grandson prior to their arrival that Tuesday in late March. They lived in San Francisco and visited only rarely, and before the old man's memory of his family closed over completely, he'd told Seini that his son was just too busy, "like his pops." The son had been a great athlete in his youth, the old man said, a baseball player—Seini should have seen him pitch. The old woman had laughed at this and told Seini that the son had been rather mediocre, but that he loved his father more than anything, and the reason he came so infrequently was that it was too painful to see the old man in his dementia. She said this without any bitterness, and Seini understood that she was also speaking for herself.

Given what she knew of the son, Seini had been surprised to hear from the old woman that he would be coming to live with them. But the son, she also learned, had been in the process of getting a divorce when the epidemic struck, and after a week, the couple had found the prospect of further close confinement unbearable. So the son had returned to live with his parents, and brought with him the little boy, who had difficulties with attention and impulsivity, and who, all parties agreed, couldn't last in the San Francisco apartment without his friends, his school, the parks. Seini was aware, listening to the old woman explain this, that there was even more that was not being shared about the son and the boy, and the mother who would assent to giving up her child. But she didn't ask. She'd long ago discovered that she could learn much more about her patients and their families by quietly waiting and watching the outlines fill in.

· · ·

So there were five of them in the house at the end of the valley of oak and laurel. Before the outbreak, Seini drove home weekly to stay with her husband and their youngest daughter in their home in Redwood City. She had two older girls, too—one who was a nurse and one who worked at a supermarket—and a boy, *her* little boy, who now was twenty-eight and stood six foot five and was a security guard at San Francisco General. When the outbreak began to spread, the old woman took Seini aside and asked about her home situation, whether it was possible to control whom she came in contact with. Seini thought of her youngest daughter's friends, and her other children's jobs. It was not possible, Seini said, and so she came to live with the old man and woman, and in the evenings FaceTimed with her family, and when this wasn't enough to fill the growing emptiness inside her, once a week, she got in her car and drove the wooded streets, the rolling grasslands, the double-barreled tunnel, the snaking highways, the long, bay-skimming bridge—an hour for a trip that usually took two—and she would park first outside her sister's apartment, and then her own, and talk. On the block where they lived, the buildings were close together, packs of teenage girls roamed in defiance of the isolation orders, and her sister jokingly asked her how it was "out in the woods." But Seini was hardly the only one among their friends who had come to live apart from their family because the people they cared for were frail and they didn't want to bring the disease into those homes.

Prior to the son's arrival, Seini had slept upstairs in the room next to the old man, who because of his nighttime wandering and confusion no longer shared a bed with his wife. It was a big room, with a view of a great backyard fig tree planted when the old man and woman first moved there, and then to the mountain beyond. Long ago, it had been the son's room, and for a moment Seini worried the son would take it back. But he chose a smaller guest room near the kitchen, where he spent his days in front of a laptop. It was clear from the start that whatever animosities had fueled his divorce were far from cooling, and when the son wasn't working, he walked up and down the street outside, arguing into his phone. It was better that he kept his distance from his father, thought Seini. For while the old man no longer recognized these new arrivals, he understood intuitively that there was unhappiness about them, and this confused and frightened him. When the son joined them for dinner, he couldn't resist correcting his father, or looking off when the old man got food on his face, or when he talked endlessly about cardiology and told them the same stories, over and over, about how much the field had changed since he was a medical student. To avoid scaring the old man or the child, they didn't talk about the epidemic, and so the old man repeated his difficult-to-follow stories, and all the others were lost in thought. All the others, that is, except the little boy, who was transfixed.

Seini's realization that the boy did not see his grandfather as she did came surprisingly slowly for someone who prided herself on her implicit understanding of families. She would have thought that anyone would eventually tire of hearing, for the eighth time, how the first EKG, devised by Einthoven, was the size of a small car and required the patient to sit with three limbs in buckets of water, or how the old man had been an intern at Stanford when Shumway performed the first heart transplant in the United States, or how, before the development of echocardiograms, he could estimate the ejection fraction of the left ventricle just by placing his palm on a patient's chest. But the boy—who in most contexts couldn't sit still for three seconds without reaching out and grabbing something, or making a joke, or rocking back and forth in his chair until it almost tipped over, who always talked too loud, too fast, who interrupted or abruptly left the table—the boy was captivated by the stories, loved the repetitions, just like her own son had asked his father to repeat the same tales from his childhood in Tonga. Sometimes, between the old man's stories,

grandmother sat with him and tried to read to him or talk to him, but the moment he was cornered, he climbed onto the top of the couch and tumbled off, or spun in circles, or suddenly decided he wanted ice from the ice maker, filling a glass so violently that the cubes went skidding across the floor.

It was Seini's idea to take the boy on her walks with the old man, and then, because her middle daughter had begun to call her crying each afternoon, to let them go on alone. Her daughter had been a dialysis nurse, but when the outbreak started, she was reassigned to the emergency room. Now, every day, she told her mother she couldn't take it, couldn't take the death, couldn't take the families threatening her when they weren't allowed into the hospital, couldn't take the feeling that her clothes, her hair, her skin, were covered with a poison that would infect her husband and her children. The street was long and mostly empty, and Seini listened as she watched the boy and man ahead of her. She didn't have an answer. But she knew her daughter knew this, knew that if she wanted an answer she would have called her father. "It's fucking unreal," her daughter said, over and over. Seini didn't like cussing and, after several days of tolerance, reminded her. "It's unreal," her daughter said.

In the street, they sometimes passed dog walkers in masks, but there were few cars and the shoulder was wide. At first, Seini felt guilty for hanging back and letting the two of them walk on together, though she didn't know if she was entrusting the child to the old man or the old man to the child. What was clear was that both were happiest in each other's presence, away from the scolding son and the fretting old woman. They made a funny pair. The old man was stocky and broad chested, had thick, gray eyebrows, and wore pressed dress shirts Seini chose for him each morning, an old trick she'd learned to make her patients feel like they were preparing for an occasion, just as she daily shaved their faces and trimmed their hair. The little boy, gangly and mop haired, had come with seven T-shirts, all of which bore the image of either Harry Potter or a character from *Star Wars*. Even after a month had passed, she couldn't say whether the old man knew that the leaping, loud, endlessly inquisitive child was his grandson, or whether the boy knew that the old man had no memory of what they'd discussed the day before.

The old man, despite his difficulties bathing or dressing, was steady with a pair of hiking poles, and though Seini worried that the child, who skipped and ran circles around him as they walked, would leap onto his grandfather or knock him over, this never happened. What did happen, one day, was that the boy dashed into the street to examine the body of a flattened squirrel, and was nearly hit by a passing car. Seini told no one, but from then on, they took the little path out of the backyard that led down into the valley. She felt less comfortable there: she saw the scat of wild animals, and turkey vultures wobbling in the sky above. But the ease of the old man reassured her. There, she understood, he could rely on instinct, habit, and she reminded herself that he'd known the mountain longer than she'd been alive. Other times, however, she thought of another story he'd told her, this one from his childhood, about a great black wolf that dragged a boy out of his schoolhouse in Circassia while the other children watched. Later, his wife had come and found her in the kitchen to tell her that he'd invented this one, too. The old man was born in Queens, New York; she'd always guessed the story came from his father, who'd passed through Central Asia after his internment in a gulag during the Second World War. A gulag, she added, was a labor camp.

"And did the boy survive?" Seini had asked her.

"The boy?"

"The boy in the story."

"Oh," said the old woman. She paused for a moment and looked at Seini in a way that she hadn't before. "You know, I never asked. But I'm not even sure there was a boy. His father also made things up."

May passed. The leaves grew thick on the walnuts, and green figs budded on the backyard tree. The valley bloomed with California poppy, then white flowers that reminded Seini of the morning glories she would pick in Tonga, and then, in thick patches, a small, blue-violet blossom whose name she didn't know. The days turned warmer, and her asthma flared, and she found herself needing to stop and rest on a long, recumbent branch of laurel, behind a bench that had been wrapped with yellow warning tape. There, the signal was good, and she could listen to her daughter while the old man and the little boy continued along the trail, ten, fifteen minutes to the gate at the end of the valley and back. Soon, she unrolled a little blanket, took off her shoes, and massaged her feet. Fierce, bristling caterpillars stalked among the waving grass, little black-caped birds warily inspected her, and a pair of mushrooms broke the hard clay earth, grew tall, and shriveled in the heat. In the distance, she could hear the boy shouting, or singing, but there was no one nearby to admonish him. If she didn't worry about the old man or his wife, or the little boy, or her son, or her husband or her daughters, she realized she was almost happy.

When the man and boy would return, she'd find them talking about exactly the same things as when they'd left. Sometimes, they were so lost in conversation, or in parallel worlds that didn't involve one another, that they didn't even seem to notice her waiting, and she had to hurry to catch them. Back at the house, the old man would nap and the boy would disappear into his Kindle. And after dinner, they would go out again, each day like the last, the time dissolving, Einthoven, Shumway, and magic portals, until the June evening when Seini lay down beneath the laurel, amid the garrulous company of the birds, and somehow, thoughts slowing in the dry and golden heat, drifted off to sleep.

. . .

She was awakened by the scuttling of a squirrel and a cool breeze rising through the valley. At first, she didn't know where she was, and took a moment to register the laurel and the dimming sky. It wasn't the first time she'd fallen asleep there, but it was the deepest she'd slept in a long while, deep enough to dream that she was back in Tonga, only now with the old man and the little boy. They were in the ocean, bobbing up and down, and she was watching from the shore. There was nothing unusual in this; almost all her dreams were about caring for others, seeing them in danger, and trying—with legs that wouldn't move, a voice that couldn't cry for help—to save them. In this one, there was something beautiful about the way they floated in the swells, but the moment that she tried to reach them was the moment she awoke.

She sat up. Dusk was falling. The birds had vanished. Her eyes followed the trail to the final turn before it disappeared behind the oaks, but it was empty. Slipping on her shoes, she stood and gathered the blanket. They must have passed her, as they often did, she thought, and with this thought she felt suddenly faint, and wondered if she had stood too quickly. There was no reason to worry, she told herself, but then her chest was very tight. Instinctively, she rummaged through her purse for her inhaler, until she recalled that with the pandemic her pharmacy had been unable to refill her prescription.

It was only ten minutes back to the house, but with her shortening breath she had to stop twice, and she reached the yard in darkness. Almost instantly, she knew they weren't home yet. Inside, the house was too quiet, and the old man's hiking poles weren't resting against the stairs, where he usually left them. The boy's father was at his laptop, and the old woman was upstairs, talking to one of two different book clubs that gathered over the computer on certain evenings, though when Seini listened, she heard the old woman talking only about her husband. Seini thought of interrupting, of asking for help, and yet she knew that would mean admitting more than just a momentary lapse, it would mean renouncing a central premise that had sustained her, that the world was something that could be tended. She returned outside, and went around to the front of the house. But the street was also empty, empty of the masked dog walkers; even the neighbors' homes seemed abandoned. In her pocket, her phone buzzed, and she fumbled for it, as if the person calling might have an answer for her predicament. But when she looked, she realized she had only imagined it. There was just the time, and the lock-screen photo of her middle daughter sticking out her tongue, a prank she'd played long ago when Seini was still learning to use the iPhone, but an image that, for so much carelessness and joy, she kept.

Still holding her phone, she circled back to the yard, and then beyond to the path, as the view of the peak opened before her. She was walking faster now, down into the valley, where she paused once more. Possibilities rose about her. Wolves pawed the fresh snow; bodies broke through the wave curl; between earth and sky, a magic portal opened. The world turned slowly around the axis of the mountain. Far away, her daughter was laughing again. A wind came over the hills, the trees, the valleys. Her lungs returned and she began to run.

Tere Dávila

Translated from the Spanish by Rebecca Hanssens-Reed

Mercedes's Special Talent

S HE WAS BALANCING THE CIGARETTE between her fingers
 and shouting at my father's corpse.

"Jorge! Wake up! I need a light!"

"He's dead now," I said, my voice groggy.

"No, no, it's his depression," Mercedes answered from the
orthopedic bed. "Jorge! The lighter!"

She extended her arm and waited. She was a tenacious smoker
and just a little emphysema wasn't going to make her quit in her
old age.

For years she'd spent more than half the day lying down, coughing and incessantly asking for someone to adjust her back pillow.
As my father always said, Mercedes was born to be sick, just like
someone who's born to write, or to paint, or to be a father.

"I've been unwell since I was little," her story went. "Mom
went through hell when she had me; I didn't sleep or eat and I
was allergic to everything. I couldn't even keep down goat milk."

As a child, Mercedes had suffered from colic, reflux, vomiting,
diarrhea, and every cold that was ever going around. Her adolescence was overwhelmed with doctors who were so ignorant they
never realized that what she had was not a nervous stomach, but

a fragile uterus. Adulthood didn't bring her better health, but gestational diabetes, complications with birth, insomnia, migraines, herniated discs, edema, and thyroid problems. Her life was a relentless chain of ailments leading all the way up to the sickly present.

"Jorge, come on and light my cigarette, my arthritis is killing me."

According to my father, they met at college, when she walked into the library one afternoon. He said she was slim, which apparently people weren't as wild about then as they are now, but she was wearing an eye-catching blue jacket. She moved to sit on one of the sofas in the lobby, but paused, and stood regarding the chair with unusual intensity. He wouldn't have guessed that Mercedes was calculating the number of germs lurking in the upholstery. He merely found it curious, endearing even, that she didn't sit down and instead chose to open her book right there and read standing up.

For some reason, this image was enough for him to fall in love with her and, two years later, ask her to marry him. That first encounter was all the explanation my father needed to justify forty-five years with the same woman. Mercedes, however, would tense up with cynicism at the slightest provocation.

"I don't know why I'm still with your father, he's so clueless and he thinks I'm a lunatic."

My whole life I was witness to her myriad manias. When I was little, she wore high heels even if she was at home watching TV, and she always kept her girdle on, as if at any moment she would have to rush off to lunch with the civil ladies' society. She applied moisturizing creams several times throughout the day and ceaselessly took inventory of her wrinkles. She never let me call her Mother or Mom; she insisted on *Mercedes* because it was more elegant. She was also compulsive about cleaning and organization: every decoration, lamp, book, or ashtray had its place, and once she decided where it belonged, there it stayed forever. She arranged clothes in the wardrobes by color, the food in the fridge and cupboards by expiration date.

"Where are the Coca-Colas?"

Mercedes didn't drink soda, of course, but my father and I loved it, and, unable to find any one afternoon, I asked if she knew where the Coke was, hoping to pair it with some popcorn while we watched the soccer match on TV.

"Are you insane? Do you want to die poisoned by rat piss?"

Not only were all soft drinks banned in the house after that, but so was anything that came in a can. My mother spent her entire life convinced that rats crawled with free rein all over pallets of canned food in warehouses around the world, and that this exact place was also where they emptied their bladders. She swore that even if only one batch ever turned out to be contaminated, she would be the one to get it. She also had other fears: she refused to eat chicken (to avoid the estrogen), red meat (because of the carcinogens), butter (because it made her triglycerides skyrocket), and no dairy product was to ever pass her lips (or it would exacerbate her irritable bowel syndrome). She didn't consume flour or white refined sugars either, both of which could increase the buildup of acid in the brain. She preferred only to smoke. One pack a day of Dunhills, pricey and hard to find, and which were never to blame for her dizziness, coughing, asthma, allergies, poor digestion, nor migraines. My father, on his end, handled this ongoing string of maladies with the attuned wisdom of in-one-ear-and-out-the-other.

One night, after Mercedes went to bed, my father signaled to me to follow him to the garage. He opened the cabinet and removed a hefty black box where the electric saw was kept. He lifted the lid and there, at the bottom of the container, a dozen of our coveted Coca-Colas were hiding. We gleefully drank a few each while we watched a movie. If Mercedes, who kept fastidious track of every nook and cranny in the house, at some point learned of our contraband sodas, she never said anything.

"I need to talk to you about your mother."

My father called me on the phone one morning to say this. He never called to talk about her, or anything else. Keeping in touch with family was one of the matters his wife took care of. I was also perplexed by the hushed manner in which he spoke into the phone. Usually, he vociferated—he was one of those people who, when excited, gradually raises his voice until everyone around him has no choice but to listen to his story. That's how he made friends sitting in waiting rooms whenever he took Mercedes to her doctors' appointments. But I sensed he wasn't feeling his usual jovial self that day when he asked me to get lunch with him.

"I'm naming you executor and we need to get the papers in order." Then he told me about the biopsy and diagnosis of lung cancer. When we were saying goodbye he added, "Don't say anything to Mercedes. I don't want her to know I'm sick."

My father never interpreted his wife's neuroses as anything other than frailty, a delicateness of spirit that was his duty to care for and that prevented her from having reasons to torment him. With everything Mercedes-related, my father had the tolerance of a Buddhist monk.

Except for when it came to jealousy. He couldn't stand it if a man so much as looked at her. Mercedes was a tall and still quite elegant woman; when she was younger she'd been a swimmer and her body, as though refuting her hypochondria, had maintained that rigid posture of an athlete. Even still, at her age it wasn't like she had admirers lining up for her. My father, nonetheless, looked at her like she was still the young woman he'd met that first day in the college library. If they went out together and a friend commented on how nice Mercedes looked, my father would fume, and later, when they got home, they would fight. After his diagnosis, it got worse and he started imagining she was having an affair with a younger man.

A few years back, my parents decided to rent out the studio apartment behind the house. The structure had had various lives before: as a guest bedroom, a tool shed, and for a few years, as my room, with its own private entrance, for the times I came home from college over break. When I moved away, they rented it out to a guy a few years younger than me who was still in college. There weren't any issues until my father's medications, prescribed to help with the pain, had the side effect of near-fits of rage. So he got it into his head that Mercedes and that literal kid were sneaking around.

I happened to be present for one of these arguments. He was reproaching her for a supposed infidelity while she defended herself.

"You're being ridiculous, he's younger than our son!"

Then my father collapsed into the sofa, buried his face in his hands, and started sobbing. This disarmed her. She sat next to him, put a hand on one of his thighs, and with the other caressed his bald head.

"Oh, Jorge. Can't you see that I'm an old woman?"

He started to kiss her. It wasn't the typical scene of chaste affection that parents enact in front of their children, but something much more desperate. I backed away into the kitchen. I didn't have the stomach to witness that drama.

While my father's lungs were wasting away, Mercedes, the smoker, was diagnosed with the early stages of emphysema. The doctor ordered her to quit smoking, even though he knew she wouldn't bother.

"It's something else for me. It's too easy for a doctor to just blame it all on cigarettes."

The origin of her suffering might have been a mystery, but if there was anything Mercedes was certain about it was the imminence of her own death. Even when I was still really young, she talked about how she hoped she would make it to the next major life event: "I only ask God to let me live long enough to see you graduate from high school. God willing I'm still alive to see you finish college. To see you get your first job. To visit you in your own house. To watch you get married . . ."

"I'm gay!" I blurted out one afternoon, sick of Mercedes's incessantly asking me about girlfriends, which to the rest of the world it was obvious I would never have.

"You don't have to yell," she answered coolly. "Christ, I'm not blind—I am your mother."

My admission didn't have a very lasting effect, though. She still wouldn't let herself be deprived of the fantasy of my future wedding.

I respected my father's wish to not reveal his condition for about two months. During that time, Mercedes continued complaining about her back, her chronic fatigue, her low blood sugar, all apparently without noticing that her husband was shedding hair and losing weight. But soon his complexion turned gray, then he barely weighed a hundred pounds, and I had to tell her. She did something unusual then: she said nothing. She locked herself in her bedroom the rest of the day and through the night. Finally, by the following morning she'd come up with her own theory.

"Your father isn't sick. Not in the way he believes. It's depression; what he's feeling is the product of his weak character. And having negative thoughts can be dangerous."

From that day to the very last, not once did she acknowledge the cancer. Instead, she talked about "Jorge's depression."

Eventually, one Saturday, my father couldn't get out of bed. The following Tuesday he stopped speaking. Since he didn't want to die in the hospital, we administered the morphine at home. I requested time off from work and set up an armchair between two beds: my father, on the verge of unconsciousness, to my right, and

Mercedes to my left, refusing to accept that her husband might need more attention than her. This was the dynamic, until the morning when he stopped breathing.

"Wake up, Jorge, I need a light!"

"He's dead, Mercedes."

"Oh please!"

Then I saw what I'd believed was my father's corpse shudder. Slowly, he extended an arm beyond the bed, and offered an imaginary lighter.

"Light, Jorge!" my mother insisted again.

The cigarette trembled in the space between husband and wife. Mercedes waited as he tried with his right hand to make a fist, flexing his thumb to turn a spark wheel that wasn't there.

Always, always, for more than forty-five years, he had lit Mercedes's cigarettes. Until, for the first time, he couldn't: he opened his hand and let the imaginary lighter fall to the floor.

"That's it," Mercedes sighed.

Joseph O'Neill

Rainbows

I CAME TO THIS COUNTRY—FROM IRELAND, at the age of twenty-three—unaware of the existence of mentors. I'm certain that I had never heard the word "mentee." The words in Ireland were not exactly the same as the words in America. When a classmate told me that she was going to meet her "mentor," I had to ask her to explain. In America, she informed me, there was a social practice in which an older, experienced person donated time and knowledge to a younger, relatively foolish person in order to help the latter better understand the world's perils and pathways. I was filled with a suspicion that bordered on disbelief. I probably said, "Ah, go away." Ireland has changed, everyone tells me, and maybe this sort of suspiciousness is no longer current. I doubt it, however.

I audited an undergraduate class in anthropology. I needed a break from the dreariness and difficulty of my master's degree, which was in applied analytics. The class was titled "Animals & People." The pet, the pest, the hunting asset, livestock, the endangered animal: we investigated the social and ideological aspects of these phenomena. I found it interesting. I may not have been an anthropologist, but I did own a kitten. The professor whose class this was, Paola Visintin, became my mentor.

Let me say that Paola was my elder by almost twenty years but was cool in a way that made professors closer to me in age seem gauche and youthless. Her style was important to me. She was thin, of course. She wore her brown hair in a slightly scruffy shoulder-length cut, with bangs, and she casually wore clothes by Martin Margiela—including a deconstructed gray wool jacket that I thought about for years with a feeling of bitter loss. Margiela, a recluse of great mystique, was rumored to be Paola's personal friend, and that was about the coolest thing possible. Mystique was important to me at that time, and some nationalities had more mystique than others. Paola was Italian, from Trieste—a city, she once suggested to me, that still belonged to an invisible Austria-Hungary. She was left-wing to a degree that seemed almost unlawful. She emanated a worldliness in which significant intellectual and sexual powers converged. She spoke with a strong and beautiful Italian accent. She was unafraid.

Our relationship began when I asked if it would be OK for me, a mere auditor, to see her during "office hours" (another new concept). She agreed, on the condition that we meet at a coffee shop on West 141st Street. This was near her apartment, the precise location of which, it was somehow understood, would never be mine to know. Of course, I found out. We met about six times over the course of two years, always at my instigation, always at the same coffee shop. We sat at a particular table in the smoking section. I was honored that she made time to see me, and I speculated that the honor had to do with a shared European identity. Paola seemed to be well disposed toward Ireland, a country, she once told me, that was incomparably supplied with rainbows. Exactly what we discussed I no longer recall, but I have a surviving sense of the excitement I felt when traveling to those meetings from Brooklyn. Many quandaries and crossroads characterized my life in those days, and I took pleasure in telling Paola about them. There was a lot to talk about, it seemed to me. I had not yet found a career, or love, or a home, or money.

Simply to think about the foregoing—all of it, even the departure from Ireland—for some reason fills me with shame.

The meeting that I think about was our last one.

Paola was already at the coffee shop when I arrived. She immediately asked, "What has happened?"

With tears in my eyes, I outlined the events of the night before. Certain details were too embarrassing and awful to relate, especially the details of how I'd come to find myself in the situation that produced what had happened, details that made me furious not only at my personal weakness but also at my naïve and counterproductive upbringing in rural County Limerick.

Paola wasn't one to offer solutions. Her conversational practice was austere and consistent: she listened, she asked specific questions, and she took seriously what one had to say. When she lit a cigarette, it usually meant that she was about to offer her thoughts. These were always brief. She seemed to have disdain for her own opinions. More than once she cast doubt on the very idea of wisdom, which made her seem wiser than ever.

Therefore I put my question to her with no real expectation of receiving an answer. "Should I report him?" I asked.

"Report?"

"Yes," I said. "To the authorities."

"The authorities?" I had the impression that a private joke was passing through her thoughts. "I have a better idea, Clodagh," she said, stubbing out her cigarette. "Now, listen to me very carefully." She looked squarely into my eyes. "Are you listening?" I nodded. She had never been so definite. She said, "Get over it."

My kitten grew into a cat, turned into an old lady, died. The obstetrician lifted a red-blue creature from behind a blue paper curtain—and, flash, the creature, Aoife, turned eighteen. This last milestone was reached in the final semester of her senior year, in January.

One Monday evening in February, my husband, Ian, became aware that our daughter was involved in a prolonged phone drama in her bedroom. He knocked on her door and went in. Aoife, who had been crying, told him that a boy at her school was harassing her. Harassing as in doing what? Ian asked. Aoife told him harassing as in direct-messaging her on Instagram after she'd told him more than once to stop, harassing as in following her around at school all day long and making her dread going anywhere. Following you around? Ian asked. Why? Dad, he's obsessed, Aoife said. Ian asked Aoife if she wanted him to call the parents of this boy, James. Aoife told him that she did not want him to do that. I'll take care of it, Aoife said. OK, Ian said.

I was in Columbus, working, when Ian reported this conversation. I told him, "I don't know any James. Keep an eye on her. I'll handle it tomorrow." By the time I landed in New York, early on Tuesday evening, there had been further developments. In the taxi home, I called Ian and learned that our daughter had not gone to school that day. She had contacted the school to explain her absence and stated that she felt fearful about going in so long as James Wang was there.

"James is James Wang?" I said.

The school had asked Aoife if she wished to file a complaint.

I said, "A complaint? What kind of complaint?"

"There's a complaints procedure, apparently," Ian said. "There are regulations."

"Go on," I said.

After consulting with a friend—

"Which friend?" I asked.

"Some friend, I don't know," Ian said.

"Go on," I said. Ian didn't keep track of the friends. I did. My money was on Mei.

—Aoife had told the school that, yes, she wished to file an official complaint for harassment and intimidation against James Wang. She wouldn't go to school unless he was stopped.

I was nearly home. "I'll talk to her," I said.

"I'm not sure she wants to discuss it right now," Ian said.

I have spent twenty years in business talking to people, almost all of them men, who have not wanted to talk to me or, if they have, then not about the things I've wanted to talk about. This skill of making people talk to me against their will comes in handy in relation to my daughter. Aoife is a sensible girl, a very good student, but she is headstrong and furtive about certain things, and sometimes the issue must be forced. The issue is almost always the same: what the facts of her life are, and what she is minded to do about those facts, and whether what she's minded to do will or won't serve her interests.

When I got home I said, "Where is she?"

Ian said, "She has some friends with her right now. In her bedroom."

"Who?" I was hanging up my coat.

"Some girlfriends," Ian said helplessly.

I knocked on Aoife's door and went in. She and Mei and Sophie were sitting on the bed, backs to the wall, looking at Aoife's phone. "Hey, guys," I said.

The visitors understood me. After some demonstrative hugging, Mei and Sophie left.

I had wanted Aoife to tell me the facts, because I was sure that Ian had not been told the whole story, but when I sat down next to my daughter I took her into my arms and said, "I know, love, I know," as if I already knew the facts.

Aoife's guidance counselor was Ms. Vincenzullo. I rang her that night. There was some difficulty getting hold of her private number, but I got there. I explained that Aoife was distressed and feared returning to school. Ms. Vincenzullo said that she was aware of the situation. I insisted that precautions be taken to protect our daughter. Ian was sitting nearby, listening. I told Ms. Vincenzullo that we, Aoife's parents, would be watching the school very closely. I said this ominously. My experience has been that

American institutions respond only to the danger of litigation. That is awful, if you think about it. I said to Ms. Vincenzullo, "An unsafe environment for our child is not an option." That was my language.

"Aoife will be safe," Ms. Vincenzullo said. "James will be absent for a while."

The next day, Aoife went back to school. I offered to drive her there, but she said she would be OK. She was right about that. The boy, James Wang, didn't bother her again. The authorities had done their job.

For about ten years we had been using a nearby laundromat. Their full-service wash was efficient, and for a small extra charge, they would deliver clean, folded clothes to your home. If you were a regular customer, like our family, they'd stick a tag on your bag that said "VIP."

The business was operated by a family from somewhere in the interior of China—I can't remember the place they once told me. The husband was a cheerful simpleton who barked at customers in very basic English and played practical jokes with the laundry bags. The wife was obviously a lot smarter and spoke much better English. It seemed incredible that she was married to the husband, but needs must, I suppose. Even though I never asked them their names, I came to know the family well enough. They lived in an old tenement building just a block from ours. They employed various friends and relations, most intriguingly a teenage girl—she had been farmed out to the couple, I suspected, as used to be common in Ireland—who gradually transitioned into a good-looking, mannish young person. If this had caused any major problems, I didn't see it. These people had other things to worry about.

The couple had one child—a son. I met him when he was

five or six years old. He'd sit under a table among laundry bags, absorbed by a gaming console. You'd see him there at all hours. His father told me that the boy was number one in his class at math. That seemed unlikely, given that he always appeared to be in the laundromat, playing video games. But time proved the father right: a few years later, he proudly informed me that his son was the only student in his year to test into a specialized high school. I was thrilled. I had watched the lad grow up. I had seen him working the begloomed washing machines on sunny afternoons and, after he turned twelve, making weekend deliveries. How many times had I buzzed him up to our floor? A hundred? Two hundred? I had seen his parents working night and day for their boy. The laundromat stayed open from seven in the morning until ten at night, every day of the year save New Year's Day. What a triumph for the family.

One Sunday, I stopped by the laundromat. The bag of whites we'd dropped off two weeks earlier hadn't been delivered. I wanted to check up on it.

The laundromat presented a familiar and reassuring drama, with a double stroller occupied by a pair of oversized children, some harassed moms, a disheveled man, and two hipsters. In the dimness at the back, behind a table piled high with bags, the mother and the trans or nonbinary young person were going through a basket heaped with clean brights. I surveyed the bags stacked up against the wall. When I didn't see mine, I asked the mother, "The purple one?"

She whispered something to the young person, whose shortish black-and-purple hair had been fixed into cute little tufts. This person went into the storage room and brought out my sack. The tag on it said "VIP $30." When I got out my wallet, the mother made a gesture of refusal. "No—no money," she said.

I was insistent, however. This was the first time that they'd failed to deliver as promised. That was hardly a reason not to pay.

The mother said, "No money. You don't come back here again. Finished." She stood with her hands clenched at her sides.

I didn't understand. I looked to the young person for guidance, but the person was examining me as if I were the curious specimen.

"Your family bad to my son," the mother said. "Please get out now."

"Your son?" I said. What was she talking about?

"You know my son—James," the mother said.

"James?" I said—and, to my horror, I understood.

Unconsciously I had slung my bag over my shoulder. Now it was too heavy. I put it down. I said, "I didn't know. I had no idea. I'm so sorry." I wished I knew her name. Then I realized that I did know her name. "Mrs. Wang," I said, "I didn't know."

"I tell the school, this big year for college. Grades important. James study hard. I tell the school, James sixteen. Junior. Doesn't know girls. Not one kiss. The school not listen. Suspend him." More aggressively Mrs. Wang went on, "Your daughter senior. Eighteen years old. Grades done. College application done. Everything easy." I tried to reply, but she kept going. James's grades had crashed. He was shunned by his friends. He didn't want to go back to school. They took him to a doctor, and the doctor said he was suicidal. "What we do now?" she said to me. "You tell me what we do now."

Her husband peeked out from behind the screen at the very back, then hid again.

"I'm very sorry, Mrs. Wang," I said.

The mother smiled bitterly. "Easy to say."

These things have a limit. The mother had every right to be upset, but I was not going to be forced into a conversation of this kind. "James will be fine," I said. "You'll see." I hoisted my bag over my shoulder like Santa.

"Your family finished here," Mrs. Wang said. "I protect James."

The bag was heavier than ever. After a short block, the muscles in my hands and fingers burned. I put the bag down and called Aoife.

I could tell from her voice that she'd been sleeping. "It's noon," I said. "Up, please."

She muttered something.

"Listen to me," I said. "Why didn't you say it was the boy from the laundromat who was bothering you?"

"I did tell you," she lied.

"You told us it was James Wang. Why didn't you say who he was?"

"I thought you knew," she said. "Anyway, why does it matter?"

I said, "We could have sorted this out with his parents. We didn't need to bring the school into it. We could have handled it family to family."

Aoife said nothing.

"What happened to him, exactly? Was he suspended? Aoife? Hello?"

"What?" she said angrily.

"How long was he suspended for?"

"I don't know."

"Well, estimate." I was raging. There were so many things I had to stop myself from saying to her.

"I don't know, Mom," she shouted. "Maybe two weeks. Mom, he's a creep. He kept following me around. Not just at the school—around here, too. Ask Mei."

"Tell me exactly what he did," I said.

My daughter told me that James had been stalking her. He would hang around the subway station until she appeared and then get on the train with her, sometimes in the same car. He'd walk behind her on the way home, always keeping her in his sights, never overtaking her. He started to show up wherever she went at school—the hallways, the food truck where she bought lunch. He was always there, hanging around, staring at her. Aoife told him repeatedly to leave her alone, but he didn't comply. He messaged her on Instagram, and after she blocked him he messaged her again from a friend's account.

"How many messages?" I said.

"I don't know, Mom. Two."

"What did they say?"

"Just dumb stuff. 'You're pretty.'" She had raised her voice again. "This is someone who comes into my home, Mom." One time, she told me, she had instructed James through the intercom to leave the washing in the lobby. When she went down to collect it, he was still there, waiting for her. According to Aoife, he had a very weird, threatening look in his eye. "He's seen my bras, Mom," she yelled through the phone. "He's kept some of my panties, I know he has, there's two at least that are missing. He's a weirdo. He shouldn't be working with people's private things."

"OK," I said. "Thanks." I know when my daughter is lying and when she isn't. The missing-panties detail was absurd, but the rest of it added up. It didn't add up to much, to my mind, because James was a child. He had feelings that he couldn't understand or manage. The important thing was that I was informed. Information enables action.

Right there, on the sidewalk, I called Ms. Vincenzullo. It was a Sunday, but it couldn't wait. That is my core skill, I believe: making phone calls promptly and persistently. It is a surprisingly rare skill. I left a message. I wasn't optimistic about hearing back.

But Ms. Vincenzullo did ring back, right away. It took me by surprise. I hesitated to accept the call.

The action I'd had in mind was to advocate on behalf of James and to ask if the complaint could be struck from his record. But I knew how American organizations worked. It was a dark wood of decision trees. Either Aoife had had a well-founded grievance or she hadn't. Either she would have to retract her complaint or the school would have to retract its decision. The school would not retract, and neither, I knew, would my daughter, nor would I advise her to. To admit to second thoughts would be to invite trouble.

Everything was a mess, everything was wrong. I didn't answer Ms. Vincenzullo.

The laundry bag hadn't grown any lighter. I had two blocks to go. Men and women were striding past me. Cars and trucks were hurtling down the avenue. I struggled onward. In Ireland, if I needed a lift, I had had only to raise a hand at the side of the lane and someone, usually a stranger, almost always a man, would stop and bring me closer to my destination.

When I got home, Aoife was ensconced in her bedroom. Later she emerged in order to leave the house and see friends. Ian came back in the early evening, bearing takeout. He set out the paper plates and split two pairs of chopsticks. He helped himself to a huge portion of everything. I joined him at the table but ignored the food. I said, "There's something I need to tell you. I don't know where to begin." With that I began.

Afterward Ian said, "Jesus Christ—that's the kid? He looks like he's thirteen."

Ian rarely sees me distraught. I don't like it when he does.

"Hey," he said. "It's going to be OK."

He was asking me to fantasize. He was asking me to invent a world made up of different facts.

"We did what we had to do," Ian bullishly continued. "We protected our daughter. What the school did or didn't do—well, that's the school's business."

This was American of him—the obsession with liability. I wanted to tell him, Either you do the right thing or you do the wrong thing.

But I said nothing. Some things can't be usefully discussed. At nine o'clock, I went to bed. Later that week, Ian found us a new laundromat. Later that year, Aoife got into Wesleyan. In the fall, we drove her up to Middletown in a rented van big enough to accommodate her bicycle and her mini-fridge and her cello.

We had a client in Albany. It was my job to travel up there once or twice a month. I went by train, along the Hudson River. The three-hour journey goes by quickly, because the river is always differently beautiful. I like it best on those still, gray mornings when you raise your eyes from your laptop and the water is as tranquil as the floor of a palace. The return trip, especially in the winter dark, feels long and dreary. I usually try to get more work done.

I was at the Albany station one night in early March, waiting for the train, when I saw a figure in an ankle-length wool coat and a wool pompom hat standing alone at the end of the platform. She was smoking a cigarette. Then the Maple Leaf, come all the way from Toronto, arrived with lights blazing and two conductors gallantly teetering in open doorways. The figure slowly approached, hands held behind her back, contemplating the ground. She was content to be the last passenger to board. I knew that silhouette from somewhere. Looking more closely, I saw the face of Paola Visintin.

A train car's small staircase fell out with a thud. I sprang up the metal steps and turned left and kept going down the aisle until I reached the front of the train. I didn't want her to see me. I believe that I was embarrassed about what I'd turned into—a middle-aged, slightly overweight American woman in business attire, with no mystique and no Margiela. This wasn't an ordinary emotion for me. My self-accusations are usually about day-to-day failings. I have no large regrets about what I have made of my life. It is a worthwhile life. It is a worthwhile body, too.

Soon my panic was replaced by a contrary feeling: a euphoric, almost romantic desire to talk with Paola. Contemporaneously I understood that what I wanted wasn't only to reconnect with my old mentor but to inhabit the self I had been when I was Irish and young. This was also unusual. Looking backward isn't a trait of mine. It requires a kind of courage that I don't have and don't want.

Hastily I Googled Paola and learned that she had left Columbia, currently taught at SUNY Albany, and had published a book titled *The Urbane* (2007). Then I got to my feet and walked along the aisle, scanning the passengers to my left and right. They had come from mythic upstate places—Syracuse, Rome, Utica—and yet here they sat like ordinary twenty-first-century mortals, watching movies or trying to sleep. I reached the café car. Paola sat alone at a table, reading a book in French. Her free hand held a bottle of beer.

I continued to the bar, got a drink, and came back. "May I sit here?" I said.

Paola glanced upward and said, "Of course."

Her hair was darker than ever, but finer and cut a little shorter. Silver roots gleamed at the parting. She wore a black cashmere sweater and a bracelet made of large gold links. Her face had the wrinkles of a long-term smoker. She was thin, thin. She hadn't recognized me.

I stirred my double Bloody Mary with self-confidence. I said joyfully, "Paola, it's me. Clodagh."

Paola looked up from her book. She removed her reading glasses. She was having difficulty placing me. "Ah, yes—Clodagh."

"How are you, Paola?"

With a wry motion of the eyes and mouth, she signaled that everything was as well as could be expected. She said, "So how has your life turned out?"

I laughed. It was a thrilling question from a thrilling questioner. To answer Paola, to hear myself narrate how things had gone for me, made my life seem coherent and adventurous. The scene felt charmed. Our conversation on a speeding and brilliant Amtrak train was linked, as distant events are linked in a folktale, to those long-ago conversations on 141st Street. Somewhere south of Rhinecliff, I offered to buy the drinks. Paola pointed at the remnants of my Bloody Mary and said, "I'll have one of those." I was proud. I had influenced her.

When I returned from the bar, two men at the neighboring table laughed coarsely. Paola and I glanced at them—big, overloud, beer-drinking, sprawling white guys in their fifties—then looked away. There was no need to spell out the politics of the situation, and indeed our conversation had been happily free of any mention of the stupid, evil president. I was conscious that I had no real sense of what Paola's ideas on that topic might be. She had never been someone to think what everybody else was thinking.

Over our Bloody Marys, I found myself telling her the story of Aoife and James. She listened, as of old, with calm interest. She expressed curiosity about the technicalities of the complaint procedure—"Does the school write the rules, or is it the Department of Education?"—but otherwise said very little.

When I was done, Paola raised her eyebrows. After a few moments she said, "Aoife must be an Irish name. It's beautiful."

This oblique response was in character, but I needed more from her. Surely she saw how ashamed and anguished I was.

The men across the aisle broke out once again into noisy laughter. It drew Paola's attention. "Have you noticed," she said suddenly, "how degenerate the so-called Irish and Italians are in this country? It really is quite interesting." Her voice was almost certainly audible to the two men, although I didn't dare look to see if they were listening. How tenaciously, Paola said, Irish- and Italian-Americans clung to their so-called heritage, and yet how little resemblance their mores and outlooks bore to those in the old countries. There was, she said, a certain pathos in the situation of communities morally misshapen, presumably, by their ancestors' brutalizing experience of poverty, emigration, and assimilation. Notable, also, was the recent and deepening fusion of these two ethnic groups by intermarriage, which had had the effect of creating a hybrid identity founded on comical and grotesque notions of racial self-worth. She was thinking of writing some-thing about it. It would involve, Paola said, a lot of research on Long Island, a part of the country that had long fascinated her.

She said with a small smile, "You look puzzled, Clodagh."

Was she testing me? Did she suspect me of Irish-American degeneracy? I felt under scrutiny—that I'd disappointed her, with my story of my business career and my maternal ups and downs. Had she always been such a snob?

"Sorry," I said. "I was distracted. This thing with the boy from the laundromat . . ." I shook my head.

Paola asked, "He's not making trouble anymore?"

"Well—Aoife's at college. We've had no contact."

"So it's a happy ending," she said.

Was she being ironic? Was she bored? "It isn't Aoife I'm worried about," I said. "It's James. He's got a suspension on his record. For sexual harassment, of all things."

Paola rattled the ice cubes in her plastic glass. "He will be fine. He will survive. People survive, Clodagh." She drained what was left of her drink. Her hand had drifted to her book.

She was condescending to me, and the encounter now felt fully anachronistic. I wasn't that girl from Newcastle West, and Paola was no longer the cool professor who jingled keys to an enigmatic adult world. My former self would have wanted to know what she was thinking—about me, about everything—would have wanted to assure her that I wasn't in the habit of ambushing near-strangers with autobiographical monologues. But I felt sorry for her, this childless, too-thin woman in her sixties who couldn't quit smok-ing and was still interested in her air of mystery.

I finished my drink and smiled. Quite amiably I said, "It was very nice to see you, Paola."

"Goodbye, Clodagh," Paola said, just as amiably. Giving noth-ing away, she smiled once again. She picked up her book.

I went back to my seat. The train stormed on and on. Time

stormed onward, too. In the spring, I went into our local Duane Reade. There I ran into someone I didn't want to see.

The checkout staff—one woman—had temporarily absented herself, and this had resulted in a long line of customers that wound around belt barriers and from there into an aisle enclosed by tall racks. I joined the line and waited. Soon enough everyone shuffled forward, and I progressed beyond the racks and into the open area with the barriers. Facing me in the winding line, in effect approaching me on my right, was Mrs. Wang.

There was no question of fleeing. You make your bed and you lie in it.

Away from that hot, dark laundry, she looked a lot younger. She was in her midthirties, I realized. Then a movement of the line placed us alongside each other. We exchanged polite nods.

"Hello, Mrs. Wang," I said. "How is your family?"

"Good," she said. "Your family?"

"Good, thank you," I said.

She gave me a more searching look. She said, "Your daughter good?"

"Yes," I said. I forced myself to utter the sentence "How is James?"

"Good," she said. "Accepted by number one college." She smiled. It was an amazing smile. She said, "University of Pennsylvania. Ivy League."

"Congratulations," I said. "He's a good lad."

Mrs. Wang said, "Yes. Work hard." Then the line quickened and she was called forward to make payment.

When Ian came home that evening, I told him that I wanted to visit Ireland again, to see my brother.

"Sure," he said. "It was fun last time."

The last time had been when Aoife was four years old. She was anxious about going, until I promised her that we'd see rainbows.

After that she would not stop talking about the rainbows of Ireland. It worried Ian a little. "There had better be rainbows," he said.

"There will be," I said. But I was worried, too.

On the airplane, Aoife asked me, "Are rainbows real?" She was suspicious.

"They are," I said.

We landed at Shannon in the morning. In the rental car, Aoife was wide awake and inspecting the sky. It was a windy spring day, with white and gray and blue clouds speeding in from the west.

We had not been driving for more than a few minutes when Ian said, "Aoife, look."

A rainbow faintly showed above the estuary. "Rainbow," Aoife shouted.

We drove from County Clare into Limerick, then back out toward Newcastle West. There were so many rainbows that we stopped looking for them before we reached Adare.

Shanteka Sigers

A Way with Bea

Bea walks into the classroom wearing the clothes she had on the day before. The Teacher understands that this is going to be a bad day. Bea's hair is uncombed, face unwashed. She arrives precisely twelve seconds late. Not so late that the Teacher *has* to make a big deal about it. But not on time. Bea walks like a prisoner forcibly escorted, snatching herself along, step by step, then pouring her thin body into the seat. She has no books, no pencil or paper. She drapes herself over the desk and waits for the Teacher to continue or challenge.

The Teacher rides the L two stops from the school and into an entirely different country. Chicago pieces itself together that way. The platform at her station offers a clear view of the rear deck of her condo and she always looks. Sometimes she hopes to catch her husband there with a woman, a stranger or a friend, his hand invading the buttons of this woman's shirt, taking a fistful of her breast. This has never happened. She is relieved and disappointed. Occasionally she catches him grilling in the brown sandals she hates. She feels like a spy trying to decipher her own life.

. . .

The Teacher grew up in the country and has seen things die the right way. You can't die right in the city. There's no place to take yourself off to be alone with your thoughts and the last wind you will ever feel. In the living room, her husband reads a magazine with his ancient cat on his lap. She has told him that it is far past time for that cat. He was disgusted by her cruelty. She shouldn't have married a man from the city.

The Teacher dissects Bea as the girl walks toward her classroom. *She looks like a doll made for tea parties that was thrown outside to fend for itself.* A nobility lives in Bea's bones, an ancient, undiluted beauty that most eyes have forgotten. She grows in angles. The broadness of her nose and the wide, sculpted divot leading down to her lips and the deep, delicate hollows behind her collarbones. The disorder of her swarming hair, misshapen and dusty, but still a laurel.

The Teacher raises a glass to her friend the Engineer, who has been promoted. The Teacher can't afford this restaurant, but the Advertising Executive will pay. She always pays. They crowd around a laptop, perfumes mingling, to watch her latest car commercial. The waiters weave around the obstruction. Someone asks about the Lawyer's big case that has not been decided yet. The Other Lawyer handles lucrative but ethically disgusting cases that no one asks about. The Teacher knows how her friends imagine her in class, as sure as a mother goose, with students trailing obediently behind. Every gathering, she is sainted anew for her work. She regains a bit of purpose and savors it as long as she can, until it evaporates, processed into the air of the school.

Bea announces that the endoplasmic reticulum has been drawn in the wrong place. She walks up to the board, showing the class her fearless back, and wipes at the drawing of a cell. She rakes the chalk across the blackboard with the concentration of a doctor repairing a beating heart. This happens with these children. Every now and again, their bellies are full enough, a lesson hits them in the right way, or they have paused their channel-surfing to learn about it in a documentary. The Teacher knows better than to get too excited. Next week, Bea will be hungry and fallible.

Bea's brother is Aldous. Which means her mother is Flora. Flora is regarded as less a person than a familiar, chaotic fixture of the neighborhood. A tiny woman singing in a drunken chorus with men or a scabby statue sleeping soundly in empty lots. Bea doesn't have to bring home a report card. Ever. No one will make generic parental demands for better grades. The Teacher returns to herself at Bea's age and begins crafting infinite versions of her life. She wonders what terrible things such freedom would have done to her.

The Teacher considers asking Bea if she can comb her hair for her. *Girl, sit down and let me give you some twists.* The Teacher thinks of Bea arriving early in the morning. She will bring her own counter-size vats and silos of grease and gel. She will give her architect-straight parts. She will oil the girl's scalp, her finger pointing down each tender row. And then the girl will go to Stanford and then Flora will get off drugs. No. Too much, even for fantasy. The ask curdles on her tongue.

The Teacher stands in the laundry closet and fishes the net bag containing her bras out of the washing machine. Her gaze falls on the domed hood of the litter box and she starts. She has not seen the cat for days. In fact, she forgot that they even had a cat. Her husband jumps when she races into the bedroom. "Where's the cat?" she pants. He holds the information for a beat as her punishment, then points to his closet. Did this man put a dead cat in the closet? The fact that she has to wonder makes her feel such embarrassment for him that she turns away. She walks to the closet and unfolds the fan doors slowly, so as to not disturb sleep or death. On the bottom of the shallow closet the cat seems flat and shapeless like the discarded clothes surrounding it, an abandoned vessel that life no longer occupies. But the cat has looked this way for months now so the Teacher reaches out to gently, gently rub an ear.

Lately when the Teacher receives her most cherished compliment, a toneless voice in her mind responds with such swiftness that the words feel like facts. You're a great teacher. *Not as great as your grandmother, your great-aunt, or your cousin.* You're a great teacher. *Not as great as the National Teacher of the Year.* You're a great teacher. *You aren't even the best in this shitty little school.* You're a great teacher. *There is absolutely no proof of that. You teach science. There has to be proof or it can't be true.*

Bea does not walk into the classroom and the Teacher is afraid. Bea only comes to school because it is a relatively safe place to be during the day. Girls who find other safe places for the day usually return multiplied into two people in one way or another.

The Teacher walks into her empty classroom and the urge to throw a tantrum is so strong her arms shoot up from her sides before she stops them. She had been so proud that she had made her classroom pleasing to the eye. She had been just *biblically* prideful that she had found a modern design that organized the chaos of the body into three colors and three harmonious fonts. Against Bea's empty seat, Bea's crisped edges, every lesson the Teacher has to teach seems trivial. The bell rings. The Teacher allows her arms to soften.

The Teacher puts down her fork and stares at her husband. A worn white tablecloth edged in lace tries to put her in the spirit of their honeymoon. But it is hard to remember the man who grinned at her across lopsided wooden tables in tiny restaurants in the

Caribbean while looking at him here with his mouth only half lifted in a smirk. She leans back, withdrawing from him. "I am aware that teaching is not going to be like a made-for-TV movie or an after-school special, and fuck you," says the Teacher.

The next morning the Teacher feels a little better about herself because Bea has never brought her to tears. The English Teacher is getting out of her Jetta. Bea has wrung tears out of her, twice. As expected, the tears improved nothing for anyone. The Teacher's Blackness has given her the gift of mastery over her tear ducts. In her entire life there has been no benefit to expressing sorrow or anger or frustration or pain, so the Teacher offers Bea none. She understands that Bea cannot offer her any. They will have to find something else to exchange.

Bea walks into class without a look in the Teacher's direction. She wears clothes from the emergency closet. A pair of purple corduroy pants cut in a reasonably popular fashion. A white sweater that has lost all its comforting softness. The Teacher wonders if Bea knows what it is like to find comfort in the things wrapped around your body.

The next day, Bea walks into class in a dress a size too small, with tiny yellow and green flowers on a bright blue background. It is a strange juxtaposition with her feline face. The impatience of her eyes. If other students do not answer questions to her liking, she raises her hand. She has the right answer or a sullen question that shows that she understands the complex interactions of the brain. When Bea's arm climbs into the air, the Teacher worries that the too-small dress will give and she will burst in the classroom, petals everywhere.

On the way to the train the Teacher speed-walks through the corner store to buy a certain thick, grape-flavored drink her husband loves. When her friends call it Ghetto Grape, the Teacher feels her face tighten. She moves through the store so fast that she almost misses Aldous, Bea's brother. Slow and ponderous in front of the Hostess cupcakes. He stares at the selection, brand-new in their packages and already stale.

The Teacher and her husband wander Home Depot. Her husband loves Home Depot but she has no idea why. He is limited to sections he can choose completed items from, like plants, appliances, or grills. He buys nothing here that has to come from here. The Teacher walks away from him and into the aisles of more challenging equipment. The Teacher eavesdrops on the men around her, agreeing and disagreeing with their assessments of the best tool for the job. She touches the soft splinters in lumber, rattles a bin of nails, cups her palm around pipes. Her father and great-aunts taught her how to fix things. She finds her husband, tall and handsome, carrying a box of lightbulbs and looking for her.

Bea has been confined in the Principal's conference room. The Teacher considers sneaking in but watches through the glass panel instead. The girl carefully unwraps a Hershey's Kiss. She uses a dirty nail with streaks of mucus-green polish to scrape the foil away, then tugs lightly at the branded ribbon still stuck to the chocolate. The Teacher feels a soul-deep respect for this girl's calm.

Down the hall, the faculty lounge crackles with some new sin. The English Teacher says, "Did you hear about Bea? She cut up a bird with scissors." The Teacher pauses. Imagines a bird. Imagines Bea. Imagines scissors. Silver with lightly pockmarked black handles. She hears the metal open and close. She tries to turn it into a weapon. She can't put these pieces together. But she can feel the teachers' fear under the hissing indignation. She is embarrassed for them.

. . .

The clump of skin and tissue and organs smeared across a paper plate on the desk seems to demand that everyone in the Principal's office remain standing as they discuss what to do about Bea. The Teacher pushes hard against people a teacher isn't supposed to push against. "This thing has been dead for days," she says. She pounds her fist on the desk and sends shame vibrating through them all. The featherless oddity bounces in agreement. "Did anyone see her kill it? Send that girl back to class."

Bea is snapping her gum. The powerful cracks echo off the smooth surfaces in the classroom, incorrectly punctuating the Teacher's lesson. For a while, Bea entertains herself by leaving the air empty and then firing off a round, making the girl next to her jump. This is a direct challenge and the Teacher gets angry. She has an unspoken agreement with Bea, built on respect that she is not at all sure is mutual. She is supposed to have a way with Bea.

Bea does not walk into the classroom and has not walked into the classroom for four days now. The Teacher closes her eyes, feeling her worth orbiting that one empty seat. She knows she shouldn't be thinking this way.

The Teacher attempts to be honest with herself about why she sent Bea to the office five days ago. When she examines the moment, she hears the sound of Bea's final snap of gum, as sharp as clapping hands. When she examines her anger, she detects the unprofessional residue of feeling betrayed. She assumes that Bea will not come walking into her classroom for a fifth day, but she does. Bea is so attentive in class that the Teacher is afraid the girl is setting her up.

For three weeks straight, Bea arrives on time. Her supplies are in a black canvas satchel with a flap over the top. It is the first time the Teacher has seen her hold anything close and carefully. It sits on her lap the entire class. She is clean underneath a new, age-inappropriate veneer. Her hair has been seized and shaped into a stiff box of weave on her head, and cheap, bright pink lipstick streaks across her mouth. She has been cared for. The Teacher unearths another thought: she wishes that the girl's caretakers were classier. That evening on the L she brings that thought out again and again and lets it sit, stinking, beside her.

Bea waits for the Teacher in the classroom. The Teacher is shocked, shocked. Thudding heart. She has not thought out a play. She busies herself at her desk after a short greeting. They are alone for thirty long seconds. It occurs to the Teacher that maybe Bea has something to say and she lifts her head and raises her eyebrows, ready to receive. The moment is gone.

The Gym Teacher does not shake easily but she is shaken. She says, "I think that girl has an eyeball in her book bag. An *eyeball.*" A laugh rises from the Teacher's throat before she can stop it.

Bea walks into class thirty seconds early without her prized black canvas satchel. Instead, she has a plastic grocery bag with a chorus of "thank you"s printed on the side. She comes to the Teacher's desk like a doe to a fence. Today, she wears clean clothes and the Teacher's wish has been granted. Bea's face is washed. There is no ridiculous weave.

The Teacher's husband has flown to the other side of the planet on business. His cat chooses four days after his departure as the day to leak shit on the carpet and die.

The Teacher knows of two ways to get animal bones so smooth and glossy they seem unreal, almost manufactured. She remembers her great-aunts, the unsentimental efficiency of their land, soft denim coveralls and a summertime discovery of luminous little skulls. The life in good Alabama soil can do all the work, reclaiming the meat and polishing the bones. That's one way. The other is to boil them.

Aldous cups his hands under the brown running water and over and over he pours water into Bea's hair. He has placed a slightly sour towel across her shoulders. He adds a gummy, clear hair gel that was abandoned in the bathroom by a girl who doesn't come over anymore. Most of the hairbrush's milky-blue plastic handle has broken off, but he clutches the stump in an underhand fist. He brushes until her hair goes limp across his wide fingers. He loops a rubber band around the handful of hair, suspicious of his work, wondering if it will hold. He steps away. Bea does not smile but she does not take it down. Both children slink into the morning.

The Teacher had offered Bea a window of time to pick up irresistible contraband, a biology textbook from a better school district. In preparation for the girl's visit, she has manufactured a number of coincidences. Inside her refrigerator ten sandwiches in wax paper form a sacred tower. The oaty fullness of good wheat bread, the sharp tang of mustard, the smooth paper with creases like gifts, all carefully conjured from her own childhood. She is practicing a casual, *I made too many for my nephew, you wanna try one? Take a few home?* A plump yellow timer on the stove will ting at the end of the lesson. *Would you like to stay for dinner?* In the closet is an almost-new denim satchel with a flap over the top. *Oh, you need something to carry all this stuff.* She gives last looks around her home, her classroom, the set. Everything is pulled taut and ready to snare.

The Teacher will tell her husband that she took care of his cat.

Olga Tokarczuk

Translated from the Polish by Jennifer Croft

Seams

THE WHOLE THING STARTED one morning when B., having wrestled the sheets off himself, toddled as usual to the bathroom. He had slept poorly of late, nights breaking him apart into pieces as small as the beads on his wife's necklace that he'd found in a drawer after she'd died. He had held that necklace in the palm of his hand, and the ancient string had broken, and the faded spheres had scattered, tiny, all across the floor. Most of them he had not managed to find, and ever since, during his sleepless nights, he had often wondered where they might be leading their globular, insensate lives, in what clumps of dust they might have nested, which minute crevices might have become their lodgings now.

That morning, as he was sitting on the toilet, he noticed that each of his socks had a seam that ran down its middle—an expertly done seam, machine-made, that led from the toe to the cuff.

It seemed like a small thing, but it did intrigue him. Evidently he had put them on without paying much attention, allowing this quirk to escape him. Socks with full-length seams, from the toes up through the insteps all the way to the cuffs. And so, once he had done with his morning ablutions, he stomped straight over to the wardrobe, where his socks resided in the bottom drawer in a dense gray-black clump. He disentangled the first one he came upon, brought it up to eye level, and unfurled it. He had landed on a black one, and the room was fairly dark, so he could not quite discern it. He had to go back to his bedroom to get his glasses, and only then was he able to see that the black sock, too, had the same kind of seam. Soon he had pulled all his socks out, taking the opportunity to try to find their mates—each and every one of them had a seam that ran from the toe to the cuff. Suddenly it felt as though this seam must be inherent to the sock, an obvious part of it, inseparable from the idea of sockhood.

At first he felt angry—whether at himself or at the socks, he wasn't sure. Total strangers to him were such socks, with such seams, spanning their entireties. As far as he had ever known, socks had seams that ran crosswise at toenail level, but beyond that, they were smooth. Smooth! He put the black one on, but it looked so odd he threw it aside in disgust. He started to try on others, but he tired fast, and for a second he felt he could not breathe. Never before had he seen such a seam on a sock. How could this be happening?

He decided to forget about the whole thing with the socks; lately he had done so often: whatever overwhelmed him, he took care to store in the attic of his mind, knowing it wasn't likely he'd need access to it again, anyway. Now he began the complicated ritual of brewing his morning tea, into which he sprinkled herbs for his prostate. The blend overflowed its strainer twice. While the liquid trickled through, B. cut bread and spread butter over two meager pieces. The strawberry jam he'd made himself had spoiled—the mold's blue-gray eye gazed out at him provocatively, shamelessly, from inside the jar. He ate his bread with butter alone.

He did think of the thing with the socks several more times, but he was already treating it as merely a necessary evil, just like the leaky faucet, the torn-off cupboard handle, or the broken zipper on his jacket. Handling such matters would have been beyond him now. When he was finished with breakfast he marked what he planned to watch later on the television schedule. He tried to occupy the day completely, leaving only a little empty time to cook lunch and go to the store. Though he almost never managed to comply with the TV's regime. Instead, he'd fall asleep in his chair and come to suddenly, without any awareness of the hour, attempting to orient himself according to whatever was then on the screen, to see what part of the day he had landed in that time.

At the store on the corner where he bought his groceries there was a woman who was called the Manager. She was a big, strong woman with very light-colored skin and well-defined eyebrows that were as thin as threads. He was already bagging his bread and a can of pasztet when he suddenly felt an urge. He asked, almost in spite of himself, for socks.

"I'd recommend the non-constricting," said the Manager, handing him a pair of brown socks tightly packed in cellophane. B. clumsily turned them over and over in his hands, trying to see if he could tell through the packaging. The Manager took them from him, swiftly stripped them of their cellophane. Then she laid out one of the socks in the palm of her manicured hand with its attractive artificial nails and held it up for B. to see.

"Look at that, they don't have cuffs, they don't constrict, so the blood flows normally through your legs into your feet. At your age . . . ," she began, but she didn't finish, no doubt realizing that age was not a good subject for small talk.

B. leaned over her hand like he intended to kiss it.

Down the middle of the sock ran a seam.

"You don't have any without that seam there, do you?" he asked, as though as an afterthought, as he paid.

"What do you mean, without a seam?" The Manager startled.

"Just for them to be completely smooth."

"But what do you mean? That's impossible. How would that work? How would the sock stay together?"

So he decided to definitively leave the thing alone. As a person starts to age, there are lots of things they miss—the world goes full steam ahead, people always coming up with something new, the next amenities. When socks had changed, he hadn't noticed. Who knew, maybe they had been this way awhile. You can't be an expert in everything, he thought, cheering himself, as he toddled on home. His trolley bag rattled after him, joyful on its wheels, and the sun was shining, and the neighbor woman from down below was washing her windows, and that reminded him he was meaning to ask her if she could recommend a window washer for his place. Now he saw his windows from the outside—gray, just like the curtains. You might think the person who lived in his apartment had already passed. But he chased those silly thoughts away and made small talk with the neighbor lady for a bit.

Seeing her spring cleaning made him anxious that he ought to be doing something, too. He set his groceries down on the kitchen floor and went into his wife's room, where he slept now, his own room having been relegated to storage: old TV schedules, and boxes, and empty yogurt containers, and other things that might yet come in handy.

He glanced around. It was pleasant and still feminine, and he found that everything was as it ought to be: the curtains were drawn, the light was low, and the bed was neatly made, with just one corner of the comforter turned down, as though he slept motionless. In the glossy cabinet stood the teacups with their decorative gold and cobalt bands, the crystal glasses, the barometer brought back from the seaside. His blood pressure monitor lay on the bedside table. On the other side of the bed, the large wardrobe had been calling him for months, but since her death, he'd hardly even opened it. Her clothing was still hanging there, and he had promised himself time and time again that he'd get rid of it, but it was a thing he'd not quite managed yet. But now a brave new thought came to him: what if he just gave these things to the woman who lived downstairs? And he could take the opportunity to ask about a window washer.

For lunch, he made himself some instant soup—asparagus—that was actually really good. As main course, yesterday's new potatoes, fried, which he washed down with kefir. After the nap that naturally followed from lunch, B. went into his room, and over the next two frenzied hours, he cleaned up all the old television schedules that had been set in there week after week, fifty-something of them yearly; and so some four hundred issues had gathered in those wobbly, dusty stacks. Throwing them away would be symbolic: B. needed to kick off this year—years began in the spring, after all, not on some number on a calendar—with an act of cleansing, like a ritual bath. He managed to get all of them out to the dumpster and to heave them over the side of the yellow container labeled "paper," but then he panicked—he'd just eliminated a part of his life, amputated his time, his own history. On tiptoe, he peered down desperately, trying to spot his TV schedules. But they had vanished into oblivion. On the staircase, as he climbed back up to his floor, he sobbed—briefly, shamefully—and then he felt weak, which must have meant his blood pressure had shot up.

The next morning, when he sat down after breakfast as usual to mark the television programs worth watching, he found his pen was really getting on his nerves. The mark it left was brown, was ugly. At first he thought it was the paper's fault, so he grabbed a different page from something else and furiously started trying to circle stuff, but those circles, too, came out brown. He decided the ink in this pen must have changed color, from old age or for some other reason. Upset that he had to disrupt his favorite ritual to go and find something else to write with, he stomped over to the glossy cabinet where he and his wife had amassed many pens over the years. There were an awful lot of them, and of course many were no longer usable—the ink had dried up, the little pathways in their cartridges had clogged. He rummaged around in that trove awhile, till he had amassed two handfuls, returning to his paper certain he would find at least one that would write as it was supposed to: in blue, in black, push come to shove in red or green. But none of them did. All of them left behind them a hideous trail the color of crap or rotting leaves or floor polish or moist rust, a color to make a person vomit. B. sat for a long time without moving, except that his hands trembled slightly. Then he leaped up and swung open the cubby in the old wall unit where he kept his documents; he grabbed the first letter from the row but instantly set it back down; it and all the rest of them—statements, bills, notices—had been written on computers. Only when he had managed to pull out some hand-addressed envelope from the very end did he understand that he had to give up: the ink on this envelope, too, was brown.

He sat down in his favorite armchair for watching TV, pulled out the leg rest, and sat still like that, breathing and gazing up at the indifferent white of the ceiling. Only after a while did other thoughts begin to storm his mind; he entertained and discarded them in turn:

—that there might be something in the ink of pens that loses its true color with time and turns brown;

—that there was something in the air now, some toxin, that made the ink change color;

and finally:

—that it was his eyesight that had changed, maybe that yellow spot, and if not, cataracts, and that that was causing him to see color in a different way.

But the ceiling was still white. B. stood and went about

marking his programs—the color didn't really matter, after all. It turned out *Secrets of the Second World War* was going to be on later, along with a movie about bees on Planète+. He had wanted to keep bees, once.

Next it was the stamps. One day he pulled his letters out of the mailbox and froze, seeing that all the stamps on them were round. Dentate, colorful, the size of a zloty coin. He felt hot. Without concern for his knee pain, he raced up the stairs, opened the door, and without even taking off his shoes ran to the cubby where he kept his correspondence. He got dizzy. He saw the stamps were round on all the envelopes, even the older ones.

He sat down in his armchair and riffled through his memories trying to find one true picture of a stamp. He knew he hadn't lost his mind—so why did these round stamps look so outrageous? Maybe he simply hadn't paid attention to stamps before now. The tongue, that sweet adhesive, that little piece of paper his fingers would attach onto an envelope . . . Letters had been fat once, even bulging. Envelopes had been light blue, and your tongue would follow along their adhesive trail, and then you'd press the two halves of the envelope together with your fingers. You'd turn over the envelope and . . . —yes, the stamp had been square. That was certain. And now it was round. How was that possible? He covered his face in his hands and sat like that for a moment in the soothing emptiness that was always there under his eyelids, just waiting to be summoned back. Then he went into the kitchen and put away his groceries.

The neighbor was hesitant to accept his gift. Suspiciously, she examined the sweaters and silk blouses so carefully folded and placed in a box. But she could not conceal the flash of lust when her gaze fell on the fur. B. hung it up for her from the door.

When they had sat down at the table and eaten their pieces of cake and drunk their tea, B. got up the courage.

"Stasia," he began dramatically, in a hushed tone. The woman looked up at him, her curiosity piqued, though her lively brown eyes were drowning in the depths of her wrinkles. "Stasia," he continued. "Something is wrong. Can you tell me whether socks are supposed to have seams—that is, seams that run all up and down them?"

She said nothing, apparently taken aback by the question, reclining slightly in her chair.

"What are you talking about, friend? What do you mean, do they have seams? Of course they do."

"But have they always?"

"But what are you talking about, 'have they always'? Of course they always have."

In a somewhat nervous motion, the woman flicked some cake crumbs off the table and smoothed out the cloth.

"Stasia, what color do pens write in?" he asked now.

She hadn't had time to reply when he added impatiently: "Blue, right? Pens, ever since they were invented, have always written in blue."

The smile was slowly disappearing from the woman's rumpled face.

"It's nothing to get so worked up over. They can also write in red and green."

"Oh, I know that, but they're usually blue, aren't they?"

"Do you want something a little stronger? A little liqueur, maybe?"

He was about to say no because he wasn't supposed to drink alcohol, but of course he realized the situation was exceptional. He said yes.

The woman turned to the wall unit and took a bottle out from the cubby there. She meted out two glasses' worth. Her hands trembled slightly. In this room of hers everything was white and light blue: wallpaper with thin blue stripes, a white cover and white throw pillows on the sofa. On the table stood a bouquet of fake blue and white flowers. The liqueur released a sweetness in their mouths, sent back dangerous words into the depths of their bodies.

With great caution, he began again. "Tell me, though. Doesn't it seem to you the world has changed? That"—he sought out the right words—"it's hard to get ahold of it these days?"

She smiled again now, as though in relief.

"Of course, my dear, but of course. Time has sped up, that's why. That is, it has not sped up, but our minds have worn out, and we can't catch the time as it goes by like we could have, once."

He shook his head helplessly, and this showed her he didn't understand.

"We're like old hourglasses, you know? I've read on this. The grains of sand get rounder the more they trickle, and they slowly rub away, which makes the sand flow faster. Old hourglasses always run fast. Did you know that? It's the same with our nervous system, it's also used up, you know, tired out, and stimuli flow through it like through a sieve that's filled with holes, and that's what makes us feel like time is flowing faster."

"And other things?"

"What other things?"

"Oh, you know . . ." He tried to come up with some ruse, but nothing came to mind, so he came out with it directly: "Have you ever heard of rectangular postage stamps?"

"Interesting," she answered, refilling their glasses. "No, I never have."

"Or of glasses that have spouts on them? I mean, well, you know, like this one. They didn't use to have those . . ."

"But—" she started, but he interrupted her.

"Or jars that open if you turn to the left, or clocks having a zero now instead of a twelve, or, and also . . ." He fell silent, too distraught to finish his list.

She was sitting across from him with her hands folded on her lap, suddenly resigned, polite, correct, as though all the wind had been taken out of her. Only her furrowed brow suggested how very uncomfortable it was for her to be in this position, and her eyes, which gazed out at him in stress and disappointment.

In the evening, as usual, he lay down in his wife's bed, which was where he had slept since her funeral. He pulled the duvet up to his nose and lay on his back, gazing into the darkness and listening to his own heartbeat. Sleep was not forthcoming, so he stood up to open the wardrobe and take out his wife's pink nightgown. He held it to his chest, and one short sob burst out of his throat. The nightgown helped—but then sleep came and annihilated everything.

Yohanca Delgado

The Little Widow from the Capital

THE WIDOW ARRIVED AT LAGUARDIA on a Sunday, but the rumors about the woman who had rented a big apartment, sight unseen, had taken an earlier flight. We had already reviewed, on many occasions and in hushed tones, in the quiet that comes after long hours of visiting, what little we knew about the widow and her dead husband.

About her life in the old country, we asked the obvious questions: Were there children? Cheryl heard from a friend who still lived in the Dominican Republic that they had only been married a year when he died. Had her husband been rich? No, our sources in the old country said, poor as a church mouse, with a big family to support out in el campo. Had the husband been handsome? Yes, in a rakish sort of way. And with what we knew we created him in our minds: medium height with a mop of curly hair and an easy laugh, walking down Saona Beach in a white linen guayabera, dropping suddenly to one knee. We ourselves felt a flutter in our hearts.

On the day the widow finally arrived in New York, the rain came in fast, heavy drops that sounded like tiny birds slamming into our windows. She emerged from the taxi with a single battered suitcase and, little-girl small, stared up at our building as the rain pelted her face. Behind us our men and children called out for their dinners, but we ignored them. We would wonder later if she had seen our faces pressed up against the windows, on all six floors, peering out over flowerpots full of barren dirt.

We watched her until she made her way out of the rain and into the lobby. Those of us lucky enough to live on the fourth floor squinted through our peepholes or cracked open our doors as the super carried her suitcase to the three-bedroom apartment she was renting. How could she afford it?

The little widow walked behind the super, her gait slow and steady on the black-and-white tiles of the hallway. He was rambling about garbage pickup and the rent. She was younger than we expected her to be, thirty, maybe. The amber outfit was all wrong for the chilly autumn weather. She was from Santo Domingo, but she looked like a campesina visiting the city for the first time, everything hand-sewn and outdated by decades. She wore an old-fashioned skirt suit, tailored and nipped at her round waist, and a pair of low-heeled black leather pumps. Seeing them made us glance down at our own scuffed sneakers and leggings. On her head, she wore a pillbox hat, in matching yellow wool sculpted butter-smooth. She dressed her short, plump body as though she adored it.

Instantly, we took a dislike.

We ourselves had been raised on a diet of telenovelas and American magazines, and we knew what beauty was. We gathered after dinner to laugh at her peculiar clothes. We murmured with fake sympathy about her loneliness, and joked that she might turn our husbands' heads. When we ran into her, though, we smiled and asked her how she was finding New York.

We began to invent stories about the little widow's life: torrid affairs that had driven her husband to die of heartbreak, a refusal to give him children, a penchant for hoarding money—we repeated the tales until we half believed them. The drama of the little widow's previous life became richer and denser, like a thicket of fast-growing ivy. Who did she think she was, anyway? Living alone in that big apartment?

The little widow seemed to understand what we expected of her: she muttered only quiet thank-yous when we held the door open as she struggled with her groceries, or when we helped her up after she slipped on a patch of ice in front of the building and landed flat on her back. As briskly as she could, she composed herself and disappeared, her head bowed low into the collar of her quaint amber coat.

When we heard that the little widow could sew, we started bringing her dresses and pants to hem, mostly because we wanted to know how she lived. The little widow's three-bedroom apartment was laid out like the others, but as she worked, our eyes darted hungrily between her and the contents of her sewing room.

Her hair was curly, dyed reddish brown, and cut short around a pointed chin. When we got to see her up close, we noted that though she did have deep creases at the corners of her eyes, she did not have a widow's peak. Her eyes were a dark hazel, and her pupils so small they looked like pinpricks.

The little widow had wallpapered her sewing room with a cheap burlap. When one of us slipped a fingernail underneath a panel and discovered that the rough cloth was glued on, we crossed ourselves and said a quick prayer for the little widow's security deposit.

On that burlap the little widow had embroidered massive, swaying palm trees, so finely detailed that we could almost feel a salty breeze warm our faces as we stood on her tailor's pedestal. Running our fingertips across the embroidered walls, we could feel the braille of her labor; the grains of sand were individually stitched, as if the little widow knew each one. The ocean seemed to ripple and surge as the little widow worked around us in meditative silence, kneeling near our ankles with a pin between her lips. She was so gentle and fluid in her movements, her soft skin creasing like a plump baby's around the pincushion she wore on her wrist.

We liked her in those moments, but even so, we didn't invite her to our birthday parties or gatherings at Christmas, though we knew she was alone in that large apartment, watching the passing of the seasons, just as we did, through black-barred windows.

We imagined she would soon have to take in a subletter to make ends meet. We mentioned that a cousin was coming to work at a coffee-filter factory and needed a place to live. She didn't have a lot of money yet, we explained, but she would be able to pay back rent on a room once she started collecting paychecks. And that could be a good source of extra income!

The little widow tilted her head to one side and appeared to think about it. She said yes, and Lucy, a single girl from Higüey, moved into the little widow's spare bedroom.

The goodwill the little widow won among us was short-lived. On a visit to get a skirt hemmed, Sonia asked to use the bathroom and snuck into the little widow's bedroom. Like the wall of her sewing room, the wall across from her bed was covered with burlap, and on that canvas the little widow had hand-stitched tidy rows of Limé dolls.

The faceless dolls looked just like the clay figurines tourists bought as souvenirs. They varied in hair and clothing—some wore their hair in a single thick plait, draped down the side of their necks, and some wore it down around their shoulders. Their dresses were every color of the rainbow and some wore Sunday hats and carried baskets of flowers. But rendered in the little widow's hand, these familiar dolls took on an eerie quality. Sonia studied the wall for a long time and became convinced that the dolls represented us.

She took a picture and texted it to the group. We looked at the faceless dolls, with their caramel skin and their ink-black hair styled into bouffants and braids and pigtails. Then we looked at each other, with our jeans and winter boots and blond highlights.

The resemblances are uncanny, we said. And so a rumor spread that the little widow was a witch come from Santo Domingo to ensorcell us and steal our husbands. We rummaged in our drawers for our old evil-eye bracelets. We started going to the dry cleaner's down on Broadway to get our clothes hemmed.

When we ran into the little widow in the halls, she smiled at us sadly, but said nothing.

To this day, we do not know how Andrés and the little widow met, but the rumor is that it happened through mutual relations from the capital.

Unlike the little widow, Andrés was a New Yorker, born and bred, and he spoke in a brambly, chaotic Spanish that she seemed to find charming. On their first date, the little widow wore a silk slip dress, hand-embroidered with small, delicate birds. He wore a blazer, jeans, and dress shoes. They stayed out until two in the morning, and when they came home, we heard her laugh ringing in the halls, a lovely, alien sound.

The next day he delivered to her a bouquet of radiant, limp-necked sunflowers. She arranged them in a giant vase by the window in her sewing room. Then in the weeks that followed, he could be heard in the small hours of the morning, serenading her on his guitar. He wrote her poetry, and according to Gladys—who took to pressing a glass against the wall she shared with the little widow—it wasn't half bad.

He was about thirty, like the little widow. But unlike her, he wore his age gaily. He was boyish and relaxed, and we often spied him leaning on doors and smoking cigarettes near the trash cans. He kept his hair cut in a neat fade that he refreshed every two weeks. He used the creaky metal ladder on the fire escape to do pull-ups until the super told him to stop. We decided that we liked him, tsk-tsked that he was too good for the little widow, with her opaque melancholy and insufferable pride.

It is said that he proposed to her right in her sewing room. Relieved that she was finally on the right track, heading toward a life we understood, we flocked in a squealing, air-kissing mob to her apartment to admire the ring: a small round diamond on a simple gold band. The way she wore it made it look like something Elizabeth Taylor would have been proud to own. There was a new lightness in the little widow that we liked to see, in spite of ourselves.

She smiled often, sometimes for no apparent reason, and it was a strange, unfamiliar smile that made us think of sunlight bursting through a cloud-choked sky. The wedding was set for the following month and the weeks flitted by. Lucy told us the little widow was hard at work on a wedding dress and that she mooned around the house, dreamy, distracted, and in love.

It all fell apart as quickly as it had come together. Five days before the wedding, Lucy woke up in the middle of the night to find Andrés standing at the foot of her bed. He had come in with the little widow's key, he said, and he had come in to see her.

Lucy leaped up and, assuming he was drunk, tried to walk him back to the door. But he refused to go and instead pinned her against the wall, which the little widow had recently embroidered with sunflowers. He attempted to unfasten his pants. Now scared in earnest, Lucy screamed and shoved him to the floor.

The little widow appeared quickly and without sound, like a ghost. She had been working; she had a needle pressed between her lips, and one lip was bleeding. She looked from Andrés to Lucy and understood everything.

Without a word, the little widow took Lucy by the hand and

led her into her own bedroom until Andrés was gone, and then she dead-bolted them into the apartment for safety. The little widow kept vigil by Lucy's bed until she fell asleep, then locked herself in her own room.

For two days, the little widow didn't speak, or eat, or sleep. She subsisted on a nightly glass of morir soñando, which she drank to appease Lucy. The girl blamed herself for everything and thought it a small penance to squeeze the orange juice for the little widow's drink.

Because we didn't know yet that the little widow was rich, we assumed Andrés returned two nights later because he loved her.

Florencia spotted him from her window on the first floor and it only took a few minutes on the phone to spread the news. By the time he was at the little widow's door, we all hovered at ours, swatting away needy children and chatty husbands.

On every floor, we cracked our doors. His pleas reverberated through the tiled hallways, filling even the central stairwell. Our hungry ears consumed every sound: The wet, racking sobs. The thud of his knees dropping onto her welcome mat. The wailing against the hard wood of the little widow's door.

He was sorry, he insisted. It hadn't meant anything. Who was Lucy to him?

After nearly an hour, it seemed to us that he planned to spend the night there, performing this noisy contrition. Then the little widow flung open her door with a whip-sharp bang that sent an echo all the way down to the first floor.

"What," she said, her voice a small, cold blade, "do you think is going to happen next?"

All through the building, our ears pricked up.

"You're the love of my life," he moaned. Cheryl, watching from her apartment across the hall, could attest to the fact that he was still, at this point, on his knees.

"And are you mine?" The little widow crossed her arms over her chest. She wore a silk dressing gown, embroidered with human hearts the size of silver dollars.

"Yes, yes," he cried, pressing his face to her bare feet.

The little widow stepped back to free her feet, and then stepped around him, out into the hallway. "Let these busybodies witness," she said. And now we could see that her eyes were red and her curls ravaged by nights of insomnia.

Andrés hobbled after her, on his knees, making mournful sounds.

"Let these chismosas be my witnesses," she said again, waving her hand and locking eyes with Cheryl, who later told us that she had nearly died of shame. "If you bother me again, you will not live to tell about it."

Andrés clasped his hands together in a prayer motion and mutely held them up to her.

The little widow looked at him as if he were a turd on the sidewalk. She shoved him aside, walked back to her door. "You heard me," she said, one hand on her doorknob. "Not a single knock."

She closed the door and left Andrés to gather himself off the floor and wipe the snot from his face. We thought we'd never seen a man renounce his dignity quite so definitively and that realization seemed to hit him at the same time. Grimacing, he wiped his mouth, and cursed under his breath. He kicked the door as hard as he could. Once, twice.

"You think you can control me," he said. "I'll show you control. And Lucy, too." He slammed the heel of his hand on the door.

Only Cheryl—who slowly and silently slipped the chain lock into place, all while holding her door ajar and keeping one eye firmly on Andrés—can describe what happened next, and only you can decide if you believe it.

Andrés raised his arm again, and as he drew it back for another blow, it froze. The arm appeared to be stuck to his head, as if glued there. His back still to Cheryl, Andrés shook himself and tried to use his other hand to pry it loose, but that one became attached, too, and then it looked like he was holding his hands to his head, the way men do when their baseball team is losing. He began to make a frantic humming sound.

When he turned to Cheryl, with the purest, most desperate panic she had ever seen blazing in his eyes, she discovered that his lips had been sewn shut with large, sloppy stitches.

He dropped to his knees with a grunt, and then bent in half at the waist. He kept folding in on himself, over and over, becoming smaller and smaller, his moans of distress more and more distant, until he was just a small scrap of cream fabric that fluttered to the floor in front of apartment 4E.

No one knocked on the little widow's door after that. Three days passed in shallow breaths.

In our apartments, huddled together over coffee, we discussed what we knew and filled in what we didn't. We imagined the little widow, dead-eyed and small in her cavernous apartment, punching a threaded needle through cloth—until she folded the entire building in on itself, apartment after apartment, life after life, collapsing together—until she could tuck it all into her little silk coin purse and carry us away forever inside her handbag.

We pretended we were innocent. Weren't we like an old fan, just moving the air around? We tipped over our coffee cups and saw in our fortunes an angry darkness that threatened to swallow us. And hadn't we sensed it from the beginning?

For the first time, it occurred to us to call our families, the ones back in the old country, to find out the full story. We pooled our facts together. We knew the story people liked to tell, but now we were detectives. We dug deeper, asked our distant aunts to ask their cousins what they knew, and were stunned at how shallowly buried the truth was.

The little widow had married for love right out of high school, to a man who was primarily interested in her family's money but liked her well enough besides. When the new couple said they wanted to move from the capital to the beach, her parents bought them a big, sprawling house on the coast near Bávaro, and hired three live-in servants to work there. And the little widow was happy! She loved the beach; it was said that she went swimming twice a day, that she walked up and down the shore as if she wanted to memorize every gull, every seashell, every grain of sand. It was at this time that the little widow began to embroider seascapes and mermaids, her head bent low over her needle and hoop.

But middling affection does not a good man make. The husband began to throw his weight around the house, speaking cruelly to the servants, punching walls, breaking things. The little widow miscarried their first child under mysterious circumstances and mourned the loss in private. She focused more than ever on her work; sometimes the light in her sewing room burned through the night.

Less than a year later, a servant filed a police report against the husband, saying that he had forced himself on her and she had become pregnant. The husband's proximity to the little widow's influential family allowed him to avoid serious charges. But he did not live to see another year; the servant's husband shot him, point-blank, as he walked down the beach near the house.

The little widow's parents swiftly stepped in, at their daughter's request, to scatter the tragedies of the story in the wind. They paid the hefty bribes required to free the servant's husband and sold the beach house to American tourists. The little widow quietly went away.

Her wedding to Andrés had been scheduled to take place at Our Lady of Lourdes, the crumbling, majestic old church we attended, and on that day, we dressed for Sunday mass.

Someone's mother-in-law in Queens said she spotted someone

who looked like Andrés slinking out of a bodega, but who could be sure? The tiny scrap of cream fabric had long since disappeared in the building's hustle and bustle. We knew for certain that the wedding was canceled. But for reasons we still can't explain, we sent our husbands and kids ahead to Sunday school and lingered in the building. The wedding had been scheduled for four in the afternoon, and when the time came, we opened our doors and, like cuckoos from their clocks, stepped out of our apartments and crowded into the narrow fourth-floor hallway.

By then we knew her name, and we started slowly calling it, in unison. Lucy came out first, dressed in sweatpants and looking like a wrung-out dishcloth. When we asked her if the little widow had spoken to her, she shook her head sadly.

A thud inside, the sound of footsteps, and our murmurs dissipated into a tense silence. When the little widow opened her door, she wore an enormous white silk wedding dress.

On her head, she had crowned herself with a ring of white silk flowers, embroidered with red drops of blood, delicate as anything we'd ever seen. Her face seemed younger than we remembered, though her undereyes were bruise-blue from lack of sleep.

She maneuvered the seemingly boundless skirts of her dress through the tight door frame and began making her way to the elevator. With a gasp, we parted like a sea to let her pass. At least six feet of heavy, layered skirts embroidered to the last inch with small, careful cursive letters trailed behind her.

Unfamiliar-yet-familiar names were scattered densely across the silk like polka dots. Women's names from the old country: the Dominican *y*'s, the florid, delirious layering of syllables. We knew our people.

We did not recognize these specific names and we did not dare ask anything of the little widow. Instead—and without thinking—we formed two lines and picked up the train of the dress to keep it from getting soiled as the little widow walked slowly down the long corridor with her head bowed and her hands clasped.

Mutely, we helped her enter the elevator and passed her the skirts, which foamed up around her, rising well past her shoulders. As the heavy door slid closed, she gave us the brokenhearted smile we had come to recognize.

"Up," we half whispered, half barked, after pressing our ears to the door. We ran toward the stairs, taking them two at a time to keep up with the old elevator, jostling one another at each landing—until we saw that the little widow was going up to the roof.

She walked out onto the silver-painted cement with us trailing behind. The air was cold but we hardly noticed. We elbowed each other and pushed to get close enough to see her without touching her, though when one of us shoved through and blurted, "Don't jump, viudita! Don't do it!"—she spoke for all of us.

The little widow turned to look at us, like a somnambulist shaken brutally awake.

Then, before anyone had a chance to stop her, she sprinted across the silver roof, clutching her frothing skirts to her sides. She climbed onto the ledge and we saw, or thought we saw, the cream soles of her naked feet.

She turned to face us. Behind her the sun had begun its plunge to earth, the sky ripe-mango orange behind needle-sharp skyscrapers. The little widow's dress lathered all around her, making her look ten feet tall. Why hadn't we seen before how beautiful she was?

The little widow's eyes shone. It was as if she were recognizing us, each of us, across a crowded room. Afraid to approach, we formed a semicircle around her, willing her to stay.

For a long moment we were mesmerized, frozen where we stood, in our regret.

When we came to our senses and reached for her, surging forward together—to grab hold of her dress, at least, to keep her from falling the seven stories to the street below, we didn't move fast enough. She took up her dress again, great big fistfuls of it, and with her back to the sky, let herself fall.

The whine of a car alarm below halted our hearts. We rushed to the edge and peered over. And what we saw—how to even describe it? The dress dissolved into a thousand pigeons, and they filled the space between our building and the next with brown and gray and white, with the sound of wings flapping. The air was thick with the feathery thrum of their wings as they flew away in different directions, toward downtown, toward the river, toward the Bronx, and skyward, toward heaven.

The little widow was gone. All we had left—as we huddled together for warmth on that silver roof and watched the sky deepen to the bruised plum of Manhattan night—was the story. And so we told it again, and again, until we had stitched the details into our memory.

We carried the story back to the patios of Santo Domingo, where we sat at dusk with the yellow light of our old family homes behind us, listening to the crickets and the slow creak of our wicker rocking chairs, and told the tale again, except this time it ended like this: in some far-flung town, maybe here in the old country, maybe back in the new, the little widow appeared with a small suitcase in hand.

Here, our eyes brightened and we leaned forward.

This time she arrived without fanfare, we said, and her neighbors liked her right away. The little widow wore an amber-colored dress, hand-sewn. Perhaps a little older than we remembered, but still recognizable, with her full cheeks and shiny curls. She signed a lease for a house by the beach. She was already picturing the magic she would create on these new walls, and we, too, thrilled to imagine it.

Eshkol Nevo

Translated from the Hebrew by Sondra Silverston

Lemonade

W E NEVER TALKED ABOUT what happened, not even once. In fact, when it was all over, people tried hard to forget.

The minute they put us both on vacation without pay and closed schools for the kids, Gavri started wandering around at home, like a kind of iRobot, and he kept repeating the same thing over and over again: We have to make lemonade from the lemons, we have to make lemonade from the lemons.

The first week, he had the idea of marketing online workshops to teach acting in front of a camera. There's nothing like it, it's a bonanza; he tried to convince me in order to convince himself. Everyone's home in front of their screens all day long, everyone has a camera on their phone or computer, people will die for it.

Honey, don't say "people will die," I told him, it's not appropriate now. And he got angry: Why do you always pour cold water on my ideas? You're the only person I said it to. Of course I won't write anything like that when I advertise it.

The ad was something he posted on his Facebook page. *Theater director (winner of the Golden Porcupine Award) is giving a workshop for acting in front of a camera. Possibility of private or group sessions. Number of places limited.*

He couldn't decide whether to add a picture of a camera or one of himself, and in the end (I knew it), he posted one of himself. Taken ten years ago. He debated whether to invest money in promotion, and in the end (I knew it, but I didn't say a word so that after it failed, he wouldn't blame me), he decided not to invest. Because that wasn't a good time for investing.

The post got a lot of likes, and a few shares. But in actual fact, only one woman showed an interest in signing up. She was about twenty-five. And basically, she just wanted to flirt a little with the idol of her youth and not really sign up.

Gavri didn't give up. For another few weeks, he tried, unsuccessfully, to organize and sell to event companies the concept of Zoom birthdays for kids; to interest an army buddy in developing an app that would enable people to send and receive virtual hugs; to offer my services as a Skype financial advisor to self-employed people in crisis.

Meanwhile, our money was running out. His parents are kibbutzniks, and mine are dead, so there was no one we could ask for help. Over the last few years, we'd spent the small reserve we had because Gavri decided he was sick and tired of performing in kids' shows and TV series for teenagers. He wanted to switch professions and become a director. That's just how it is, baby, he told me, when you go into a new field, you start from the bottom. Salary-wise too. So pretty quickly—two months after the epidemic broke out—we reached the point where our bank started offering us loans. Anyone who understands a little about finance—and, after all, I am a money manager—knows that this is the point when things start deteriorating.

And then Gavri came up with an idea. Or more accurately, did everything so I would suggest it, not him. The little ones had finally fallen asleep and Yuvi was in his room with Fortnite, so we locked our door and watched live porn. We usually only watched other people doing things, and didn't do them ourselves because Gavri was too tired and too down. But that night, his hand stroked my thigh as we watched—which is our signal—so I turned off Andy and Laurel, from Toronto. And we had sex. I didn't come, but I enjoyed the touching. Any physical contact was welcomed those days.

Later, we went out to the small balcony off our bedroom and smoked a joint. Gavri took a drag and said, That Andy and Laurel, they probably make tens of thousands of dollars a month, and passed me the joint. Think about it, if every person pays three dollars for a weekly subscription and they have ten thousand subscribers—he took the joint from me—and what expenses can they possibly have? They probably pay something to the site and that's it—he kept the joint a little too long and said, I could get hold of a good camera—he handed me the joint—and didn't say anything else. And waited for me to say something. When I didn't, he retreated quickly and rejected his own idea. No way, no way, it's like that movie, *Indecent Proposal*, except that instead of one Robert Redford, there'll be thousands of perverts who'll look at you.

At me? I took a drag—Why only at me?—and held on to the joint a long time. Deliberately.

Someone has to film it, Gavri said.

I didn't think of that, I said, and handed him the joint. But what exactly will you film?

You, doing that trick of yours, he said, and crushed the butt in the ashtray even though it still had a few drags left in it.

I didn't say anything. Even though the waste drove me crazy. Every bit of waste drove me crazy in those days. I angrily turned off every light left on for no reason. Any kid who didn't finish his food got a speech from me.

And what about the kids? I asked.

We'll only film at night. After they fall asleep.

What about the people who know me?

We'll put a wig on you, and a kind of mask for your eyes.

I'm a thirty-nine-year-old woman, honey, who gave birth three times. Who will want to see the body of a thirty-nine-year-old woman who gave birth three times?

You have a fantastic body, baby. And . . . you have that trick.

We didn't talk about it for a few days. But one evening after sitting for an hour trying to make an online order for groceries and after filling out all the credit card details, I received a message saying that the purchase was not approved. When I called the credit card company, they suggested that I take an emergency loan that would cover our overdraft.

So that night, I said to Gavri, Let's go for it. And I didn't have to say what "it" was. Clearly, he'd been waiting for me to give the green light, and I saw that he was happy and I saw that he was trying not to show it.

Are you sure? he asked, putting his hand on mine. In the end, it's your body, and only you can decide what you want to do with it.

Yes, I'm sure, I said, and pulled my hand away. I won't let my children go hungry. And I added, But on one condition.

What? Gavri asked.

That no one ever knows about it.

Of course, he said.

I looked him in the eye and said, And that includes transformations, Gavri.

Because ever since he decided he wanted to be a "creator" and not "a slave to the theater," everything he writes, all the skits and plays and proposals for TV series, have all been inspired by our real relationship and the real problems of our children, and every time I complain about it, he says, But, baby, I made transformations.

Including transformations, Gavri said. Done.

From that moment on, everything happened pretty fast.

He got hold of a camera (don't know how and don't want to know). Lighting. A wig. An eye mask. We signed up on a site. And agreed to their draconian conditions. I picked a fake name for myself: Lemonade. And one night, after the kids fell asleep, he filmed me live. In order to do the trick, I have to concentrate, and it was hard to concentrate when I knew that people all over the world were looking at me. So I closed my eyes and pictured the young salesman at Eye Contact. He always complimented me when I tried on glasses, and even though I knew he was flirting with me so I'd buy another pair I didn't need, I sometimes caught him staring at my breasts. So I imagined that I was doing the trick for him. I imagined that he was in his bedroom now watching Lemonade. And that helped me concentrate.

When I finished, Gavri said, Listen, that was fantastic. You were amazing. And I told him to turn off the camera already, and felt as empty and sad as I had in my Tel Aviv period, which I liked to call my wild time, but which was actually my humiliating time, and I started to cry.

Gavri lay down beside me on the bed. You don't have to do it, baby, if it makes you feel so bad. We'll manage somehow. How, exactly, I asked. And he didn't answer.

We broadcasted every night for almost a month. The first week, we only made five hundred dollars, because most of the subscribers were the type that took advantage of the site's first-week-free policy. The next week, we went up to seven hundred. The third week, we jumped exponentially to three thousand. And for the three days of the fourth week when we managed to broadcast, we reached ten thousand. Dollars. Which is twenty-five thousand shekels after taxes. Finally I could order summer clothes for the kids. Which arrived the next morning.

I went into Yuvi's room to arrange his on the shelf, so he would have a nice surprise when he woke up. He was sleeping without a shirt, and the blanket covered him to his waist.

How beautiful he is, I thought. Like Gavri, when we met. Actually, more than Gavri. He got the best of both of us. What a heartbreaker he'll be when he stops being eleven, I thought. I reached down to stroke his head—because I can only do that when he's sleeping—and accidentally stepped on his computer cable. The screen was pulled slightly toward me. Which woke it up.

He didn't know that Lemonade was me. I'm sure of that. A mother knows her son, and if he had known it was me, I would have seen it on him right away. He didn't know. He continued being hostile and needy at the same time, just like before, and continued to look at me in exactly the same clear way he always did. But we stopped broadcasting anyway. Obviously.

Gavri dared once to say that it was a great time to buy an apartment as an investment for anyone who had a little money put away. And he added, as if there was no connection, that we had to block those kinds of programs on Yuvi's computer, who would have believed that a kid his age . . . What has the world come to?

I yelled at him quietly—parents learn how to yell quietly so their kids won't hear—that if he even hinted at it one more time, I'd make a transformation in my life and leave him. And I didn't care that we weren't allowed to go out of the house without permission. That whole business had turned me off him anyway, big-time.

That scared him. He got down on his knees, grabbed my hand, and kissed it. Baby, he said, I'm so sorry. You're the love of my life, baby, I can't live without you. I stroked his head and thought, Once an actor, always an actor.

A few weeks later, they lifted the lockdown and sent the kids back to school, and they said on TV that it would take the economy a while to recover, it wouldn't happen all at once. One Friday, when Gavri was at rehearsal for the new play he was in, I went to Eye Contact. On the way there, I thought, If the young salesman is there, and if he flirts with me, I'll ask him to give me my annual eye test, and in the small room, I'll press him up against the chart with the lines of numbers and kiss him and tell him that I'm ready to leave everything for him, and I'll mean it.

But the store was closed, and in the window, where eyeglasses no one could afford had been displayed, there was only a small sign saying that a touch therapy center was coming soon.

So I drove to pick Yuvi up from school and we went to the supermarket together. By the time we got home, Gavri was already there, and they both carried all the bags from the car while I put the groceries away in the cabinets and the fridge. Since then, we've never talked about it, not even once. In any case, when it was all over, people tried hard to forget.

'Pemi Aguda

Breastmilk

THE WARM, SLIMY CREATURE that is my son is placed in my arms. He is crying a grating, lusty soprano. I stretch my mouth into the likeness of a smile. I don't look down at the baby. I hold him loosely: too tight and he might squirt out of my grip and ricochet off the white walls of my hospital room.

"We're going to cut the cord now, Mummy," one of the nurses says, and I nod. She says "Mummy" in that patronizing tone I use when I tell my cousin's children that they are so big and tall and grown now.

"Can I cut it?" Timi asks.

I don't hear what they say to him, how these efficient women tell him no. But I see him step back, his head lowered like he's been chastised. I could have told him that this is not one of those New Age hospitals that allow men to actively participate in the birth, that the father is merely a bystander here, a witness. But I didn't. There are many things I don't say to my husband.

The baby is taken from me so he can be cleaned, so I can be cleaned too. Through the haze of twelve-hour labor pains, I watch my husband reach out to receive our baby from the nurse, now swaddled in the ewedu-colored cloth we bought. I am tired. My gritty eyes want to close against the world, and my aching body wants to gather its leaking, melting shape into itself so I can recover from all the pushing and groaning and bloody catastrophes of childbirth. But I want to watch Timi's first moments of fatherhood. His body is stiff, in the practiced hold they taught us in prenatal classes: baby's neck in the crook of your elbow, the other hand supporting the rest of the weight. He swings his head toward me—the only part of his body he releases from this wooden stance that proclaims fierce responsibility and a dash of pride—and smiles. Through mine, I see the sheen of his tears.

I turn away and settle back into the pillow.

In the morning, my mother shows up. She is telling me that she came as soon as she could, that my father would be proud of this feat of mine, bringing new life into the world. And am I glad? Am I relieved? Am I fine? Am I proud?

I am excused from responding to her barrage because I am a woman who just had a baby, an exhausted woman who endured earth-shifting contractions, who thrashed through a forest of clawing pain, whose pelvic region throbs as if pounded by a pestle. My mother doesn't sit; she hovers above me, tucking a braid away, stroking my cheek.

I roll my eyes. "What of the conference?"

"Bah," she says, waving fingers as if she didn't spend the last six months putting the event together. "I have a grandchild!"

The headliner of the conference is a friend of hers, a woman who is combining her research on chemosignals in some Netherlands university with knowledge from her grandmother's traditional beliefs and claiming that with practice, we can all smell emotions. When my concern doesn't fade, my mother adds that her assistant is very capable.

A nurse comes to save me from my mother's goodwilled pawing. "Da-Silva?"

Her uniform is so white, her waist so small. She looks like a cardboard cutout, this nurse. She also looks faintly like someone I have seen on Timi's Facebook when I hit "Load More" so that his life appears before me in grainy frozen smiles with strangers. Why do some Nigerian hospitals insist on these silly white caps for their nurses? Her cap looks like a diamondless tiara tucked into her Afro bun.

"Yes," my mother answers for me. "This is her."

There are many times I have wished my mother were present to speak for me, with her impassioned activist's voice. Like the night Timi confessed his affair, thirty-eight weeks ago. But am I not an adult?

"Your baby is scheduled to receive formula again in thirty minutes," the nurse says, "but I came to see if there are any changes. Any thick liquid? Clear? Yellow?"

As she reaches for the neck of my hospital gown, I catch her wrist. Her face rearranges itself in surprise, and I think she isn't that pretty; her eyes are too close together. "There's no change," I say.

She twists free and brushes the rescued limb against the front of her dress, as if to restore her composure. "Okay, but I still need to take a look, Mrs. Da-Silva—"

"Ms.," my mother corrects. "*Mizzz.*"

What does "Mrs." really mean? is a question I grew up hearing my mother pose to people who could only stutter in response.

The nurse's frown deepens; she is unsettled by this interaction with me and my mother. "I'm sorry, *Miz* Da-Silva. Your son isn't pooping as much as we'd like. He's okay, but to be safe, I'm going to have to feel around for colostrum, milk."

That's all I did last night while Timi slept in a chair beside me. I prodded and tugged and massaged, but my breasts have stayed swollen to unfamiliar D-cups, nipples stubbornly dry. They told me milk, or something like it, would come a few months into pregnancy, or around birth.

"I said there's nothing." I jerk the top of the gray sack of a gown they have put me in. I turn away from the nurse's unpretty face to my mother's, which is now contemplating me with a frown.

Timi holds my hand, and my mother caresses my shoulder while she cradles our baby in one elbow. Another day has passed, and the doctor is asking questions before discharging us. I hang limp in Timi's clasp. His palms are always so dry. How do I trust a man whose sweat glands won't betray him? His palms were dry then too, when he stroked my arm and informed me he was going to Abuja for business, just business. But should this man trust his wife who claims she forgives his affair, who pardons his cheating so easily, a wife who says everything is forgotten and buried? A wife who kisses those dry palms the morning after his confession and says, "We're good, babe." Should he trust this woman if she doesn't believe the truth of her own forgiveness?

I wriggle free from Timi's hold and reach for the baby we have not yet named; we have two more days till the naming ceremony. My mother lowers him into my arms.

"And don't worry about lactating," the doctor is saying. "I don't want you to worry at all. Lactation happens late for some women, others not at all. Some women even say breastfeeding is old-fashioned! But everything is fine as long as baby is loving the delicious formula."

I want to ask the doctor how he knows the formula is delicious, if it is more delicious than breastmilk, if the baby can tell the difference.

When we saw the baby's penis for the first time, pointed out to us in the jumble that is an ultrasound, the nurse gave a practiced chuckle. "See how he's proud of that penis!" she said. Timi's eyes liquefied. I turned away from him and away from my son's penis, to look at the fetal growth chart on the wall. A son? My heart broke a little. A son who could grow up to become a man, a man who might hurt other people no matter how well I raise him because a man is a man, even when he is the best man—as Timi has shown me. I gathered myself and turned back to smile at the monitor.

Maybe it started there, my body's rejection of my child, visiting the sins of father on son?

I lower my head to blow air into my baby's face, my mouth a soft O. My smile is not forced when he wrinkles his face and blinks at me.

"If you want to see our lactation consultant," the doctor adds, "you're welcome to do so. He's not in-house, though well recommended. Give it some time, I'd say. Baby is fine, poop is fine, all is fine!" The doctor has three horizontal tribal marks on each cheek that squirm when he speaks. My baby's cheeks look extra smooth in comparison. I press my lips to that smoothness. Timi beams at this picture and asks if I'm ready to go home.

All of our family members come out for the naming ceremony. Their voices ring loud as they celebrate me, celebrate Timi. A first child, a son! Someone has dropped a thick white envelope into my lap—for my hard work, they say. I let the insulting thing slide off.

Timi strolls around in his agbada made from the matching guinea brocade his mother bought for us, a baby-blue shade of sky we haven't seen since harmattan started. He stops to laugh at someone's joke, the cloth billowing around him, so natural, so *man,* so *Timi.* He has been cradling our baby all day, as if eager to show off how modern he is, a rare Nigerian man who "allowed" his wife to keep her mother's name, a man who will be involved in the care of his child. I want to yank the baby from him, but I do not have the right. The one bond that ties baby to mother, at least for the first year, is missing. My breasts oppress me with their emptiness.

We name him Fikayo; we call him Fi. Olufikayo. All the names

I suggested were Finn, Fenton, Fran, because my love of *F* names had lingered from devouring all that angsty British literature when I was a teenager. But Timi reminded me that we are Yoruba, not English, and the name should reflect that.

Is there a Yoruba name for "this child was conceived in the throes of hurt and anger"? An Egun name for "this boy is a result of your forgiveness sex after your husband confessed his wrong"?

I acquiesced easily to his sensible argument about the names, remembering how he had quietly rebutted my reservations about becoming his girlfriend six years ago, an elevation from our casual fling. "Come on, we have the same views on the important things, Aduke!" he said. "That's what's important ni t'ori Ọlọrun. That's a foundation not many folks have."

Timi's mother's pastor calls out the names, Olufikayo Olujimi Olatunde. The people cheer and toast with glasses of wine and zobo under the canopy we rented for the day. When the robed pastor dabs anointing oil on Fikayo's head, the baby begins to cry. I jump up to snatch him.

"He's hungry," I murmur to no one in particular, and retreat into the house. I hear music pick up behind me, Sunny Adé blasting from rented speakers, my cousin's children screaming at each other, Timi's mother shouting for the caterer to start serving small chops. The woman's Christian benevolence is what prevents friction between her and my mother, between me and her, between her and Timi. "Love thy neighbor as thyself," she mutters to herself frequently, like a calming mantra, shrugging in acceptance even when she doesn't understand why her son is acting "like a woman," doing household chores and sharing the financial decision-making with me. The microphone screeches and I close the nursery door behind me, but the door is not thick enough to drown them out.

One of my aunties has tied my iro for me, insisting that the tighter the wrapper, the faster my pregnancy pouch will shrink. I release my belly now and flop down into the armchair. I shift Fi in my arms and draw the diaper bag closer with a foot. It is an awkward process; I haven't yet perfected the juggling acts of motherhood.

He quiets when the nib fills his mouth, and I am envious of a plastic bottle.

My aunt finds me dozing off while Fi feeds.

"Ahn ahn, feeding bottle kẹ?" Her gele is green and gold, and the light from the window reflects against the scaly material. I squint and look down at Fi. He has fallen asleep.

"Aunty," I say.

"But kilode? Why are you not breastfeeding, mgbọ?" She crosses her arms under her own breasts. "Deyemi's wife had the nerve to tell me she was not breastfeeding so her breasts won't sag. Sag! You too, Aduke? Does your mother know about this decision?"

"Aunty, Aunty!" I check to make sure Fi is still sleeping and lower my voice. "There's no milk, Aunty." I have begun to cry.

My aunt's face relaxes. She moves to pick Fi up, places him in his cot. She leans forward then, as if to hug me.

"I know what to do. Jumoke had this same problem, but you should see her now! The baby girl is three, and we're begging her to stop. I will send you one agbo that my sister makes in Ijebu. You will rub it like . . ." She reaches for my breasts, through the baby-blue brocade, through my bra, and begins to knead. I feel myself leaving my body through a frustrated sigh, floating to the ceiling of the lilac nursery with the white silhouettes, above my own gele, above my aunty's gele, which dips forward in rhythm with her hands, above my body, above my shame.

Our friends visit with gifts that are not newborn-baby appropriate. Only Sandra, who writes an annoyingly wholesome mummy blog with a large readership, shows up without a hard-edged toy, but she also brings along a pious look to throw at the feeding bottle and formulas. If I were to check, I would probably find an irate blog post railing against them. Timi tells her I need to rest when he catches the glance. The others bring laughter and warmth and kisses for Fi, but I am grateful when I walk the last person out the front door and return to the silence of our living room. Timi is sitting on the edge of an armchair, and I know he wants to speak with me. I grab a bib from the floor and head to the nursery, to my baby, to hide.

"Aduke."

I turn to look at my husband, his wide nose, the Cupid's bow that would fight Rihanna's for perfection. The first time I kissed him, I let my tongue trace that dip, recarving it with my lust.

"Are you okay?" he asks now.

"Yeah, why?"

"You've been kind of distant."

What I should say is: I don't care about your stupid ex; I care that I don't know how to be angry about her. What I say instead is: "We just had a baby, Timi. Have you read any of Sandra's articles about motherhood?" The laugh that punctuates my sentence is a weak sputter.

Timi points at me, then at himself. "We're okay?" He wants my eyes to meet his; I hear it in his question. They meet. Mine skitter away.

"We're great," I say. I look down to find my baby's bib crumpled in my fist. I straighten out the butterflies on soft white cotton, blue and orange and pink. "I'm just tired, you know?"

"But you—"

I look up, afraid he will say that I am not even breastfeeding, that he will ask me what is making me tired.

"You don't even let me help with Fikayo. You're always sleeping in the damn nursery. This wasn't our plan o, Aduke."

Of course, Timi is not insensitive. He rises right along with me when Fi cries us awake. I keep shushing him away, back to sleep, away from the nursery. "I just feel a bit guilty about the breastmilk thing. Maybe I'm overcompensating." I push the fiction out of my lungs easily.

Back in Sunday school, where my mother used to send me before she decided religion hated women, the teacher would pipe, "To err is human, to forgive is divine," even if we kids didn't know what it meant to err. Now that Timi has shown me what it means, the homily taunts me. If to forgive is divine, why am I resisting my own divinity? I want to feel the righteousness that comes with forgiving infidelity, but all I feel is shame at my lack of backbone, my lack of indignation, and fear that if it happens again, I will just as easily forgive Timi.

My husband is good, has been good. This was a fluke, and he confessed immediately because he knew I would want to know immediately, and he was sorry, and he is sorry every day, and I could see his heart breaking because he knew he had broken mine, and he is so very sorry, sorry in a way that I believe?

Am I even my mother's daughter, to be thinking about forgiveness?

Now Timi is asking if I think this is postpartum depression. "I'm not depressed. Just tired."

"Come back to bed," he begs. "I miss you."

I flinch.

"God, I'm not talking about sex. I'm not a monster!"

I raise both hands in surrender. "Yeah, we can move his cot to our room tomorrow. How about that?"

When Timi lets out a dissatisfied breath, covering his face, its beautiful features, with his hands, I flee into the nursery, closing the door that is only wood, not metal, not thick enough to protect me. But why do I need protection? Why shouldn't *he* be seeking protection from *me*? I want to be the type of woman who turned into a pillar of flames when Timi told me about sex with the ex in Abuja. I want to have singed the confession off his tongue until the smell of his own burning choked him, robbing him of oxygen till he was flat on his face, at my feet, melting in my fury. I want to be a woman like my mother. There are YouTube videos of my mother cutting down the governor at a rally organized by her nonprofit for women's development. The governor had said she should leave politics to men. "Don't you dare, Mr. Olusegun Adetula!" my mother screamed, spittle gathering in the corner of her Ruby Woo–painted lips. "Don't you dare belittle the women who carry this society. We carry it!" But no, I went straight into his arms. Mine was a faltering anger: here, then gone. My mother would be disgusted to see the weakness in her spawn.

We're in the nursery. I am seated on the floor between my mother's knees on a folded blanket, feeding Fikayo while my mother lines my scalp with oil. The smell of the coconut oil meets the smell of formula in my nostrils. Fi is naked against my bare breasts, skin-to-skin bonding my mother scoffed at the first time she saw us in this position. "Bonding?" She laughed. "Where did you read about this one now?" But this proximity to his sucking mouth, even if the milk doesn't come, has me flushed with feeling. Fi tugs on the bottle against my breasts while my mother tugs softly at my hair, plaiting straight cornrows. This is what it is like to be a mother and a daughter.

Timi is cooking okra soup in the kitchen, and when a waft strays into the room, I hear my mother's belly rumble. We laugh. A husband who shares the kitchen with me is something I am proud of, a way of life my mother approves of, preaches. She works through a tangled section, and I stiffen my neck in discomfort.

"Sorry, does it hurt?"

I shake my head.

"How's the copywriting?"

"Fine. I submitted June's calendar yesterday."

"It's stupid they didn't give you time off."

"It's fine. If I stop, they'll find some mass comm student to do it for cheaper. It's just words; I can handle it."

"And Timi's work?"

"Good. He's building a website for Coke with Deji."

"And"—she continues to plait my hair—"are the two of you okay?"

I take a deep breath and try to relax my shoulders so my mother doesn't sense the tension this question evokes.

"Why?"

I feel her shrug. I wonder if she has somehow smelled the strain through my scalp.

Maybe her professor friend has taught her nose a trick or two. And if so, what emotion is she identifying? Shame? Resentment? Anger? How do I tell my mother, the woman who told me never to stay with a man who disrespects me in any way, that I am doing just that? That not only did Timi disrespect me with this affair, but I couldn't even flare up in response?

Whenever we heard a story of a husband who left, who hit, who had another family in a village somewhere, my mother would joke that my father—"that one who died to escape my wahala"—knew dying was better than misbehaving. That he knew she wouldn't have stayed a minute longer, that her blood was thicker than that. He had met her on the streets of Unilag waving a placard that read, *Women Are Students, Too! Students Not Maids! Students Not Sex Objects!* He joined the protest that day, later finding out she was the last daughter from a polygamous family she never completely forgave for their lack of attention. "That's your mama's origin story," he used to say to me when I sat on his lap and pulled at his full beard, "our superhero." Joking about my father's death made me squirm, even though I understood the dark humor for the coping mechanism it was. But she would look at me with those blazing eyes that want all the good in the world for me and say, "Women suffer enough. Don't add man problem on top. Keep your shoes beside the door."

I can't tell her now that maybe her superior blood thinned with me.

"We're fine," I say. But I have waited too long. She knows I am hedging.

She will not push it, though. Instead, she will scoot her chair away from the table later at dinner, announcing her departure, leaving a full bowl of delicious food untouched, leaving Timi thinking that he has offended her with too much salt. But I will know it is my mother bringing her protests from the streets of Lagos into my home.

My mother is gone and Timi wants to talk again; he wants to hammer this out once and for all. He wants to be sure we are good, are we good, are we good, are-we-good-arewegood? Timi wants to know, Timi wants.

I walk into our bedroom, where we have moved the cot, away from Timi's questioning voice. I want to look down into my baby's face with his always-puckered brows, to have his lustrous brown eyes look back into mine, his chubby puff-puff cheeks reassure me with their fullness, his plastered curls remind me of newness and freshness and growth.

Instead I find my baby turning blue in the face. His fingers are fisted tight; his arms are flailing little sticks. Has the strain hanging in the air of our bedroom asphyxiated our son?

When the doctor tells me that Fikayo has a gastroesophageal reflux, an allergic reaction to the formula, that breastmilk would be ideal at this point, I feel a sharp pain in my breasts. Can guilt be felt physically, like a blade on a finger, like a cramp in the calf, like biting your own tongue?

.   .   .

The lactation consultant's office is in the boys' quarters. We squeeze past two Jeeps in the narrow driveway to get to the one-room office at the back of the main house. The signage is lopsided, dusty, but my doctor said Dr. Laoye is good at what he does.

Timi and I sit on the couch while he paces.

"Have you taken any cod liver oil?" he asks after I tell our story, that a fourth formula is being tested on Fi, that my baby is now bones in a bag of soft skin, that my aunty's agbo didn't work.

I shake my head.

Dr. Laoye reminds me of those boys I loved when I was thirteen. The older boys in our estate who looked big and tall and bounced with a swagger to buy Guinness from the shop where I would be buying matches or Maggi or cotton wool. They looked like the epitome of adulthood to me with their loud, uncontained laughter and colorful rubber wristbands, as if they knew exactly what they wanted and how to get it: beer, life.

And that had been Timi too, so dogged in his pursuit of me, his want of me. What fractured this want, insinuated a pause long enough for Abuja to happen?

"This isn't about you," is what my mother might say in this situation, as she has done before, those days I came home crying about a boy who didn't love me back, a friend who stopped talking to me, a job I didn't get. How she would straighten my shoulders and wipe my face and insist, "It isn't about you. Roll it off. Those who appreciate you will come." How she would embrace me, "my gentle, sensitive baby" whispered into my hair in a voice I thought sounded mournful or scared, and I would go back into the world trying to be less gentle, bolder, demanding more from life once I saw things through the filter of my mother's opinions.

Dr. Laoye asks me to sit on the consultation chair and take off my blouse and bra. I like that he has not looked to Timi for permission or acknowledgment, unlike many nurses at the hospital who ask about my husband before attending to me.

I look nowhere as the cool from the air conditioner tightens my now-bare nipples. Not at Timi, not at the doctor. I pin my arms down, fighting the urge to cover myself.

Dr. Laoye peers at my breasts, then cups them in his gloved hands, latex against breasts.

This is the first time a man has touched my breasts since the night of confession. That night with Timi that brought us Fi, that angry night when I allowed my nails to dig into his back, scratch at his skin, draw blood, when he held my breasts and bit them, and I arched into the violence of his mouth, asking him to press down harder, longer, forever.

Could my confused pleasure of that night have ruined me for my child?

The doctor squeezes gel into his palm and gets to work on my breasts. The gloves glide over my skin with the slippery tingly gel, with a soft sound, his fingers moving first in an elliptical motion from the sternum, round and round, till he tugs at the nipples.

As the tugs become harder, I hunch over. Dr. Laoye lightly grazes my shoulder, tender, an unspoken *relax*. My eyes shoot up to find Timi's. His face is blank, too straight, and I know he is struggling to show me nothing.

I think: Look at another man touching me, Timi.

And then I feel it, a warm trickle out of my left nipple. The milk feels like a living creature crawling out of me. I look down at my chest, then up to share this moment with Timi, but he has turned away.

The hospital wants to test my breastmilk before they introduce it to Fi. *My* breastmilk. Fi's. Even while the doctor explains milk content to me, why they are testing, how the mother passes on more than fat and protein, how toxicity the mother has been exposed to can be a risk to the baby, all I can hear is *your* breastmilk. Timi's gaze keeps drifting down to my unbound breasts under the boubou.

Later, my mother shows up at the hospital with the woman from her conference, the smell professor. The woman has decided to take up a visiting professorship from Unilag, and they have just come back from lunch. I reach for my mother's hands. "We're waiting to hear," I say.

"Timi?" I can see my mother's nose wrinkle when she says his name. I will not confirm her suspicions.

"With Fi," I reply.

Another nurse comes to stand by the bed. "It's time to pump again, madam."

The nurse pulls apart the flaps of the hospital gown and starts to apply lubrication to my nipples. I do not move to help. I do not move away. I just lie there, a body. When the pump has been attached and turned on, my mother's professor friend stands to leave the room. The swish of her colorful kimono disappears around the door. My mother goes out after her.

I am now alone with the nurse, who is intently watching the liquid stream down the tubes into the bottle. *What are you looking for?* I want to ask. This feeling of milk out of my breasts is so strange, like a string is being unspooled out and out and out. *What can you see?* I want to ask.

When I stir from sleep, my mother and her professor friend have returned to the room. My mother rushes to fuss over me. "Mummy," I say, shifting my face away from her pesky touches. "Do you want to check on Timi and Fi?"

"Yes, yes." She hurries out of the room, happy to be useful, leaving me with the professor.

"Good evening," I whisper, remembering my manners.

She turns toward me. Her face looks sunken, the wrinkles fanned around like the lines on a palm to be read. She nods at my greeting and walks closer to the bed, almost regal in carriage. She stops before she reaches me.

I am curious: What is it about me that is repellent to her? Why won't she come closer? Can her trained nose smell my shame? My failing motherhood, wifehood? My failed daughterhood, too?

She is quiet for so long that I think she has not heard. But then she takes two steps closer. When she speaks, her accent is a flavored reflection of all the places she has lived, nasal and clipped and flat and lyrical all at once. "Good evening." She shifts. "What is it?"

I am not surprised at her question. "What can you smell?" I ask, doing the Nigerian thing of responding to a question with another.

She laughs, but her face is sad. "Darling," she says, and this endearment, which I would find annoying coming from anyone else, fits. "But, darling, you smell a lot like your mother."

My mother walks her friend out to get a taxi, and I slip out of bed. I move down the corridor, climb the flight of stairs that will bring me to my baby's ward. I find Timi asleep on a chair next to Fi's cot, a thin curtain their only privacy from the rest of the room. I stand there staring at my family.

"Timi," I whisper, and he jerks awake.

"Hey," he says, rubbing his eyes. He looks at my breasts, and I follow his gaze. There are splotches where milk has leaked onto my gown.

"Timi," I say again.

He stands and leads me out of the ward to the dim corridor. A fluorescent light farther down blinks every few seconds.

"Hey, what's wrong?" His hands rest on my shoulders. He runs them down my arms, slides them back up.

"I've forgiven you," I say. For my job, I rely on the thesaurus, finding new ways to say old things, fancy ways to turn the client's directives into copy the consumers can relate to. But for my own life, the words are flat. I can say only what I can say.

He becomes still. He swallows. "You said you had."

"I have. I swear." I raise my hands to trap his on my shoulders. While my belly swelled with our baby, I would smile at my beautiful husband, who was the first man I felt confident enough about to introduce to my mother, a man I was sure wouldn't misbehave. Surely I must have suckled some fire from my own mother's breasts, even if just a trace. I press down on Timi. Hard. "I just hate that it was so easy."

I feel him go rigid. This is the first time I am allowing us to discuss the affair since he dropped that suitcase and knelt in front of me, crying, begging for forgiveness. "What are you saying, Aduke?"

There is a scar on Timi's chin, a small diagonal line hidden mostly by his beard, and I like to rub my thumb against the slight elevation. He says he doesn't know how it got there. But what would the scar say if it could speak? If the body could tell what it doesn't forget, doesn't process? I reach out to touch it now.

"I'm saying I am angry that it was so easy," I tell him. "I needed to say that to you."

The doctor says toxicity passes unto the child through breastmilk. If I don't tell Timi these things, will my fluids flood with unvocalized coarse emotions? Will I choke my son with the force of them?

My hands fall to my sides; I release Timi. He drops to a squat. He is trembling; he holds his face. "Give me something to do. Give me a list, anything. What can I do?" His voice thickens. "What can I do?" He loses balance and latches on to my knee. I look down at my husband's head. There isn't anything he can do differently. This is about me, was always about me.

The fluorescent bulb flickers again, like a flashlight panning an abandoned room, lighting up things that have stayed in the dark too long.

.   .   .

The next morning, my milk is declared safe for Fi by the doctor with the tribal marks. He smiles wide, all those scarred commas stretching at me.

When Fi is placed into my arms, when his lips and gums circle and clamp onto my nipple, I cannot stop crying. Emotion rises up my chest, hot and forceful, up my neck, up my head, then crashes over me. I pull him closer to my heavy breasts. I hold him tight. My wet kisses slobber all over his forehead. Does that nose look like mine? Those eyes, like my mother's? "My sweet baby," I cry. "I love you," I weep. "I love you," I sob.

My mother sits by my head, letting me cry, stroking my braids. Timi shows up just outside the door, keeping his distance, still reeling from yesterday's talk. My mother stops stroking. She stands up, smiles at me, says, "Look, my baby is a mother. Her own woman." Her voice is gentle—no mourning, no concern, no fear.

I nod at Timi to come closer, and he stumbles across the threshold to join my mother and me, my baby and me.

Amar Mitra

Translated from the Bengali by Anish Gupta

The Old Man of Kusumpur

FAKIRCHAND OF KUSUMPUR set out on his way to meet the
Big Man. A bundle of meager belongings hung on his back
from one end of a cane stick that rested on his shoulder. Old
Fakirchand walked with a slight stoop.

It was moments before sunrise, and the March morning was
soft and cool with a genial air and the earth still pleasant to walk
on. The cocks were still crowing. Swarms of little children were
already out in the open. Old Fakirchand walked slowly, as though
measuring each step, and raised both hands to his forehead in
obeisance or "pranam" to the rising sun. Yes, his eyes felt better
and so did his body. In the brisk morning air, he touched his
rheumy eyes with his cold hands.

Fakirchand was about three-times-twenty, but already the
world appeared hazy to him, his limbs trembled, his skin hung
loose, and innumerable wrinkles crossed his face. At this age, the
ripe old man felt the desire to meet the Big Man of Kanyadihi,
situated on the bank of the river Subarnarekha, some twenty miles
away, beyond the forest of Durgadiha.

Of late he was passing through a state of mental turmoil. He
decided to go and see the Big Man, whom he had never met

before, because his sorrows were not one but many. His eyes, for instance. Fakirchand knew the Big Man would refer him to a village doctor, a wizard, the very sight of whom would heal his eyes. Of what good was it to remove a cataract, he thought: Clear it once and it comes back again! But the Big Man had many medicines, he knew of many wild herbs. Oh, it was ages since he had last seen the good earth with clear, transparent vision.

His son, too, caused him much pain. The fellow had eloped with a village wench to distant Chakulia, where he managed to get himself a job of sorts. But life at this age, without a son, was not worth living. What point was there in having given the boy life if, at this fragile age, he was to be left to fend for himself, old Fakirchand brooded as he walked along. He knew the Big Man would have an answer. He expected him to find a way to bring his son hurrying back, abandoning his woman of love.

And about his plot of land, the Big Man's advice, he knew, would be providential. Fakirchand was a loner. His wife was long dead. Keeping possession of his land was driving him to his wit's end. His enemies did as they pleased; they carried away every sheaf of unhusked rice that stood on his field. Just one word from the Big Man and Fakirchand would know how to treat the rascals!

And even though his wife was dead and gone, Fakirchand's sixty-year-old blood still ran warm in his veins. If only the Big Man named a good girl: even now the old man's eyes lit up, his mouth watered, passion swelled within him at the sight of a well-formed woman.

Hence Fakirchand had braced himself for a meeting with the Big Man of Kanyadihi. The night before, he had dreamed his own death. The villagers, a bumptious lot, were hovering like a bunch of vultures, waiting for him to die. The moment he breathed his last, they swooped down, tearing at his possessions. But Fakirchand would not let that happen. He would meet the Big Man and tell him all.

Fakirchand had been hearing of the Big Man ever since he moved to Kusumpur fifteen years ago from beyond Parihati. It was only after he moved to Kusumpur that he found a home and a patch of land. The village was rife with tales of the Big Man's great deeds. All things moved, it was said, according to his wishes, everything changed according to his dictates. He had never before cared for the Big Man, but now he did. He felt restless.

One could never tell how the mind would behave when the body grew old and infirm.

Fakirchand's wife had gone to heaven, his son had run away with a wench, leaving him lonely to guard his own little kingdom—a thatch hut and a piece of land—like the Yaksha of the legends. Many in the village wished him dead, but he was not a person to give in easily. If only his eyes were healed, he would once more live it up with the warmth of his blood, he mused as he walked.

Leaving the dusty bushes and the dry ponds of Kusumpur behind, Fakirchand found himself in a gently undulating, open, barren field of saffron gravel. The sky soared infinitely above, the moor stretched unhindered to the horizon, and the light poured down from the heavens in a warm, incessant stream. In that thick light, the old man made his way, charting his course to a distant destination that lay beyond the moor, beyond the villages, and beyond the forests.

Fakirchand's mind grew dim. He remembered with difficulty the days when he first came to this region. It seemed a long, long time ago. It was when an awesome flying machine of war had broken apart in the sky and come crashing down on the plains of Nishchinta. Fakirchand now heard a drone, like that of one of those machines of yore, approaching from afar. He turned his head and looked heavenward, into a brilliant and dazzling sky. A helicopter, hanging on its revolving blades, flew by toward the air base of Kalaikunda.

The sun changed color, the light thinned into a brassy glare.

Fakirchand crossed the field. The day was still cool, but the sky seemed to have receded far, as he approached a narrow dirt track winding through a wilderness of tall grass and thorny shrubs.

He crossed that, too, and stood before a canal in which waist-deep water still flowed. With summer advancing, it would be reduced to a mere trickle, but after the rains, it would again swell to a height greater than that of a man and a half.

There used to be a bridge across the canal. But it had disappeared. Fakirchand looked left and right, but found no trace of it. Had he come the wrong way? No, not quite, he thought. The old banyan tree stood all right at the crossing of the Baburbani canal. The tree was there, but the bridge was gone, without a trace.

Fakirchand studied the water with his foggy eyes and sensed a sharp current beneath. He stood helpless on the banks of the canal, which was the only source of water in a sprawling, drought-prone place. He knew there were layers of silt beneath the water and a treacherous current. He remembered old Nakphuri, who died of drowning while fishing in the canal one monsoon month and was washed five miles away to Kadamdihi.

It was a hopeless case, thought Fakirchand, surveying the surroundings. His body was too infirm, his eyes too weak, to brave a crossing. Memories of Nakphuri came repeatedly back like horrid and cautioning visions, making him sink into a stupor. And as he stood transfixed, not knowing what to do next, the day grew brighter as the sun rose higher in the sky. It was just then that the notes of a flute wafted into his ears, bringing him back to his senses. He scanned the surroundings for the one who played so sweetly, and, before much time had passed, a black man appeared with the flute like an apparition from the void. At long last, Fakirchand had found someone.

"Where are you going, old man?" the black man asked, lowering the flute from his lips.

"To meet the Big Man," Fakirchand said, taking a step forward.

"The Big Man? Who on earth is he?"

It was Fakirchand's turn to be surprised, and he let off a jeering giggle at the black man's ignorance. How was he to describe the Big Man—it was as impossible as divulging the secrets of the bird and the bee. So he broke into a song, hoping that the black man would understand the allegory.

Who spreads the smell when the flowers bloom?
Who brings rain borne by the clouds?
The flowers blossom and He makes the smell waft.
The clouds gather and He makes the rain come down.

The black man listened with wonder, and Fakirchand told him many, many things about the Big Man.

"Are you telling the truth?"

"Yes, I have no reason to lie. You don't know of my sorrows. My son has deserted me; my wife is dead. I have no one at home. My eyes don't see well. But I know the Big Man will set everything right."

"Oh! Then he must be as powerful as God!" exclaimed the black man, whose skin was as lustrous as the first clouds of monsoon.

"Yes, very much," Fakirchand agreed.

"Then proceed," said the black man, and turned to take his leave. But Fakirchand held him by the arm.

"How will I cross the canal?" Fakirchand asked.

"How do I know?" The black man tried freeing himself.

"Carry me across," Fakirchand pleaded with a tremulous voice.

"What will you give me in return?"

Fakirchand promised everything! He would tell the Big Man about him so that the black man was left without sorrows. "I'll request the Big Man to make you happy."

"Really?"

"Yes, of course, I am mentioning the Big Man not for nothing."

With a quick, effortless jerk, the black man lifted Fakirchand onto his shoulder and went down into the canal. As he waded through the waist-deep water, the black man told Fakirchand, in bits and pieces, the tales of his woe.

The black man's name was Chhotosona Mandi, whose life seemed as barren as the fields of March. He was deeply in love, with the daughter of one Bankim Hansda, and the girl loved him, too. But it meant nothing. Hansda would not give him his daughter's hand, never.

Fakirchand's body quivered with pleasure at the thought of marriage. "But why wouldn't he marry his daughter to you?"

"Because I have no house, no land."

Ah, the greedy swine, thought Fakirchand with laughter building up inside him as Chhotosona Mandi stepped out of the water onto the canal's other bank.

"I've helped you cross, so be sure to tell the Big Man about me," said Chhotosona Mandi. "Tell him that a youth as fresh as the clouds loves a woman of Asanbani whose name is Bishnupriya."

If only the Big Man brought them together, his sorrows would be over. He wished he could go along with Fakirchand, but his hands were tied, he had to go and work as a laborer. But he would be at the same spot the next day, waiting for Fakirchand's return. He would help him across the canal again and would expect to hear the good word.

Saying this, Chhotosona Mandi let himself go in the bright sunlight and blew into the flute again, the strains of which were carried far by the wind as he disappeared out of sight on the other side of the canal.

Chhotosona Mandi's affair was indeed a sad one, thought Fakirchand, and resolved to tell the Big Man everything, as he resumed his journey. The old man made a slow headway along the dry, saffron dirt track, on the one side of which was a low-lying field, and on the other a small thickly wooded hillock. The day was warm. It was the last day of March. The wind was laden with the smell of sal, mahua, and myriad flowers.

Twenty years ago, he had been strong as a buffalo. Some of that strength must have still lingered; otherwise, how could he come this far on a hot day? With his limpid body, hazy eyes, he waddled along doggedly.

Gradually, the day grew white with heat. Unfiltered sunlight struck his dark, glistening body and broke up into flares as though from sparklers. He felt his throat drying up, his face felt hard and baked, his mouth tasted bitter, and his body burned like desert sand.

The old man's eyes became dimmer still and flights of hallucination crossed his fading vision. He was in the midst of a wood and ravines. His progress slowed down. He gasped for breath. With his tongue he sought more air and wetted his dry, parched lips. He knew it was still a long way to the Big Man's house and felt intimidated.

Then a strange thing happened. Old Fakirchand heard people singing. He wondered who were the joyous lot who sang when the sky rained fire. He followed the sound, and the forest soon thinned, revealing a clearing. Men and women, Santhals all of them, were gathered there, singing without a care in the world despite the oppressive heat. Fakirchand silently drew closer, his head dizzy and darkness enveloping his eyes.

"What's happening here?" he asked, running out of breath.

The Santhals looked at him curiously.

"Where does it come from?" asked one man.

"Would you like some rice cake?" asked another.

Fakirchand felt as though his skull would crack because of the heat. He sat down in the shade of a young neem tree.

"We are performing 'salui' puja," he heard someone say.

"Give me some water to drink before I die," mumbled Fakirchand, loud enough to be heard.

Some of those who stood around called for water and others brought it in a shiny pail.

Fakirchand first applied some to his scalp before drinking to his heart's satisfaction. His sight came back to him and he took a long, deep breath.

"Why is your puja being held here?" Fakirchand asked.

Someone said something but he was too drunk to be coherent. The women started singing again.

Fakirchand skewed his eyes to have a look. Just then someone ordered the singing to stop.

"An alien has come among us. We must speak to him. No singing now, please," the voice said.

"Where are you going?" asked a veteran Santhal, too drunk to stop swaying.

"Kanyadihi."

"Where do you come from?"

"Kusumpur."

"Kusumpur to Kanyadihi—that's a long way to go! But why are you going there anyway?" The Santhals seemed eager to know.

Fakirchand felt more at ease now. He ran his eyes over the faces that crowded round. All the eyes that stared at him were bloodshot.

"I am going to meet the Big Man."

"Who is he, the forester, a forest ranger?"

"Rubbish." Fakirchand snubbed them, surprised at their ignorance. So he told them all that he knew about the Big Man and his greatness.

"Why? We don't need any Big Man; we are happy without him," said one.

"Shut up," another cut him short.

"We have our sorrows," he continued, "our sorrows pile up to the skies."

Old Fakirchand batted his eyelids and cast sly glances at the shapely young women. "Tell me of your sorrows and they will all be over," he said absentmindedly.

"Yes, we'll speak. Would you care for a drink?" asked one, nudging him by the hand.

"How can I? I am going to see the Big Man."

"Then listen. Bad times have overtaken us. The salui festival can no longer be observed with pomp. We don't get good sal trees anymore. The forester sends them all to Kharagpur. We can no longer sacrifice a boar at the ceremonies and my daughter will, in all likelihood, run away with an outsider. We don't get timber, we don't get game to hunt. The Marang Buru is not happy with us. If we drink, police get after us and pack us off to Jhargram."

The man hid his face between his knees and cried. Those who stood around cried too.

"Look, old man, you are like a god to us. Don't go away without accepting our offerings. If you don't like handia, have rice; if you don't like rice, have water," they pleaded.

They forced Fakirchand to have rice. But he had no taste for it. He felt like throwing up, but it was good that his belly was full. He stood up, ready to depart. The Santhals followed him. "Tell the Big Man about us; tell him to give us back our good days," they said as they saw him off.

"Be here tomorrow. On my way back, I will have a word for you," Fakirchand assured them.

The old man set out again. He had not gone much farther when he squeaked with suppressed laughter, but fell pensive again. He was moved by the sadness all around. "I must carry these words of sadness to the Big Man," he said to himself. The sun had slanted already. A deep booming sound reverberated through the somnolent wilderness. Were the clouds bursting? No, bombs were going off in Kalaikunda. A mock battle was on, ripping the silence apart.

The sun was going down fast when Fakirchand neared the forest of Durgahuri. He still had the forest to cross and two villages and a field beyond that before he could reach the banks of the Subarnarekha on which Kanyadihi was situated. The Big Man lived there—tall, fair, and in the pink of health. He must have grayed by now, Fakirchand tried to figure out. He had not seen the Big Man ever; whatever he knew was all based on hearsay.

He recounted the things he had to say to the Big Man—about Chhotosona Mandi, the Santhals, and about himself. There was no point in surviving like the Yaksha—either he must have a wife or his son must come back, Fakirchand thought as he walked, without realizing the sky had disappeared behind thick foliage overhead.

He was deep inside a forest. Beams of sunlight pierced through the cover of leaves here and there amid vast pools of darkness. These forests had contained so much to fear in the days gone by; now they were different. Yet, there were mysteries galore. God Baram still made his rounds of the forests silently, invisibly, riding on his favorite animals. Beneath the towering sal trees lay heaps of horses and elephants made of burnt clay; somewhere in the forest's elusive depths one could still run into the seat of the demon goddess Rankini.

The old man walked along the eerie path and found himself in trouble again. Three distinct tracks branched off in different directions and Fakirchand did not know which one to take. He was faced with yet another confounding predicament. Again, he stopped and looked left and right as he often did when helpless, not knowing what to do next. And, then, he noticed something move at the foot of a sal tree. A man, was it? he wondered.

"Who is it that comes this way?" Fakirchand called out, feeling nervous.

The figure waved back at him, beckoning him near, he distinctly saw with his hazy eyes. His heart began to pound in fear. A ghost, a genie, moving like a man? Fakirchand asked himself. But there was nothing he could do. He was lost in the forest and had to seek help.

He moved closer and what he saw made his hair stand on end. Yes, it was a man indeed, who spoke in whispers. He looked hideous, his body dismembering from leprosy. His face appeared moist and bulbous and he lay limp on the forest floor.

"Which village do you belong to?" Fakirchand asked as he threw a coin toward the ill-fated man.

The man did not care to touch it. Other coins lay where they had fallen. He had been forsaken by society; of what use was money to him? Fakirchand stood transfixed and quiet.

"Death has had me," moaned the man. "Where are you going, to which village?"

"Kanyadihi, to meet the Big Man."

The man sat up, but said nothing.

"How long has it been?" asked Fakirchand.

"It will be five years this May."

Fakirchand felt uneasy standing near him. He could not bear the sight of that horrid, disintegrating face.

"Which way is Kanyadihi?" he asked the leper.

The man did not answer. "If you saw the Big Man he would surely prescribe good medicines," Fakirchand said.

"Who is he?" asked the leper, this time his voice echoing in the forest.

A chill ran down Fakirchand's spine. He told him slowly, haltingly, all that he knew about the people of Kanyadihi. The leper listened with distended eyes and stretched forward to feel the old man, but Fakirchand stepped back, avoiding his touch.

"I'll tell you the road to Kanyadihi, but promise me you will tell the Big Man about my misfortune. If I am cured, I would like to roam the village streets again," the leper said, his voice becoming increasingly hoarse.

He showed Fakirchand the way and the old man promised the leper to return with the medicine the very next day.

"If only the Big Man touched you once, your body would be healed," he repeated.

Fakirchand resumed his march with haste. His heart was heavy. A fine youth wrecked by a terrible disease; the thought kept turning in his mind. He will tell the Big Man about him, too. Had they not helped him, Fakirchand would never have found the way to Kanyadihi, where the Big Man lived. He was sure that the Big Man would provide succor to them all.

The sun slanted toward the river in the west. The old man walked listlessly on, and then, suddenly, not far away, he saw the sandbanks of the Subarnarekha spreading like an endless white band across the earth. Kanyadihi must be there, the Big Man's house must be there! The exclamations involuntarily went off within him.

He walked even faster now. Oh, what immense suffering people endure! he thought as he walked. But without suffering who would know what happiness is? It was only in search of happiness that he had come all this way, hadn't he?

The evening grew sullen. Fakirchand ran out of breath with excitement. With his lean body, sagging skin, and weak eyesight, he had endured much strain. He felt awfully tired. His body seemed to bend and break. If only he could rest awhile! And if in that place of rest his wife were with him and his son by his side, his pain would disappear. He would once more sit back and stare at the world with ethereal pleasure. He would go and have the cataract removed, and if it reappeared, he would go to Kanyadihi with his son. His son would carry him on his shoulder, or would arrange a palanquin, if possible. The Big Man of Kanyadihi would then heal his eyes and make the world appear sharp and clear. But that was not to be. So, at the twilight of his life, he came to meet the Big Man all alone, risking his body and soul in an arduous trek on a terrible day in March.

He walked with a tremulous heart. Shadows stretched far and long. The sun went down in a pool of blackish red. Old Fakirchand felt melancholic, remembering his ruined family as the day neared its end.

He at last reached the banks of the Subarnarekha. But was it Kanyadihi? Was it the place where the Big Man lived? The sullen wind had no answer; it only blew hissing past.

The river had swallowed up much of the village. A few structures stood scattered, reminiscent of a hearth. Babla trees crowded the place and wild bushes grew in abundance, and not a soul was in sight. The old man strained his eyes in the hope of seeing somebody, for this must have been the Big Man's village. Beyond, no village could exist; the river had taken a fearsome bend.

Fatigue and hopelessness began to overcome him. His body felt limp and bloodless. Perhaps this was not Kanyadihi at all, he thought; maybe, he had come the wrong way. Maybe, it was somewhere else, somewhere around.

Gradually, darkness spread itself. The wind from across the river blew hard into the old man's face as he felt the darkness thicken around him. The footloose old villager still looked for people and he did chance to spot someone, coming his way with a lantern in hand. Fakirchand pumped all the strength into his lungs and called out at the passing man, asking him to stop for a while.

"In which village does the Big Man live?" Fakirchand asked.

"The Big Man?" The stranger stood askance in the dark.

With a quivering voice, Fakirchand told the man about the munificence of the Big Man, one who gave shelter to the tired, unendingly spoke of life, solved insurmountable problems with inconceivable ease, the one to whom people went seeking succor for all suffering.

The stranger broke into a harsh metallic laughter.

"You dream of such a man on earth, old fellow? Such men don't live anymore." The stranger shook his head and went his way, leaving Fakirchand standing alone.

A pale moon rose like an ocher egg. There was nobody in the vast expanse that lay between the moon and Fakirchand, not even the Big Man; only the sand dunes and the river seemed familiar. Everything seemed shrouded in mystery. The old man's mind began to fail, everything seemed to go wrong. "You didn't wait for me, Big Man. They say people like you don't exist anymore. How will my suffering or that of Chhotosona or the leper or of the Santhals ever end, if you are not there?" Fakirchand muttered to himself.

He walked down to the sand dunes, where the grains of sand glittered in the faint moonlight. Standing on a sea of sand beneath a benevolent sky, Fakirchand cried out in frustration and anguish, "How can I sit on guard eternally like the old Yaksha, how will I live with my hazy eyes, Big Man?"

The river was there, but the man was gone. He had departed silently, leaving behind all the sorrows and sufferings; and yet faith persisted in the old man's mind.

"If you had to go away, why didn't you carry all human miseries with you?" The old man spoke to the river in whispers. He perked up his ears and listened to something—the sound of feet wading through water. "Who goes, Big Man?"

Fakirchand tried to dash toward the sound, but fell spread-eagled on the sand. He lay on the dune like the sky lies on the earth and all stirrings sank into a cosmic silence. Only much later, a flying machine, flashing its red and green light in the elemental darkness, broke the silence.

The following day the others waited where Fakirchand had asked them to, in the forest and by the canal. But the old man did not return that day as he had promised. He did not come the next day either, or on the day that followed.

But he will, one day, they thought.

Christos Ikonomou

Translated from the Greek by Karen Emmerich

Where They Always Meet

G OOD EVENING, I'M STALIN'S granddaughter. Putin is after me, wants me dead. You have to help me.

It's Christmas Eve, snowing outside, and Marina Orologitis is working the night shift at HNN.gr, the Hellenic News Network. It's been quiet—a while ago she edited an item about a strange glow that appeared in the sky over Siberia, then put up photographs from Prince Harry's Christmas trip to New York with his new girlfriend—and now she's sunk back into her reading, surrounded by computer and TV screens, the hum of the air duct, and voices from the radio echoing in the empty, dimly lit room. She's experienced in the art of reading, doesn't let herself get distracted, because she knows that for a book to work its miracle the writer's voice on the page has to become the reader's voice in her head. She also knows that reading means tossing an anchor into deep waters, that reading is the third dimension of a two-dimensional person.

The book before her is a biography of Franklin Pierce, fourteenth president of the United States of America. Considered one of the worst American presidents in history, he died an alcoholic at sixty-four. His wife, Jane, who abhorred politics, was sickly and suffered from chronic depression. They had three sons. The first died when he was just a few days old, the second of typhus at age four, and the third, Benny, was killed in a train accident before his parents' eyes when he was eleven years old. The couple never got over their grief. Franklin started drinking more than ever, and Jane, who wore black for the rest of her life, wrote letters to her poor Benny, begging his forgiveness for having failed as a mother to protect him. She died of consumption a decade later. Pierce, who'd left the White House by that time, told a friend, "There's nothing left to do but get drunk."

Marina lifts her eyes and looks out the window at the bluish snow, which is silently covering the sidewalks, the cars, the roofs of houses. She watches the flakes slowly twirling in the air—big white flakes, so big they seem to cast shadows as they fall. She wonders if everything she's reading is true, if all that could possibly have happened to a predecessor of Trump, Bush, Nixon. Of course it's been almost two centuries since then, but still. You don't expect an American president to say that the only thing left for him to do is drink himself to death, or a First Lady to send letters to her dead son apologizing for not having been a good mother.

She watches the snow fall and wonders. Wonders and remembers. She remembers how she once believed, truly believed, that she'd never again have to work a night shift, and how twenty-five years ago—a quarter of a century, that is—she thought she wanted to become a journalist because it would allow her to do the two things she really loved in life: write and read. Her face smiling wryly with bitter wisdom in the breath-steamed windowpane, she remembers the days when people didn't just read newspapers; they treated them as a kind of refuge. She remembers and wonders how it must feel for a mother to lose three children, one after another, and why there's a word for a child who loses a parent, but not for a parent who loses a child. And as she's thinking about all this, she sees out the corner of her eye a shadow moving between the empty desks. The shadow comes closer and takes the form of a woman, who stands in front of her and says, "Good evening, I'm Stalin's granddaughter. Putin is after me, he wants me dead. You have to help me."

The woman has a foreign accent, dark blond hair, and eyes the color of ash. She says "Gud evenink," "granddautter." She's dressed as if on her way to a holiday party—heavy perfume, a black coat, patent leather heels. Her skinny, bowlegged calves look like bowling pins through her mesh stockings.

Marina puts her book aside and stands up. The woman takes a step forward. On her cheeks, beneath her heavy makeup, her freckles look red, like marks from shrapnel. She takes off her gloves and reaches out a hand. Marina hesitates for a moment, then takes it. It's small, warm, and trembling—like holding a frightened bird in your palm.

"What can I do for you?"

"I'm Stalin's granddaughter. Putin is—"

"I heard that part. But what do you want?"

"To talk to you. It's very important. I need help."

"Listen, right now I don't—"

The woman gestures for her to be quiet, gently takes her arm, and points out the window.

"That car," she says. "That one there, the black one. Do you see it? There are KGB agents inside."

There's no snow on the car, and white smoke is rising from the exhaust pipe. Through the window Marina can't tell whether there's anyone inside. She observes the woman and tries to detect some other scent apart from the heavy perfume of her evening-wear—booze, weed, pills. But there's nothing. All she smells is cardamom, wood, and incense, maybe Oud Royal or the old Cashmere.

The woman pulls a crumpled tissue from her evening bag and wipes her eyes, and a tear that rolled down to one corner of her mouth. "I'm sorry," she says, reaching out a hand. "How rude of me. I'm Marina Alliluyeva. Svetlana's daughter, you know."

Marina hears a muted ringing. The woman pulls a cell phone out of her pocket and turns the screen toward her.

"It's them," she says. "They're showing me that they know where I am."

She turns off the phone, puts it back in her pocket, and fixes her gaze out the window.

"Christ, what am I supposed to do? How am I going to get through another night of this?"

Then her face lights up; she turns and looks at Marina.

"I wasn't sure, you know. About tonight, I mean. So many newspapers, so many channels, and no one would help me, everyone's afraid. But then the man at the entrance told me your name was Marina, and I said, Well, that's a good sign. In Russia we have a saying: the enemy of a lucky man dies, the enemy of an unlucky man becomes his friend. But not me, never. I'll never become their friend. The man at the entrance agreed, it's a good sign: we're both Marinas. He said you'd help me for sure. He said, 'Oh, of course, she's our best journalist.' And it's Christmas, too. So I'm very happy. I looked for you on earth, but found you in the skies. So you'll help me. I'll tell you an incredible story. You'll help me, right?"

She talks and talks, shows me photographs, watches my hand as I write it down on the page. She knows how it must seem, realizes it sounds unbelievable, but swears it's all true.

"And don't forget," she tells me, "what Dostoyevsky said: 'There is nothing as unreal as reality itself.'"

I write sloppily, mechanically, observing her gestures, how she rolls a tissue between her fingers, how she crosses and uncrosses her legs, sitting opposite me. I keep an eye out every time she opens her bag—who knows what she might be hiding in there: a knife, a gun, pepper spray—and keep an eye on the door, too. I keep thinking that any minute now someone might come bursting in, not the KGB agents with their black suits and Kalashnikovs, but guys in white uniforms with tranquilizer guns and nets.

I met plenty of people like her in my day, back when newspapers (at least the smaller ones) were something like a refuge for the kind of person who would later end up in the studios of marginal TV stations. People who came and went almost every day in journalists' offices asking for money so they could send their sick children to hospitals abroad or begging for reporters to turn their pain into a story—addict sons, annoying neighbors, greedy landladies. Some wanted to report scams, unlawful acts, corrupt politicians, or lying civil servants. Others came with envelopes and stacks of paper—reduced pensions, inflated bills, bureaucracy. There were, of course, more serious cases. I still remember the guy from Petroupoli and the mysterious patent that NASA had stolen from him; the old lady from Megara whose grandchildren were trying to kill her to get their hands on her property; a kid from Piraeus with razor marks like tic-tac-toe on his arms, who was convinced that his neighborhood barber was Jim Morrison. But I've never come across a granddaughter of Stalin before.

Now she shows me a color photograph of a woman with a little girl on her lap. The girl is her and the woman is her mother, Stalin's daughter, Svetlana Alliluyeva, who became famous in the sixties for defecting to the United States, but died a few years back, forgotten and impoverished in an old folks' home in Washington. She says her mother was a tortured woman who from a young age had been burdened with a sadness as big as Greece's national debt. A woman who was constantly changing names, husbands, countries, religions. A woman who, when she arrived in the United States, sent a long letter to her children, whom she had abandoned in Moscow, explaining that she'd had to leave her family and country because the Soviet system was not only financially but also morally bankrupt: "With one hand we're trying to grab hold of the moon," she wrote, "and with the other we're still plowing our fields the way people did a century ago."

The other Marina explains that she never met her grandfather, although her mother told her all about him. She says Stalin loved Svetlana very much—the way cats love mice. People who say that the fundamental difference between Stalin and Genghis Khan was that Genghis Khan didn't have a telephone are right, she says. She claims that she could speak for days about her grandfather, but she won't, because even the thought of him makes her sick.

"I'll just tell you one thing," she says. "My grandmother accused her husband of spoiling my mother because he called her 'little sparrow,' gave her lots of gifts, and let her watch American movies. Just imagine a family in which Stalin is considered the more affectionate parent, and you can guess how my mother was raised, and how she in turn raised me and my siblings.

"Don't bother looking online to learn more about me," she remarks. "You won't find anything. They've erased all traces of me. I don't exist. I'm a ghost that's chasing them, that's why they want to kill me. But ghosts don't die, isn't that so?

"The eyes," she says, "that's the worst part. My poor mother said anyone who looked her in the eye was always searching for Stalin's eyes in hers. She looked for his eyes in mine, and I in hers. And then, at some point, we realized we'd both been making the same mistake. We weren't looking to find Stalin's eyes in one another's; we were looking to find the eyes of everyone he killed. That was more or less why we stopped meeting one another's eyes, then stopped looking at one another altogether. And finally we just lost touch. You're doing it now, too, I know, looking for my mother's and grandfather's eyes in mine, searching for the eyes of a monster in the eyes of a human. No, no, it's fine, I understand. But that's the help I'm looking for. To not be a monster, or a ghost."

She shows me some more photographs, still talking. She says that when she was little, the stories her mother told weren't about princes and princesses, but about a French king who thought he was made of glass, or about the Haitian dictator Papa Doc, who thought one of his enemies had been turned into a black dog and ordered all the black dogs on the island to be killed, or about a usurper to the Chinese throne who died, and the emperor's soldiers burned the body, mixed the ashes together with gunpowder, and shot them out of a cannon so nothing of that terrible man would be left on earth. She thinks this should have been Stalin's fate, and the fate of all dictators: to be shattered like glass or to have their ashes scattered by cannons.

Every so often she stands and looks out the window at the black car, which is still parked across the street. With tears in her eyes she begs me to help her, to write her story and publish it, today, tomorrow at the very least—no one else dares to write anything, everyone's afraid, and she's tired, how much time does she have left?

For a moment I'm tempted to ask where she was born, who her father is, how and when she came to Greece, how she makes a living, why they want to kill her, how it's possible for the entire world to be unaware of her existence, but of course I don't. I know there's no point, you don't ask people like this questions, you don't challenge them, don't doubt them, because if you back them into a corner, they can become truly dangerous.

Now she's overcome by some kind of spasm: her hands shake, her breathing is shallow. I make her sit down, give her some water. When she has calmed down a bit, she gets to her feet and goes and stands in front of the window again.

"You know," she says, "the night before they executed Lacenaire it snowed in Paris. He looked out the prison window at the snow and said, 'Tomorrow the earth will be very frozen.' And from the neighboring cell someone called, 'Ask them to bury you in a fur.'"

She turns toward me and stretches her arms out to either side. "And I went out tonight dressed for spring," she says. "But I don't like furs at all."

I make her sit down again, I tell her everything is going to be okay, that her coat is very nice. She asks me if I believe in miracles and then begs me to write down that, contrary to what most people believe, miracles are entirely logical phenomena. Nature and science are governed by laws, but there are exceptions to those laws, and each miracle constitutes one such exception. Miracles imply the triumphant confirmation of logic.

"Only crazy people don't believe in miracles," she concludes, and leans over to make sure I'm writing it all down correctly.

History narrates the struggle of humankind to become the third power between good and evil, she tells me. Only those who believe in eternal life can live their life on earth without having already died. Trying to approach God in a logical manner is like trying to assign a color to a musical note. Asking someone to prove the existence of God is like asking Prince Myshkin to prove the existence of Dostoyevsky.

I listen and write, feeling her breath on my cheek. I jot all this down, too, just like everything else she's told me up to now. I'll write down whatever she tells me, I'll assure her that tomorrow or the next day it will all be published, I'll tell her everything is going to be okay and not to worry, and then she'll leave, and I'll never see her again. And if she comes back, which she almost certainly won't, I'll have informed the blockhead of a security guard and my colleagues to get rid of her.

It's a slightly more complicated situation than the usual, the ones I used to deal with—it's not just technology that's constantly developing, right?—but I know how to handle her. She'll haunt me, though. That much is sure. When she leaves here in a bit, I'll remember her. I'll see her walking alone in the night, in the snowy darkness, dressed for a Christmas party that will never take place, constantly looking over her shoulder, checking to see whether the black car is following her. I'll remember her and wonder where she came from and where she went, just as I still wonder, all these years later, where the guy with the patent that NASA stole went, and the old lady from Megara, and the guy who let an old barber with Parkinson's cut his hair because he believed he was Jim Morrison. Not shadows, not monsters, not ghosts, but living people. I remember them and wonder where they come from and where they go.

She asks for some more water, and then gets up and goes to look out the window again.

"Can you make them leave?" she asks. "That's all. Could you at least do that?"

"Don't be afraid," I assure her. "Everything's going to be fine."

"Fear," she says. "Fear gives rise to hate. You hate out of fear, you hate yourself for being afraid, you hate the people who are making you afraid, and those who don't do anything to help you stop being afraid. But you'll do something, won't you? You'll help me, right?"

"OK," I respond.

"Can I stay here a while longer? It's so cold tonight. And tomorrow the earth will be very frozen."

Before I have time to answer, she takes off her coat, folds it carefully, and drapes it over the back of a chair. Her shoulders, skinny and smooth, are covered in freckles, just like her arms. Her perfume now spreads even more strongly in the air, as if it was trapped all this time under her coat. She glances around, and for the first time I see her smile. Her teeth are white, shiny, and straight.

"You're pretty cozy here," she says. "It's warm, quiet."

Then she looks at the papers with my notes.

"So, where were we?"

The woman speaks, Marina writes. She scribbles hurriedly, crosses words out and changes them—as if she's trying to solve a crossword puzzle with no clues, with no squares, a crossword puzzle fated never to be solved, a crisscrossword puzzle, an uncrossword puzzle.

"You should put a period in here and there," the woman jokes. "Babel wrote that no iron can strike through a human heart with the power of a well-placed period. He was one of our greatest writers. My grandfather sent him before the firing squad, too."

She glances at Marina's notes and then her gaze falls to the book open on the desk: the biography of Pierce.

"Do you know why people read? We read because we want to live more than one life. Well, now you've got plenty to read about," she says to Marina, pointing toward the pile of papers.

"That's my gift to you," she continues. "A Christmas gift."

It's past midnight. The woman gets to her feet and stands in front of the window, her arms hugging her body. Outside the snow is falling thickly, the flakes twirling like an enormous flock of starlings constantly changing formation and direction.

Marina goes over and stands next to her. The black car is gone, the spot where it was already covered with snow. She starts to say something, but thinks twice and says something else instead.

"Thank you. And merry Christmas, Marina. Happy holidays."

The woman reaches out a hand to work Marina's hair free where it's gotten tangled in the zipper of her blouse, high up on the back. Marina is confused, thinks she's going in for a hug, leans over awkwardly, and when she understands her mistake, apologizes, but the woman also laughs awkwardly, and then they hug and kiss three times on the cheek, there, in front of the big window, which bears the traces of their breath, their palms, the snowflakes that are melting and running down the pane like traces of fingers trying to find something to grab hold of.

"They're gone, but they'll be back," the woman says. "Can I stay a little bit longer?"

"What about your party?" Marina asks. The woman looks at her, confused.

"Sorry, my mistake," Marina says. "Sit down, I'll be right back." She goes to the kitchen at the back of the room and brings out the plastic containers she brought from home with her Christmas meal. Christmas bread, salad, cheese pies, leek and celery purée, a few Christmas cookies, a bottle of Cretan wine. She lays it all out on a nearby desk, brings over the chairs, lights an old candle she finds in her desk drawer.

"Happy holidays!" she exclaims, and raises her glass. "Merry Christmas and a happy New Year to us both."

"To our health!" the woman says. "Christ consecrated a new life, not a new religion."

And then, smiling, "Don't write that down. People don't want to read things like that. Just remember it."

They eat and drink with appetite, looking at one another frequently but speaking little—about the food, about Marina's job, about the weather, which is supposed to change tomorrow. When they're finished, the stranger raises her glass and declares in a steady voice, "I'd like to sing."

With her lips half closed, she begins to murmur something like a lullaby. Her voice grows stronger. Eyes closed, she sings in a language I don't understand, a language I'm not even sure exists, but I close my eyes, too, and add my voice to hers, and we sing together. At first I'm hesitant, but the woman encourages me, squeezing my hand, and so I set myself free to sing in this unknown language, while outside the window the snowflakes twirl as if they're now following the rhythm of the song—big white flakes that glow in the dark and come together in a delirious silent dance somewhere in the space between sky and earth, where they always meet, all those that descend from up high and all those that rise from below.

Janika Oza

Fish Stories

ON THE DAY MY DEAD BROTHER came home I awoke to the smell of salty broth, mushrooms swollen with water and heat, the tang of sugared limes. My mother entered my bedroom, pulled me from sleep with cool fingers. He's home, she said. Who? Your brother. When she said his name, I pushed away the thought of the boy I had once known, glasses round and thick, framing eyes whose lashes I never stopped envying, a checkered shirt or perhaps his Manchester United polo, a missing canine that had never grown in. Instead, I rolled over and said, My brother is dead. Let me sleep. Patiently, my mother peeled back the covers, waited for the February air to work its way under my pajama shirt. He's in the living room, she said. He needs a change of clothes. Give him something of yours.

When she left the room, I heard her speaking to someone, asking my brother if he was hungry, when was the last time he ate. When I stepped into the living room with a sweatshirt and shorts folded in my arms, my mother was seated on the low sofa, rubbing her hands over a flowered pillow. He's soaking, she said, give him the clothes so he can change. I placed the clothes next to her and asked why he was wet. It's a storm, she said, and as she said so

I heard the drum of rain against the window. Also, he had to swim so far to get here. He can't swim, I said.

My brother had drowned years ago when we first arrived in this country where children learned to swim before they could walk, burbling mounds of fat and feathery hair dropped into communal swimming pools like coins, careless wishes tossed by believing parents. My mother looked at me. He learned, of course, she said. He had to swim all that way.

What's that smell, I asked, my nostrils pricking at the acidic cloud that was drifting from the kitchen. I'm making soup, my mother said. Help him change while I go check on it. She left the room, and I heard the clicking of a spoon against a pot, the splatter of garlic and mustard seed frying in oil. They're just ripe enough, I heard her say, followed by the whack and tear of plantain skin peeling from body. Moving to the couch, I sat where my mother had been and fingered the pile of clothes next to me. My brother was older than I, but he had always been slight, his cheekbones carving his face into delicacy, his collarbones knocking against mine whenever we hugged. Which wasn't often, but I remember him slinging his arm over my shoulder as we walked home from school, whispering low into my ear to drown out the calls of the kids on the field. Where did you even come from, they would call. What happened to your dad? My brother would stroll over with an easy cool, nod his head at the boys who were doubled over in cruel laughter, and steer me away. Just like that.

Something was crackling in the kitchen, maybe dried chilies added to the pot, the ticking of the back burner that never quite worked. Almost ready, my mother called, her voice high-pitched, singsong, like it wasn't past midnight and she didn't have to be up for work in five hours to stand on her feet in a cold hospital waiting room all day. OK, I called back, then picked up the pile of clothes and shoved them under the pillow.

One day, I had arrived at school to find that no one was interested in bothering me. Instead, I found a crowd of sixth-grade boys around my brother, and my brother recounting story after story, his hands shaping the air into mountains, rivers, elephants, swords. Yes, we rode lions to school, and for dinner my mother would kill a monkey, crack open its skull for us to feast on fresh brains. Yes, for my last birthday I had tea with the king of Uganda; we shared a cake made of mango flesh studded with passion fruit seeds like jewels. Yes, he sent my family on a mission to far-off Canada. We swam here; it took us a whole year. Yes, a few days into our journey my father realized he had forgotten to bring our money, so he had to turn back to fetch it. He'll arrive any day now, with our money, too. The boys were nodding, nodding, what looked like hesitant admiration in their eyes. Later, I would understand it as jealousy.

I heard my mother humming over the stove. In the kitchen I found that she had coiled her hair into a high bun atop her head and that sweat was speckling her nose from the steam rising out of the three steel pots. She had her arm nearly all the way into one of them, working a fork over the matoke, grunting with effort. Do you need help? I asked, but she shook her head, her back turned to me. You just keep your brother company for now, she said. He's missed you. She pulled a wide bowl from the cabinet, ladled in broth and heat-drunk vegetables, sprinkled a palmful of salt over the sticky mound. He never liked spicy much, but— she said, adding a green chili. Then, balancing the vessels in her arms, she turned around to face me and my brother. Oh, she said. Where did he go? I looked beside me, at the seat that I had pulled out. My mother walked over and lined up the two bowls and the mug, folding a sheet of paper towel under the spoon. Steam curled up around the empty chair, thick with oil and salt. Just as the plate had sat seven years ago when we waited for my brother to come home from school, the spoon untouched, the napkin to be folded up and placed back in the cutlery drawer, though the food would be left out all night. In the morning we had found bugs feasting on the corn, an upturned fly floating in the orange grease, its belly swollen, glutted. Later we would learn that some of the boys had challenged my brother to prove that he had swum across the world, leading him down to the creek after school. If only he had mentioned the airplane, or the boat, or even the life jackets. My mother sat down in the chair across from the brimming bowls, wiped her wet fingers across her stomach. Never mind, she said. He'll be back any day now. We'll just leave this out until morning.

Vladimir Sorokin

Translated from the Russian by Max Lawton

Horse Soup

HOW DID IT BEGIN? Simply, like all that which is inevitable. July 1980, a train from Simferopol to Moscow, 2:35 p.m., a packed restaurant car, tomato sauce stains on the overstarched tablecloths, someone's forgotten box of Lviv-brand matches, cigarette ash, bottles of Narzan tinkling in their metal cupholders by the window, a fluttering curtain, hyperboloids of thick sunbeams, Olya's forearm peeling from a sunburn, Volodya's faded polo shirt, two poppy heads embroidered on Vitka's jean skirt.

The fat waiter rustled his greasy notepad. "Guys, please, hurry it up. I've got a line of people here to last me all the way to Moscow."

"What do you have—" Volodya began to ask. But he was interrupted by a sudden torrent of words spewing from the waiter's froggy lips.

"We're out of salad and solyanka, but we've got kharcho, pike perch with mashed potatoes, and steak and eggs."

"There's no beer?"

"There is!" The waiter clapped with a sweaty bang. "Two? Three?"

"Four." Volodya relaxed. "And we'll all have the steak."

"Do you have any ice cream?" Vitka put on her dark glasses.

"No." The waiter scribbled his pencil on the pad and walked his portly, seal-like body over to the barmaid, who was watching over the line of people waiting. "One more over here, Lyuban!"

"Maybe we don't neeeed one? Because we're so cooommfy!" Olya sang, lighting her last cigarette, but there was a man already walking down the aisle, chocolatey with sunburn, dressed in white pants and a blue shirt.

"Hello." The man gave the three of them a quick smile and sat down, looking each of them in the eyes. He had no defining characteristics other than being bald, and no visible age.

"A veterinarian," Volodya decided, taking the cigarette from Olya.

"Dynin in the flesh," Olya thought, remembering the character from *Welcome, or No Trespassing,* the Klimov film.

"Some dickhead on his way back from a bachelor party at a resort," thought Vitka, curling her beautiful lips.

The waiter was muttering something to himself when he remembered the new arrival and turned around, but before he could say anything the bald man handed him three rubles.

"Nothing for me, please."

The waiter took the money and frowned, not understanding.

"But, um . . ."

"Nothing, nothing . . ." The stranger waved his fingers, with their devoured nails. "I'll just sit . . . for a little while. It's nice and comfy here."

"But maybe . . . a drink? A beer? A glass of Psou? Some Ararat cognac?"

"Nothing, nothing. For now—nothing." The waiter sailed back into the kitchen.

"A veterinarian, but a fucking weird one," Volodya thought, squinting at the stranger. "Probably some yokel from Siberia. Breaks his back all winter long without complaining, then ships off to the south in the summer to make his pockets a little lighter."

"He left his wife back in their compartment," Olya said to herself, grabbing the cigarette from Volodya and taking a drag. "He should've given us those three rubles. Volodka is blowing our last five right now. We'll get back, nothing at home but tumbleweeds, all our elders away at the sanatorium, a week till they get back, horrible . . ."

"This guy let loose in the south and now he can't get it back together," Vitka thought, looking out the window. "Why do assholes like this always have so much money?"

The train crawled through the torrid Ukrainian heat.

"How is it that the summer has already been somehow so hot this year?" the bald man said, attempting to look all three of them in the eyes again. "Can it be that in the fair capital of our homeland the temperature has also reached such catastrophic heights?"

"We don't have a clue," Vitka said, speaking for all of them. She gave the man's nails a squeamish look.

"Where were you vacationing?" The bald man smiled with his small, dirty teeth.

"In your mom's pussy!" Volodya thought to himself angrily. "You know what," he said, "we're overheated and want to sleep. And when we want to sleep, we also want to eat, but we do not, under any circumstances, want to talk."

Olya and Vitka responded with satisfied chuckles.

"A siesta, you mean?" The bald man squinted ingratiatingly.

"A siesta." Volodya put out his cigarette butt, remembering a Hemingway novel he'd started but never finished that had a similar title.

"For me it's just the opposite," the stranger said, bending down to the table like a doomed man drawn to the scaffold. "Whenever I get a sunburn, an incredible cheerfulness comes over me, an incredible strength rushes through my body—"

Just then, without warning, he broke off his sentence and froze, as if bitten by a snake.

The waiter put three plates onto the table with overcooked

pieces of meat, callused sticks of potato that were supposedly *fries*, limp feathers of dill, green peas, and three fried eggs. The eggs, it must be said, weren't overcooked or runny. They looked rather appetizing. From the pockets of his dirty white apron the waiter took out four bottles of cold Simferopol beer, set them down loudly, opened them, and sailed off once again.

"Thanks be to labor!" Volodya said to himself. He picked up a bottle that had already begun to sweat, a palpable feeling of relief washing over him. "He was really chewing our ears off with all that cheerfulness of his," he thought.

Having forgotten about their neighbor, who was now silent, all three of them began to eat their food. They hadn't eaten anything since morning and they'd been drinking in their compartment since the previous day. They had begun when the train departed and continued well into the night, finishing three bottles of Mukuzani, lacquered over with a quarter bottle of local "Russian" rotgut, all of which was severely affecting their well-being today.

Each of them ate in different ways.

Volodya poured a heap of salt and pepper onto his egg and speared it with his fork, put it into his mouth whole, and washed it down with beer; he then put three potato sticks onto his fork, stuck the fork into the tough meat, cut off a decent-size piece, placed five peas onto the meat using his knife, put the entire edifice into his mouth, crammed in a piece of white bread, and began to chew while looking out the window at the cables flashing by and thinking about what might come to pass if, suddenly, Bryan Ferry and David Bowie got together and decided to form a band.

"They would call it something weird." He chewed with so much pleasure that tears came to his eyes. "Maybe BB. Or Rose of Blue. Or, like, Miracle No. 7."

Vitka placed the egg onto her meat, nervously mashed it with her fork, speared a potato stick, dipped it in the yolk, put it into her mouth, cut off a piece of meat, dipped that in the yolk, put the eggy meat into her mouth, had a drink, and, while chewing, began to quickly collect disobedient peas and pass them through her lips, which were by now yellow with egg. She stared at the silver ring on the ring finger of the bald man's left hand.

"That ring is all I need to see," she said to herself. "I've had it up to here with divorcés. I wonder if he boned anyone down in Crimea. Some kind of Aunt Klava from a sanatorium cafeteria. Or, no, maybe a single mother, a fat-ass Jewish mama. He was holding her a space in line to buy cherries, then she gave it to him on the sly, on a nude beach . . ."

Olya ate calmly, cutting her meat into little pieces and washing down every bite with beer, pinching off bits of white bread and completely ignoring her side dish. Her gaze swam absentmindedly over her plate.

"I wonder if my headache will go away after this beer," she told herself. "I'm never gonna drink that disgusting vodka again, but Vovik seems like he'd drink anything in sight. I have to call Natashka right away. I wonder if she xeroxed the sheet music. If not, I'm not gonna return that Bartók to her, on principle. It's impossible to get her to do anything. But then whenever she needs something, we all have to hop to it, like that one time with the ensemble . . . God, why is he looking at me like that?"

Olya stopped chewing.

The bald man stared at her with his crazy, watery, greenish-blue eyes. His face wasn't just pale but deeply ghoulish, as if he were bearing witness to something terrifying, contrary to his very nature.

"An overthrown face," Olya thought, laying her knife and fork down at the edge of her plate. "Why are you . . . watching me like that?"

Vitka and Volodya also stopped eating and stared at the bald man. A grimace passed over his face. He clutched at his temples, he was blinking furiously, his whole body was shuddering.

"Forgive me . . . I . . . this . . ."

The train was going over a bridge, steel pillars flashed by with a roar, it smelled of cinder.

The stranger rubbed his pale cheeks with a furious motion, then reached into the breast pocket of his shirt and pulled out a piece of paper, which he handed to Volodya in silence. It was a certificate of release from a correctional labor colony issued to one Boris Ilyich Burmistrov. Olya and Vitka stared at the paper.

"Seven years, guys, seven years. And all because of some stupid bag of citric acid," the bald man said before taking back the paper. "Forgive me, I don't want to disturb . . . to interfere . . . and so on. I just have one large request. A very big one."

"D'you need money?" Volodya asked, imagining that the three rubles he'd given to the waiter had been a trick.

"Whaddya think?" Burmistrov smirked, pulling a thick leather wallet out of his pants and throwing it onto the table. "I'm made of money."

The three of them stared silently at the wallet, from which protruded bills of various denominations.

"Money is generally . . . well . . ." The stranger waved his hand nervously. "It comes, it goes, and so on. But the request. Well . . . I dunno. First lemme tell you a story."

"He won't let us eat!" Volodya said to himself, looking longingly at what remained of his steak.

"Weird dude," Vitka thought, sipping her beer.

"A criminal! How about that!" Olya gave him a distrustful look.

Burmistrov put his wallet away and rubbed his small chin.

"Well, as for the circumstances of the case, let's leave them to the side. I'll say just one thing: I'm a construction manager by trade and a businessman by vocation. But times are hard. Is there such a thing as honest business? Well . . . underground there is. Yes. That's how they were able to do away with seven years of my life. It's been two months since I was released. Our camp was forgotten by God, all the way in Kazakhstan. Ah, forgive me! Not *ours* any longer!" He laughed delicately. "Now it's only *theirs* . . . This is how I, a man with two degrees, began to work at a brick factory. It wasn't the only thing I did there, but I mostly just shaped bricks. Yep. A little bit later, just before I got released, I started work in a killer spot: the kitchen. But our camp, God I was sick of it, had a big problem—it was too small. Only two hundred sixty-two people. And none of us should have been there in the first place. We were inside for financial crimes of mild severity, so to speak. Long sentences. Calm, serious people. We didn't rebel, didn't take drugs, didn't try to run away . . . And the provisions were disgusting. Yes . . . generally speaking, every day for those seven years I only ate one thing—horse meat stew. Horse soup we called it. There was a big stud farm right next to us and they sent their defective horses over and into our pots."

He grinned and looked out the window.

"What else was in the soup?" asked Vitka.

"Millet, rice, or flour," said Burmistrov with a smile. "The ratios changed all the time. But there was always horse in it, the main *by-product,* so to speak. Our daily ration. And every day our little camp would eat a whole horse. A skinny, old horse."

"Where did they find so many horses?" asked Volodya.

"Are you kidding me? Kazakhstan is full of horses. A lot more than they have in Moscow!" Burmistrov laughed, and Olya and Vitka smiled.

"Isn't that unhealthy—horse every day?" Volodya asked.

"No, horse meat is the healthiest. Much better than beef or pork."

"And you really ate only that for seven years?" Olya looked at his restless forehead, the freckles hidden by sunburn.

"Is that so hard to believe?" He looked into her eyes.

"It is," she responded gravely.

"It's hard for me too. But, look—" He spread out his hands. "Seven years have vanished into thin air, two regiments of horses have been devoured, and I'm alive!"

"That's so depressing—every day exactly the same!" Vitka shook her head. "Even if they made me eat this steak every day, I'd go insane!"

"Well, humans can get used to anything." Burmistrov shook his bald head. "In the beginning, I ate everything, then I stopped being able to eat the meat, picked it out of the soup, and drank only the broth. Then I did the opposite and started to eat the meat on its own, with bread. Then I stopped caring and started eating it all, but by the end of my sentence . . . it's hard to explain."

He thought for a moment.

"If he isn't lying, this is fuckin' crazy," Volodya said to himself. He poured some beer into his glass.

"Now he must want to gobble up everything he sees," Vitka thought, looking at Burmistrov as if he were a strange reptile. "But he didn't order anything! He probably had too much to eat in Crimea, the poor thing."

"I just can't . . . figure him out . . . ," thought Olya. "He's acting like he's on his way back from a funeral."

"You know, when they moved me to the kitchen," Burmistrov continued, "I saw the whole process of how the food got cooked. Every day. It started early in the morning. They'd bring in a horse carcass from the freezer on a cart and we'd put it on three wooden blocks that were slammed together. Then the cook would call for Vasya Two-Axe. Vasya was a convict who'd once worked as a butcher in Alma-Ata, but got locked up *big-time*. A robust man, with two axes. He would come and start cutting up the skinny, frozen carcass like a head of cabbage. This was his greatest pleasure. He cut it up like an artist, each cut came from the heart. Then he left and we dumped the meat into cauldrons, boiled it, poured in the grains . . . We boiled it for a long time, until the meat came right off the bones. And then . . . then . . . forgive me, what's your name?"

He stared at Olya fixedly.

"Olga," she replied calmly.

"Olga, can I ask you a favor? Only you."

"That depends."

Burmistrov clutched the table with his hands, as if he were preparing to rip it off the ground.

"Can you eat for me? Here. Now."

"What do you mean 'for you'?"

"So that I can watch. I just want to watch."

Olya exchanged a look with Volodya.

"I knew he was a nut," Volodya thought, sighing emphatically.

"You know, we came here with a concrete—"

"I understand, I understand, I understand." Burmistrov frowned. "I don't want to bother you, I don't want to do anything but watch you, that's all I need, really. I don't have a family, don't have relatives, and now I don't even have any friends, don't have a home or a hearth." He gestured toward the plate with his lips in a cautious way, like a dog: "That's all I have left."

"What? Food?" asked Vitka.

"No, no, no!" He shook his head. "Not food! Just to watch how a good person eats. How a beautiful person eats. To see how Olga eats. Yes. Now, please, I don't want to answer any more questions . . ." He took out his wallet again, pulled out a twenty-five-ruble note, and put it down on the table.

"Here we go!" Vitka thought, covering her mouth with her hand so as not to burst out laughing. "Mother of God, if we try to tell anyone in Moscow about this, no one will believe it . . ."

Olya looked at the money. "He's seriously crazy," she said to herself.

"What nonsense," Volodya thought, smirking.

"I'm going back to our compartment." Olya stood up.

Burmistrov shuddered as if he'd been hit with an electric shock. "Olga, I'm asking you, begging you, please don't go!"

"Thanks, but I'm already full." Olga began to squeeze her way out from between Volodya and the table.

"I'm begging you! I'm begging you!" Burmistrov cried out.

The guests at the neighboring tables turned to look at them.

"Hold on." Volodya grabbed her by the arm. "This is interesting."

"Yeah, very!" She snorted.

"Please believe me, Olga, this minute of you eating will be enough to last me a whole year," Burmistrov mumbled, pressing his head against the table and looking up into her eyes. "You . . . you eat in such a remarkable way . . . it's simply divine . . . it's as if, it's as if . . . I've got something here that . . ." He pressed his hands to his sunken chest. "Here it's . . . it's just that it . . . so strongly, so strongly that . . . that I don't see anything . . ."

His voice was quivering.

"It's hard not to feel for him," Olya thought, "but he's crazy." She looked at him sideways.

The train car was silent but for the rumbling of the wheels.

"What's the problem, then?" Volodya blurted out. "What's the big deal if someone wants to watch you eat?"

"I don't like it when people look at my mouth. And also, I . . ." She looked out the window. "I try to avoid crazy people."

"I'm not a lunatic, Olga, please believe me!" Burmistrov waved his hands. "I'm a totally normal Soviet man."

"I can tell!" she said with a chuckle.

"Maybe I could eat for you instead?" Vitka glanced at the twenty-five-ruble note on the table, fluttering in the drafty train car.

"You . . . forgive me, what's your name?"

"Vita."

"Vita . . . Vitochka, understand, I only experience this with certain people, please don't be offended! Generally speaking . . . this is the first time I've felt it. Don't be offended."

"I rarely get offended. I'm more likely to offend." Vita straightened her dark glasses. "Ol, eat that meat. Give the guy what he's looking for."

"I'm begging you, Olga, just for a few minutes! It would be

such a joy for me! This . . . this would be . . . I don't know . . . more than joy." Burmistrov's voice was quivering once more.

"Now he'll start crying again," Olya thought. She looked at the passengers glancing furtively in their direction. "It's Murphy's Law. Of course they sat him here with us, and not with the two fat ladies over there . . ."

"All right, I'll finish my food," she said. She sat back down without looking at Burmistrov. "But put your money away."

"Olga, I'm begging you!" He pressed his hands to his chest. "Don't offend me. I really want you to take the money, just you, only you!"

"You can pretend that she took it," Volodya said, reaching for the money. But Burmistrov quickly covered the bill with his palm. It was a warning, as if he were protecting a candle from the wind.

"No, no, no! I'm asking that Olga take it, only Olga! To take it out of the kindliness in her heart, to take it simply . . . as an ordinary . . . well . . . like a . . . like nothing at all!"

"Take it, Ol." Vitka nodded. "Don't upset the man."

"Olga, take it, I'm begging you!"

"Take it, take it . . . ," said Volodya with a frown.

Hesitating for a minute longer, Olya finally took the money and put it away into the pocket of her jeans.

"Thank you, thank you so so much!" said Burmistrov, shaking his bald head.

Olga frowned and brought her fork and knife over to the steak, but as if there were a piece of dumb metal lying on her plate.

The train rocked violently.

She gulped, stuck her fork into the meat, and cut off a piece with a decisive motion.

"Just don't rush, I'm begging you, don't rush!" whispered Burmistrov. Volodya poured Olya some beer. She speared the meat with her fork, brought it to her lips, plucked it off the fork with her teeth, and began to chew slowly while looking down at the plate.

Burmistrov's dark, sinewy body seemed to have turned to stone. Clutching the edges of the table, he stared directly at Olya's mouth. His murky eyes rolled around and glazed over, as if this unhandsome man had been injected with a large dose of narcotics.

"And this is na . . ." His gray lip began to twist. "And this is na . . ." Vitka and Volodya stared at him, wide-eyed with shock.

"The guy's really getting his rocks off, huh?!" Vitka thought. "What a show . . ."

"Fuck this!" Volodya said to himself. "Just, fuck this . . ."

Olya ate, having promised herself not to look at Burmistrov even once. This worked at first. She wasn't even in a rush to finish her food, forking up potato sticks and green peas. But Burmistrov's babbling became even more insistent, as if there were something tearing itself out of his chest, forcing its way through his clenched teeth. His shoulders trembled and his head shivered gently.

"This is na! And this is naaaaoo! And this is naaaaoo!"

"Don't look!" Olya ordered herself, spearing another piece of meat, cutting it off, and dipping it into the viscous yolk of the cool egg.

Burmistrov moaned and shivered more and more violently as foam appeared at the corners of his bloodless lips.

"And this is naaaaoo! This is naaaaoo! And this is naaaaoo!"

Not able to stop herself, Olga looked over. She shrank back from his glazed eyes in an instant and began to choke, remembering *Ivan the Terrible and His Son Ivan,* the Repin painting. Volodya held out a glass of beer.

"Don't look, you idiot!" she said to herself angrily, taking a drink from the glass.

Through the yellow beer, Burmistrov's blue shirt was the color of seaweed.

"And this is naaaaoo! This is naaaaoo!"

Olya felt like she was about to vomit.

"Think about the sea!" She fixed her eyes on the "seaweed" and remembered how she and Volodya had swum out onto an ichthyologists' platform one evening and made love on its steel floor, which was still warm from the sun. Vitka stayed on the shore and cooked mussels over a bonfire with two local guys. Volodya forced Olya onto her knees and entered her from behind; Olya pressed her cheek to the smooth floor, listening to the weak nocturnal waves beat against the platform . . .

She speared the last piece of meat, rubbed it in the egg yolk, and put it in her mouth.

Burmistrov trembled and roared with such force that the restaurant car got quiet and the waiter rushed over to their table. "And this is naaaaaaoooo!"

"What's going on?" He bent over to them with a furrowed brow.

"Everything's . . . fine," said Volodya, the first one to shake off his stupor.

Burmistrov went limp, his lip drooped, his face was sweaty, but he was still staring at Olya's mouth.

"Is something the matter with you?" The waiter frowned.

"No, everything's fine," Volodya answered for him. "Could we . . . pay?"

"Four twenty," the waiter declared at once.

Volodya handed him five rubles and began to rise from the table. Vitka and Olya stood up as soon as he did.

Burmistrov was now hunched over and moving his wet lips soundlessly. He was dripping with sweat.

"Let me by," Volodya said.

Burmistrov stood up like a robot and walked into the aisle. The waiter gave Volodya his change, but he refused it. He led Olya over to the exit. Vitka hurried after them, grinning and wagging her skinny hips. Burmistrov stood there, hunched over. He looked down at the floor.

"You need to lie down," the waiter said to him, touching his sweaty back, having finally decided that what was happening to

Burmistrov was normal, that he'd just gotten caught up in a prolonged holiday binge.

"Huh?" Burmistrov raised his eyes to look at him.

"Get some rest is what I'm saying," the waiter whispered to
him. "And this evening, right before we get into Moscow, come
find me for some hair of the dog."

Burmistrov turned around and walked away.

Back in their compartment, Olga closed her eyes and dozed off.
*She dreams that she is in Kratovo, where the administration at the
Gnessin Institute has organized a secret end-of-the-year competition,
over which Pavel Kogan will be presiding; she is riding her cousin
Vanya's mountain bike down Chekhov Street with a violin case over
her shoulder, making her way to the home of the elderly Fatyanovs,
who breed tulips; she rides easily and freely, manipulating the obedi-
ent pedals, offering her face to the warm country breeze, the fresh
country breeze, accelerating up the hill near the Gornostaevs' dacha,
then allowing herself to roll down it, past moldering, winding fences,
behind which an endless pack of dogs lies in wait, nursing their torpid
anger, then turning onto Marshal Zhukov Street; she sees that the
entire street has been converted into a very deep trench, from fence to
fence, its every inch, and that over this trench, right in the center of the
street, is a monorail; it is completely straight and sparkles in the sun;
"How will I get past? I'm already late!" she thinks in horror, braking
sharply; sand, country sand, fine white sand, is ground down by the
bicycle tires, the roots of a pine tree are in the bicycle's way, cabbage-
white butterflies zoom into her eyes, then fly off into the nettles, while
down below, in the gloomy trench, people waiting in line for kvass
fidget in the dark; the line is small, silent, and unfamiliar; Olya looks
at the monorail; "Hey, miss, you've gotta take off your tires," someone
suggests from down below; "How can I take them off? I don't have any
tools!" she responds, beginning to grow cold; "Ask the mechanic!"; Olya
raises her head and looks up; there, high up in the pine trees, high up*

*in the orange-blue pines, lives a group of mechanics with steel claws
on their feet; one comes down to her from his tree; "We each have two
axes," he says, and takes out two enormous axes; they shine in the sun;
the mechanic grunts and deftly hacks the tires off the bicycle wheels;
"Thank you!" she says, overjoyed; "Now pay me!" says the mechanic,
who reeks of vodka and sausage, blocking her path toward the monorail; "How can I pay you?"; "With cooked meat! You're wearin' ridin'
breeches made of meat! You've been growin' 'em all summer, you li'l
dragonfly!" Olya looks down at her legs, in shorts; on her thighs are
giant growths made of cooked meat; she touches them, palpating them
with horror and fascination; "Stand still!" the mechanic orders, and
cuts off the growths with two sharp blows; "Now I'm gonna bake 'em
in dough and make me some capital chow!" he shouts in Olya's face;
the meat disappears into the mechanic's bottomless pockets; "Get outta
here! Don't dawdle! I changed the tracks!" the mechanic shouts; Olya
puts the rim of her front wheel onto the monorail, pushes one foot
against the ground to gain speed, and begins to ride over the bottomless, dark trench, at first with uncertainty—unsteadily—then more
and more freely, accelerating as the wind whistles in her ears.*

Jerk.

Clang.

Jerk.

Olya woke up and wiped her wet mouth with her hand.

The train jerked again, then quietly came to a crawl. The sun
had grown weaker. Their compartment was stuffy, dusty, and
smelled of sausages. Volodya was sleeping on the bed across from
her. Olya found her sandals and went out into the hallway. She
entered the bathroom and slammed the door behind her.

"I had a dream . . . about Kratovo . . ." She tried to remember
her dream. "God, three more hours of getting jostled around in
here . . . Something about Kogan . . . Oh yeah! Meat breeches!"

She laughed and stroked her tanned hip. Having finished pee-
ing, she moved her hand across her genitals, rubbed the urine
collected there onto her hand, stood up, rinsed her hand, zipped

up her pants, and looked at herself in the spattered mirror: a pink, Hungarian tank top with spaghetti straps; blond, shoulder-length hair; a broad face with chestnut eyes; and a hickey from Volodya above her collarbone.

"And that was my trip to Crimea," she declared, and opened the door. Standing directly in front of the bathroom was Burmistrov.

She looked at him without surprise.

"Now he's gonna ask for his money back," she thought. "The crazy idiot!"

"Forgive me, please, Olga, but I wanted to talk to you . . . I really need to."

"In the bathroom?"

"No, no, if you want, we could go over to my compartment in the seventh car . . . if . . . or . . . here . . ." He moved to the side to let her pass by.

"And if I don't want to?" She walked out of the bathroom and gave Burmistrov a scornful look. "Of course it couldn't end that easily!" she said to herself. "Now he won't leave me alone . . . what a sleazeball . . ."

She pulled out the twenty-five-ruble note and quickly placed it in his shirt pocket, from which a few papers and a pair of dark glasses were sticking out.

"Take this back and let me be."

"No . . . no, please . . ." He reached into his pocket as he tried to come to his senses. "Why are you . . ."

Olya turned away from him and began to walk away, but he grabbed her by the arm.

"I'm begging you, please don't go!"

"I'm gonna call my husband over," she said, immediately getting angry with herself for this cowardly lie. "Now I'm married too!" she thought.

"What do you want from me?!"

"I'm begging you, I'm begging you . . ." He noticed a man in the hallway walking over to them. "I'll just say two words, let's go . . . well . . . over to the vestibule."

Burmistrov didn't scare her at all; Olga understood that this man wasn't capable of doing anything violent or frightening, but that didn't make him any less unbearable.

"Which vestibule do you mean exactly?" she said with a scornful smirk, nodding at the approaching man; he had a bushy mustache and striped pajamas and was carrying a transparent cellophane bag of food scraps in both hands while purring to himself. Olya attempted to avoid the bag, which was filled with chicken bones, eggshells, and apple cores, then began to walk over to the vestibule. Burmistrov hurried after her.

It was dirty and dark in the vestibule, and thunderously loud.

Leaning against the cool, muddy-green wall, Olya folded her arms over her beautiful bosom and looked at Burmistrov. He fumbled around in his breast pocket in a feverish search for the money.

"Why did you . . . I did this in all honesty . . . and you . . ."

In pulling out the bill, he accidentally hooked several other papers, which fell out onto the floor. He bent over to pick them up. A photograph landed at Olya's feet. She lifted it up into the air with her foot, caught it in her hands, and gave it a close look: Burmistrov embracing a lean, dark-complexioned young man with close-set eyes, with the Swallow's Nest, a castle in Crimea, in the background; the young man was wearing a sailor-striped tank top and had several tattoos on his shoulders and arms. One of them, of a snake crawling up his wrist, stood out: it was emblazoned with the name "Ira" in the same spot where it was pierced through with a sword.

"Your . . . *friend*?" Olya gave back the picture.

"Well, yes, yes, my friend. We saw each other in Yalta."

"He was in jail, too?"

"Yes, but not with me. He had . . . he did . . . something else . . ."

"What'd he do? Kill Ira? Or just love her too much?"

"Ah—you want to talk about that!" Burmistrov gave her an exhausted smile. "Well, no, it has nothing to do with a person named Ira. It's a prison tattoo. 'I Ruin Actives.'"

"What's an actives?"

"They're big burgers, bad guys."

"Big burgers?"

"Olga," he said sternly, and held out the money. "Take it. Please don't offend me."

"Tell me what it is you need from me." She stuck her hands into her armpits.

"I need . . ." He began to speak in a decisive manner, but immediately got down onto his knees. "I saw you in Yalta, Olga."

"What?"

"I . . . back in Yalta . . . at a seaside café . . . the Anchor. It was the first time. You were there with your husband. You were eating tomato salad and . . . hmmm . . . chicken . . . Chicken Kiev . . . You ate there two more times. And then on the beach, you ate cherries. I gave them to you."

"Hold on." Olya tried to remember. "On the beach . . . cherries . . . a bucket of cherries! That was you? You gave them to us? In the newspaper cone?"

"Me, me, me!" He put his bald head into his hands.

Olya remembered a strange resortgoer with an ingratiating smile who poured her yellow cherries from a bucket and mumbled something to her with a laugh.

And suddenly, at that moment, for some reason she remembered her whole dream about Kratovo: the monorail, the trench, and the mechanic with the two axes.

"God, what a vision!" she said, laughing.

This fit of laughter shook her young, slender body, but Burmistrov, still on his knees, kept staring at her with his pitiful smile.

"That was you?" she repeated after she was done laughing.

"Yes! Yes! Yes!" He was nearly screaming. He rubbed his face with his fist, the twenty-five-ruble note still clenched in it. "I . . .

forgive me . . . Olga . . . I haven't been able to sleep for four nights. Since Yalta."

"You . . . because of me?"

"Yes."

"And you were, what? Following me?"

"No, well . . . I just found out when you were leaving. Just . . . from the landlady, where you were staying."

"Why?"

"So I could see you eat again."

Olya stared at him in silence. The door opened and a heavyset man with five bottles of beer pressed to his naked chest stepped out into the vestibule. Burmistrov did not get up off his knees. Glancing at him and Olya, the man passed by.

"Get up," sighed Olya.

Burmistrov stood up heavily.

"What do you want from me?"

"I . . . Olga . . . please don't misunderstand . . ."

"What do you want from me?"

He took a deep inhale of vestibule air, which smelled of creosote.

"I want us to see each other once a month and for you to eat for me."

"And what will I get out of it?"

"One hundred rubles. Every time."

She reflected on it.

"This won't be in a public place," Burmistrov muttered. "It will be in a safe, secluded spot and the food won't be anything like—"

"I'll do it," Olya interrupted him. "Once a month. Only once a month."

"Only once a month," he repeated in an ecstatic whisper, and, closing his eyes, leaned against the vibrating wall with total relief. "Oh, I'm so happy!"

"I'm not going to give you my address or my phone number."

"You don't need to, no need . . . We'll find somewhere to

meet . . . we'll establish a time and a place . . . that'll be better, much better. When's a good time for you?"

"Well . . . ," she said, "I'm done early on Mondays. At one ten. Let's meet at one thirty . . . in front of the Pushkin Monument."

"In front of the Pushkin Monument . . ." He echoed her words.

"Yeah . . . and do you live in Moscow?"

"I'll be living in Golutvin. They won't let me register in the capital."

"That's all, then. And please, don't follow me to the bathroom again!"

She turned and grabbed hold of the door handle.

"Wait . . . which Monday?" he asked, not yet opening his eyes.

"Which? Well . . . at the start of the month. On the first Monday of the month."

"The first Monday of every month."

Nodding, Olya walked out.

Volodya had woken up and was waiting for her in the compartment with a puffy face and disheveled hair. Vitka was still sleeping.

They climbed onto one of the top beds and kissed for a little while, then lay in silence.

The train was entering the Moscow suburbs.

"I forgot to take back the money," Olya remembered, ruffling Volodya's hair. "Once a month. So what? Let him watch. OK, enough, time to get our stuff together, we're almost there . . ."

The dusty pillow of a sun-kissed Moscow summer tumbled down onto Olya. She spent August at her family's dacha in Kratovo. A hammock; pine trees; Sibelius's violin concerto, which she was learning for an exam; an old pond; a new edition of Proust; afternoon tea with fresh cherry jam; Volodya coming to visit, which invariably ended with a hurried sex act in the old fir grove; games of badminton with their timid neighbor, a mathematician who was always covered in burrs; bike rides with stupid Tamara and nervous Larissa; long evenings spent around the table at the Petrovskys'; an afternoon nap in the hammock; and a good night's sleep in the attic on Grandpa's lumpy sofa.

During the whole of August she never once thought about her adventure on the train and would probably have completely forgotten about it had it not been for one unexpected event. On the first Monday of September, she was performing the first part of the Sibelius concerto for her teacher Mikhail Yakovlevich, a small, round man who resembled a restless hamster. She was halfway through the piece when he interrupted her, snapping his tiny, plump fingers, as he often did.

"Nao, nao, nao. Naot like that. Too typical—naot like that!" he mumbled with the Georgian accent that often came out when his students were playing badly. "Olenka—there's something going on with the sound here that's nao, nao, nao. You're not throwing yourself into the music. You're not taking yourself in hand, darling. You must throw yourself into it, throw yourself right in, my child, and don't just sit there on the rests. The sound is good, but there's no meat to it. No meat to it, my golden darling! You're sleeping on the rests. Throw yourself into it, throw yourself into it and don't look back, that's what I'm saying. It's better to overdo it than not to give enough. And here . . ." He leafed through the music. "Your chords went off, rang out, rang out . . . and then you got lost on the neck! Got looost! Totally lost! Push yourself forward! Push yourself! Push yourself to the climax! If you don't, you'll cripple the sound, slow the tempo, and we're left with nao tempo and nao sound, you unddeerrstand? And this is na . . . and this is na . . . !"

"Why is this *na* so familiar?" Olya began to think, looking over the violin's tuning pegs at Mikhail Yakovlevich's wide forehead. "And this is na . . . steak and eggs!"

At that moment, she remembered the steak and eggs, the train, and Burmistrov, and her mouth broke into a broad grin.

"Why're you so happy?" Mikhail Yakovlevich reached both hands into his pockets to look for his cigarettes. "Summer's over and your piece hasn't budged . . ."

At half past one, Olya was standing in front of the Pushkin Monument with her violin case over her shoulder. She saw Burmistrov get up immediately from the crowd of people sitting on benches by the statue and walk toward her, his gait rushed and awkward. He was still skinny and bald, though he now wore a beige raincoat.

"He lost his tan awfully fast," Olya said to herself, watching Burmistrov with great interest. It was as if he were an exotic plant who had not only managed *not* to wilt in the last month and a half, but also to grow, to lead his own mysterious life, to eat, to drink, to sleep, and to wear a raincoat, a turtleneck, and a new pair of suede boots.

"A construction manager . . ." She began to remember his words on the train. "Two degrees. The Tin Man has a brain, then."

Burmistrov approached her.

"Hello, Olga," he said, bowing his head but not offering his hand. "Hello."

His face was calmer and more balanced than when she last saw him, and his greenish-blue eyes stared at her with benevolent attention.

"I thought that you were out of town back in August, and that was why you didn't show up."

"It's true."

"I wasn't very worried."

"Why not?"

"I was sure that you'd show up in September." He gave her a tense and shy smile.

"Why?" Olya laughed, playing with her hair. "Such confidence!"

"Are you . . . a musician?" He had noticed the violin case.

"Almost."

"Are you studying at a conservatory?"

"Almost."

"What do you mean 'almost'?"

"You're asking too many questions."

"Forgive me . . ." He began to get restless in his usual way. "Let's . . . over there . . . we'll get a cab . . ."

He walked ahead of Olya toward the boulevard.

"I wonder if he's got a woman," Olga thought as she studied his long, nervous stride, his gray pants, and his suede boots. "Guys like him have either had a lot of 'em or nobody."

On the boulevard, Burmistrov caught a banana-colored Zaporozhets, helped Olya into the backseat, sat down next to the frowning driver, and then, thirty minutes later, helped Olya get out when the car stopped across the street from Avtozavodskaya Station.

"Is it far?" asked Olya, getting out of the Zaporozhets.

"Two steps from here, that building there," he said, gesturing to it with his hand.

They walked into a nine-story apartment block and took the elevator to the sixth floor. The door to apartment number twenty-four was upholstered with cheap fabric. Burmistrov opened it and let Olya lead the way. She entered the one-room apartment, which was poorly furnished but had been carefully cleaned. In the middle of the room stood a table set for one person, covered with a white tablecloth. There was not yet any food on the table.

"Right . . . here." Burmistrov gestured to the table and fidgeted continuously. "Come in, please . . . take your coat off."

He helped her take off her jacket. She put the violin case on top of the refrigerator in the hallway and walked into the main room. Burmistrov quickly took off his own raincoat and ran his palms through the few hairs sprouting from his almost completely bald head.

"Olga, please, sit down."

"May I wash my hands?"

"Yes, of course . . ."

He turned on the bathroom light and opened the door for her. Washing her hands in the rust-streaked sink, Olya looked at herself in the mirror.

"You crazy idiot, ge-ge-get ready for the hap-p-py blade . . . He's getting ready to cut you up with it . . . Right when the st-st-starlight is scattered and night and darkness come down onto the si-si-silent world . . . No. He won't cut me. He's peaceful. Peaceful like pa-papa. Or like Pa-Pa-Pavel . . . Don't be afraid, Ole Lukøje."

She wiped her hands off with an old washcloth, left the bathroom, and sat down at the table. Burmistrov disappeared into the kitchen and came back holding a serving dish. On the dish were pieces of cooked chicken, boiled potatoes, and pickles. He walked over to the right of Olya and began to carefully fill her plate.

"Did you cook this yourself?" asked Olya.

"No, of course not . . . I can't really . . . cook . . . this . . ." He disappeared into the kitchen with the serving dish, scurried back, took a pillow off the bed, and stood facing Olya, holding the pillow in front of him.

"Why do you need that?" She looked at the pillow.

"It's . . . so . . . that I'm not too loud . . . ," he muttered, his voice beginning to quiver. "Please . . . can . . . please . . . I'm asking you . . ."

"Do you have anything to drink?"

"You don't need it . . . can't have it . . . ," Burmistrov pronounced harshly. "Eat, please. Please only eat."

"That's a new one!" Olya thought. She chose the tastiest-looking bit of chicken, cut a piece from it, and put it into her mouth.

Burmistrov's face immediately went pale and his eyes rolled up into his head.

"And this . . . and this . . . ," he mumbled pitifully.

Olya began to eat. The chicken wasn't bad at all.

"And this is naaaaoo . . . And this is naaaaoo!" Burmistrov muttered, clutching the pillow.

"It's probably chicken from the farmer's market, steamed

chicken . . . ," Olya thought, chewing and swallowing the meat slowly. "I wonder if he rents this apartment? Or if it just belongs to his friends . . . No work's been done on it for at least twenty years . . . and the furniture . . . 'Hey, Slavs! We stand firm-iture!'"

Burmistrov's body was quaking uncontrollably. He was drawing in air with a whistle and roaring "This is na!" into the pillow, his gaze fixed on the pieces of meat, which were disappearing between Olya's lips. His trembling legs gave out and he fell to his knees.

"Look around him, not at him . . . ," Olya ordered herself.

There was a plastic donkey sitting on top of the old television.

"Eeyore!" She looked at Burmistrov and almost choked. "You don't have anything to drink . . . eat slowly, you idiot . . ."

Burmistrov's cries gained strength and became an unintelligible roar, his bald head trembling.

Olya swallowed the last piece and pushed the plate away.

Burmistrov went silent and limp and let the pillow fall from his hands. He caught his breath, took a handkerchief from his pocket, and began to wipe off his sweaty face.

"Is that all?" asked Olya.

"Yes, yes . . ." He blew his nose loudly.

She stood up from the table, walked into the hallway, and began putting on her coat.

"Just a sec . . ." Burmistrov put his hands onto the floor, attempting to get up.

He walked to the corridor, helped Olya into her jacket, and handed her the money: 125 rubles.

"You forgot to take it the first time."

"He remembered . . . ," Olya thought. She took the money and realized all at once how important she was to this sleazy, half-crazed man. "It's like a dream . . ."

"Forgive me, Olga . . . I . . . can't . . . I won't be able to take you back . . . ," Burmistrov muttered. He looked pitiful.

"The metro's right here," Olya said, visibly relieved. She put the violin case over her shoulder.

"In a month . . . I'm begging you . . ." He looked down beneath his feet at the shabby hardwood floor.

Olya nodded silently and took her leave.

She took the elevator down, dumbly reading the vulgar graffiti on the wooden doors, walked out through the dim entryway, and set off for the metro.

It was a cloudy September day, but it wasn't raining.

"I want a drink," Olya said to herself, and noticed a soda machine in the middle distance.

The machine was working, but there were no cups left. Olya walked into a grocery store. There was a big line in the meat section. One woman was shouting angrily. Someone pushed someone else away from the counter. A flushed, finely dressed woman emerged from the crowd, holding a string bag. Four pairs of yellow chicken legs were sticking out of it. The woman half-turned back to everyone else as she walked away and made a pronouncement: "This lady wanted poultry! You worthless trash!"

She walked out of the store triumphantly.

A fit of laughter came over Olya. She bent down and began to howl, covering her mouth with both hands and staggering around, coming to a stop in the grocer's section; she doubled over with laughter, her violin case flew off her shoulder, and she barely managed to catch it, now laughing so much that everyone around her in the almost empty grocer's section went quiet. Tears streamed from her eyes. Olya leaned against a column decorated with white tiles and laughed, moaned, then shook her head.

"Someone's got the giggles!" the canned-food seller called out to her.

Olya wiped away her tears.

"Have you got mineral water?"

"Only Drogobych."

"And . . . do you serve it in a glass?"

"No." He looked at her with a smile.

Olya walked out of the market. She took the metro to Oktyabrsky Station, got on bus number thirty-three, got off near the Mineral Waters store, and went in and drank two glasses of Borjomi thirstily.

"One hundred twenty-five rubles! And he didn't give me any bread," she thought, walking home along Gubkina Street. "He wouldn't let me drink either. Why? He didn't ask me to eat more than what I did, even though there was still some food left . . . oh well. If someone's an idiot, then that's forever. One hundred twenty-five rubles . . . how horrible! It all began on that beach in Yalta. He was sitting next to us, just sitting there with his newspaper cap and a bucket of cherries, and he turned to me and said, 'Help yourself.' And I did."

Awaiting her arrival at home were her quiet mother (her loud mathematician father was at the university where he taught); their Irish setter, named Ready; Polish perch with rice, which she immediately refused; and her endless Proust.

Olya went to her room, dialed Volodya's number to tell him everything that had happened, but hung up the phone as soon as he answered. "Why would I?" she asked her reflection in the mirror on the shelf. "Better no one knows."

The following day she went to a black marketeer and bought two Pirastro strings (an A and an E) for forty rubles each and bought a blue-and-white French scarf for thirty-two rubles at a vintage store on Sretenka.

. . .

One month later at one thirty p.m., she was standing in front of the Pushkin Monument.

Burmistrov arrived a little late, then took her to the same apartment, and, having given her a plate of cooked pork with vegetables and roared to his heart's content, paid her the hundred rubles.

Olya decided to begin saving up for a good violin. She put the banknote inside a volume of Proust that she'd finished. She moved the book to the upper level of her bookshelf.

"It's too bad I can only do this once a month," she thought as she fell asleep. "Imagine if I could do it once a week! I'd have a Schneider by junior year!"

A year passed. Olya began her third year at the Gnessin Institute; broke up with Volodya, who'd been pushed to the side by the beautiful and phlegmatic pianist Ilya; learned a Mozart concerto; played reasonably well with a quartet in a university contest; read Nabokov's *Lolita*; plus tried hash and anal sex.

Her meetings with Burmistrov happened regularly on the first Monday of every month.

In December, she arrived at the monument with a fever of a hundred degrees and, dripping snot, was barely able to finish the meat ragout accompanied by Burmistrov's moans; in April, she felt very nauseous after eating a fatty piece of sturgeon; in May, after eating quail with cranberries, she awoke with a cry: she had dreamed that Burmistrov had an enormously fat python coming out of his mouth; in July, after eating liver in sour cream, she was tormented by sharp pains in her stomach. But in August, she tanned on the beach in Koktebel, resting on Ilya's plump chest, which was overgrown with red hair.

Olya thought of Burmistrov sometimes, usually referring to him as "Horse Soup." She felt that he played an important role in her life, but she wasn't sure what it was. The phrase "this is na" stayed with her, however; she used it often, mumbling it when something surprised or disappointed her.

"Well, this is na!" she would say as she stomped her foot when her fingers didn't obey the notes as she played violin.

"This is na!" she would say, shaking her head when she saw a long line leading out of a store.

"This is naaaaa . . . ," she would whisper into Ilya's ear after he brought her to orgasm.

One day, rushing off to meet Burmistrov, she declined to go to a closed screening of *From Russia with Love* with Ilya.

"Have you met someone else?" asked Ilya sharply.

"Horse Soup," she replied cheerfully.

"What's that?"

"You wouldn't understand."

As with Volodya, she didn't tell Ilya anything.

It was 1982. Brezhnev died. Ready also died, after eating rat poison. Olya started her senior year at the institute and bought herself a violin made by the German master Schneider for 1,600 rubles, telling her poor parents that a girlfriend who'd dropped out of school and married a Georgian had given it to her. She continued to meet Burmistrov at the same apartment. She was so used to Horse Soup's screaming that she no longer paid any attention to it, focusing only on the food in front of her.

"Not enough garnish here . . . the cauliflower is boiled and not fried in bread crumbs . . . but the meat is good . . . and the salad is fresh . . ."

Having received her money, she would go to a nearby cafeteria, ask for a glass of compote, and drink it quickly without sitting down. She wasn't saving money anymore, instead spending it on whatever she fancied.

So passed another six months.

Then something began to happen to the food Burmistrov

served her. There was no less of it, and it was still of the same high quality, but it was now presented to her in particulate form. The meat, fish, and vegetables were cut into small pieces, and all of these pieces were mixed together, as if it were a Russian salad. Olya ate without asking any questions and Horse Soup howled his habitual "This is naaaaoo!" Eventually, the food was cut up so finely that it was hard for Olya to figure out what exactly was in the fastidious mix of meat (or fish) and vegetables on the plate in front of her.

"What's he having me eat now . . . ," she thought as she studied the food with a distrustful look. But then, having tasted it, she calmed down once she realized that it was still normal food.

One day, Burmistrov's monthly concoction of foods only took up one half of the plate he put in front of her—the other half was completely empty.

"What can he mean by this?" Olya thought, frowning. "Did he eat the other half himself?"

She picked up her fork and began to eat the mixture of turkey, salad, and boiled potatoes. This time, Burmistrov's howling was especially protracted. His bald head quivered and his hands squeezed the pillow convulsively.

"And this is naaaaaaaaaoooo! Naaaaaaoo!" he bleated.

Having finished her food, Olya put down her fork and stood up.

"You haven't finished yet . . . ," Horse Soup muttered huskily, looking out from behind his pillow. "Finish, please . . ."

Olya looked at the empty plate.

"I *have* finished."

"You haven't touched one half of the plate."

"I ate everything. Look. Can you not see?"

"I see better than you do!" he cried shrilly. "You didn't touch one half of the plate! There's food on that side too! Eat!"

Olya gave him a dumb look.

"Has he lost his mind?" she thought.

Burmistrov writhed around on the floor.

"Don't torment me like this, Olga, please eat!"

"But there's nothing there . . ." She smiled nervously.

"Stop tormenting me!" he cried.

She sank back into her chair.

"Eat, eat, eat!"

"He really has lost his marbles!" Olya thought. She sighed, picked up the fork, scooped up the invisible food, and put it in her mouth.

"And this is naaaaoo! And this is naaaaaaaaoooo!" Burmistrov howled.

"I'm a mime now!" Olya said to herself, and grinned. She slowly lifted the fork to her mouth, took the invisible food off it with her lips, chewed it, then swallowed.

She was enjoying this game. After a little while, she put down her fork.

"There's still some left . . . but that's OK . . . actually . . . why rush?" muttered Burmistrov, still moaning.

"What a pain in the ass!" Olya calmly *finished* the invisible food.

He paid her a hundred rubles as usual and, helping her with her coat, said: "We're going to meet in a different apartment from now on, Olga, so next month don't go to the Pushkin Monument. Go to Tsvetnoy Boulevard."

"Where will we meet there?"

"Outside the market. Same day, same time."

Olya nodded and left.

The apartment on Tsvetnoy Boulevard was much nicer than the previous one: three comfortable rooms with high ceilings, luxuriously furnished. Burmistrov entertained Olya in the living room. The table was set tastefully: silver utensils on crystal couverts de table, porcelain plates, napkins in silver rings. There was still neither bread nor water, though, and Olya's plate was still only half-full. Burmistrov stood in front of the table holding a silvery-pink silk pillow at the ready.

"It's like a test," she said to herself as she glanced over at Burmistrov. She began to eat. "OK . . . meat and mushrooms . . . and he has a new suit . . . did he get rich or something?"

Horse Soup howled into the pillow.

She ate the visible food. Then the invisible food. She ate calmly, not hurrying at all.

Burmistrov didn't say anything and blew his nose as he usually did, wiped off his sweaty face, and gave Olya her money.

"Still I don't get it—why me?" she thought, walking to the metro. "It's been two years . . . It's a miracle I haven't lost it! And it's only me . . . So many women in Moscow . . . He's a real sicko . . . Schizophrenic, maybe? I think there's another name for his condition . . . I should go shopping at Passage, my tights are a catastrophe . . . It's nice out today . . ."

Their meetings continued with businesslike regularity. But every time there was less and less visible food on her plate. The invisible half expanded, and Olya diligently mimed her meals, bending down to the plate carefully so as not to drop any food, bringing it to her mouth, wiping her lips, chewing, and, finally, scraping what was left onto her fork and putting the final bite into her mouth.

On February 7, 1983, a slushy Monday, she sat down at the table as expected. Burmistrov came out of the kitchen with a serving dish. There was no food on the dish—only the silver spatula he typically used to serve Olya. Burmistrov put the serving dish down on the edge of the table and began to carefully mete out the invisible food to Olya.

"So, this is what it's come to . . . ," she thought, and smiled. "I should get a bonus for my artistry."

Burmistrov left with the serving dish and came back with his pillow.

Olya looked at the empty plate.

"And this . . . And this . . . ," mumbled Burmistrov.

"In your hooouse, I spent my yoooouth, its gooolden dreams . . . ," Olya sang to herself, scooping emptiness from her empty plate with an empty fork.

Two more years passed duskily by. Andropov and Chernenko died. Olya's family got a spaniel named Artaud. Her father left his post at Moscow State University. Vitka got married. Perestroika began. Olya completed her degree at the Gnessin Institute and, thanks to an advantageous connection, joined the regional philharmonic orchestra. Ilya moved away to Israel with his family. Olya had two lovers—a tall, skinny, long-haired guitarist named Oleg and a calm, thorough doctor and cosmetologist named Zhenya. Zhenya had a wife and a car. Olya made love with Oleg in his artist friend's studio. She and Zhenya made love wherever they could—mostly in his car.

Nothing changed with Burmistrov: she ate a plate of invisible food, he roared and gave her money.

After her father's departure from MSU, the family had almost no money, so the hundred rubles she got from Horse Soup every month were very useful. She also got ninety-six rubles a month from the orchestra.

Perestroika flew off clumsily into the night, leaving the stormy and merciless nineties in its stead. Olya's mother had her right breast removed; Olya's scandalous grandmother died, finally freeing up her two-room apartment near the VDNKh; Olya had her second abortion and left the orchestra in order to become a music teacher at a school for foreign students.

Something began to happen with Burmistrov: he changed their meeting place several times, sometimes feeding her in a stand-alone office at the Hotel Metropol, sometimes in half-empty apartments that reeked of renovation in the "European" style. Burmistrov now roared without a pillow, apparently no longer worried about anyone overhearing. He drove Olya around in a Lada, then in a Honda, then in the backseat of a Jeep, as he now had a fat-necked chauffeur at his disposal. Burmistrov began to dress like a New Russian, if not an especially young one, and started shaving his head. The sum he gave Olya accumulated more and more *Russian* zeroes and then, like a butterfly caught in a glass, petrified into an American hundred-dollar bill.

Olya ate her invisible food with great appetite and Burmistrov howled "This is na," writhing and spattering his expensive suit with foamy spittle.

On October 19, 1994, Olya married Alyosha, a cosmetologist and a colleague of her ex-boyfriend Zhenya. They began to remodel her grandma's apartment, which was filthy and run-down because of the old woman's six cats, bought new furniture, a huge television, and an Irish setter named Karo. Alyosha, a broad-shouldered red-head, loved Olya, French cinema, sports, and cars, and made good money. She left her job at the music school and wanted to have kids. That summer, the couple prepared to set off for a twenty-four-day trip around Europe organized by Alyosha's father, a functionary in the department of foreign affairs. Olya had never been abroad before. Alyosha, on the other hand, had spent his childhood in France and was very excited to show his wife around Europe.

As she finished packing her bags, Olya remembered that she had a meeting with Burmistrov the next day.

"I won't be there . . . I'm done chewing air . . . ," she thought. "Basta, Horse Soup . . ."

They penetrated Europe's soft body through the quiet expanse of Finland, passed through Sweden, Denmark, Norway, Iceland, witnessed the crass beauty of London, crossed the English Channel, nibbled their way across the deliciousness of France, and ended up in immaculate Switzerland.

Olya was incredibly happy right up until Geneva, where she began to feel ill. One evening, she and Alyosha were sitting at a restaurant with a view of the lake and slowly eating a huge grilled lobster, washing down the juicy snow-white meat with Fendant les Murettes from the south of Switzerland. Slightly tanned from two weeks of traveling, Alyosha was telling Olya about the problems they had with theft at his father's dacha in Barvikha.

"The people around there have lost it—and that's putting it mildly! You can't leave the gate unlocked for even a minute, otherwise they fly in and take everything they can. Maybe there's a hammock, they cut it off the trees, maybe there're some linens, they drag those away. If there's a shovel, they take the shovel, if there's a barrel . . . hey, you OK?"

Now deathly pale, Olya stared glassily at the piece of lobster on the end of her fork. It was as if an enormous orb had burst inside her head, leaving behind only a resounding and infinite emptiness. For the first time in her life, Olya *saw* the food that people ate. The sight of this food was horrifying. Worst of all was that it was so heavy, endowed with its own grievous and *final* weight. The lobster, which seemed to have been formed from white lead, reeked of death. In a cold sweat, Olya raised herself up on her stiff arms and vomited onto the table. It felt like she was throwing up gravestones. Alyosha paid twenty francs for les dégâts and took her back to the hotel. She vomited three times on the way. That night she got turned inside out by her illness, but Alyosha was afraid to call a doctor because of the risk of getting stuck in Geneva.

"It's just a little bug, bunny." He pressed ice against her temple. "We shared all our food. If something was off, then I would've thrown up too. Take deep breaths and think about snow, snow, snow, newly fallen Russian snow."

Olya fell asleep toward morning, woke up at two p.m., rubbed her heavy brow, and opened her dry lips. The nausea had passed. She wanted orange juice and toast with strawberry jam. Alyosha was asleep next to her.

"Let's go eat, big boy." She stood up.

"You're OK, bunny?" He stretched. "I told you—just a little bug. But I'm surprised that there're any bugs at all in Switzerland! You could eat off the sidewalk here!"

Olya took a shower and did her makeup.

"Sometimes it's good to throw up," Alyosha said. "It helps with wrinkles."

Downstairs in the cool foyer, they were greeted by a glorious Swiss buffet with an abundance of fruit and seafood. Olya served herself juice, toast, an egg, and a kiwi. As usual, Alyosha filled his plate with salad and covered it with dressing.

They sat down at their favorite table on the terrace, which was covered with ferns and calla lilies.

"When the heat breaks, let's go to Chillon Castle," Alyosha said. "No more locking ourselves away, 'K, bunny?"

"OK." Olya drank her juice thirstily, hit the egg with her spoon, peeled off the shell, poked it, watched the yolk run out of it with pleasure, salted it, put both yolk and trembling white onto her spoon, and brought the spoon to her mouth. Then she froze: the egg reeked of death. That same resounding emptiness rang out once more in Olya's head. She moved her crazed eyes away from it. The kiwi lying next to the egg seemed to her to be a heavy, moss-covered rock, and the toast lay on the plate like a tombstone. Olya dropped the spoon and put her hands over her face.

"No . . ."

"Is it happening again, bunny?" Alyosha stopped his cheerful chewing.

"No, no, no . . ."

Olya stood up and walked to the elevator. Alyosha came fast on her heels.

"Could I be pregnant?" She stroked her belly as she lay on the hotel bed. "No—it's never felt like this before."

"You should've stayed in bed, bunny. Stay here. I'll order us lunch here."

"Don't talk to me about lunch!" she panted.

"Have some juice."

There was no minibar in their room, so Alyosha went downstairs and came back with a portly yellow bottle.

Juice flowed into the glass. Olya brought it to her mouth and swallowed with great difficulty. It felt like drinking melted butter. She put the heavy glass onto her bedside table.

"Later."

But, later, she couldn't even bring herself to sip it. Any thought of food put her into a stupor and filled her body with a terrifying heaviness that swiftly turned to nausea.

"It's nothing but a nervous condition," Alyosha thought aloud. "Anorexia brought on by a sudden change of scenery. I have Relanium. I always take it for hangovers. Take two. It'll calm you down."

Olya took the two pills, flipped through a copy of *Vogue,* and dozed off. She woke up four hours later, took another shower, and got dressed.

"You know what, big boy, I just won't eat today. Let's go to that castle."

They spent the evening in Montreux. Alyosha ate a sausage and potato salad and drank a glass of beer. While he ate, Olya strolled along the embankment. They got back to Geneva at midnight and went to sleep. In the morning, Olya woke up at seven, quietly got ready, and, not waking her husband, went downstairs: she had a strong desire to eat. She walked out of the elevator and said "morning" to the waitresses in their white aprons and took a big warm plate and a fork and knife wrapped in a napkin and moved toward the food. She had barely caught sight of the fatal mounds of salad, cheese, ham, fish, and fruit before her legs buckled and her plate fell from her hands. She vomited bile onto the carpet.

Even though everything was in order with their insurance, Alyosha was still afraid to call a local doctor.

"They'll say she has some horrible infectious disease and send her straight to the hospital," he thought.

Instead, he found the addresses of three local psychiatrists.

"I'm not going to see a shrink." Olya pushed away the card in Alyosha's hand. "Get me some water."

Alyosha handed her a glass. She could still drink water.

"When are we leaving for Italy?" she asked, sitting on the bed and leaning against the wall.

"The day after tomorrow."

"What's the plan for today?"

"Le Valais. A wine cellar in Vétroz."

"Let's go then." She stood up decisively.

The air was cool in Serge Roh's wine cellar. Moldy stacks of bottles under brick arches, just like in Burgundy, called forth a feeling of peace and security in Olya. But, still, she couldn't bring herself to drink the wine. The glass of ruby-red cornalin seemed to weigh a whole ton as Olya swirled it around lethargically, a liquid nightmare that engulfed any and all safe, familiar feelings. Its thick, ominous glare made her heart stop.

Meanwhile, Alyosha drank so much that Olya had to prop him up as they walked to the train station.

That night in their hotel room, as she was giving herself to Alyosha, who was still not entirely sober, Olya fixed her gaze on the spots of light on the ceiling and tried to understand what was happening to her.

"Maybe I'm just overtired?" she thought to herself. "Or traumatized by the West? Marina Vlady wrote that Vysotsky vomited when he first went to Berlin and saw how affluent it was. 'Who won the war, goddamn it?!' he cried out. Or maybe we're traveling too much . . . Or it's an abnormal pregnancy . . . Meaning, I'm going to have a baby . . .'"

Instead, two days later in Rome, Olya got her period. She was very sick. She hadn't eaten anything in three days and lay in bed trembling, drinking only water. Alyosha called his father in Moscow, who got in touch with the Russian embassy. Soon, a somber embassy doctor was taking Olya's weak pulse. Having examined her, he went out into the hallway to talk to her husband.

"It could be exhaustion, but it could also be depression." He rubbed the bridge of his thick nose as he talked to Alyosha in the hotel hallway.

"What about . . . our trip?" Alyosha said thoughtfully, looking at a reproduction of one of Leonardo's drawings in a tacky frame.

"Tell you what, friend, I'll give your wife an injection of Seduxen with a touch of Barbital. Then let her sleep. You can start giving her Relanium and continue your trip. But, in Moscow, you *must* take her to a psychiatrist."

Olya slept for fourteen hours and woke up calm and visibly well rested. Alyosha gave her a pill. She took it. She ate nothing for breakfast and set off with her husband for some sightseeing around the city.

"Let's just pretend I'm on a diet!" she joked.

But she was terribly tired and very hungry by the time evening rolled around.

"Order me some tea and a sandwich from room service," she said.

Alyosha ordered for her. When the food arrived, Olya gave the cup of tea and the sliced roll, ham protruding from the cut along its side, a distrustful look.

"Could you leave me alone for a minute, big boy?"

Alyosha kissed her and walked out of the room.

"What's going on with me?" Olya said to herself. She looked down at the food. "Please just eat!"

She walked over to the table decisively. Two steps later, though, her legs seemed to have turned to clay, but this clay, made up of viscous fear, was melting. The fatal sandwich was grinning, sticking out its dead, leaden tongue at her. Olya collapsed onto the bed and began to sob.

"How's it going, bunny?" Alyosha came back into the room a little while later.

"Take it away . . . take it away . . . ," she sobbed.

Alyosha took the food into the bathroom, sat down on the toilet, ate the sandwich, washed it down with tea, and, still chewing, came back into the room.

"Just let me lie here . . ." Olya stared at the cheap white material covering the wall with her wet eyes.

Alyosha sat next to her on the bed and wiped the tears from her cheek.

"What if you tried eating with a blindfold?"

"Just let me lie here . . . ," she repeated.

"I'll go down to the square, OK?"

"Mmhmm."

Alyosha left.

"Of course it would happen here, in this ugly room . . . Murphy's Law . . . What have I done to deserve this?" She touched the wall.

The feebleness that comes after tears quickly put her to sleep.

Olya dreams that she is in the hospital where her mother had her breast removed; she is walking down the hallway to her; she enters room number sixteen and sees her mother sitting on the bed and looking at herself in Olya's grandmother's circular hand mirror; her mother is completely naked and very cheerful; "Look what they've done to me, Olenka!" she says, handing her the mirror; but even without the mirror, Olya can see that both of her mother's breasts are intact; "They've tricked you, Mom, they haven't done anything," Olya says as she palpates her mother's right breast indignantly and feels the hard tumor still inside it; "You're not looking at it right," her mother says, and insists she take the mirror. "Look over there!"; Olya looks at her mother's body in the mirror and sees that she has a hideous chunk carved out of her body—her right breast and shoulder have simply vanished. "Now you need to look from this angle," her mother says, smiling, "that way you can see the most important thing. What needs to be done." Olya shifts her view and begins to see everything very differently, everything as it truly is; she moves the image of her mother's body like a magnifying glass and superimposes it over the view of Moscow through the window; she sees a neon sign that reads MIXED FEED. *"Hurry up, they close at five," her mother insists. "Run straight through the dump." Olya runs through the enormous dump, the stinking waste reaching her waist, makes it out onto the street, and finds herself in front of the enormous building with the neon sign—* MIXED FEED; *Olya tries the door handle, but it's locked; "I'm going to starve to death," Olya thinks with horror, and knocks on the door; "Why are you banging down the door, miss! They always close at five!" a voice says nearby; Olya sees an old woman; "I'm dying of hunger," Olya sobs; "Go to the back door and talk to the shopkeeper," the old woman suggests; Olya slides into the darkness through the cracked door and finds herself in a huge storage room filled with all manner of objects; she walks and walks, then suddenly sees a small table in the corner; Horse Soup is sitting at the table with a can of food in his hand; he is young and handsome in a sad, solemn way; paying no attention to Olya, he opens the can of food in his hand with a knife; the can is empty, but this emptiness is also real chow; an unbelievably strong and intoxicatingly delicious smell wafts over to her; Horse Soup takes out a spoon and begins to eat from the can; "Gimme some! Gimme some!" Olya cries out, getting down onto her knees, but he doesn't hear or see her; she tries to catch the spoon with her mouth, but it's moving as fast as a propeller; can to mouth, can to mouth, can to mouth; Olya puts her mouth even closer and is hit very hard by the spoon, which knocks out several of her teeth.*

"Bunny! Bunny! Bunny!" Alyosha was shaking her.

"What?" She raised herself up.

"You were screaming. Can I give you another pill?"

Olya sat up and wiped tears from her face. She understood everything. This feeling of understanding didn't frighten her; on the contrary, it was soothing.

"We need to go back to Moscow, big boy."

"What about Greece?"

"I'm really ill. I need to go back."

"But . . . we'll waste our tickets and have to buy new ones. Another thousand bucks."

"Then I'll go back alone."

"Don't be silly, bunny!"

"Then let's pack and go."

"C'mon, bunny, let's put our heads together a li'l more, let's not do anything ra—"

"I need to go to Moscow!!!" Olya screamed.

They caught a flight that evening.

Moscow greeted them with the striking darkness of its dusty streets and its deeply familiar but also wild smells.

That night she got to sleep with a Reladorm, and the next morning she'd barely woken up when Alyosha made an announcement.

"I'm going to get the doctor, bunny."

"I don't need a doctor." She stretched out her tired body.

"He's a good neuropathologist—he'll figure out what's wrong. Lie down and wait for me to come back." Alyosha left.

Olya quickly got up, got dressed, combed her hair, had a drink of water, got some money, and left the apartment. She was dizzy, but still thinking clearly and quickly. Olya was aware of the weakness in her body, but was also experiencing the tender satisfaction of feeling a lot younger.

She hailed a taxi on Korolyov Avenue.

"Myasnitskaya Street."

She remembered that Horse Soup had once stopped the car there and run into his office for something.

Getting out of the car on Myasnitskaya, she quickly found a grayish-pink building, recently remodeled, with a metal plaque polished until it looked like a mirror. On the plaque was engraved:

PRAGMAS

JOINT-STOCK COMPANY

She went in through the door. A security guard in a black uniform was creeping around in the large, bright entryway, and a young receptionist sat behind the desk.

"Hello, who are you here to see?" she asked with a smile.

"I'm here to see your . . . boss," Olya said, and realized that she had forgotten Horse Soup's last name, remembering only his first: Boris.

"We have two of those." The receptionist smiled. "Do you want to see the director or the chairman?"

"I'm here for Boris—" Olya began.

"Boris Ilyich?" the receptionist interrupted her. "Does he know you're here?"

"No. It's . . . a personal matter."

"You're lucky he's in. Who shall I say is here to see him?"

"Just say it's Olya."

"OK." The receptionist picked up the phone. "Marina Vasilievna, I have a visitor here for Boris Ilyich on a personal matter. Her name's Olya . . . Yes, just Olya."

The receptionist waited for a minute, nodding politely at Olya, then put down the phone.

"You can go up now. Second floor. Last office on your right."

Olya climbed the marble staircase with no trouble, but in the hallway she became dizzy and had to lean against the wall for support.

"Please don't kick me out, Horse Soup . . ."

Coming back to her senses, she made her way to Burmistrov's waiting room.

"Head on in, Boris Ilyich is waiting for you." His secretary opened the door.

Olya walked into the office holding her breath. Burmistrov was sitting at his desk and talking on the phone. He took a quick look at Olya, raised his index finger, and began to stand up from his chair as he finished his conversation.

"I'm telling you for the third time—they don't need gas masks, they only need the metal things and the filters, do you understand? What? Well, tell him to stick those masks up his ass! What? What??? Vitya! Were you born yesterday or something? Just get twenty suckers, put 'em on the barge, and they'll take it apart in a day! Throw the masks over the side. End of conversation. Goodbye."

He slammed down the phone.

Olya was standing in the center of his office.

Burmistrov walked around his desk with a frown, moved over to Olya, and stared at her silently for a long time. Olya's lips and knees were shaking.

"So, were you trying to cash in your chips?" he asked her good-naturedly, and slapped her across the face.

Olya fell to the floor, completely exhausted.

"How many days has it been since you last ate?"

"Four . . . Five . . . ," she mumbled.

"Idiot!" He picked up the phone and dialed a number. "Polina Andreyevna? Hello. I need you today. Yes. Please get there as fast as you can, start cooking right now. We'll see you in . . . how much time do you need? Let's say an hour. Yes. Thank you."

Still on the floor, Olya sat up.

"Sit over there." Burmistrov nodded at two armchairs by a coffee table.

She stood up, walked over, and sat down.

Burmistrov sat on the edge of his desk and folded his arms across his chest.

"Where were you?"

"I was traveling with my husband."

"You got married?"

"Yes."

"What was the last thing you ate?"

"I . . . don't remember . . . lobster."

"Tasty . . . You fuckin' idiot. You wanna die?"

"No . . . ," whispered Olya, leaning back into the armchair exhaustedly. Sweet tears began to flow down her face.

"A sow, a total sow . . ." Burmistrov shook his head.

A smug brown-haired man in a white blazer walked in without knocking.

"It's coming up roses, Boris!"

"What the hell?" Boris grunted with a scowl.

"They're taking thirty in cash and eighteen in bonds. And the Ukrainian piece of shit is still gonna get twenty to twenty-five from his stupid friends."

"What about Larin?"

"What do we need Larin for? He got his piece of the pie, that's how it goes."

"But he's their underwriter now."

"What's he gotta dick around like that for?" the man replied with a big smile, then squinted over at Olya. "There's no reason for it. Get Malakov to knock out a new contract. We'll get the wholesalers to sign today, why wait?"

Burmistrov bit his lip, looking down at the hardwood floor.

"You know what . . . here. I'll go have a chat with the old man myself. In the meantime, you get started with Zhenka, got it?"

"Got it." The man left.

Burmistrov picked up the phone.

"Oleg, hello again! We gotta talk terms. They just put a good offer in front of me. Yes. Yes, just now . . . Almost . . . No, those are Vitya's wholesalers. Yes. Yes. Listen, let's meet by the pipe? Yep. Fantastic! OK, I'm leaving now."

He walked out of the office.

Sweet tears once again began streaming down Olya's face as soon as the door shut behind him. She wept silently, leaning her head against the cool, soft leather of the armchair. Her successful reunion with Horse Soup filled her body, heretofore so tormented by fear and hunger, with the smooth oil of tenderness. She was no longer afraid to spill this oil.

"This is na . . . This is na . . ." She repeated Burmistrov's words like a baby, smiling through her tears.

Burmistrov returned an hour later—cheerful and satisfied. "Let's go!"

Her face puffy from crying, Olya stood up.

"Were you crying?" He glanced at her eyes.

She nodded.

"How wonderful!" He grinned and opened the door.

Downstairs, a big black Jeep was waiting for them with both a chauffeur and a security guard inside. Olya sat in the backseat with Burmistrov. The Jeep turned onto the Garden Ring and sped up.

"We're headed toward Kursk Boulevard," she realized.

Kursk was where the Stalin-era building with the highest arch in Moscow was located, the place where she had been eating invisible food for the past six months. She also knew that Sakharov, the famous academic, had lived in that building not long ago.

Burmistrov looked out through his tinted window. His smoothly shaven head, his plain features, his murky eyes, his fiddly hands—all of this was deeply familiar to her.

Olya suddenly realized that she was truly happy.

"Thank God he forgave me," she thought, taking a deep breath. "What if he hadn't? What would I do then? May pedestrians stumble awkwardly through horror." She improvised this last line on the theme of the Russian birthday song.

"Oh yeah . . ." Burmistrov suddenly remembered something, took out his cell phone, and started to type in a number.

The driver made a sharp turn to overtake another car and Burmistrov's cell phone flew out of his hand and onto the floor.

"Forgive me, Boris Ilyich," the driver mumbled.

"I'll fuckin' fire you, Vasya!" Burmistrov looked down at his feet with a broad grin.

"I'll get it." Olya bent down happily.

This was the first time that Olya had ever seen a cell phone up close, which added ever so slightly to her general feeling of happiness. Looking under the seat, she saw it immediately. The phone had an illuminated keypad, like a nocturnal insect from a faraway tropical land that no one had discovered yet. It was lying near Burmistrov's beautiful boots. Olya moved over to the phone and touched Horse Soup's thin, bony ankle with quiet joy.

"Strong *and* intelligent," she thought.

She suddenly heard a sound that made her think the car had driven into a dead tree. Then the dead branches started pitter-pattering over the roof.

"Fuck!" the driver said loudly.

The Jeep swerved violently. Olya sprawled forward, right next to Burmistrov's boots.

The dry branches continued to knock into the car. Bits of glass from the windows fell inside.

The car swerved again, then came to a shrieking halt, then started to move again very slowly. Burmistrov's boots gave Olya a violent kick.

"What's he doing?" she thought, and started to get up.

The car was going very slowly.

Olya lifted up her head and looked around.

Ten narrow rays of sunshine pierced the car's murky light. Dust gathered in the rays.

Olya looked around, not immediately realizing that the sun was shining through ten neat little holes.

Burmistrov's face was monstrously deformed, swollen with bubbles of blood. His hands were trembling very slightly, his legs twitched like a doll's. The driver had five tiny holes in his neck and shoulders and had fallen onto the steering wheel, his body still shuddering. The security guard leaned against the window, one cheek gone.

Olya watched.

The car continued crawling forward for a little while, hit a scaffold, and came to a halt.

Burmistrov's legs were still.

Absolute silence reigned inside the car.

But something was moving.

Olya looked over.

Bits of Burmistrov's brain were sliding down the tinted window. Olya felt for the door handle, squeezed it, jerked the door open, and tumbled out of the Jeep.

"So flat . . ." She pressed her cheek to the calm and dusty asphalt.

And, suddenly, all around her, cars were braking, doors were slamming, and legs, legs, legs were running.

"Flat, but not familiar . . ." Olya got up onto all fours, began to stand up, and, surprising herself, sprinted off, still hunched over and covering her mouth with her hand.

She ran through an alleyway on her half-bent legs and remembered how, during her junior year, she and Lena Kopteyeva had once raced from the barberry bushes to the gate and back, and how Lenka had moaned when she fell behind.

"She looks like Tatyana Doronina . . . ," Olya thought, spotting a full-figured woman carrying tightly wrapped rolls of wallpaper.

The woman looked Olya over with a gloomy gaze.

"What's the number for the police?" Olya asked as she stopped running.

She was clutching the cell phone in her left hand and holding the purse hanging from her shoulder with her right.

"Oh-two?" she asked, already beginning to dial it on the phone.

But the phone could only buzz when it made any sound at all.

"What now?" Olya looked at a grayish-white cat sitting in the window.

The cat licked its paw.

"Let's go, let's go, let's go . . ." She put the phone into her purse and began to walk quickly through the alleyway, making it to Chistoprudny Boulevard in a few minutes.

"I need something to drink," she said to herself. She saw a street vendor, walked over, and bought a plastic bottle of Coca-Cola, beginning to twist off the red cap as she walked. Pink foam rose up from under the cap. Olya stopped to look at the foam and felt the fatal heaviness that had been slumbering inside of her for the past few days begin to rise up from her stomach and into her esophagus like mercury. Olya vomited bile. Dropping the bottle, she made her way to a bench and sat down.

"He's dead," she said, and the whole world shrank.

She could see everything in the world. Everything was heavy and everything was dead. No one in this wretched, leaden world could help her. To whom could she turn? In a daze, she went through friends and relatives, doctors and pets, businessmen and street magicians: but none of them, none of them, had any *food*. Nobody on earth could feed Olya. Not even God? Olya didn't believe in God and had never understood religious people.

And suddenly she remembered the apartment where Horse Soup fed her invisible food.

"There's food there!" Olya whispered in a hoarse voice. "There . . . of course! There and only there!"

She stood up, walked to the metro station, hailed a taxi, and, in a daze, was driven to the building with the highest arch in Moscow. She went up in the elevator and found the apartment and rang the doorbell.

A short, elderly woman with a calm, sweet face opened the door. "Hello! The food's been ready for a long time."

Polina Andreyevna cooked the food, but always left before the *eating process* began. Olya entered the spacious foyer.

"And where is Boris Ilyich?" Polina Andreyevna walked into the kitchen.

"He's . . . currently . . ." Olya looked into the dining room. She saw the old familiar table set for one.

"I've been waiting! Waiting!" Polina Andreyevna said loudly from the kitchen. "I thought he'd canceled! But then he would have called, right?"

Olya went over to the kitchen. A dry emptiness was ringing out inside her head. Her heart beat hungrily and heavily. Polina

Andreyevna put something away in the refrigerator, shut it, and noticed Olya standing in the doorway.

"What?"

Olya walked in silently, moving her eyes hungrily from side to side.

"Are you looking for something?" asked Polina Andreyevna.

"Where's the food?"

"What food?"

"My food."

Polina Andreyevna looked at her with an uncomprehending smile.

"Uhh . . . We have apples and kefir in the fridge. Shall I wash an apple for you?"

Olya looked at her spitefully. Polina Andreyevna went quiet and stopped smiling.

Olya noticed something on the kitchen table with a dish towel over it. She removed the dish towel. Under it was the porcelain dish from which Horse Soup served invisible food. Now, however, there was only emptiness.

Olya looked into the refrigerator. She saw apples, a lemon, two packets of margarine, and an open bottle of kefir. The only thing in the freezer was ice.

Olya began to open cupboards and rifle through drawers.

But her food was nowhere to be found.

She was overwhelmed by fear. Her face turned green and she froze in the middle of the kitchen.

Polina Andreyevna slowly moved into a corner of the room.

Olya examined the electric stove. There were three empty pots, with a frying pan next to them. In the frying pan was a can with no label. Olya picked up the can. It was heavy, slightly larger than an average can.

Olya's heart beat heavily and a gruff, inarticulate moan escaped from her lips. Her whole body now shivering, Olya began to search for a can opener. But she couldn't find one anywhere. Then, putting the can onto the table, she pulled out the largest knife from the wooden knife block. It was as heavy as a hammer and as sharp as a razor. Olya picked it up with both of her hands and clutched its comfortable black handle. She tried to suppress her trembling as she drew back and plunged the knife into the can.

The heavy knife sliced through the tin like paper.

"You didn't know!" Olya grinned wickedly and stared back at Polina Andreyevna, who had been struck dumb. She kept pressing down on the knife.

Olya had never before opened a can this way. Jerking the knife a couple of times and jaggedly cutting the tin, she trembled and stamped her foot with impatience. She pushed the knife in the other direction in an attempt to make a bigger hole. She was using her left hand to clutch the edge of the can, but it slipped off and collided with the knife. Blood flowed onto the table and the can. Olya paid no attention to the blood, looking instead at the slowly expanding slit she'd made. It looked like the Tin Man's mouth.

"Trying to hide it . . . bitch . . ."

The tin lips spread slowly apart.

The Tin Man's mouth was filled with liquid shit.

Olya's hair stood on end: the can was filled with eggplant spread.

"No!" She smiled and looked at Polina Andreyevna. "No, this . . . no . . ."

Polina Andreyevna looked at her with quiet horror.

Olya exhaled, noticed how bloody her hand was, pulled another dish towel off the hook, and wrapped it around her hand. On the towel there was a hedgehog carrying a mushroom. She left the apartment.

She descended the chill staircase.

The cell phone rang gently in her purse. Olya took it out, looked at it, pressed the red button with a picture of a telephone on it, and pressed it to her ear.

"Borya?" someone said through the phone.

Spreading open her dry lips, Olya made an indefinable guttural sound.

"OK, so I got sixteen guys and they estimated, well, they guessed that they'd take it apart within the day. But, here's why I'm calling: we threw the masks into the water and they won't fucking sink! You see the problem, six thousand masks . . . This could be bad, it's the Moscow River, the water cops could come and, well . . . I can't even get the car to the docks 'cause of these huge mountains of trash! Bor', you gotta just get in touch with Samsonov so that he can drive a couple of those shit-suckers out to us, we'll throw the masks to the bank of the river, and the shit-suckers'll, well, suck 'em up with their pipes, right out of the water, and then . . ."

Olya dropped the phone down the building's garbage chute.

Outside, the sun had gone behind the clouds and an occasional drop of drizzle fell down onto the city.

Olya wandered aimlessly, squeezing her left hand with her right. The dead world flowed around her and parted heavily and indifferently before her. She made it to Paveletskaya Station, saw the tram tracks spattered with rain beneath her feet, and froze.

It was pleasant to look at the steel bars of the tram tracks. They calmed her down. They were calming. They flowed, flowed, and flowed. They were cold and heavy. They were in no rush. They moved properly and steadily, one always parallel to the next. They were like a ski run laid down by good, kind people, honest and reliable people, brave and attentive, who knew how to have a good laugh, knew many, oh so many! proper and heroic stories, who knew many physical and chemical formulas, who knew many, oh so many! wonderful songs to play on the guitar, songs about geologists and climbers, about beautiful and inaccessible alpine peaks, peaks covered over in snow, white snow, sparkling snow, snow that never melts, cold snow, kind snow, eternal snow.

Olya walked along the tram tracks toward the center of the city.

Her legs moved of their own accord, taking her deeper and deeper into the rain-washed metropolis.

The rain stopped and the timid sun peeked out from behind the clouds.

Olya slowly made her way to Novy Arbat Avenue, bought ice cream, looked at it, threw it into the trash, turned, walked past the Shchukin institute, and turned down a lane.

Suddenly, something blankly familiar drew her gaze. She saw a redbrick café, recently built. In the window sat the man in a white blazer Olya had seen in Burmistrov's office.

She stopped.

Two other men were sitting at the table with White Jacket: a tall, broad-shouldered, blond man and a skinny man with close-set eyes. Olya recognized the second man right away: Simferopol–Moscow, the vestibule, Burmistrov on his knees, the picture lying at Olya's feet. A tattoo on his wrist.

"IRA . . ." pronounced Olya.

The three of them were eating and chatting.

Olya walked into the café. The bartender gave her an indifferent look as he poured a beer.

The café was filled with cigarette smoke and ugly people. There were many open places to sit. The table where White Jacket and IRA were sitting was in the corner. Olya sat at an uncleared table nearby, her back turned to them.

The blondie stood up and left.

White Jacket finished his beer and lit up. IRA was chewing.

"With the first one, everything's cool, so don't resend anything. Got it? But you should resend the second one, the white one."

"Yeah, I get that, but why the fuck . . ."

"Stop wasting time, we don't have much of it."

"Right when they get it, right away."

"That's right, motherfucker."

They stopped talking. The blondie came back not long after, wiping his wet hands with a napkin.

"I always take a dump after I do *business*."

"That's just fuckin' natural law . . ." IRA chewed. "I took a shit this morning. Hey, didn't he have a dacha too?"

"Yeah. In Malakhovka," replied White Jacket. "But I don't remember the address. And anyway it wasn't that . . . I guess it was all right. The house wasn't great, but it was on a good piece of land."

"Find the address."

"It's not goin' anywhere."

"OK, let's have a little drink then . . ."

The carafe made a glugging sound as they poured the vodka. "Here's to Boris the Sucker havin' somethin' to drink and someone to fuck on the other side!"

"Mhmm . . ."

"Cheers."

They drank and began to eat.

Olya looked at the dirty, sauce-covered butter knife next to her hand. Touched its rounded edge. Then opened her purse, rummaged through it, pulled out a pair of nail clippers, stood up, walked over to White Jacket, who was still chewing, and with all her remaining strength stabbed him in the neck with the clippers.

"Ow!" cried the man, as if he'd been stung by a bee, and grabbed the clippers buried in his neck with both hands.

The blond man jumped up like lightning, knocking down his chair in the process. He leaped over to Olya, brought his hands to his chest like a kangaroo, and, with terrifying force, kicked her in her left side. Nobody had ever injured Olya like that. She flew back, hit the wall, and slid down to the floor. IRA stood up, a pistol suddenly in his hand.

"Ow! Ow! O-w-w!" White Jacket cried, getting up from the table. Everyone in the café was silent, staring dumbly at the events unfolding in front of them.

Olya didn't lose consciousness from the brutal kick, but found herself unable to breathe. Her heart throbbed. Leaning against the wall, she touched the left side of her torso. She felt a terrible and unexpected depression where her ribs seemed to have cracked. Shaking and hiccupping, Olya attempted to inhale even a drOp, even a drOp, even a drOOOOOOOOOOp of air, but the air wouldn't come in-in-into her mouth and it was like an abortion

    like an abortion

               like anesTHESIA

like anesTHESIA

and a drO

        drO

                drO

                        drO

they're pink they're red

they're burning and pEEErfect

MOMMY

anesTHESIA already?

yes

    yes

        yes

            yes

                yes

"DID THEY ANESTHETIZE SLAVINA?"

"grandma, when will my boobs grow?"

"DID THEY ANESTHETIZE SLAVINA?"

"sweetbootssweetboots."

"DID THEY ANESTHETIZE SLAVINA?"

"the little hedgehog carries the mushroom."

"DID THEY ANESTHETIZE SLAVINA?"

"don't fuckin' pull it, it'll knock out the glue!"

"DID THEY ANESTHETIZE SLAVINA?"

"Olya, what's going on with this sonatina?"

"DID THEY ANESTHETIZE SLAVINA?"

"the bitch was with him!"

"DID THEY ANESTHETIZE SLAVINA?"

"but Rudik showed Anka some stupid things."

"DID THEY ANESTHETIZE SLAVINA?"

"Should we bathe Olenka on the terrace, Nadya?"

"DID THEY ANESTHETIZE SLAVINA?"

"to the wall, assholes!"

"DID THEY ANESTHETIZE SLAVINA?"

"doll-ballerina-dreamer-gossip"

"DID THEY ANESTHETIZE SLAVINA?"

"Natashka's cat gave birth to five kittens."

"DID THEY ANESTHETIZE SLAVINA?"

"quietquietquietquietquietquiet."

"DID THEY ANESTHETIZE SLAVINA?"

"Give back the jump rope, Ol!"

"DID THEY ANESTHETIZE SLAVINA?"

"i won't do it anymore, Mommy."

"DID THEY ANESTHETIZE SLAVINA?"

"i won't anymore, Mommy."

"DID THEY ANESTHETIZE SLAVINA?"

"i won't, Mommy."

The blondie held up White Blazer, who was moaning because of the clippers sticking out of his neck. The bartender put a napkin to his busted lip. Two men in athletic clothing were chewing something or another, standing by the wall with their hands in the air. A beer bottle rolled across the floor. IRA shifted the pistol to his left hand and pulled a fluted awl out of its leather sheath. Walked over to Olya. Kneeled down precipitously. The awl went into Olya's heart.

But she couldn't feel anything anymore.

Francisco González

Clean Teen

Around the time he entered the eighth grade, Agustín began to watch pornography on a blue iMac he had salvaged from a dumpster. There was a McDonald's next door to his apartment building, and he would use its Wi-Fi to view free clips. He did this while his grandmother wasn't home.

Agustín thought he was cautious, but he often dropped his guard. One Saturday evening, during a marathon download session, he took a bathroom break and neglected to quit QuickTime Player. He didn't pause his newest video. Nor did he mute it. Instead, he left it playing in a loop.

He stepped across the hallway to the bathroom. He urinated, flushed, and washed his hands. Then he returned to find his grandmother standing just inside the threshold of his room.

For whatever reason, she had finished work early. She faced the computer screen, where two blond women performed fellatio on a bald man in a black T-shirt. It was one of those poolside scenes in someone's backyard. The man sat in a deck chair. He cursed softly at the women, who moaned and giggled.

Agustín watched his grandmother watching the video. He observed her frown, her crossed arms. Later, he couldn't help but admire the fact that she'd walked into their apartment without a sound—an impressive demonstration of stealth. In that moment, though, he was choked with shame.

His grandmother trudged away to her bedroom. Agustín heard a drawer opening, closing. She reemerged with a cardboard box containing two dozen condoms.

"When the time comes, use protection," she said. "Once you have a child, you'll never sleep again."

She handed him the box. Holding it made him feel doomed.

Agustín's grandmother barely slept. In the mornings and afternoons, she cleaned rich people's homes in Winterhaven. At night, she bused tables at a Korean restaurant that also served sushi. She often returned to their apartment in the small hours, and woke before dawn.

Agustín didn't want to end up like her. He wanted a job that was less like work and more like play. Occasionally, he considered whether he could be one of the actors in his pornographic videos. He imagined driving a fancy car to a studio in Miami or Los Angeles. He saw himself having sex with a different woman every day. The women would thank him, and the film crew would applaud his performance.

However, his fantasies always ended with him contracting a disease. This possibility frightened him so much that he decided it would be better to study hard and pursue another profession.

Agustín attended Mesquite Junior High School, an overcrowded, two-story complex in the heart of South Tucson. Rooms were crammed with as many as fifty children. The staff couldn't tell them apart, let alone remember their names. For the most part, teachers addressed students as "you."

Agustín's English class was taught in a "modular classroom"—a trailer on the far side of the athletic field. Its remoteness made him feel that he was being punished. The trailer smelled like wet paint. Agustín hated its thin walls, its fluorescent bulbs, its popcorn ceiling. It reminded him of a storage unit. Fortunately, English didn't require any effort. His teacher, Mrs. West, believed that school was pointless.

"It would make more sense for me—and all of you—to sit under a tree than to sit in this trailer," she said.

Agustín had a crush on Mrs. West, who was from Birmingham, Alabama. He liked her drawl. He felt special when she called him "sweetie." And he was fascinated by her long black hair, which had bolts of gray, despite the fact that she was in her twenties, younger than most of the other teachers.

The students looked forward to an easy A in English. Rather than make them read, write, or speak, Mrs. West allowed them to watch movies based on books.

She'd wheel a television out of the supply closet. Then she'd present the children with a pair of DVDs, and they'd choose one by a show of hands. Mostly, they got to watch Hollywood blockbusters. Whenever possible, they chose movies that were rated R.

Sometimes Mrs. West would leave the trailer for upwards of thirty minutes, claiming that she needed to find more chalk. She would return without any chalk, appearing happier than before, but also drowsier, with bags beneath her bloodshot eyes. Between class periods, a few of Agustín's friends, who had encountered similar behavior in their own homes, speculated that Mrs. West was a drunk.

And they were right. Eventually Mrs. West stopped concealing her habit. One day, while the class watched *Jurassic Park* in semidarkness, she reached inside her desk drawer and produced a bottle of whiskey, along with a steel cup. She gave herself a pour. She sniffed the liquid, sipped it, took a gulp.

"A bit woody," Mrs. West said. "Just the way I like it."

Her drinking became a matter of routine.

Every now and then, Mrs. West would nod off during a movie, and the students would nudge her awake at the end credits. When a nudge wasn't enough, they would shake her by the shoulders, or yell at her, or both. But sometimes she looked so peaceful in slumber that it seemed cruel to rouse her, and they'd tiptoe out of the trailer, to their next class period.

Out of all the movies they saw, Agustín's favorite was *Starship Troopers,* from which he learned that, instead of attending college, you should attack distant planets. He wished that he, too, could leave Earth, in order to shoot giant arachnids in outer space. It would be a small price to pay for showering with naked women, like the young male soldiers in the movie.

Word got around, and the school principal showed up at Agustín's English class, flanked by two muscular janitors. At the sight of these men, Mrs. West groaned.

"Another talk, huh? You know how much I hate it when we have to talk."

Her forehead glistened. Her nose and cheeks were pink. The janitors glanced at each other, as if they weren't sure what to do. The principal stared at the television, on which *The Beastmaster* played. His hands were balled into fists. He was so angry that he appeared to be out of breath.

"Fun's over, Stephanie. Leave your shit—we'll box it up for you."

"Fine," Mrs. West said. "Fine, then. But I'm union, and you'd better remember that."

Mrs. West stood and made her way toward the door. She had done very little to soften her boozy reek that day, and even Agustín, at the back of the trailer, could perceive it. Mrs. West couldn't walk in a straight line. The students gasped in unison when she stumbled, nearly falling to the floor, but she regained her footing at the last moment, bracing herself against the wall.

Shrugging, she said, "It's these bourbon legs." To Agustín, this sounded like an apology.

The school sent children home with letters, expressing "sincere regret" for Mrs. West's "health issues," while insisting that she was "on her way to recovery." Agustín provided a loose interpretation for his grandmother, whose grasp of English was poor. She shook her head and told him that Mrs. West had gotten off easy. "She's no better than an animal. Back in Badiraguato, we would have flogged her and joked about it later."

Agustín's English class entered a transitional phase, where a rash of stand-ins filled out the rest of the fall semester. Among them: a woman who brought a guitar to class and played her original compositions; another woman, who took the children on a field trip to Domino's, where they learned how to fold pizza boxes; and a man resembling Dick Cheney, who wore cargo pants and tie-dye shirts.

In January, at the start of the spring semester, Mrs. West returned to teach. When Agustín walked into the trailer and saw her writing "iambic pentameter" on the chalkboard, he couldn't contain his joy.

"You came back!" he cried. His classmates tittered, and he wished he hadn't been so transparent.

"Naturally," Mrs. West said. "Where else would I go?"

Within minutes, Agustín could tell that she wasn't the same. Her eyes were clear and focused. Rather than slump at her desk, she now preferred to stand upright. Her skirt and turtleneck were spotless, with hardly a fold or a crease. It was as if someone had loaded her into a machine, which spat out a cleaner, well-pressed version of her.

Mrs. West began to assign homework. Gone were the daily

movies, replaced with vocabulary quizzes, grammar lessons, and slender novels. The students waited for their teacher to revert to her old ways. When she didn't, some of them stopped showing up, and Agustín couldn't blame them. They must have found it difficult to unlearn what Mrs. West had taught them: that school didn't matter, that they'd be better off in the outside world.

Agustín didn't skip a single class, though. His attraction to Mrs. West persisted. He would arrive early, in order to make small talk, and he would always thank her on his way out the door. He loved Mrs. West's cursive annotations at the end of his compositions; sometimes they were longer than the assignment itself. He imagined that she was writing him letters, and her desire was encoded within them.

A few weeks into the semester, Mrs. West gave the class a new kind of assignment: a half-page short story.

Agustín wrote about a man who feared his microwave oven. Every evening after work, the man would place a bowl of instant noodles in the oven. Then, after setting the timer for two minutes and pressing "start," he'd flee to the living room and hide behind his couch. He did that because he thought the microwaves would give him cancer.

The day before the story was due, Agustín approached Mrs. West at the end of class. He asked if she could look at his draft and provide suggestions. He wanted to show her that he'd taken the assignment seriously. He also hoped that, by being the last student to speak to her, he could maintain a foothold in her consciousness.

They sat at Mrs. West's desk, and it only took her a minute to read the story. She praised its premise, as well as its final sentence: *Of course, no one really knows how a microwave works.* But she made many corrections. Her pen lashed the page, carving boxes, hoops, and borders around words. By the time she finished, Agustín's story contained more red ink than black. It looked mutilated. It looked like a piece of roadkill.

Ashamed, Agustín bowed his head. "It's trash, isn't it?"

"It's a first draft. We all have to start somewhere."

Mrs. West placed her hand on his. Agustín was aware of her silver wedding band, along with the dust of chalk on her skin. They were alone in the trailer. He looked up to see her smiling; her teeth were straight and white. She squeezed for several seconds before breaking contact.

"I'm happy to check out your work, anytime," she said. "If you want me, you know how to find me."

When Agustín got home, he browsed pornography on his computer. Usually, if he was attracted to a woman, he would search for porn stars who resembled her. In Mrs. West's case, it was easy to single out performers who matched her build, the shape of her face, her eyes. But Agustín found those women unsatisfactory— there was always something not quite right about them. He had memorized Mrs. West's finer features, her mannerisms, the modulations and inflections of her voice. He had come to believe that she was one of a kind.

On a February morning, snow fell in Tucson. The Catalina Mountains glittered with fresh powder. Cacti froze, sagged, and broke to pieces. It was only two-thirds of an inch, but the entire city went into shock. The school district officials, who had never faced such an unusual situation, lost their nerve and sent everyone home at midday.

As the students shuffled out of the trailer, Mrs. West asked if any of them needed a ride. Sensing an opportunity to be close to her a few minutes longer, Agustín said, "I could use a lift." He spoke quietly, intending to sound grateful, but also reluctant.

Mrs. West and Agustín walked to the parking lot. She led

him to her car, a Toyota Prius with a Jesus fish on its rear bumper. Agustín clicked his seat belt. He looked out the windshield and saw snow melting into puddles. Sunlight had overcome the clouds, and steam wafted up from the asphalt. Mrs. West put on a pair of dark glasses. She pressed the ignition button and put her car in reverse.

"Whereabouts do you live?" she asked.

Agustín mentioned his cross streets, and she raised her eyebrows. He was used to that kind of reaction; his barrio had a colorful reputation.

"Your parents will be home soon?" she asked.

"I live with my grandma. She works late."

Mrs. West grunted.

"I'm not comfortable just deserting you there. Why don't you hang with me for a while? I can whip you up some lunch."

Mrs. West lived in a development surrounded by walls. In order to access her neighborhood, you had to type a code into a PIN pad. Beyond the walls, roads were smooth and clean, as if they'd barely been used. Her community contained dozens of two-story houses, all of them white, or pink, or brown. The buildings were new enough that their orange roof tiles had not yet been bleached by the Arizona sun.

Agustín was exhilarated at being inside his teacher's home. The Wests' kitchen had marble countertops and wood floors, which were so firm that they accepted his weight without a creak. While Mrs. West rummaged through her refrigerator, Agustín explored the living room.

On a wall hung Mrs. West's diploma from Bryn Mawr College, along with photos of the Wests, together and alone. In one photo, they stood side by side on a rocky beach. Agustín's eyes lingered on Mrs. West, in her blue bikini; her husband wore only a pair of swim trunks, his belly overhanging them. Neither one of them smiled.

In another photo, a crowd of policemen stood witness while the mayor of Tucson pinned a medal on Mrs. West's husband. Beneath this was a framed newspaper clipping, which recounted an attempted bank robbery, and the role of "Detective West" in putting a stop to it. He had shot one of the thieves and single-handedly "subdued" the other, the article said. Agustín was surprised at the revelation that Mrs. West was married to a cop.

"Oh, that's just Teddy," she said, behind him. "Don't pay him any mind."

Agustín read the article again, and the word "subdued" lodged itself in his head. He could not comprehend its precise meaning. Nor could he understand whether Teddy West's gunshot had slain the first bank robber. He decided it probably had.

Mrs. West began to knead Agustín's shoulders. As she did this, her breasts pressed against his back. Agustín scarcely noticed. He was lost in his thoughts about Teddy, whose name didn't sound like it should belong to a killer.

"What are we having for lunch?" Agustín asked.

Mrs. West took hold of his arms. She turned him toward her. "You're a sweet kid, you know that?"

With her face inches from his, she smiled. Then she leaned in to kiss him. "Wait," Agustín said, or tried to say. He attempted to pull away, but Mrs. West didn't let go. Her strength caught him off guard.

The first thing that scared him was the fact that he found it hard to breathe with her mouth locked on his. He acknowledged excitement, too, weighing against the fright, but he couldn't keep track of her maneuvers. He was shocked at the coolness of her lips, the darting of her tongue, her hands moving up and down his back, underneath his T-shirt.

When Agustín felt his brain slipping into darkness, he fought to regroup. Mrs. West seemed a lot taller now than she had in class, standing before the lime-green chalkboard. And the mechanics of kissing, which had appeared simple in pornography, were laborious and counterintuitive. Mrs. West knew what to do, though, that much was clear. He kept his hands on her waist and tried to let himself relax against her. She smelled like Tide. He detected peppermint on her saliva—just a passing tingle.

Agustín shut his eyes, opened them again. He wondered if his grandmother had ever experienced these sensations, perhaps in an era when she was not yet his grandmother. Then he felt ridiculous for thinking about her at such an important moment.

Minutes later, Agustín lay with Mrs. West on the floorboards. She had removed his clothing and hers.

"Shouldn't we use a condom?" he whispered. Even in his daze, he could not forget his grandmother's advice.

"No need—I've got an IUD."

Mrs. West laughed, and Agustín felt stupid, as if she had just pointed out an obvious error in one of his papers. He had forgotten what "IUD" stood for. He didn't want to compound his embarrassment by asking.

Mrs. West grinned as she drove Agustín back to the south side. Her lipstick was smudged, and her blouse wasn't tucked into her pants anymore. She didn't seem to care.

They remained silent for several minutes. Agustín realized that his hands were trembling; he clenched and unclenched them. He craved the radio, a voice, an outside sound for his mind to lean on. When they reached a four-way stop, Mrs. West turned to look at him.

"Happy now?" she said. "Oh yeah—I bet you are."

Her tone seemed to imply that the sex was something he had planned. She lowered her sunglasses, winked at him. Agustín didn't know how to respond, so he stared at his sneakers. He quietly reviewed the sequence of events: he had asked for a ride, he had gotten into the car. Even so, their encounter didn't feel like it had been his idea. He hadn't expected it to go as far as it had gone.

Mrs. West dropped him off in an alley, a block from his building, so they wouldn't be seen. From start to finish, they had spent roughly two hours together. Agustín entered his apartment, locking the dead bolt behind him. His grandmother wouldn't be back until after midnight, so he had plenty of time to shower and change. He took tortillas out of the fridge and began to heat them on the stove. He had missed lunch. He was starving.

That was Thursday. On Friday morning, Agustín's genitals were sore. He had trouble putting on his jeans. When he walked to school, he stopped repeatedly to adjust his crotch. He was late to first period.

In class that day, Mrs. West acted like nothing had happened between them. Agustín winced, bit his tongue, crossed his legs. Meanwhile, she observed him, addressed him, corrected him, the same as any other student. She defined vocabulary words, etching them on the board. *Foreshadowing. Allegory. Hubris.* Agustín searched her face, her movements, for signs of distress, but saw nothing. He didn't mention his discomfort to Mrs. West. He was too ashamed. He reflected that perhaps he had made a mistake during sex, that the soreness was his own fault.

On Saturday, Agustín's friends stopped by the apartment and tried to lure him out for a quinceañera after-party, but he turned them away with an excuse about math homework. He took some of his grandmother's Tylenol from the bathroom cabinet. It made little difference.

The pain was complicated by his guilty conscience. He wanted to tell someone about the incident, anyone who might advise him, reassure him. But his tryst with Mrs. West was too outrageous to be believed. And if someone did believe him, they would probably end up blowing his cover. Agustín could not forget the photo of Teddy West, or the newspaper article beneath it. Again, he pondered the word "subdued," and he thought himself in danger of being arrested—shot, even. Having sex with a detective's wife seemed like the sort of thing that would get you killed.

Agustín resolved to deal with the irritation on his own. A real man, he reasoned, would get to the other side of it without making a scene. He hoped he hadn't contracted something fatal; he hoped it wasn't HIV.

He didn't worry for long, though. He was only in pain for two days and two nights. On Sunday morning, he woke up, ate a bowl of oatmeal with his grandmother, and felt fine. It was hard to believe he had ever been sore at all.

Agustín hadn't anticipated that Mrs. West would want to have sex again, but it became a once-or-twice-weekly activity. She established rules for communicating. Agustín had a Samsung flip phone, and they exchanged numbers, but, at her insistence, it was always she who called him to set up a meeting, and never the other way around. Mrs. West forbade texting. She justified this by saying that her husband could discover the messages.

Usually they would meet after school, on Tuesdays and Thursdays, while both Teddy West and Agustín's grandmother were working. There was a Quik Mart three blocks from Agustín's building, and Mrs. West would pull into its parking lot. She'd drive him to her house. On the way there, she'd trace shapes on his knee, below the hem of his basketball shorts, without taking her eyes off the road.

Mostly, they had sex on her king-sized bed in the master bedroom, although there were instances when she couldn't wait to climb the stairs, and they would do it in less conventional places.

Agustín kept a mental list of these: the dining room table, the leather armchair in the living room, the downstairs bathroom, the stairs themselves. More than once, they got no farther than the garage. Whenever they couldn't meet for a week or more, Agustín would recite the spots where they'd had sex, until he had the certainty that he was valuable to her.

Only the black upholstered couch, in the den, was off-limits. Mrs. West said that her husband spent more time there than anyplace else, perched in front of his forty-three-inch television. A sports fan, he liked to watch the Cardinals, the Diamondbacks, the Suns, for endless hours. She was afraid he'd perceive something amiss. A shifted cushion. A strand of hair. Something small that most people wouldn't notice. Something a detective would notice right away.

"If Teddy finds out about us, he'll murder me first. Then he'll come after you," she said.

Agustín had already reached that conclusion on his own, and he was glad that Mrs. West was sensible enough to fear her husband, just as he did. At the same time, he found himself becoming jealous of Teddy West. It was strange to feel this way about a man he'd never met—a man who had killed before and could kill again. Agustín wanted to displace him. He wanted Mrs. West to be his, and his alone.

Due to his growing jealousy, Agustín liked it when Mrs. West complained about the state of her marriage. Between bouts of sex, she described her husband's infidelity. Agustín learned that Teddy West had started affairs with some of his coworkers. The Tucson Police Department often hosted social functions—softball games, dinners, fundraisers—and Teddy would force his wife to attend and interact with the home-wreckers.

"I wish they would all eat shit and die," Mrs. West said.

Agustín was delighted to hear this. It nurtured his hope that Mrs. West's resentment toward her husband would increase her reliance on him. Still, he knew he couldn't crowd Teddy out completely, not unless Mrs. West took a stand and divorced the man, or at least kicked him out. Her unwillingness to do so struck Agustín as absurd, but pity kept him from telling her as much.

One day, however, unable to contain his frustration, he asked Mrs. West why she had chosen to marry such a wretched individual in the first place. As soon as he did, he cringed at his own stupidity.

"You've got balls, asking that," she said, and laughed, but Agustín sensed indignation in her voice. They lay naked on her bed, which was so large that he thought an entire family should sleep on it. Her head rested on Agustín's chest. He had no doubt that she could hear his racing heart. After a moment's pause, she said, "We met in Philly. On the subway, of all places. He was a cadet in the academy, and I had a thing for policemen. It made me blind. Actually, I think Teddy could've just as easily been a firefighter. You know how it is—men in uniform."

Agustín nodded, although he wasn't sure what she meant. In hopes of easing the tension, he changed the subject. He asked her if she got good grades when she was his age.

"In middle school? I had other, hugely important things to deal with at the time, such as getting high. But you don't get high, do you? You're a clean teen." She pinched his cheek. "You're a good boy."

Agustín didn't like being thought of as a boy. He nearly asked Mrs. West if she loved him yet, in the way that a man and a woman would love one another, but held back. He still found her intimidating. Partly, this was because he had been taught to view whites as dangerous, and she was one of the whitest people he had ever seen outside of a pornographic movie. Her skin made the bedsheets appear beige by comparison.

Then, too, Agustín was conscious of her black-and-silver hair spilling over his arm, her smooth legs shifting against his, and it felt wrong to challenge her. He told himself he should be thankful for this type of relationship, which others enjoyed.

. . .

Days and weeks went by.

In March, Agustín's grandmother turned sixty-three. To celebrate, the two of them rode a bus to Campbell Avenue and had dinner at Chipotle, a restaurant they'd never been to. After a few bites, his grandmother dropped her burrito and scowled.

"I thought beans and tortillas were impossible to ruin, but these people wouldn't know good cooking if it kicked their teeth in." She threw up her hands. "Whose brother-in-law invented this place? Nobody could have been paid to do it!"

On the bus back to their apartment, she told Agustín about one of her coworkers, whose daughter had been admitted to Northern Arizona University.

"And Martínez keeps lording it over us. He thinks the rest of us are beneath him. Ha! You and me will show him, won't we? Where will you apply? I've heard that Harvard is the best!"

Agustín's grandmother hugged him, and he smiled, but her question left him petrified. He was unprepared to face the prospect of life at a distant college. The thought of it made him miserable. He didn't want to leave Mrs. West behind, didn't want their relationship to end. He considered whether he should find a way to marry her.

Mrs. West often praised Agustín. She once remarked that he had a rock-solid ass. Another time, she said she wanted them to stay in bed forever. She told him that he was a naturally talented kisser, that she wished she'd met him sooner. Her compliments sounded familiar, though he couldn't remember when or where he'd heard them.

By then, Agustín's anxiety was continually growing. They had been seeing each other for more than two months, and the secrecy had turned into a terrible burden. He was plagued by fits of paranoia. In class with Mrs. West, he couldn't stop asking himself if he'd left telltale evidence at her house; he expected squad cars to pull up to the trailer at any moment, sirens blaring. Whenever his grandmother asked him how school was going, he'd immediately begin to sweat through his clothing. He endured recurring nightmares, in which faceless policemen chased him around town, pistols drawn.

Occasionally, Mrs. West would disappear into the bathroom to "wash up" after they had sex in her bedroom. She would close the door behind her, and it would remain closed for several minutes. Agustín, suspecting that her husband could be hiding anywhere, would inspect his surroundings. He'd peer inside the bedroom's oak armoire, which was tall enough to stand in. He'd look under the mattress, behind the curtains, and out the bay window. He'd check the hallway, too. Even after assuring himself that nobody was hiding nearby, he feared that a recording device might be planted in the room. At times, he had the urge to rip open the pillows and examine their contents.

And yet Mrs. West appeared increasingly carefree. Sometimes she'd settle down beneath the covers, close her eyes, and nap in Agustín's arms. He had seen her sleep in class, but this was different. He enjoyed her steady respiration, the rise and fall of her bare shoulders, the odd twitch as she dreamed. She didn't look like an authority figure. He could believe that she was once a child, someone vulnerable in need of protection, warmth.

One evening, while she dozed, he photographed her with his phone. He didn't think she would mind. He made a habit of looking at her picture every night when they weren't together. He thought that Mrs. West trusted him, that their relationship had deepened and was bound to deepen further.

Agustín could feel himself changing. Not only had he lost his taste for pornography, but he had also begun to regard his friends as members of a separate species. It was hard to talk to them, hard to relate to them. They bragged incessantly about making out with girls, feeling them up, getting their phone numbers. It seemed to Agustín that he had bounded ahead of them. He had become a man, while they remained locked away in time, as boys. By March, he was a confirmed loner. He spent his free periods moping in the library. At lunch, he ate by himself in a corner of the cafeteria.

Agustín avoided the girls he had once been obsessed with, but, to his bafflement, they periodically went out of their way to express interest in him. Foremost among them was Yesenia, a Guatemalan girl from PE class, who enjoyed temporary tattoos, and swore that she would cover herself in real tattoos the moment she turned eighteen. During one of Agustín's walks from science to social studies, she approached him in the hallway. She asked if he would watch a Friday-night movie with her. As Yesenia spoke, she stroked Agustín's bicep and giggled, as if they had some kind of preexisting relationship. He accepted her invitation because he couldn't improvise an excuse to decline it.

Their date, at the Loft Cinema, was dreadful. Yesenia didn't apologize for arriving twenty minutes late. With money he'd borrowed from his grandmother, Agustín paid for their tickets. He paid for Yesenia's popcorn. He paid for her lemonade, as well.

They watched *Howl's Moving Castle*. All the while, Yesenia never looked at Agustín. At one point, he touched her hand, and she yanked it away. Near the end of the film, he tried to kiss her, but she turned her head and dodged him. Irritated, he squirmed in his seat. Their interaction felt tedious, onerous, compared to the sensations he had shared with Mrs. West.

Outside the theater, Yesenia gave Agustín a quick hug, thanked him for the movie, and began to walk away. He called after her.

"It's only ten. Where you going?"

"Home."

"But why?"

"Because that's where I live, fool. You got my number, though."

Agustín was confused by her apparent lack of interest in having sex. By the time he got back to his building, the confusion had given way to anger. He wrote off the whole experience as a monumental waste of energy.

About two weeks later, Yesenia ambushed Agustín in the cafeteria. She jabbed a finger in his face.

"You never texted me. So that's it, huh?" she said. "What are you, a fuckin' faggot?"

It took him a few seconds to register that he'd offended her.

Eventually, Teddy West started working late shifts. Agustín would wait for his grandmother to begin snoring, then he'd sneak out of the apartment to meet Mrs. West.

One night, they almost got caught. They fell asleep in each other's arms, and, since Mrs. West had forgotten to set an alarm, they didn't wake up until five in the morning. They threw their clothes on in a panic. They were terrified at the knowledge that Agustín's grandmother would have noticed his absence. And Teddy was due to return at any minute.

Half-dressed, they leaped into Mrs. West's Prius. She was in such a hurry that she had gotten a shirt on, but her bra still dangled from her left shoulder, and she accidentally shut the driver's door on it. In her haste to reach Agustín's neighborhood, she ran a red light and three stop signs. With every traffic violation, Agustín imagined what would happen if a policeman pulled them over. He envisioned Teddy interrogating him, beating him, murdering him.

They reached Agustín's barrio, and he jumped out of the car. It was the cusp of monsoon season. The air tasted cool, charged with captive rain. Agustín cursed: someone had locked his building's entrance, and he hadn't brought his key with him. His apartment was on the ground floor. He tried to get in through the kitchen window, which faced the street; however, humidity had swollen the wooden frame. In the process of forcing the window open, Agustín made a tremendous racket.

He found his grandmother in the kitchen. She sat in a chair, sipping coffee, watching Telemundo. She'd been waiting for him.

"Welcome back," she said. She grabbed the remote, switched off the television set, and took a draft from her mug. "I can see right through you, m'ijo. Remember the proverb: 'The devil isn't smart because he's the devil, he's smart because he's old.' I know you were with a girl. I can smell her on you."

"Oh. Yes," Agustín stammered. "Yes, I was."

"What's her name?"

He eyed the window behind him, and saw new light edging over the mountains. He felt cornered. He couldn't bring himself to lie so brazenly to this woman, who cared only for his well-being. Steeling himself, Agustín decided to confess the truth, the whole story, from start to finish: the first visit to Mrs. West's house, the kissing, the sex. But before he had a chance to say anything, his grandmother burst out laughing.

"Ha ha ha! Don't worry, you don't have to tell me! But you took care of it?"

"Took care?"

She narrowed her eyes.

"Prevention! You left nothing to chance, right?"

Agustín remembered Mrs. West's IUD.

"That's right."

On a Friday evening, one week before the end of the spring semester, Agustín and his grandmother bumped into Mrs. West at Safeway. When Mrs. West crossed their path, Agustín was pushing a shopping cart, which contained a sack of pinto beans, a jar of Tang, and a ten-pound canister of Nescafé. He was conscious of the fact that he would appear poor.

Mrs. West wore black tights, and a pink sweatshirt with the word "princess" written across her chest. To Agustín's horror, she introduced herself to his grandmother, shook her hand, and remarked that her grandson was reading and writing far above his grade level. Agustín's grandmother smiled and nodded, pretending to understand. She said, "Thank you. Very good."

Agustín remembered his latest session at Mrs. West's home, two nights prior. She had stripped naked, but kept her pumps on. At some point during sex, she had forgotten herself and gashed Agustín's shoulders with her fingernails. Now, in the supermarket aisle containing trash bags and paper plates, Agustín was keenly aware of the red marks she had inflicted, which smarted underneath his T-shirt.

Mrs. West kept talking at his grandmother.

"Agustín has been a real joy to work with. You should be excited! If he keeps this up, he can get into any college he wants."

"Great!" his grandmother said. She knew the meaning of the word "college."

Meanwhile, Agustín hoped he was acting almost normal. His stomach surged, and he found it difficult to say anything at all. He waited for his grandmother to notice the veiled chemistry between Mrs. West and himself; he waited for her face to fall in a moment of recognition, followed by a burst of outrage. But his grandmother only continued to nod and grin, pleased by the handful of English words she could comprehend.

Agustín watched as Mrs. West waved goodbye, walked to the deli, and placed an order from a white-aproned attendant. He asked himself if she had taken up drinking again, because she appeared to enjoy making choices that invited disaster. He couldn't believe she had engaged his grandmother in conversation.

He concluded that he was expendable, and her carelessness would get him killed.

Agustín's grandmother snickered as they made their way to a checkout lane.

"So I finally got to meet that famous teacher of yours. She seems nice enough, but someone should tell her she's dressed like a woman-for-hire."

Groceries advanced along the conveyor belt. Agustín swallowed hard. He wished he could feel again the thrill of Mrs. West's hand touching his for the first time. Before, her presence held so much wonder. Now she reminded him that the world contained too many ways to die.

All he could think of that weekend was his own apprehension. He kept to himself, in his room, gritting his teeth. Mrs. West called his phone a dozen times. Agustín did not answer.

On Monday, Agustín packed his books and binders and stepped out the door, but could not bring himself to go to school, where he would see Mrs. West in English class. His intuition warned him that if he set foot in that trailer, something awful would happen. He went instead to Reid Park, a ten-minute walk from his apartment building.

He was fourteen. Years later, long after Mrs. West went to prison, he would revisit that morning in his frailest moments. He sat beneath a palo verde tree, next to the duck pond. He tried to shake his head clear. Despite sun and blue sky, he couldn't stop shivering. He thought about Teddy West and imagined that man's existence, which was better than his. He hated Teddy, wished him dead, and thought he would be content if he were him.

Agustín's phone vibrated in his front pocket. He was a liar and a monster, and his destiny was no longer his own. Suddenly he gasped, lurched forward, and vomited on the desiccated grass, heaving until tears streamed down his face.

Other lives moved on. An old man tossed hunks of bread into greenish water, where ducks fought over them. Yoga practitioners stretched on their mats. There were joggers, and homeless, and women with strollers. No one bothered to ask what a sick child was doing in the park, in the middle of a school day.

Michel Nieva

Translated from the Spanish by Natasha Wimmer

Dengue Boy

Nobody liked dengue boy. It might have been his long beak, or the constant annoying buzz of his wings rubbing together, which distracted the rest of the class, but whatever it was, when the kids rushed into the yard at recess to eat sandwiches, talk, and joke, poor Dengue Boy sat alone at his desk in the classroom, staring into space, pretending to focus intently on a page of notes to spare himself the embarrassment of going outside and revealing that he didn't have a single friend to talk to.

There were all kinds of rumors about how he got the way he was. Some blamed the pestilential lot where his family lived, full of rusty cans, old tires, and festering pools of rainwater. They said a mutant species had bred there, a giant insect, and that it had raped and impregnated his mother after killing her husband in gruesome fashion. Others claimed the giant insect must have raped and infected his father, who upon ejaculating into his mother had sired the misfit creature, only to run off the minute he got a glimpse of the baby, disappearing forever.

People had plenty of other theories about the poor kid, but there's no need to go into them now. Whatever had happened, when his classmates got bored and saw that Dengue Boy had stayed behind in the classroom pretending to work, they were sure to tease him.

"Hey, Dengue Boy, is it true your mom was raped by a mosquito?"

"Ho, bug boy, what's it like to be born from rotting bug scum?"

"Hey, fly crud, is it true your mom's cunt is a smelly hole full of worms and cockroaches and other bugs and that's why you came out the way you did?"

Immediately Dengue Boy's little antennae would begin to quiver with rage and indignation, and his tormentors would run off laughing, leaving Dengue Boy behind to nurse his sorrows.

Dengue Boy's life wasn't much better at home. His mother considered him a burden—he was sure of it—a freak of nature who had ruined her life forever. Wasn't she a single mother with a kid? Raising children alone is hard, of course, but as the years go by a mother's efforts are more than repaid. Eventually the boy becomes a young man and then an adult, a companion and a source of support for his mother, who in her old age thinks back nostalgically on their beautiful shared past, filled with pride by the accomplishments of her firstborn. But a mutant child, a dengue kid? He's a monster she'll have to feed and care for until she dies. A genetic mistake, a sick cross between human and insect who in the disgusted gaze of acquaintances and strangers will bring only shame, never once granting his mother the slightest achievement or satisfaction.

That's why his mother hated and resented him—he was sure of it.

In fact, she worked from sunrise to sunset to provide for him. Every day, even weekends and holidays, she rode a crowded ferry the wearisome 150 kilometers to Santa Rosa. During the week she worked as a cleaner in the financial district, while on Saturdays and Sundays she was a nanny for wealthy families in Santa Rosa's residential districts. When she got home at night she was too tired to do much, and having endured her bosses' rough treatment all day she had no patience left. Sometimes when she opened the door and saw the mess Dengue Boy had left on the table and the floor (he didn't mean to but he had no hands), she would scream, "Stupid bug! Look what you've done!"

And she would clean up resignedly, eyeing him with bitter hatred—he was sure of it.

Dengue Boy's mother was still young and pretty, and since she didn't have time to go out and meet anyone, she went on virtual dates in her room when she thought her son was asleep. From his own bed, Dengue Boy could hear her talking animatedly and even laughing.

Laughing!

The sound of wonderful happiness: something he never heard when she was with him. Dengue Boy was so curious that he flitted stealthily from the kitchen to his mother's door (making a great effort to control his buzzing), and put one of the ommatidia of his compound eye to the keyhole. As he suspected, his mother looked happy. She was wearing a beautiful flowered dress, laughing and telling jokes, almost like a stranger or even a new person, since in their everyday lives she was always worried, tired, or sad.

As he spied through the keyhole, Dengue Boy grew somber, and thought how much better his mother's life would have been if a mosquito had never invaded her vagina and given her a repulsive mutant child.

The ghastly horror of the bitter truth!

He was a monster, and he had ruined his mother's life forever!

It was then, unable to sleep and in the dawning light, that Dengue Boy went back to his room and looked at himself in the mirror, shrinking in disgust.

Where his mother had surely hoped for sweet little ears, Dengue Boy had big hairy antennae.

Where his mother had surely hoped for a sweet little nose, Dengue Boy had a long beak, black and brittle as a charred stick.

Where his mother had surely hoped for a sweet little mouth, Dengue Boy had misshapen flesh bristling with maxillary palps.

Where his mother had surely hoped for pretty eyes the color of hers, Dengue Boy had two grotesque brown globes composed of hundreds of ommatidia moving constantly and out of sync, to the disgust and loathing of all.

Where his mother had surely hoped for fat little feet with darling baby toes, Dengue Boy had spindly bicolored claws, sharp as four needles.

Where his mother had surely hoped for a cute little tummy, Dengue Boy had a rough abdomen, rigid and translucent, containing a clump of reeking greenish guts.

Where his mother had surely hoped for sweet little arms, his wings sprouted, their ribbing like the varicose veins of a disgusting old man. And where his mother must have hoped for little giggles and enchanting burbles, there was that constant, maddening buzz, grating on the nerves of even the calmest person.

His reflection in the mirror thus confirmed what he had always known: his body was revolting.

Brooding over this awful certainty, Dengue Boy wondered whether he wasn't only a repulsive monster, whether he might also be destined to one day become a deadly threat.

He knew that his mother's great worry—it tormented her day and night—was that when her little Dengue Boy grew up and became Dengue Man, he would be unable to control his impulses. That he would begin to bite everyone and infect them with dengue, including herself or some friend from school. Not only would he be a mutant carrier of the virus, he would become its deliberate transmitter, its gleeful homicidal vehicle, dooming her to an even more terrible suffering. And so, when Dengue Boy left for school in the morning, his mother would hand him an extra Tupperware container along with his lunch, whispering sorrowfully in his ear, "Remember, my little bug: if you feel any strange new urge, you can suck on this."

Poor Dengue Boy would look down in consternation and nod, trying in vain to hold back the tears falling from his ommatidia onto his maxillary palps. Humiliated, he would set the box on his back and go flying off to school, enduring the shame of being thought a potentially dangerous criminal, contagious vector of incurable ills. Which is why, when he was far enough from home, he would angrily fling the Tupperware container in some ditch. And when the container hit the ground and came open, Dengue Boy, never looking down, his eyes still filled with tears, went right on flying. Dengue Boy didn't look down because there was no need to confirm, no need to verify what he already knew was in the mortifying container: a blood sausage, quivering, greasy, and still warm, slowly coming apart and trickling into the cracks in the gutter.

Cooked blood, coagulated blood, black blood, thick blood. Blood sausage!

That was what his mother thought would sate his shameful insect instincts.

And so poor Dengue Boy persisted as best he could, back and forth between school and home, until one day it was summer vacation. Since his mother worked all day and had no time to care for him, she sent him to a summer camp for boys along with the children of other working-class families. For Dengue Boy, the camp was an ordeal even worse than school. School might have been a nightmare of persecution and abuse, the kids boundlessly cruel, but at least they were always the same kids. Dengue Boy was used to his classmates and could guess what they would do; he knew all their nasty tricks. Bloodsucker. Bug boy. Fly scum, they called him. He could even predict when they would spray his seat with bug repellent. But the camp was a whole new world with dozens of strange kids, and the risk was that they would be even more aggressive and spiteful, or at least unpredictable in their tactics.

The camp was on one of the dirtiest and most desolate public beaches of Victorica. For those unfamiliar with the southern reaches of South America, think back to 2197, year of the massive Antarctic ice melt. With the unprecedented rise in sea level, Patagonia (once known for its forests, lakes, and glaciers) became a random scattering of little islands. But what no one could have guessed was that this long-foretold environmental and humanitarian catastrophe would miraculously give the province of La Pampa a new outlet to the sea, utterly transforming it. One day it was an arid, moribund desert at the end of the Earth, exhausted by centuries of sunflower and soybean monocropping, and the next it was the continent's sole alternative to the Panama Canal for interoceanic travel. This unexpected metamorphosis breathed life into the regional economy with a constant juicy influx of cash from port tariffs, while endowing it with idyllic new beaches that attracted vacationers from all over the world. But the best beaches, the ones closest to Santa Rosa, were the exclusive property of private hotels and the mansions of summering foreigners. Common folk like Dengue Boy were only allowed on the public beaches, near the Victorica interoceanic canal, where all the port debris washed up: a miserable repository of plastic and junk incubating all kinds of freakish things.

The camp was the perfect solution for mothers and fathers who worked from sunup to sundown, like Dengue Boy's mother. Crucially, the camp bus came by very early to pick up the kids and returned them punctually at eight p.m. Since this was the camp's most important service, it was the best-oiled part of the business, and everything else took second place. So the kids got nothing but stale bread and boiled maté for breakfast, and buttered polenta and juice drink for lunch. As for the recreational activities the camp promised, they consisted of a paunchy retired gym teacher slouching in the sand smoking, blowing his whistle when he saw one of the kids swimming out too far or scaling a mound of sharp-edged trash.

And so the kids, far from watchful eyes, did whatever they wanted. They ran and played ball or swam and basked on the smelly beach. And in the absence of responsible adult supervision there was one kid in particular who became the leader of the pack. Everybody called him El Dulce. El Dulce was a fat, hyperactive boy, maybe twelve years old. His father worked at a chicken-processing plant, and El Dulce, who sometimes visited him at work, had won the admiration of the group by describing in great detail how the birds were slaughtered and gutted.

"At the plant," said El Dulce, "there's a remote-controlled super-robot machine called the Eviscerator 3000, and my father runs it. All you have to do is push a button and it sticks a hook up the chicken's butthole and pulls its guts out." A reverential silence fell as El Dulce spoke. "The crazy part is that the chickens are still alive. The only way to make sure the meat is tender is to steam their feathers off, then pull their guts out through their buttholes. Their heads aren't chopped off until the very end, when they get cut into pieces. That's why you have to use earplugs," El Dulce went on, touching his ears, "so you don't lose your mind listening to their death squawks while the Eviscerator rips up their buttholes."

Once he had finished his story, and the other boys were quietly imagining the chickens' agonized shrieks, El Dulce, who by now had become a kind of master of ceremonies, led the group to a distant corner of the beach and without further ado dropped his trunks to his ankles.

"Speaking of meat," he said.

And as everyone watched, El Dulce began to furiously jerk his weenie with his thumb and index finger. After a few minutes, before the group's riveted eyes, a skinny clear streamer shot from it, falling into the sand like a glob of snot.

"What about the rest of you? Aren't you going to beat the meat?"

Confused and terrified, the other kids, suddenly envisioning themselves gutted and plucked like chickens, proceeded to imitate El Dulce. They pulled down their suits hesitantly, and standing in a circle they brought their thumb and index finger to the zone and got to work. It goes without saying that this was a highly embarrassing moment for most of them, since they were at that in-between age when some have entered puberty and others haven't, and bodies start to change against their owners' will, turning erratic and clumsy. But for better or worse they were all human children, and their bodies, no matter their differences and idiosyncrasies, resembled each other. Except for Dengue Boy, of course. It is a well-known fact that the genitalia of male mosquitoes lacks a penis. Internal testicles in the abdomen connect to the cloaca, a small ejaculatory tract. And so Dengue Boy, horrified at the idea of revealing his difference, was the only one who didn't follow El Dulce's orders. Naturally, his disobedience did not go unnoticed. The little dictator, trunks still around his ankles and fists on hips, watched in satisfaction as each of the boys did as he was told. But when El Dulce's gaze fell upon Dengue Boy, standing there frozen and staring shyly at the sand, he jeered:

"What's wrong, Dengue Boy? Scared to show your dick?"

When Dengue Boy didn't answer, hunching instead over his four delicate legs and sheepishly poking at a few grains of sand with his beak, El Dulce dialed up the attack. And that was where things got out of hand.

"Look! Look!" El Dulce pointed, yelling to call the attention of the other kids, absorbed in their onanistic labors. "The insect is a eunuch!"

In fact, nobody knew what "eunuch" meant—not even El Dulce—but that only made it more satisfying and effective.

"The insect is a eunuch!"

"The insect is a eunuch!"

"The insect is a eunuch!" they shouted over and over again gleefully, repetition making the words even more magical and mysterious. And so, unexpectedly, the glories of language called poetry by some were revealed to them, and with arms on shoulders and shorts still around ankles—though guided by El Dulce as if being led by Virgil into purgatory—they put Dengue Boy in the middle of the circle and began to yell in unison, unleashing a wealth of language they never could have dreamed they possessed, though it flowed from their hearts like divine bardic inspiration:

"Hermaphroditic bug boy!"

"Androgynous grub!"

"Dickless invertebrate!"

"Emasculated dung fly!"

And then all together like hooligans at a soccer match, in a chant led by El Dulce, who kept time with his baton hand: "Eu-nuch bug!"

"Eu-nuch bug!"

"Eu-nuch bug!"

And then the chorus again: "Eu-nuch bug!"

"Eu-nuch bug!"

"Eu-nuch bug!"

Oh how hard it is to describe the exact, fleeting moment of initiation!

Thousands of coming-of-age novels have been written, of course, attempting it with varying degrees of skill. But is it possible to account in words for the chilling instant when a child commits the decisive act, no matter how blind or muddled, that will braid together past and future, stamping him with the brand of fire or blood that some call destiny?

In any case, this time Dengue Boy didn't react as he usually did to taunts about his mixed parentage: he didn't despair, he didn't wish to be dead, and his hairy little antennae didn't tremble with rage or pain. The cruel chanting (rising to notable poetic heights, it must be admitted) of the circle of boys led by El Dulce didn't shake him at all. This time it was a very different kind of adrenaline that coursed through every branch of his veined wings. When Dengue Boy turned the gaze of his compound eye on El Dulce, who stood there with his pants still down, pointing and laughing at him, he no longer saw an antagonist, a peer, a human. All that Dengue Boy and his fearsome needle saw was a luscious gulp of flesh, a quivering slice of succulent blood sausage. Carried away by the thrill of this new and unquenchable thirst, a sudden idea crossed Dengue Boy's antennae with great clarity and sharpness despite the mindless babble all around. I'm not a boy, I'm a girl, he reasoned, perhaps with some incongruence. Dengue Girl. In fact, it is the female of the species *Aedes aegypti*—of which he (or she) was a singular specimen—that bites, sucks, and transmits disease, while the male performs the routine business of copulation and procreation. With relief, with filial reverence, he realized that he'd been subject to a grammatical error all his life, and if he was Girl, not Boy, he could never rape his mother, nor repeat the crime of which his classmates accused his father. And so, blazing like one who discovers a humbling truth, Dengue Girl hurled herself at the body of El Dulce, naked to the ankles, tumbling him onto the sand. With surgical precision she immobilized him. She lowered her beak and like someone slitting a blood sausage to get at the insides, she sliced open his belly. Deaf to the hysterical shrieks of the other boys, who had swung from festive chanting to a state of terror and stampeded off in search of help (as best they could, of course, with their shorts still around their ankles), Dengue Girl stuck her beak into El Dulce's ruptured gut and pulled out a bloody portion of entrails. Before the horrified eyes of the gym teacher, who by now had appeared on the scene, too shocked to do anything but stupidly blow his whistle, Dengue Girl raised a beakful of El Dulce's clean, blue guts up to the sun as if offering a sacrifice to her god. Straightaway, like someone flinging a top, she gave a jerk. A spurt of blood, excrement, and bitter bile splashed the gym teacher's stunned face, then stained the sand, and, finally, the waves as they rolled slowly in and out.

Dengue Girl sipped at the luscious brew welling uncontainably from El Dulce's guts. El Dulce was shaking in a strange kind of seizure, surely from the sinister disease he had just contracted. Remember: mosquito saliva contains powerful anticoagulants and vasodilators that cause hemorrhaging, which is why the blood flowed ceaselessly like a great fountain.

Once Dengue Girl had swallowed the last drop from El Dulce's freshly dead body, she brought things to a close with something strangely like a bad joke:

"El Dulce was delicious!"

She looked defiantly at the gym teacher, who, frozen in horror, wasn't even blowing his whistle anymore, and declared:

"Not like the pathetic scrap of bread with maté you give us in the mornings!"

With sudden vehemence, Dengue Girl approached the dazed gym teacher, and, with a thrust of her beak, split his forehead open like a watermelon, sucking out the contents of his brain in a few slurps.

There was nothing left to do on that filthy beach.

Taking pity, or perhaps revenge, on the other boys, who by now had pulled up their suits but were still running and sobbing, she decided it made no sense to kill them. She just bit them. As soon as they felt the bite, they fell and were seized by the dread shakes.

She decided there was no sense saying goodbye to her mother either, since the poor woman would hear about her transformation from the newspapers or the other boys' mothers. All that was left for her now was to flee to the beaches of Santa Rosa in search of revenge, to kill and infect the rich people and foreign tourists who had caused her mother so much suffering, and so made her suffer too.

She took flight, shaking the blood from her wings, and set off enveloped in her trademark annoying buzz, until she was an imaginary dot on the gorgeous horizon of the Pampas Caribbean.

Hail, Dengue Girl!

Chimamanda Ngozi Adichie
Zikora

ALL THROUGH THE NIGHT my mother sat near me but never touched me.

Once, I screamed, a short scream that lanced the air in the hospital room, and she said, "That's how labor is," in Igbo, and I wanted to say, "No shit," but of course she didn't understand colloquial Americanisms. I had prepared for pain but this was not mere pain. It was something like pain and different from pain. It sat like fire in my back, spreading to my thighs, squeezing and crushing my insides, pulling downward, spiraling. It felt like the Old Testament. A plague. A primitive wind blowing at will, evil but purposelessly so, an overcoming in my body that didn't need to be. Hour after hour of this, and yet the nurses said I wasn't progressing. "You're not progressing," the smaller nurse said as though it were my fault.

The room felt too warm and then too cold. My arms itched, my scalp itched, and malaise lay over me like a mist. I wanted nothing touching my body. I yanked off my hospital gown, the flimsy blue fabric with its effete dangling ropes that gaped open at the back as if designed to humiliate. Naked, I perched on the edge of the bed and retched. Relief was impossible; everything was impossible. I stood up, sat down, and then I got on my hands and knees, my taut belly hanging in between. The clenching in my lower body came and went, random, irregular, like mean surprises.

The bigger nurse was saying something.

I shouted at her, "I need it now!"

"You'll get the epidural soon," she said.

The smaller nurse needed to check me. I rolled onto my back. An invasion of fingers. She was gloved and I couldn't see her nails, but her false eyelashes, curving from her upper lids like black feathers, made me worry that her nails were long and sharp and would pierce through the latex and puncture my uterus. I tensed up.

"Bring your feet up and let your legs fall apart," she said.

"What?"

"Bring your feet up and let your legs fall apart."

Let your legs fall apart.

What did that even mean? How could legs fall apart? I began to laugh. From somewhere outside myself I heard the hysteria in my laughter. The nurse looked at me with the resigned expression of a person who had seen all the forms of madness that overtook birthing women lying on their backs with their bodies open to the world.

"You're not progressing," she said.

Then came a wave of exhaustion, a tiredness limp and bloodless. I was leaving my body. I could die. I could die here, now, today, like Chinyere died in a fancy Lagos hospital that had flat-screen TVs in the labor ward. It was her third childbirth and she was walking, chatting with the nurses, stopping to breathe through each contraction, and then midsentence, she paused and collapsed and died. She was my cousin's cousin. I had not liked her but I had mourned her.

My heart was beating fast. I'd read somewhere that maternal mortality was higher in America than anywhere else in the

Western world—or was it just higher for Black women? The subject had never really interested me. I'd felt at most a faraway concern, as though it was something that happened to other people. I should have paid more attention. Now I would die in this hospital room with its rolling table and its picture of faded flowers on the wall, and become a tiny nameless dot in the data, and somebody somewhere would read a new report on maternal mortality and mildly wonder if it was Black women who died more often.

My doctor came in, looking unbearably calm.

"Dr. K, something is wrong. I just know something is wrong," I said.

My body was turning on me in spasms and wrenches I had never before known, each with a dark promise of its own return. Something had to be wrong; childbirth could not be this gratuitous and cruel.

"Nothing is wrong, Zikora, it's all normal."

"I'm tired, I'm so tired," I said, in my mind the image of Chinyere pregnant and dead on a hospital floor.

"Epidural is almost here. I know it's difficult, but what you are feeling is perfectly normal."

"You don't know how it *feels,*" I said. Before today, he was the lovely Iranian doctor I'd chosen for the compassion in his eyes. Today, he was a monstrous man pontificating opaquely about things he would never experience. What was "normal"? That Nature traded in unnecessary pain? It wasn't *his* intestines being set on fire, after all.

I caught my mother's glance, that icy expression she had when I was a child and did something in public where she couldn't slap me right away as she would have liked.

Once, I was about nine, and my father's second wife, Aunty Nwanneka, had just had a baby, my brother Ugonna ("Your *half brother,*" my mother always said). To visit the baby, my mother asked me to wear a going-out dress, red and full skirted, as though for church. Aunty Nwanneka offered us plantain and fish, the house smelled of delicious frying, and my mother said no thank you, that we had just eaten, but when I went to pee, I told Aunty Nwanneka I was hungry, and she brought me a plate, smiling, her face plump and fresh. Later, as we walked to the car, my mother slapped me. "Don't disgrace me like that again," she said calmly, and for a long time I remembered the sudden vertigo, feeling surprise rather than pain as her palm struck the back of my head.

I was disgracing her now; I was not facing labor with laced-up dignity. She wanted me to meet each rush of pain with a mute grinding of teeth, to endure pain with pride, to embrace pain, even. When I had severe cramps as a teenager, she would say, "Bear it, that is what it means to be a woman," and it was years before I knew that girls took Buscopan for period pain.

The epidural person, a pale-faced man with a reddish mustache, was saying, "I need your help to get this done, okay? I need you to be very still, okay?"

He did not inspire confidence, with his false cheer and his saying "okay?" so often. I began to wonder if he was qualified, where he had trained, whether his animation was a shield for incompetence.

"That's your mom?" he asked. "Hi, Mom! I'd like you to help us out here, okay? If you can hold her so she doesn't move . . ."

Before he finished speaking, my mother, still seated on the armchair, said, "She can manage."

The smaller nurse raised her eyebrows. It made no sense to be angry with the nurse, but I was angry with the nurse. Why did she have to make that face? Did it really surprise her? Did other mothers sit there overnight as my mother had, still as a coffin, glasses gold framed, face perfectly powdered in MAC NC45? Was she thinking that it should have been the father of my baby here with me? How dare she judge me? Was the father of *her* children in their life, what with her outlandish lashes and all? She probably had three children, each with a different father, and here she was judging me for having a cold mother instead of a husband by my side. I would write a complaint about her ridiculous lashes. The labor and delivery ward needed to have a false-eyelash policy. I would have chosen a different hospital if my health insurance company hadn't been so difficult about things. I felt angry and I felt ugly and I welcomed both like a bitter refuge.

The epidural man would not stop talking. "As still as you can, okay? Don't flinch, okay?"

I bent over and hugged the pillow and held still. There was the cold smear of a liquid on my back and the brief prick of a needle. Tears filled my eyes; my anger began to curdle into a darkness close to grief. It really should have been Kwame there with me, holding me, sitting on the chair my mother was in, finding a way to make a joke about "nutty." In a rush I reached for my cell phone and sent him a text: I'm in labor at East Memorial. I held on to my phone in the delivery room, and I kept checking it, willing Kwame's reply to appear on the screen, until my doctor asked me to push.

We met at a book launch that I almost didn't go to. A woman I worked with had left the firm to write a cookbook, and she launched it downtown in a rooftop space, with someone at the microphone describing each complicated canapé served. After the author introduced us, Kwame leaned toward me and said with a casual intimacy that wasn't inappropriate, as though we already knew each other but only as good friends, "When they say something tastes nutty, do we know which nut they mean? Because a walnut tastes nothing like a cashew nut."

"I think they mean a texture, not a taste," I said, then laughed, a little too eagerly, because I hadn't expected to meet anyone and now here was a clean-looking Black man and a thrill in the air.

On our first date he said, "Looking nutty good!"

He had a boyish quality, which was not, as in some men, mere cover for immaturity; he was a grown-up who could still touch in himself the wonder and innocence of childhood. "Nutty" became our word, an adverb, an endearment, an adjective, and even when it wasn't funny, it was still ours.

On the day we broke up he said, looking me over, "Nutty dress." Neither of us knew we would break up that evening as we went to his law firm's gala, holding hands, him in a dark suit, me in an emerald dress, my hair in a bouncy twist-out, a young Black couple in Washington, D.C., with glittering promise spread before us. I had never met a man like him, so attentive, so free of restlessness. He volunteered details about his life, and at first his openness confused me, because I dated men who were so guarded they made secrets of simple things. When Kwame saw me, he let his face show its light—he didn't hide, he didn't pretend not to care too much. He said "I love you" before I did. He was supposed to be like other single, straight, successful Black men in Washington, D.C.: intoxicated by their own rarity, replete with romance opportunities, always holding out for the next better thing. For the first few weeks, I held my breath, waiting. He was too much what I wanted, it was too good, he would change, crack open and reveal the sinister center. But he didn't change, and soon I unfurled wholly into our life together.

I was a little older than him, but sometimes I *felt* older, as though I knew better than he how uneven life's seams could be. It puzzled me that he could not see the insincerity in people or the ill will of some friends, which was often as obvious to me as a brightly colored stain. He said jokingly that I needed to vet his friends, to protect him, a joke with the undertones of truth. "You would have probably warned me about Jamila," he said once with a laugh. Jamila, the long-term girlfriend from college and into law school, who cheated on him and left him reeling, single and celibate for years. He said he loved how I "got" him, and what was unsaid was that Jamila hadn't. He said how similar our backgrounds were, and yet it felt to me that his American childhood was more restrained, and more fraught, than my African one. He grew up with his dreams already dreamed for him. There was his Ghanaian father's immigrant intensity, and there was his African American mother from Virginia, determined to open for him some of the many doors that had been closed to her. He and his younger brother had violin lessons and went to private school in formal uniforms, and every summer, his father pasted reading lists on the refrigerator and arranged tutors on the weekends. He had barely gotten his acceptance to Cornell before his father was talking about law school. The first time he took me to Sunday lunch at his parents' house in Bethesda, I was surprised by his father's effusive warmth, his mother's deliciously sly humor. I hadn't quite expected to *enjoy* them, and to be at ease with them, but I knew, too, that their approval would have come slower had I not had the right bona fides, my Georgetown degree, my wealthy Nigerian family. We went in the summer to his mother's family reunion, and I was moved that Kwame had ordered a T-shirt for me too, with their family name printed beside an image of a multibranched tree. I watched him throw a Frisbee with the teenage boys, and I could see how much they liked and looked up to him, this handsome older cousin, a D.C. lawyer with his pockets full of cool. I was sitting in the shade eating watermelon with his parents and saw the pride in the eloquence of their body language: he had turned out as they had hoped. The women relatives flirted with him and he, generously, harmlessly, paid them lavish compliments. He charmed people without trying. I felt myself sitting up straighter, as though I had won a prize I was not sure I deserved, and so needed to prove my worthiness. He was the kind of man you married, the kind people called, minutes into meeting him, "a good man." We didn't talk about marriage itself, but we talked often of the future, what we would do and wouldn't do in five years, in ten years, as though we both knew it was inevitable that we would be together.

"Water, this is why it's best to wait for the right person, and not just settle," I said over FaceTime to my cousin Mmiliaku.

I was boasting actually, a callous boast. Only days before, Mmiliaku had said, "Emmanuel still waits until I'm asleep, then he climbs on me, and of course I'm dry and I wake up in pain. Sixteen years."

She had settled. She had been living at home after university graduation, working as contract staff in telecom customer service, the kind of middling job that asked little of her and promised nothing to her. Her parents expected her home before nine p.m. every day, her penniless boyfriend lived in his uncle's boys' quarters and was looking for money to go to China and try his luck in import-export. And then came Emmanuel, older and wealthy, holding his intentions like jewels.

To marry Emmanuel was her only way into the world of adults.

I did not understand this then. I had moved to America for college, and after a few years away, the pressures of Nigerian life seemed easier to overcome. Why didn't she run off to China with the guy she loved? What did "It's time to get married" mean, anyway? Why did she have to marry at all?

She had laughed at me. "Please, I am not in America like you. Daddy will never allow me to get my own place. And Emmanuel is nice."

Nice. "I don't think that is how to describe a man you want to marry," I told her. *Nice.*

And Mmiliaku laughed some more. Mmiliaku, my cousin with the beautiful name, water of wealth, wealth's water, wealth like a river. The cousin that was like a sister, clever. Mmiliaku, who had advised me and taught me things, was now marrying a man who had asked her to stop working because he could afford to keep her at home. They had been married only a few weeks when Emmanuel said he didn't want her best friend to visit them anymore because married women shouldn't keep single friends.

I once told Kwame the story, and he rolled his eyes in a kind of disbelieving amusement. "What, the single friend will seduce the husband, or the single friend will make the wife want to be single again?"

"Maybe both?"

"He sounds like a sad specimen," Kwame said.

I liked the description "sad specimen," because it cast Emmanuel as apart, a different species of man, and therefore completely removed from Kwame himself.

On the day we broke up, we went back to my apartment after the gala, and I told Kwame, "So I'm very late and I'm never late."

He looked confused.

"I might be pregnant." I was so certain of his delight that I made my tone playful, almost singsong. But his face didn't relax, instead it went still, as though all his features had paused, and suddenly this communicative man retreated into the cryptic.

He said, "We're at different places in our lives."

He said, "I'll take care of everything," in a voice that belonged to someone else, in words that he had heard somewhere else. *Take care of everything.* How absurd; we were both lawyers, and I earned a little more than he did.

He said, "It's a shock."

I said, "You came inside me."

He said, "I thought you let me because you had protection."

I said, "What are you talking about? You know I stopped taking the pill because it made me fat, and I assumed you knew what it meant, what it could mean."

He said, "There was miscommunication."

"Kwame," I said finally, in a plea and a prayer, looking at him, loving him. Our conversation felt juvenile; an unreal air hung over us. I wanted to say, "I'm thirty-nine and you're thirty-seven, employed and stable, I have a key to your apartment, your clothes are in my closet, and I'm not sure what conversation we should be having but it shouldn't be this one."

I wanted to rewind and redo. Have us walk into my apartment again, laughing, me saying, Let's make margaritas, and him saying, I really want a burger; I don't know what that tiny Chilean bass thing at dinner was about. Then I saw it, the almost imperceptible shrug. A shrug. He shrugged. His response was a shrug. From the deepest vaults of his being, a shrug.

"I think I should leave. Is that okay?" he asked as though he needed my permission to abandon me. He would kill you, but he would do it courteously.

The pregnancy websites said no soft cheese, and I stopped eating all cheese. They said don't take any medicines for nausea, and so I sucked natural ginger sweets, but I always felt a mere breath away from vomiting. Day after slow day, I nursed nausea, until I no longer remembered what it felt like to be free of my biliousness. I took breaks from meetings to throw up in the toilet, and then walked back in with perfect aplomb, as though I had just gone to retouch my lipstick. At first I wore stylish loose-fitting dresses that hid my burgeoning middle, and when I couldn't hide it anymore, I stayed late every day, noisily late, and at morning meetings I made sure to note with false casualness how traffic thinned after nine p.m. My colleague Donna was my closest competitor for making partner, the only woman as senior as me, and everyone knew the partners wanted a woman next. Donna was "child-free," an expression she used often; she was thin and vegan and did yoga and wore dresses cut for flat-chested women. She watched me with the eyes of a person willing you to stumble.

"Do you need anything, Zikora?" she asked often, especially when the men could hear, her eyes hard and bright.

"I don't have a debilitating illness, Donna. I'm only pregnant," I would say. I made jokes about pregnancy. *See, I can balance files on the belly!* I told her I still drank once in a while, because my mother had drunk Guinness stout throughout her pregnancy with me. It was a lie, my mother had not drunk, nor did I, but I wanted to seem, to Donna, in control, even slightly reckless, as though my pregnancy were a glamorous adventure that would certainly not affect my work.

"I figured I better have this baby, because it might be my last chance. I probably wouldn't want to keep it if it were ten years ago," I told her breezily. "It's funny how pregnancy is like body hair. We scrub and scrape our armpits and upper lip and legs because we hate to have hair there. Then we pamper and treat the hair on our heads because we love hair there. But it's all hair. It's the wanting that makes the difference."

"I can't believe you're saying a baby is like body hair," Donna said.

She was being deliberate, and her lips had that downward curve of the righteous, the same curve as when she spoke of people who ate beef.

"Oh, come on, I'm not saying a child is like body hair. I'm saying our relationship with body hair is similar to our relationship with pregnancy. It could be the thing we most desperately want and also the thing we most desperately don't want."

Donna, lips still downward turned, changed the subject. "Are you sleeping okay?" she asked.

"I'm sleeping really well," I said.

In fact I barely slept, propped up on three pillows, tossing this way and that, seeking an elusive comfort, my chest aflame with heartburn, and a stubborn throbbing ache in the joints of my fingers.

Each morning, I coated concealer on the dark bags under my eyes. Most days, I caressed a bottle of Advil, longing for the translucent green pills, but knowing that I would never take them. I poured glasses of merlot and tipped them over to watch the redness trickle down my kitchen drain. It was a sweet-and-sour time, a time of exquisite paradoxes. I raged at Nature but wanted to appease Nature, to secure the safety of my pregnancy. I obeyed the rules, dutiful and seething. On weekends, I lay blankly on my couch reading Kwame's past text messages, as the hours slid one into another. Time spent on remembering, time lost on remembering.

I lingered on the messages he had sent when he stopped at my favorite Indian restaurant to buy me pakoras. **No veg today, babes. Meat okay?** Or when he drove to the Middle Eastern place in Silver Spring to get me hummus. **They ran out of regular, just red pepper, sorry babes.** How well he knew me. It was real hummus or nothing for me, none of those flavors invented to appeal to the American obsession for variety. I read somewhere that love was about this, the nuggets of knowledge about our beloved that we so fluently hold.

"Stop reading his texts," Mmiliaku told me on FaceTime. "You'll start questioning everything, and wondering if any of it was even real."

"Yes," I said, but I didn't question whether it was real, because I knew it was. I questioned where it had gone. How could emotions just change? Where did it go, the thing that used to be?

Each time I called, I felt newly surprised at the burr-burr-burr of his phone ringing unanswered. How could he have turned, and so quickly? I knew him well, but I could not have known him well. He was lovely, he truly was. Silence was not his fighting tool; he was a man who talked things through. But he ignored my calls and texts, and sent back my apartment key in an envelope, the lone metal key wrapped in plain paper.

. . .

Some days I was fine and some days I was underwater, barely breathing. At my twenty-week checkup, I smiled at the moving grainy gray image on the ultrasound screen, flush with well-being, and I waved at the front-desk women as I left, but in the elevator, I burst into tears, a sudden sense of dissolving all around me. I sent Kwame a text: I'm 20 weeks today.

He replied three days later: It's manipulative to send me this. You know you made a decision that excluded me. I didn't want things to end this way. I'm hurting too.

I read it over and over; it felt like something written by somebody who was not Kwame, like an exercise from law school, an argument about case law, hard and elegant and empty. To my Can we please at least talk? Kwame did not respond. Ours was an ancient story, the woman wants the baby and the man doesn't want the baby and a middle ground does not exist.

What would a middle ground be? We couldn't have half a baby.

"Water, everyone at work knows I was dumped while pregnant," I told Mmiliaku. "I hate the way they look at me."

"It's all in your head," Mmiliaku said.

Maybe she was right and I was merely suffering from the paranoia of the abandoned. I cared now what people thought, and I had never cared before.

"I just want them to know I can handle it, I can do it alone," I said.

"Some of us have men and are still doing it alone," Mmiliaku said. She could have gloated. She could have asked, "Isn't this the perfect man you won by deciding not to settle?" She could have been passive-aggressive, or resentful, or lectured me in that world-weary way of a woman who believed that men would be men. But she didn't, and so with the light streaming through my apartment window, I began to weep because my cousin had grace and I lacked grace. I cried and cried. I no longer had friends, all my time so focused on Kwame. I cried and cried, and even though people said crying made them feel better, it made me feel frightened and small.

I sifted through my memories, as though through debris, trying to find a reason. Was it how I had told him? Was it because I said it so lightly, so playfully, that there was no question of how I felt? Did he know, too, as I knew, that I was pregnant even as I was telling him that I *might* be? It had never occurred to me not to have the baby, and he must have heard it in my voice. The knowledge came to him as an already-sealed box.

He said so often that we had to make decisions together, and it amused me sometimes, how seriously he meant this, even for small things like which table to select when making a restaurant reservation online. "Okay, babes?" he would ask, and wait for my nod. Was he recoiling because I had made this decision already? If he was going to have a child, of course he should have a say, but how much of a say, since the body was mine, since in creating a child, Nature demanded so much of the woman and so little of the man. I remembered taking him to visit a relative in Delaware who had come from Lagos to have her baby. She had brought her toddler, too, and a nanny, and it surprised me how quickly Kwame displaced the nanny for the length of our visit and was on his knees, slipping his palm into a puppet and wiggling his fingers, his voice tuned to a funny high pitch. I had watched the two-year-old, who was riveted and adorably giggly, and saw the father Kwame would be.

"I just don't understand it. It's as if an artery burst inside him and suddenly his whole body is wired differently and he is no longer the person he was," I told Mmiliaku. "I don't understand how we could have unprotected sex for so long and then when I get pregnant, he reacts like he never knew it could happen."

"Zikky, have you considered that maybe he didn't know?"

"What do you mean?"

"Men know very little about women's bodies."

I felt betrayed by her. I was annoyed, and wanted to tell her that not everyone was her Emmanuel, warped and stunted, raping her while she slept.

"How can you say that?" I asked.

"Seriously. Men don't know how women's bodies work. Remember Amaka, my friend from university? She moved to Canada some years ago. She has a blog where she interviews men anonymously. You should read it."

Kwame thought I couldn't get pregnant because I hadn't explained that stopping birth control pills and not using condoms meant I could get pregnant? How ludicrous. I hung up, my dark day further darkened.

Yet I began to think about it. On the blog, I read about men who as boys were separated from the girls in sex ed class, and were never taught about the bodies of girls. They learned instead from mainstream pornography, where women were always shaved smooth and never had periods, and so they became men who thought the contrived histrionics onscreen were How Things Were Done. The blog annoyed me, and I resisted it while also seeing its sense. It was possible that a sophisticated, well-educated man with a healthy sex life could still harbor a naivety, a shrunken knowledge, about the inner workings of female bodies. Could it be that Kwame was fuzzy about this, that it had not occurred to him that I might get pregnant, that when he said "Okay, babes" to my "I'm stopping the pill," it was not what I thought it was?

One sleepy weekend morning in his apartment, after slow sex, and a slower brunch of eggs I made and pancakes he made, he was playing a video game with lots of noise and flashes, and I was reading the news online, and I looked up and said, "Can you believe an elected U.S. official actually asked why women can't hold their periods in?" I laughed, and so did he, but I remembered now his first fleeting reaction, the slightest of hesitations, as though he was holding back from saying, "You mean they can't?"

And I thought about the night I was patting cream on my face and examining again the ugly brown-purple patch that had appeared on my cheek. "It has to be my birth control pills causing this," I said, and there was again that small hesitation from him, a restraint, from discomfort rather than deceit. I could have been clearer when I stopped the pill, we could have talked plainly, as we talked about so much. Did I choose to assume he understood, because I didn't want to give him the chance to say he didn't want a child? Now I was blaming myself. I was bearing the responsibility of a full-grown man. It felt self-flagellating, as though I were looking for a reason to excuse him, but the alternative was to accept that the Kwame I knew was a lie. My head pounded and throbbed, and my vision fogged over. I worried that my stress was harming the baby, and the worry added layers to my stress. I called Mmiliaku again sobbing, saying I was scared to do it alone, I was scared to be alone, I was so secure in my relationship with Kwame that I just never considered being alone.

For a while, she let me cry.

"Zikky, it won't be easy, but it won't be as hard as you think. How you imagine something will be is always worse than how it actually ends up being," she said. The easy wisdom, her emollient words slipping out so smoothly, rankled rather than soothed me. As if Mmiliaku sensed this, she asked, "Remember when I called you from NITEL?"

When I called you from NITEL.

Years had passed since that phone call, and Mmiliaku had never referred to it; we had picked up and continued as though the phone call had never happened. She had gone to a NITEL office in central Lagos to call from a grimy public phone because she was worried that Emmanuel—who was not even home— would somehow hear our conversation if she used her cell phone. A bright winter morning in Washington, D.C. I was sweeping pillows of snow from the top of my car and missed the first call as my gloved hand fumbled in my coat pocket, and then I almost didn't answer, because I thought the strange number was a telemarketer.

"Zikky," she said.

"Water!" I said. "What number is this?"

"I'm pregnant," she said.

Right away something felt off, her flat tone didn't match her news.

"Ah-ah," I said. Her fifth child was six months old.

"I should have put in the coil, but I was waiting for my stitches to heal well first, and then I had to deal with the nipple infection and then Baby's pneumonia, and I just forgot."

She was crying.

"Water, calm down."

"*Amuchago m*," she said. "I'm done having children."

We mostly spoke English; Igbo was for mimicking relatives and for saying painful things. When our grandmother died, Mmiliaku had called me and said, "*Mama-Nnukwu anwugo*," with a firmness that gave no room. I had no choice but to accept the news. She sounded the same now as she said, "*Amuchago m.*"

I pictured her from my last visit at Christmas, in her harried living room, little children stumbling about, the eldest just six, an endless loop of cartoons on television, and the faint smell of urine in the slightly warm air. Emmanuel traveled a lot, she said, and when he was in a bad mood, he refused to pay the oldest child's school fees. "I don't understand that," I said, and she looked at me blankly as if to say, "How do you expect *me* to understand it?" She had a nanny, but she seemed always to be laboring, distracted by tasks and things unfinished. *Why is this diaper leaking again? Let's add banana to the sweet potato puree. If he doesn't sleep now, he will be unmanageable this evening. This rash is getting worse.*

"*Amuchago m*," she said again.

"Water, I understand. Do you know where you'll go?"

"I'll ask Dr. Ngozi. I trust her."

"It will be okay. I'll send the money today. I wish I could be there with you."

Nigerian banks were not yet modernized, online transfers didn't exist, and so I drove, windscreen frosted with ice, to a Western Union. I sent her the money in dollars, so she could get the best rates on the black market, and she hid it in her daughter's underwear drawer, where Emmanuel would never go, until she went to a discreet doctor's clinic.

I pushed out a baby boy. Wrinkled and silent, scaly skinned, wet black curls plastered on his head. He came out with his mouth full of shit, and the bigger nurse, chuckling, said, "Not the best first meal," while somebody swiftly took him away to suction the feces from his mouth.

Now here he was wrapped like a tidy sausage roll and placed on my chest. He was warm and so very small. I held him with stiff hands. I was suspended in a place of no feeling, waiting to feel. I could not separate this moment from the stories of this moment—years of stories and films and books about this scene, mother and child, mother meeting child, child in mother's arms. I knew how I was supposed to feel, but I did not know how I felt. It was not transcendent. There was a festering red pain between my legs. Somewhere in my consciousness, a mild triumph hovered, because it was over, finally it was over, and I had pushed out the baby. So animalistic, so violent—the push and pressure, the blood, the doctor urging me, the cranking and stretching of flesh and organ and bone. At the final push, I thought that here in this delivery room we are reduced, briefly and brutishly, to the animals we truly are.

"Beautiful boy," my mother said, smiling down at him.

To me she said, "Congratulations," and it stung of the perfunctory. I reached for my phone. There was no response from Kwame. In a surge of disbelief and desperation, I sent another message: **It's a boy**. Now that he knew it was no longer just about me, he might respond. Or appear at the hospital, holding a balloon and flowers, limp flowers from the supermarket because he wouldn't have had time to go to a florist. I felt pathetic.

"You've had a tear," my doctor said, needle in hand. Did it never end? Nature must not want humans to reproduce, otherwise birthing would be easy, even enjoyable: babies would easily slip out, and mothers would remain unmarked and whole, merely blessed by having bestowed life.

At the needle's pierce of tender raw skin, I cried out.

"Shouldn't the epidural still be working?" I asked.

My mother glanced at me with eloquent eyes. *Get yourself together and stop making noise.*

Then she looked away and asked the doctor a question. "Will it be possible to have his circumcision today?"

"Not until he has urinated," the doctor said. "And I don't do circumcisions. It'll be done by another doctor."

"And when can we expect him to urinate?" my mother asked.

"I won't circumcise him," I said. How could they be having a conversation while he slid needle and thread in and out of my flesh?

"Of course you will circumcise him," my mother said coolly.

"I won't!" I said, my voice raised, and for a moment I felt an intense desire to pass out and escape my life.

"Done," my doctor said, still holding the needle. "It should heal nicely."

My mother was asking about the circumcision consent forms. "Can we get them today?"

"I said I won't circumcise him."

"Why?" She trained her eyes on me.

"Barbarism," I said, surprising myself, remembering a post on a pregnancy website. You Americans may circumcise, but we don't do barbarism here in Europe. The only reason it's tolerated at all is so we don't get called Islamophobic.

I mostly ignored posts about baby boys because I thought I was having a girl, I sensed it, and all the mythical girl signs were there: I carried the pregnancy high, I had bad morning sickness, my skin turned greasy.

But I remembered the post because I had disagreed, bristled at it. Now it was convenient ammunition.

"Circumcision is barbaric," I said. "Why should I cause my child pain?"

"Cause your child pain?" my mother repeated as if I was making no sense.

I checked my phone, still nothing from Kwame. I sent another text: Your son. I felt ragged and hopeless, high on my desperation. I had already ripped up my dignity, so I might as well scatter the pieces. I called him, and his phone rang and went to voice mail, and I called again, and again, and the fourth or fifth time, I heard a beep instead of a ringing, and I knew that he had just blocked my number. I closed my eyes. In my head, there was a queue of emotions I could not name, wanting to be tried out one after the other. A fog blanketed me, a kind of deadness. I didn't cry; crying seemed too ordinary for this moment.

When my mother left the room, the smaller nurse gently asked, "Is it really about causing Baby pain?" I stared at her. Her eyelashes made her eyes doll-like and difficult to take seriously. "Baby won't remember the pain. If everyone in your culture does it, you should do it too. Kids hate being different. I used to work in a pediatrician's office and that's one thing I learned. We don't have kids yet, my fiancé is training to be a police officer, but I'm keeping that in mind for my kids."

She held the circumcision consent forms in her hand for a

moment before placing them on the table. Something about her manner made sobs gather at my throat. Compassion. She thought what I was feeling mattered. Had I missed it before or had she suddenly changed?

"Thank you," I said, wanting to say sorry, too, wanting to reach out to hold her hand, even though I knew it might be a bit too much, but she had turned to leave.

"I don't know if I want to circumcise him," I told my doctor.

"It's your decision. Boys live happy lives whether circumcised or not." It felt to me a glib thing to say.

"Are you?" I asked.

"What?"

"Are you circumcised?" I could ask him that, surely, after the shared intimacy of delivering my baby.

He smiled a small smile but did not respond. "Your mother speaks so well, she sounds almost British. I like hearing proper English. My relatives in Iran speak like that. She owns two private schools in Nigeria?"

"Yes," I said, and wondered when she had told him that.

In the nursery procedure room, he was placed on a board under a warming light, restrained, his arms and legs strapped down. It felt sacrificial. Afterward he fussed and cried.

His tiny mouth was pinkly open. From it came a high-pitched wail. My baby boy, his skin peeling, his gums bare, and between his legs, an angry raw nub. I cradled him and hushed him and pushed my nipple into his mouth and then I, too, began to cry. Why had I done it? Why had I signed those forms, with my mother looking over my shoulder? I had caused my son unnecessary pain. My son. Those words: *my son*. He was my son. He was mine. I had given birth to him and I was responsible for him and already he knew me, moving his face blindly at my breasts. He was mine, and his tiny translucent arms lay precious against my skin. He was mine.

My son. I would die for him. I thought this with a new wonder because I knew it to be true; something that had never been true in my life now suddenly was true. I would die for him. His tiny tongue quivered as he cried his high-pitched, screeching cry. My mother took him from me and paced back and forth, holding him pressed to her chest, and soon he fell asleep.

She laid him in the glass-walled crib next to my bed.

"Mummy, I would die for him," I said, partly to make peace with her and partly because I needed to speak this miraculous momentous thing that was true.

"Thank God you managed to get pregnant at your age," she said.

"What?"

"Many women find it difficult at your age."

Why was this an appropriate response? *How* was this an appropriate response? For long moments I could not find any words to fling at her.

"I've been pregnant before, so I knew very early on," I said finally.

She said nothing. She began looking through the file the lactation nurse had left on the table.

"Thank God I was able to remove that pregnancy," I said.

Her silence bruised the air between us.

"I was so relieved," I said.

"Some things are better left unsaid." She turned away.

I wanted to wound her, but I wasn't sure why I chose this to wound her with. Now her indifference grated. Did it even matter to her? And what would matter—that I ended a pregnancy, that I got pregnant at nineteen, that she hadn't known? Only Mmiliaku knew, and I never told the boy who didn't love me, the boy I was trying to make love me when I didn't yet know that you cannot nice your way into being loved. I met him in sophomore year of college, my second year in America. A basketball player. He was very dark and very beautiful, near-comical in his self-regard, tall, his head always held high, his gait something of a trot. He often said, "I don't do commitment," with a rhythm in his voice, as though miming a rap song, but I didn't hear what he said; I heard what I wanted to hear: he hadn't done commitment *yet*. From the beginning I was of no real consequence to him. At some level I knew this, because I had to have known this, but I was also nineteen and feeding the insecurities of that age. The first time I knelt naked in front of him, he yanked a fistful of my braids, then pushed at my head so that I gagged. It was a gesture replete with unkindness. He could have done it differently, had he wanted me to do things differently, but that push was punitive, an action whose theme was the word "bitch." Still, I said nothing. I made myself boneless and amenable. I spent weekends willing the landline next to my bed to ring. Often it didn't. Then he would call, before midnight, to ask if I was still up, so he could visit and leave before dawn. When my grandmother died, I called him crying, and he said, "Sorry," and then in the next breath, "Has your period ended so I can stop by?" My period had not ended and so he did not stop by. I believed then that love had to feel like hunger to be true.

"The rubber came off," he said carelessly that night. He'd been drinking and I had not.

"It's so funny how you say 'rubber,'" I tittered, wishing he weren't already distracted, reaching for his clothes, eyes on his car keys. I thought nothing of it; the condom slipping off once couldn't possibly matter.

Symptoms can mean nothing if a mind is convinced, if a thing just cannot be, and so the sore nipples, the sweeping waves of fatigue, had to have other meanings until they no longer could, and I walked to Rite Aid after class and bought a pregnancy test. How swift the moment is when your life becomes a different life. I had never considered myself getting pregnant, never imagined it, and for moments after the test showed positive, I sat drowning in disbelief. I didn't know what to do; I had never thought I would need to know. I went to the health center and lied to the nurse practitioner, telling her the condom slipped off the night before. She gave me a white morning-after pill, which I swallowed with tepid water from the dispenser in the waiting room. It was too late of course, I knew, but still I did other desperate nonsensical things: I jumped up and threw myself down on the floor, violently, and it left me stunned, too jolted to try it again. I drank cans of lemon soda, dissolved sachets of fizzy liver salts in glasses of water. I disfigured a hanger in my closet and held it steely in my hand, trying to imagine what distraught women did in old films. A clutch of emotions paralyzed me, bleeding into each other, disgust-horror-fear-panic. Like slender talismans, I lined up different pregnancy tests on my sink, and each one I urinated on I willed to turn negative. They were all positive. Something was growing inside me, alien, uninvited, and it felt like an infestation.

Some kindnesses you do not ever forget. You carry them to your grave, held warmly somewhere, brought up and savored from time to time. Such was the kindness of the African American woman with short pressed hair at the Planned Parenthood clinic on Angel Street. She smiled with all of her open face, kind, matter-of-fact, and she touched my shoulder while I settled tensely on my back. She held my hand through the long minutes. "It's okay, you'll be okay," she said. My fingers tightened around hers while cramps stabbed my lower belly. I was utterly alone, and she knew it. "Thank you," I said afterward. "Thank you." I felt light from relief, weightless, unburdened. It was done. On the bus home, I cried, looking out the window at the cars and lights of a city that knew my loneliness.

My father told jokes and laughed and charmed everyone, and broke things and walked on the shards without knowing he had broken things. He didn't call on the day my son was born; he called the day after.

"My girl!" he said to me. In the weak hospital Wi-Fi, his face froze on the screen, midsmile, and he looked for a moment like a caricature of himself, teeth bared, eyes widened.

"Daddy," I said happily. To see him, all good humor and mischief, was to remember like a brief blur my life as it once was, when I was only a daughter, not a mother.

"Congratulations, my princess! My beautiful girl!" my father said. "Where is my grandson?"

I was eight when my mother told me that my father would marry another wife, but nothing would change; we would still live in our house, but sometimes Daddy would visit her in her house, not far from ours.

"Your father will live here," my mother said with emphasis. "He will always come home to us."

She made coming home to us sound like a victory.

"But why is he marrying another wife?" I asked. "I don't want a new mummy."

"She's not your new mummy. Just your aunty."

Aunty Nwanneka. My father took me to her house, a brief visit, on our way to his tennis club. She was young, plump, skin glistening as though dipped in oil. She smiled and smiled. She slipped in and out of the parlor and each time reappeared with a new source of pleasure for me: chocolates, chin-chin, Fanta. She called me Ziko, not Zikky like everyone else, and I liked that it sounded older, that she took me seriously. I liked her. Only later did I see how, to survive, she wielded her niceness like a subtle sharp knife. In America, I began to call her my father's *other* wife, because people assumed "second wife" was the woman my father had married when he was no longer married to my mother. But with Kwame I said "second wife," because he understood. Although he had never been to Ghana, he had grown up familiar with his father's family, with relatives from a different place.

We laughed whenever I mimicked my law school classmate, a humorless American woman, face scrubbed, asking me to "acknowledge the contradiction" of my mother. It was after my presentation on traditional Igbo property laws, and I'd used my mother's story: a woman from a wealthy family marries a man from a wealthy family, has one daughter, three miscarriages, and an emergency hysterectomy, after which her husband decides to marry again because he needs to have sons, and she agrees, and it is those sons who will inherit the family property.

"My mother is uncommon but normal," I had replied to the woman, and then corrected myself with, "Uncommon *and* normal."

"Perfect response," Kwame always said each time we laughed about that story. He had an uncle in Ghana, a government minister, who had married a second wife.

"Can't have been easy for either wife," he said when he told me the story, and I nodded, agreeing, loving him for his sensitivity.

We told and retold each other stories from our past lives, until we felt as though we had been there. I felt flooded by sadness in the brightly lit hospital room. I could not imagine being with someone else, someone who was not Kwame, who did not know me as Kwame did and did not say the things that Kwame said and did not have Kwame's easy laugh.

"He looks just like me!" my father announced when my mother placed the phone above my son's face.

"Ziko, congratulations, God has blessed us," Aunty Nwanneka said, and a slice of her face appeared above my father's on the screen. "How are you feeling?"

"Tired," I said, and sensed my mother's disapproval. She would have wanted me to tell Aunty Nwanneka that I was perfectly fine.

"Aunty, congratulations," Aunty Nwanneka said to my mother. She had always called my mother "Aunty" to show respect.

"Thank you," my mother said serenely.

"My girl, is anybody else there with you apart from Mummy?" my father asked.

"No, Daddy."

Is Kwame there? Has Kwame called? Does Kwame know? The questions he wanted to ask but didn't. My mother hadn't asked either. I sensed her suspicion, as though I had not told the truth and there was more unsaid. How could Kwame have left me because I got pregnant—Kwame, who came to Lagos with me last Christmas for two weeks and tried to kneel when he met my father, until my father laughed and said, "No, no, we don't do that, that's Yoruba," and Kwame said, "I can't believe I didn't do my research better." "Do your research better" became their joke, in that blustery male way of men who felt unthreatened by each other, and the evening my father took Kwame to his club alone, it was, he joked, to do his research better. My father had liked him right away, but my mother watched him for a while before she, too, caved. On the phone I heard her say to a friend, "Zikora's fiancé."

My father was asking to see the baby's face again. My mother hovered the phone above his tiny sleeping form.

"My girl, I won't be able to make it after all, but I'll definitely see him before he's one month old," my father said.

"Okay, Daddy." I had expected it. When he said that he would come from Lagos to be there for the baby's birth, I knew it was just one more of the many promises he made.

"I have a stubborn cold," he said. "So it's best not to be around a newborn."

"Yes," I agreed, even though I knew the cold was as good a reason as any. It could have been a business meeting or a last-minute issue at work.

My mother handed me the phone and walked to the window.

"I've had this cold for almost two weeks now, and it doesn't help that this house is like a freezer," my father said. "The air conditioner is so cold, but your aunty still wants to reduce the temperature. I've told her that we have to reach a compromise because we don't have the same condition!" He was laughing, that mischievous laugh that meant he knew his joke was less than decorous. But what was the joke? I laughed a little too, because I always laughed at my father's jokes. Then I realized it was about Aunty Nwanneka's menopausal symptoms, her feeling hot when nobody else did. I looked at my mother, by the window, turned away, separate and apart from the conversation. My father would never have joked about *her* menopause. With my mother his jokes were smaller and safer; he was careful always to show her respect. Respect: a starched deference, a string of ashen rituals. It was my mother who sat beside my father at weddings and ceremonies; it was her photo that appeared above the label of "wife" in the booklet his club published in his honor. Respect was her reward for acquiescing. She could have been difficult about Aunty Nwanneka, fought with my father, quarreled with his sisters, disrupted things with relatives. Instead she always bought Christmas and birthday presents for Aunty Nwanneka's sons. She was civil, proper, restrained, running her schools, always nicely dressed, a subdued gloss in her gold-framed eyeglasses. Senior wife. My aunty Uzo, my father's sister, said "senior wife" like a title, a thing that came with a crown.

"You are the senior wife, nothing will change that," Aunty Uzo told my mother a few days after my father moved out of our house. My brother (my half brother) Ugonna, only in primary school, had been caught cheating on an exam. A teacher saw him sneak out a piece of paper from his pocket and shouted at him to hand it over, but instead of giving up the paper, Ugonna threw it in his mouth and swallowed. My father decided to move in with Aunty Nwanneka to set Ugonna right. "He needs to see me every morning when he wakes up. Boys can so easily go wrong, girls don't go wrong," he told my mother. It was a Sunday, with the slow lassitude of Sundays in the air, and we were in the living room upstairs, playing cards, as we always did after lunch, before my father left to spend the rest of the day at Aunty Nwanneka's. I remembered that afternoon in drawn-out, static images: my father blurting out the words, eyes trained on the cards in his hand, words he must have been thinking about how to say for days, and my mother staring at him, her body so rigid and still.

Later, she stood at the top of the stairs, in my father's way, as he tried to go downstairs. She reached out and pushed him backward, and he, surprised, tottered. "This is not what we agreed!" she shouted. She was a different person, shaken, splintered, and she held on to the railings as though she might fall. My father left anyway. The next day, his workers moved his clothes and books, his collection of tennis rackets, his study desk, to Aunty Nwanneka's house. For weeks I spoke to my mother only in sullen monosyllables, because I thought she could have better handled it. If she had not raised her voice, if she had not pushed him, my father would not have left. For some months my parents were estranged. My father did not visit us; he sent his driver to pick me up on weekends and bring me to his tennis club, where we drank Chapmans and he told me jokes but said nothing about moving out of our house.

Slowly, things thawed, and my mother accepted that he would no longer come home to us, that we were now the family who would merely be visited. She began to hang her newest dresses in his wardrobe, which was almost empty, a few of his unloved shirts hanging there.

I looked at my mother, standing by the window. How had I never really seen her? It was my father who destroyed, and it was my mother I blamed for the ruins left behind. My parents decided early on that I would go abroad for university, and in the evenings after school, lesson teachers came to our house to prepare me for the SATs and A levels. My father wanted me to go to America because America was the future, and my mother wanted me to go to the UK because education was more rigorous there. "I want to go to America," I said. Had I really wanted America or did I want what my father wanted or did I not want what my mother wanted? The way she said "rigorous" had irritated me. Her addiction to dignity infuriated me, alienated me, but I always looked past why she held so stiffly to her own self-possession.

"I'll call you tomorrow, my princess," my father said. "Send another photo of my grandson once we hang up."

"Okay, Daddy, I love you."

We left the hospital in the early afternoon. My mother dressed my son in the yellow onesie I had packed, newborn sized but still big for him, the sleeves flopping around his tiny arms. In the taxi, his car seat lodged between my mother and me, I felt a wind pull through me, emptying me out. An intense urge overcame me, to hide from my mother and my son, from myself. You don't know how bristly sanitary pads are until you have worn postbirth pads in the hospital and then switched to sanitary pads at home. I was constipated, and on the toilet, I tried not to strain while straining still, tentative, panic in my throat, afraid I might tear my stitches. A geyser of anxiety had erupted deep inside me and I was spurting fear. I sat in the warm sitz bath, worried that I hadn't sat for long enough, even though I set my timer for fifteen minutes. What if I got an infection? I would need medication, which would taint my breast milk and affect my son. My son. My son could not latch on to my breasts properly, always my nipple slipped out of his little hungry mouth. He wailed and wailed. His cries seared into my head and made me so jittery I wanted to smash things. My mother called a lactation nurse for a home visit, a tiny platinum-haired woman who coaxed and cooed and tried to get my son's mouth to open and close, but he pulled back and wailed. Was it something about being back home? I had breastfed him in the hospital. The nurse gave me a plastic nipple shield, to place between my nipple and my son's mouth, and for a brief moment he sucked in silence, and then began to cry again. I pumped my breasts with a machine that vibrated, funnels affixed to my nipples, spurts of thin liquid filling the attached bottles. The pumping was tortuously slow; my breasts recoiled from the machine and so gave up little of their milk. My son slept in a crib by my bed. At first, my mother slept in the next room, and then she pulled her mattress into my bedroom and set it by the couch. At night, she fed my son a bottle of breast milk with a slim curved nipple.

"Sleep, try and sleep," she said to me, but I couldn't sleep. I hardly slept, and I could hear in the silence of my luxury apartment the gurgle of my son's swallowing.

My tear itched badly. My appetite grew with a fury, and I ate whole loaves of bread, large portions of salmon. The sun slanting through the windows my mother opened every morning. The tinkly music from my son's crib mobile. The frequent flare of sad longing. I missed Kwame. I looked ahead and saw a future dead with the weight of his absence. I thought of getting a new number and calling him, to tell him we could make it work, that he could do as little as he wanted as a father just as long as he was there. But I was wearied of his rejection, his ignoring my texts, his blocking my number, and I felt translucent, so fragile that one more rejection would make me come fully undone.

"Why don't I call his parents? To inform them. They deserve to know," my mother suddenly said one morning as she fed my son, and I was startled that she could read my mind.

"Who?" I asked foolishly.

She looked at me evenly. "Kwame."

"No," I said. "Not yet."

My son began to cry. He was fed, his tiny belly tautly round, and yet he cried. He cried and cried.

"Some babies just cry," my mother said calmly.

What am I supposed to do with him? I thought to myself. It had only been a few days. There would be more days and weeks of this, not knowing what to do with a squalling person whose needs I feared I could never know. Only in my mother's arms did his wails taper off, briefly, before they began again. Only while asleep was he fully free of tears. My mother laid him in his crib and after a moment said, "Look how he's raised his arms!" She was smiling, and I had never seen delight so naked on her face. My son's tiny arms were raised up, as though in salute to sleep. It made me smile too.

"I don't know what I'll do when you leave," I said.

"My visa is long stay," she said. "I'm not going anywhere yet."

"Thank you, Mummy," I said, and I began to cry. Tears were so cheap now.

How do some memories insist on themselves? I remembered the night of Aunty Nwanneka's birthday party. A big party. Canopies ringed by balloons had been set up in her compound. My mother asked me not to go. It was shortly after my father had moved out of our house, the strain between my parents still ripe and raw.

"Stay and stand by me," my mother said, and I scoffed silently, thinking she was being dramatic. *Chill out, it's not as if this is a blood feud.* I went to the party. When I came home, unsteady from the wine Mmiliaku and I had drunk straight from the bottles, our househelp let me in. My mother was in the living room reading.

"Mummy, good evening," I greeted her, and she said nothing. She looked up from her book, as though to show she had heard me, and then turned away. A recurring image: my mother turning away, retreating, closing windows on herself.

My son woke up and began to cry. My mother hurried to his crib. I watched her cradle him and lower her head, as though to inhale him, touching the skin of his face with the skin of hers.

Gunnhild Øyehaug

Translated from the Norwegian by Kari Dickson

Apples

1

THE DOG CAME PELTING toward me. Mouth half-closed around a stick, coat rippling. *Freeze time,* I thought, so we stay like this forever, me here in the field, open and white, and him with the snow glittering and swirling around him in mid-flight.

It was afternoon by the time we turned home. The dog ran in front of me, behind me, beside me. Completely untroubled. When we got to the cabin, dusk was falling. I brushed the snow from us, gave the dog some food, water, lit the fire.

Later in the evening there was a knock at the door. It was Sonja, who owned the dog. The dog leapt to its feet, ran to its owner, and jumped up, Sonja laughed and said doggy things to the dog, Sonja looked at me with a questioning and slightly dumbfounded smile, as though she was saying to me, without saying, you could just have rung and told me. *Freeze time,* I thought, as I stood watching the dog jumping up at Sonja and Sonja looking at me with her gently quizzical smile, as though she wondered who I was, who could just take the dog like that and not say anything, again. You like the dog, Sonja said, and I nodded. You can come and visit, you know, Sonja said. I nodded again, would you like something to eat, I asked, I've just baked some rolls. Sonja looked at me, as though taken aback, either because I'd baked the rolls or because she wasn't sure what to do, OK, she said.

I put the rolls and a pot of tea on the table. Sonja looked around the cabin; the dog was lying on a blanket on the sofa, asleep. I hoped that I wasn't dreaming, that I wouldn't wake up and it would all be a romantic dream, that a person and a dog had come to visit me, that I'd made them food, that I'd put cheese on the table, that I saw a person standing there looking at my family pictures hanging on the wall, as though she was genuinely interested, and the dog lay sleeping on the sofa, and felt cared for and safe. And I liked the way I had written this, intimate and honest, and I liked the fact that Sonja was named after a variety of apple.

2

The class clapped. The author showed a page from a fruit encyclopedia on the digital blackboard, with an illustration of a round, red apple, and the text underneath said that Sonja was an autumn apple, resistant to apple scab, sweet in flavor, with a rich red color and good keeping quality. Well, the author said, that was something I wrote yesterday to show you a way to turn everything upside down at the last moment, first: a realistic story without any meta levels, where "I" has a dog and is happy and looking for moments to freeze, and then at the very end destroys everything by saying "I liked the way I had written this," so everyone falls out of the story, and knows that what they have just read is fiction. Obviously, it's not a style I would use for anything I was going to publish, said the author who was the lecturer that day. The creative writing class at the creative studies college looked at the author. They didn't actually chorus "oh," but might well have done by the look on their faces. The author was tall, had dark hair is difficult, to hold it still, to observe it. Signe glanced at Aksel, just long enough for him to realize that she wondered if he was impressed by what she'd said, before she looked at the floor. Her objection didn't come until the day was over and he was out on the street that ran like a long sentence past the creative studies college, which lay more or less in the heart of Oslo, not far from the fjord. Signe came out with her bag through the glass doors, and stepped onto the pavement where Aksel was standing lighting a cigarette. She looked at him with the same skeptical expression, pout, and eyes. Let's continue in the present tense. It's easier, when it comes to dramatic experience: I know, Aksel says, I know I shouldn't. By this, he means smoking. There was something, Signe says, something I thought about that text you read out today. I could tell, Aksel says. Signe looks surprised. Oh, she says, because she doesn't really like the author's overconfidence. What I thought was this: I liked the story without the meta sentence at the end, which just ruined the whole thing. I liked it when he was out in the snow with the dog, and he was happy, and that then he went back to the cabin and baked rolls and had a visitor. End of. What you're saying is that you like a realistic narrative, Aksel says. What I'm saying is that I like stories that are genuine, Signe says. That are not clever and pretending to be something they're not. But it was only an example, the author says. I don't believe you, Signe says. I think you liked it when you were writing it. I think you were into it. I think you were in the landscape in your head, I think you pictured the snow, and the dog, and I think you liked that there was something about the dog that the protagonist longed for, and I think you thought that if you named a person after an apple, the meta device you used to leave your own story would somehow feel less obvious because of the symbolism of the person growing out of the soil, which we all do really, in a way. AND: I don't for a second believe that you actually wanted to deconstruct it at the end, I think it's exactly what you're looking who normally catches everything, has failed to catch something so fundamental. What we are witnessing is an intellectual turning point for Signe. And Signe would no doubt wish that this entire conversation had a different outcome from the one it did, that she had not become the apricot that she naturally became for him, in fact, it took her several years to get over it, that she had gone home with him, this and that happened, in short, that in the course of a few months they went through the whole tiresome young woman/ older man relationship that inevitably follows its necessary drama-turgy based on the young woman's need to be seen and her essen-tially mature mind that finds no resonance in her male peers, and the older man's attraction to youth and constant longing to be seen, a longing that for some men is voracious and never satisfied, so constantly seeks out new, fantastic girls, but time and again these girls' lack of life experience seems to ruin the relationship for the older man, whereas the man's lack of listening ears appears to ruin the relationship for the young woman, not least, that he almost exactingly uncovers great flaws in her not yet fully devel-oped sense of self (which is exactly what provokes the need in him to carry on searching for the perfect woman who does *not* have this flaw), but the most frustrating thing of all, says Signe, and surveys her students at the University of Bergen, who are sitting listening to her story, which she has slipped into so unexpectedly, was that it ended just as I had wanted his story about the cabin and the dog to end, with fruit, that's to say, my bare arse, to put it humorously, and normally that would have been the kind of irony that I appreciate, but now I'm so old, and this is my last day as professor at this institute, and this story is what started it all for me, the reason I became a literary scholar in the first place, and I feel, actually . . . nothing. Nothing at all. The students clap uncer-tainly. Signe smiles at them, she is sixty-eight years old and a rather large lady, and she has to bend over slowly to pick up her bag from the floor. She takes her coat from the chair and leaves Auditorium A at the university for the last time:

3

Outside, the sky is blue, it's late May, and Signe walks to the bus that will take her home. She passes a flower shop, which is blooming with bouquets of tulips and roses and anemones, and bushes she does not know the name of, which are temptingly green in their own way standing there in their pots, but at the back, right against the flower shop window, on a small table, is a little tree that catches her eye, and she stops. And this is what the scene looks like from the outside: A stout, older woman stands looking at a tree. She holds her bag with both hands in front of her girth, resting the bag on her stomach, as older women with bags often do. And what is happening inside her is this, she is asking the question: What kind of tree is that? She leans over to look at the label where the name of the tree is written. And it says: Sonja.

Next scene: Signe takes the apple tree to the counter, she pays, the apple tree is given to her in a plastic bag, but that doesn't work, Signe has to carry the apple tree in her hands. Thankfully the tree is small and thin, and it's not far to the bus.

For the entire bus journey home, Signe is in a strange mood. Another line from Inger Christensen's book pops into her mind, perhaps because she is carrying an apple tree: Right at the end of the collection, there's a poem about some children sitting by a road after a war, and they have lost everything. And then the poem says: *there is no one to carry them anymore.* She sits with the apple tree on her lap and looks out at the sky. It's blue, with wispy white clouds. When she eventually gets home, she lets herself into the small, red house in a garden that is so well suited to an older woman of girth, and puts down the apple tree in the hall. Sonja? Signe calls. The story crackles with surprise. Sonja answers from one of the rooms, but Signe can't make out if it's the kitchen or the living room. Mum! Sonja shouts. Sonja comes hopping out into the hall—Sonja is Signe's forty-five-year-old daughter. She has Down syndrome and works in a sheltered workplace, where, in her own words, she makes "everything" and always finishes for the day half an hour before Signe comes home from university. Sonja is the result of the months when Signe and Aksel went through the relationship dramaturgy of young woman/older man, and Signe has been alone in her responsibility for Sonja, from the time even before she discovered she was pregnant, as Aksel disappeared in a way that no one can really hold against him: he drowned in the Mediterranean, he dove in too deep, down to a coral reef, and he should perhaps have remembered the discussion in class about the aquarium as a possible symbol, he might perhaps have seen that it was in fact a foreshadowing, but he didn't, he dove down and there he drowned, in all that blue, with fish of all colors swimming cheerfully around him. Signe hugs Sonja. Let's make dinner now, Signe says. Signe feels a lump in her throat a number of times through dinner, it must be because it was her last day as a professional, now she's a pensioner, all that's missing is the big farewell party, and so she embarks on the final stage of her life. How will Sonja get on without her is a question that has cropped up more than once, even though she's not ill, she's just old, there's no doubt about that. She tries to keep the chitchat going, asks in a thick voice: So how was it at work today? Just like normal, Sonja says. I love you, Signe wants to say. And was Andrea nice today? Signe asks. Andrea Liliane *Hamar,* Sonja corrects her. Signe smiles. Was Andrea Liliane *Hamar* nice today? Signe asks, it's easier now, she will be able to eat without crying. She is always nice, Sonja says. Oh, Signe says, I had the impression that Andrea could be a little naughty at times. Yes, Sonja says. But not today. She's learned to behave herself. That's good, Signe says.

Sonja and Signe do the washing up. Signe washes and Sonja dries. Signe looks at her, looks at her daughter who is standing there drying the plates with such care, the tears well up in her eyes, *freeze time,* Signe thinks, freeze time as I stand here looking at her! But time does not freeze, Signe hands her an already dried plate. There! Sonja says. Now we'll have coffee! Yes, Signe says, and swallows. But first, I've got a surprise for you, Signe says, wait a moment. Signe goes out into the hall, and comes back into the kitchen with the small apple tree. Oh! Sonja cries. A tree! It's an apple tree, Signe says, and it's called the same as you. Sonja Olsen? Sonja says. Just Sonja, Signe says. I thought we could plant it in the garden. Let's plant it now, Sonja says. OK, Signe says.

4

Signe and Sonja kneel in the garden and pat down the soil around the trunk of the small tree. They are both wearing gardening gloves. The story is unsure as to where it should end. If it should end here, or if it should end with Signe's young fingers that once leafed through a book and found a poem by Inger Christensen where it said that "a dreamer / must dream like trees / of fruit to the last," and she felt that this was so true that it couldn't be truer, that it was a truth that was radiant and luminous—or if it should stop with an open, white landscape where Aksel is throwing a stick to a dog that's not his, that he has borrowed, or if it should stop when the dog picks up the stick and comes running back in a way that is ridiculously happy, as though the dog is smiling (but it's actually because it has a stick in its mouth), and its long black-and-white fur ripples around the dog's body as it jumps through the circus director's Hula-Hoop-like hoop, stretched with thin greaseproof paper. Sonja, the small tree, has no answer, just a thin trunk and a few branches, and some budding leaves. And in this moment, she stands there in the garden, a tree in waiting, something that will grow, blossom, bear fruit, lose fruit, lose her leaves, be covered in snow, etc., with an astonishing patience and the peace that is particular to apple trees.

David Ryan

Warp and Weft

1

A CONSTRUCTION WORKER FALLS from the thirty-fourth
floor of a high-rise, or, rather, an unfinished thirty-fourth
level of iron and concrete girders, bundles of loose cable, wall-
board patchwork, and the improvised twist of wind so high up,
wind a muscle the altitude flexes just now, just enough to push
the man off balance and send him tumbling through the sky. His
harness had not been engaged as it should have been, he'd played
fast and loose, and he was tired, he'd been up all night with his
infant son. And here, at work, he'd gotten used to the sensation
of being barely suspended over the earth, of skating over gravity.
Along the fall to his death, his wife and baby boy wave from the
twenty-seventh floor, she's holding their favorite book, *Frederick,*
and on the nineteenth floor his son burps quietly on the shoulder of his memory, and their dog is sleeping on the sofa again
on the fifteenth, and now taking up the whole bed on the thir-
teenth. He's in Miami Beach for a millisecond with sand in his
trunks and a pretty bad sunburn on the seventh floor, and then
he's proposing to Mary on the fifth and fourth floors, but then on

the third floor he's a kid and he's holding his father's hand, and then—

A crane operator on the street below witnesses his coworker, really just a little dot of humanity above, slip and descend and in his surprise he pumps the clutch of the cab and leans into the boom's joystick, instinctually if irrationally, as if trying with the long, raised arm of the crane to catch the falling man but instead sending the arm crashing into the unfinished building. The crane groans like a dying giant, then cocks and tips on its side and topples. The operator is crushed. His final thought, which sparks through him like the final short circuit of a live wire, is of that morning's egg-and-bacon breakfast sandwich—the best he'd ever had.

2

A small, arthritic dog, who answers with exasperated glee to the name Troubles, circles with a permanent tremor, hobbling around the bed of an old woman dreaming, deep in sleep. Troubles barks once, then returns to the kitchenette just outside the woman's room, to a food bowl where even the crumbs have been lapped away, a thin, dirty puddle of old water in the bowl beside it. Troubles barks three times at the bowls, demanding satisfaction. There is a loud boom outside, then a crack, and then a groan. The dog pauses, cocks its head at the empty bowl, backs away. The old woman wakes.

She was dreaming about her husband in reverse—no, not as if time were reversing so much as falling back, falling away. Just before the dream slips off from consciousness, she recalls holding his cold hand, the warmth having left his dry, slack fingers. The machines turned off. The hospital staff giving her a moment in the room. Then, in the dream, they're checking into the hospital after she wakes in bed with him seizing. Then, in the dream, they are sharing a sea trout with root vegetables and rosemary, a nice bottle of Lambrusco. And then, dreaming, they're closing the sale of their house to a young couple—strangers—the mortgage paid off two decades ago. Then, in the dream, their daughter, who had moved out long ago, has passed her bar examination and calls on the phone. Now, the old woman, much younger, is using the slow cooker her daughter gave them for their thirtieth anniversary, and then in the dream she and her husband are fighting about their daughter, who turned thirteen a few weeks ago, arguing not with each other so much as discussing with great angry force their child's newfound angst over the slightest things, and then in this dream they are fighting about their daughter, aged six, her schooling, the cost of which is unsustainable, but the public system here is so awful. Then, he's bringing home so little, there's a brand-new mortgage—what if they want to have kids someday? And then in the dream he is a young man, with a broken ankle from sliding to third base in a college baseball game, so kneeling isn't possible—the ring extended, will you? but she says yes before he's finished his marry me. And finally, in the dream, just before she woke, they were driving on a crisp autumn night, circling the Deerfield mansions north of their own neighborhood, the high canopy of tall oaks and maples and chestnuts, the paned windows glowing a safe, warm orange. A spoon is stirring a cup of chocolate milk and in the dream, on this date, the chocolate milk is her electric joy in this car and he's the stirring spoon and already she's in love. Boom.

And she woke, and it's now, the actual now of her life, but she is still feeling the spoon inside her, the spoon stirs and then it dissolves, leaving just a lingering ache. Time before him, she forgets it now, like this dream, in waking. She hears a groan following this spoon into the ether, away, away . . .

Troubles has stopped barking and left only the sound of her heart like some ritual drum, pulling and pushing in her chest. She rises from the bed with her heart just behind the fear that wakes in her solar plexus. All that remains of the dream now is fear. In the kitchen she pours a bag of dry food into Troubles's bowl. The dog attacks the bowl with great Chihuahuaic force, or as much force as a Chihuahua with such a fragile tremor in her bones, such rheumy eyes, can muster. The old woman rinses out the water bowl and fills it with clean water, sets it beside the creature at the food bowl. It's the middle of the afternoon. The room is hot. She's recalling a time before her husband, or trying to, but lately she just comes up empty, empty like this hot room. This silence, but for an old dog devouring its food and a clock ticking, and her heart in this silence of now, her heart is so loud. The dog finishes eating, and she leashes it and takes her grocery bag from the peg by the door. She steps out, slowly descending the stairs, where memories lie cracked in the plaster walls, curled in whorls of dust and shadow in each shaky step. Troubles sniffs at the wall, hop-hop-hopping down each stair. Below they emerge onto the hot, bright avenue. An unusually windy day, blustery she'd call it were the air not so scorched. Why is she craving chocolate milk? Well. She'll add that to the grocery list.

At the corner of Fourteenth Street and Second Avenue, a gust flexes and the woman and her little dog Troubles are lifted like cinders spinning in a mote of air, rising together over the traffic, then the buildings, darting in the wind, twirling over the city like lost half-withered balloons. The woman's wig slides from its pins and she watches it tumble away from her, falling to the grid of streets below. Troubles lunges against the leash as if chasing after some airborne quarry. Now she can see Central Park, the size of a birthmark. It's cooler, and they rise and rise, until the woman's head suddenly taps against some kind of resistance, like a ceiling, though the sky is cloudless today, a surface above her, pressing both firm and soft. And then the crown of her relatively bald head pushes through. There he is, wading toward her. On the shore, all these other lost friends. A boom box is blasting "Goodnight Irene." Her head now, risen above the cool, clear lake water, her face, shining and slick in the sun, the water having washed over her thick black hair, and then her shoulders push up through the surface. He comes over, her husband, her Lancelot. He reaches out, hand extended, and their hands grab hold, and she feels the gravity of the lake release her to him, their Troubles behind them. The three wade a bit, then slowly swim-walk to the shore. "Goodnight Irene" ends and then there's this lovely silence, like no silence she's ever heard before. Someone offers her a glass, and she sips, and the silence returns, filling her, sweet and rich in her throat.

3

A man sits in front of a dead television screen imagining his own suicide so deeply that, though he's never owned a gun, his reverie—its desperation having dropped him into a kind of lucid dream—has put a dream pistol in his hand. It's a shining and tragic police revolver, the same his dad had, this dreamed gun that is all the same quite real. His despair gives it mass, substance, heft. The smooth, polished nickel finish gleams, the lacquered hickory handle pebbled and stiff in the palm of his grip. Here it is, a legacy, passed down to this moment. His father, a polished, nickel-plated barrel. The bullet, a copper-and-brass descendant.

Outside there is a boom, and the percussion enters his lucid depression, much as a bullet in a dream enters a brain, so that he believes the dream he holds in his hand has been executed, that he has pulled the trigger of the dream on himself, and when he hears the distant crack and groan, he believes it's just the sound of life leaving his body. A more proximate groan, his own. The sound of his soul wrenching free of his body. He's now entered the afterlife and it's identical to his prior life. He had been outside, twelve years old, in the backyard, playing with their dog, Champ. A fire-cracker pop came from inside the house. Champ was the smallest dog, wiry hair, bulging soulful eyes. Utterly devoted and unintelligent, Champ never ran for the ball, just stared up at him as if asking, What, please, tell me? From inside the house, his mother's

No!, as if acts could be reversed by simply scolding, and then the sobbing howl that there would be no reversing this bad behavior.

Now, here, in what he believes is the afterlife, he rises from his familiar chair, goes into a kitchen no different from the living kitchen. He takes a glass from the counter and pours tap water into it. He drinks. There is life all around him. He returns to the blank television screen and sits. He takes another sip of the water and feels the afterlife, perhaps colder than before, sliding down his throat.

4

This couple, they don't know each other that well really, they met at jury duty. Neither had to serve. But they were there, and she was reading *Anna Karenina*. He's never read Tolstoy, but he said Tolstoy, as if. And, in truth, they know each other enough because how much do you really need to know? I mean, he's young and single and she's young and single. Sometimes attraction just fills in the blanks. She looks a little like that girl in that television show. They are twisted up in bed, the window open to the chatter and hot breath of metal and city trash and jaywalking and exhaust of Sixth Avenue, the clatter and bombast in their ears like a kind of musical experiment. The girl has a lovely birthmark on her left breast and her skin smells like mown grass, and the boy hasn't smelled mown grass since he was a kid and her skin reminds him of children. A yard full of children splashing in a kiddie pool. They'd bought beer in the bodega below her apartment—to get to her door you have to enter the bodega, it's like a twenty-four-hour doorman. Nice. They are a little tipsy, sure. It's nice here. Their bodies fit nicely together. There is an egg inside her. It was nice of that judge to—I mean, basically—hook them up. And what is a stranger anyway? Aren't we all, forever? Familiar people hide in their lives for years; anniversaries pass married couples like strangers. Lovers die of old age, never realizing they spent their lives not knowing one another. That's life. And life should be lived, ergo.

The egg has just dropped inside her. She's above, straddling him. But then the egg inside her body says, no, lean down into him, kiss his forehead, then pull away and lie on your back. Then her hands reach and guide him on top. A stripe of damp hair crosses her face, the tip fallen into her parted mouth, and he reaches down and wipes it back behind her ear and this moves her. They're good together, they seem already to know each other, don't they? Like how they move together, how they both were sent home by the judge. The court had all the jurors they needed. He knows nothing of her desire for children. She knows nothing of his ambivalence. A siren on Sixth Avenue below passes her window and a truck shudders. He doesn't want kids, no, but already she maybe would, yeah, probably with the right person, the right situation. Yes, someday.

Boom comes through the open window from somewhere beyond Sixth Avenue—and then a metallic crack and groan. The girl's body begins to contract and pulse, a flux and pull guiding her now, taking control over her. The urgency of the boom and groan outside presses into this couple, though they're only vaguely aware of it, and they push deeper into each other, as if the sirens that now pass outside were rushing into their blood, their lives, the sirens a desire heightened and impelled toward some cataclysm. Life is too short, the sirens are saying. She's pulling at him now and there's this kind of laughter coming out of her body, the laughter of her musculature releasing, and then he shudders and grabs hold of her. And something between them embraces, something silent and deeper than they know, yet. Another wave of sirens passes through the open window; entering the room like spectators or thieves, then passing back outside and racing away until it sounds like no more than the whine of children's toys. And at this moment—though this couple doesn't yet know it—they will never be stranger to each other, or happier again, in their lives.

5

" 'But Frederick,' they said, 'you are a poet!' " A young mother is reading Leo Lionni to her infant son. Frederick the mouse daydreams and composes poetry all day while the other mice gather food for the winter. The child is too young to understand the words, though the mother sings to him as if he can. She wills his favorite book to be any book by Lionni, but in particular this one, because these are her favorites, this is her favorite. This son, their first (though they intend to have more children), has brought such a mortal urgency to every waking moment. Sometimes she sleeps and dreams she is holding him. He's stroking her face the way an adult might, the way Bill does sometimes. In the dream, his tiny hand is ruddy, his fingers soft with baby perspiration. Nights are often sleepless. She sometimes dreams she's holding her child even when she's half asleep, waking frequently to check the boy in the co-sleeper, to change him, feed him, the wall between sleep and wakefulness worn through, she, sitting in that thin membrane between. Bill wakes too, does what he can. She worries about his clumsiness during the day, without enough sleep. The job, so demanding of his body, he's so high in the sky these days. Manhattan Island is a rock, nearly all of it, and yet how easily it seems that one of these buildings could shift its footing, or he might stumble, or take a false step, or a breeze might wrap around him and throw him out of her life. Why does the city need so many high-rises? These disgusting luxury apartments. She dreams sometimes they're living on sand, not like a beach with palm trees, just a murky substance their feet sink into, a grounding that slows her, sets her off balance as she tries to get from one place to another. In these dreams, she's childless, entirely alone. It's like the earth is embodying the lethargy she feels when she hasn't had enough sleep. Which is, of course, all the time these days. With his construction job, she knows there are harnesses, guidelines, strict rules about safety. But the men flaunt the rules so often. Bill's admitted it, he's told her stories about the risks they take. "'But Frederick,' they said, 'you are a poet!'" she whispers again. Her little boy is asleep in her arms as the phone rings and she chooses not to pick it up, not to disturb their sleeping son.

Her dog, asleep on the sofa, wakes, startled. She lays her hands over the child's little ears. The landline, they need to get rid of it. The only callers are collection agencies, telemarketers, pollsters. The machine answers but the volume is turned down too low for her to hear anything but a murmur, a sober voice, a texture of concern perhaps. Who needs a landline these days? Bill says if a cell tower goes out in an emergency, that's why. Then the machine finishes recording the sober voice, a voice it now holds for the record. Her sleeping son in her arms. He's slept through the ringing. He won't remember this moment, asleep so soundly now. The dog is staring at the phone, as if the call were for him. He's not supposed to be on the sofa. But she hasn't the heart to kick him off most of the time.

She rereads silently to herself the last lines in the book: "When Frederick had finished, they all applauded. 'But Frederick,' they said, 'you are a poet!' Frederick blushed, took a bow, and said shyly, 'I know it.'" The phone rings again, and this too her son sleeps through in peace, her hands once more pressed against his ears, so that, as she later sees more clearly, he won't yet wake to what has just happened, will not hear what is happening to them.

Lorrie Moore

Face Time

I ASKED MY FATHER IF HE KNEW where he was and he said, "Kind of."

"You are in the hospital. Your hip surgery went well. But there is a virus and you have been found to have it. You are contagious. No one can get near. It's happening all over the world. You caught it in your assisted-living facility. The chef had it."

His blue eyes had a light that appeared to race from the back of his brain to the front. The brightness of them seemed to direct itself, with sudden power, into the screen, then straight through and past me. "The Berrywood chef?"

"Yes."

Now his eyes dulled again. "The food was not that good. I did have a glass of lemonade once that was delicious. Like in the war. Cold lemonade in a jam jar." He licked his lips. There was crust in the corner of his mouth, and he picked at it with one of his long, now thin pianist's fingers. The oxygen tubing dangled on his chest.

"Is there something you need now? After we finish FaceTiming, I can phone the nurses' desk."

"I'd like some of that lemonade."

"I'll ask them about that." Why should this patient be so thirsty? Give him a lemonade, for Christ's sake. Give him the lemonade of his memory and his dreams. "We are drying the lungs," a doctor had said last week. "We don't want him to aspirate."

"Isn't this a quality-of-life issue?" I did not say. Doctors all around the country seemed confused about whether hydration or dehydration was better. I feared that dehydration meant they were sending him off the exit ramp. A dry death. A dry death is better, someone had once told me.

"But how does anyone know?" I had protested.

"There is no death rattle. You don't hear the death rattle."

"So you mean it's better for us," I said. "The living."

Who knew what the dying felt at the end? They didn't return calls.

"That would be very kind of you to ask," my father said, delicately trying to moisten his lips with his gray tongue.

He attempted to smile but his whole dry mouth seemed unsplittable and in need of sponging.

His bottom teeth were as dark as teak and twisted in his mouth.

"When the nurse comes back in, I'll tell her."

"Did I do something wrong?" he asked. "I feel like I did something wrong."

"No. Not a thing. The nurse set up the iPad for you but then had to leave. She'll be back later."

Three times daily, visored, hazmatted nurses dressed like beekeepers popped in and out of the room, their faces indiscernible, their voices the high, chipper kind that children and the elderly are supposed to prefer. Birdlike, perhaps. Good to have the song of a bird. Even if they were frightened birds, in a rush to get out of there. Even if they were terrified of their tasks.

"Are you in any pain?" I asked.

"Oh, not really," he said defeatedly.

An exhilarating exchange of ideas was not possible on screens or in this weird dystopia. Still, I decided to make the situation as interesting as possible. "The British prime minister has this virus," I said. "So does Prince Charles. Also Tom Hanks."

His face perked up as he searched for a reply. "So I'm in good company."

"Yes, you are. And the poor are getting the virus, too, of course."

"I'm the poor!" he said. "Especially after next month's Berry-wood bill."

Later, I would accuse my quite comfortable friends of appropriating the illness from the disadvantaged, of co-opting a fear of the illness that targeted prisoners, frontline workers, meatpackers, and, of course, the elderly. "It's all unfair."

My father's sight came rushing into his eyes again and brightened up the screen. "I just hope I don't have to arm-wrestle the meek and the peacemakers for a seat in heaven. That would be awkward."

I gave him a smile, as if everything were all good, then started in with some more about the virus. I would try to make a bad situation diverting. He would be interested. "It is all over the globe," I told him. "No country was really prepared, except perhaps Finland. The Finns are a nation of doomsday preppers, so they were completely ready. They've been stockpiling for years, out of fear of Russia, so they're in pretty good shape. Also, South Korea did well. They are wary of North Korea, so are somewhat disaster-ready. Same as Taiwan, which fears the mainland."

I could see him considering this. "I guess we just weren't that afraid of Canada," he said, his eyes giving a wobbly little jump. Jokes! The very wattage of life. Performance had always been how he conversed, summoning it up from the depths. Rehearsing the recitation. Looking for the opening. There it still was, beneath the bullshit malaria drugs.

"I guess we weren't! Even though Trudeau's wife came down with this."

"Is that so? Pierre Trudeau's wife?"

"Justin Trudeau. Yup." I could see his focus change and his chest rise with sad and effortful breathing.

"I am supposed to go to the shoe store, but if I get there before the pastor I won't have the key."

I knew the hydroxychloroquine gave people hallucinations. Still, all the doctors seemed to be using it. It had the endorsement of Washington, which had invented the undrained drained swamp, and of France, which had invented pasteurization and had been dining out on that ever since, while still serving small, moldy raw-milk cheeses. "It will be OK. They are giving you medicine." The last time he'd been on it was in 1945, during the war, when he actually had malaria.

"My mother had the Spanish flu."

"Yes, I know."

"She was pregnant with my older brother and they told her to lie there and not to cough or her lungs would burst."

I wondered if lungs could really burst. I had heard this story from my dad on several occasions in my childhood and wondered about its veracity every time, though never out loud. Now to watch him sending these utterances into the light of the screen was like seeing an old man burn all his poetry in a fire.

"They were all interesting people, my family, my sister and brother and parents," he said, seemingly forgetting about his own three children: Livvy, the eldest; me, in the middle; and Delia, the baby, who had opted out of these scheduled conversations. "No-necrophilia Delia," she'd called herself. She adored our father but could not participate.

Oddly, it seemed that his daughters, at present, were not as interesting as his childhood family. Or perhaps that had always been true. His mind seemed a little rinsed of all of us, even of our mother, who had died eighteen months before, so abruptly that her vividness for me had not been interrupted. There were still things I made mental notes to tell her. She would want to know how Dad was doing.

"Now, you were born on Staten Island, isn't that right?" my father said.

I was slightly startled. "No, that was Mom." I knew I sometimes looked like her.

His head leaned back against the pillow, and then he pulled it up to look again into the iPad that the nurse had set there on a kind of tray. He had grown thinner, and silvery stubble covered his chin. He was trying to be courteous. He did not ask after me, for which I was grateful. Who wanted to share the banalities of this life right now: the low buzz of dread in the head like a broken wire; the endless YouTube links; everyone frantically not socializing; the recently furloughed male friends doing their insane air-guitar concerts on Zoom; the hours of television news interspersed with highly theatrical, mind-boggling insurance ads; the early-morning senior mixer at the supermarket; the neighborhood walks with face masks hanging from one ear like dream catchers. Women created e-mail threads of their readings of the Bible. It was all ghastly, especially the singing "Happy Birthday" twice as you washed your hands, because it might never actually be your birthday again so have at it. Well-to-do white families in large suburban homes tended to their bubbles—bubbles that intersected other bubbles so were not bubbles at all—disinfecting grocery bags and ordering from Amazon and Grubhub, and in general claiming the pandemic for themselves. The shuttered theaters and museums made the gloom of cities everywhere a harrowing one. Photos of empty boulevards and squares flooded the Internet. Pierced ears filled back in, because who wore earrings anymore? Your badly painted toenails you could say were done by a neighbor girl, home from school, on her deck—a neighbor girl who was actually you. French wine had been turned into hand sanitizer. Wisconsin milk had been turned into soap.

But some things had stayed the same, like the arrival of spring and the pastel monotony of the flowering shrubs. Who could feel how large a transformation was really occurring when the earth seemed to be enjoying itself more than ever, and who could speak of such things to a man who was clutching his plastic necklace of oxygen?

"Are you comfortable, Dad? Just lie back away from the iPad if you want. Don't make yourself uncomfortable. We can still talk." The headboard behind him was white pleather and attached to the wall. He had a bedsore and a catheter for a prolapsed bladder. I knew that. His unrehabilitated hip would never be right now, though the surgery, we'd been told, had been a great success.

His gown was slightly open in front, revealing his pink and sunken chest. He threw his head back against the pillow again, then tipped it forward. "I have to go downstairs and get the mail." And then, for a moment, he seemed to know where he was. "Am I going back to my apartment?"

The Berrywood facility would not readmit him until he had tested negative. So far, four positives.

"Not yet. You have to test negative before they can let you go."

"I don't think I got the mail today. I need to get the mail. I have to do that before I meet the pastor."

There were a lot of things he needed to do and places he needed to be. He was always announcing this. He was supposed to meet trains and people and small groups holding meetings. Perhaps, even in normal life, every place a person believed they needed to be was a kind of hallucination, and that was its power. Berrywood had, some years ago, constructed a fake bus stop for escapees. It was a way of catching a runaway pet with the lure of food. The staff would find residents sitting there, waiting, no bus ever stopping, and talk to them sympathetically, until their plans evaporated into the mist, as so many plans did, even in good times. My father had never got that bad. Before all this, he had seemed fairly with it.

"Is that music playing?" I asked. My laptop had good speakers. It sounded like massage music, a calming electronic flute, the kind of music that played on what one of the nurses called "the classical station." They had two hours' worth of music on each station, she said.

"I was hoping for Brahms," he said.

"We'll see if we can get some Brahms."

"You know, Beethoven had one great symphony, the *Eroica*. And then there's Mozart's C-minor. But then Brahms comes in third—he had four symphonies of equal quality."

"That's so interesting," I said. Whenever we spoke of music, he ignored my preference for Tchaikovsky or Duke Ellington. He would sometimes allow for Harold Arlen.

"Only four symphonies, but they were all top-notch."

I didn't always know what to say. "Well, I'm going to call the nurses' station and see if we can get some Brahms for you."

"Any of the symphonies," he added.

An aide suddenly appeared on the screen in her beekeeper's garb. "We are here for his oxygen levels and to change his dressings," she said.

"OK. Well, Dad? I'll leave you to these proceedings. But I'll hope to reach you later tonight. Livvy's going to call at some point today. Love you."

"OK, honey, good to talk to you," he said, sounding suddenly as he always had. He would never have said "Love you" back. He had fought in the Philippines. The greatest generation did not do the fey, fake "Love you, too." The greatest generation did not wear lip balm brought by the aide or don compression stockings—too feminine—and hearing aids were a lot like jewelry, and thus a problem, and were sometimes found lost amid the tangled sheets. The greatest generation had taken a lot of orders early in life and did not want to take any more. The aide peeked into the screen and waved with her gloved hand. "Bye-bye," she said.

"Thank you. Is it possible to play some Brahms?" I asked her quickly.

"This isn't Brahms?"

"No."

"Brahms? How do you spell it?" She seemed to be typing it into the iPad.

I told her, hoping I'd put the "h" in the right spot.

"I'll see what I can do."

"Also, do you have lemonade?" I asked.

"Here's this," she said, bringing a plastic cup to my father's lips. He sipped, then grimaced and waved it away. It looked to be a chartreuse-colored, watery drink made from powder.

"Bye-bye," the beekeeper said again, as she grew larger in the screen, and then turned the iPad off entirely, so that on my laptop my connection became just a lit square with my own face in it.

My father was too old to grasp technology, so the nurses were the ones to place his FaceTime calls, according to a schedule that Livvy had given them. But the nurses were frazzled and Livvy could be a pain in the neck, though she didn't know it. Her husband always called her an angel, massaging her shoulders, hoping to get laid. And Delia, of course, had refused to be a part of it. "I can't watch Dad like this," she'd said again that day.

The following afternoon, a FaceTime call came in from Livvy. "I thought I'd patch you in and share my time with you," she said.

"What do you mean? I'm scheduled for a different time." But Livvy was both bossy and retired, a bad combo. She'd retired too young.

"Watch this," she said, and spun her phone so that through my screen I saw her screen and in her screen I saw my father.

"Hi, Dad," I said.

"Hey, hi!" my dad croaked uncertainly. Then the screen switched so that I was looking into the black of Livvy's fireplace.

"Why am I looking into your fireplace?" I asked.

"It's so he can see you. The way it's patched in you can't both see each other at the same time. When he sees you, you don't see him—"

"I see the fireplace? This is too strange."

She toggled back and forth between the black hearth and my bewildered father. I didn't want to be patched in in this manner.

"Well, I thought we could sing to him," she said. I knew that one afternoon she had used the iPad as a nanny cam, watching him while she folded her laundry. She had Ferberized her children—a method that was also known as "graduated extinction"—letting them wail themselves to sleep as she watched, and I wondered if there wasn't something similar in what she was doing now.

"I suppose we could sing 'Danny Boy,'" I suggested. "It's a beautiful song and it matches his name."

"Oh, I don't think Dad likes that song. He says they're not the original words."

"What do you mean? It's a beautiful song."

"Yes, but he objects to it somehow. He says the Irish took it from the English."

"The Irish stole 'Danny Boy'? That's the most ridiculous thing I've ever heard." Now I had questioned her authority. There was always a crisis of expertise with Livvy.

"How about this?" Livvy said. She sang into the phone, "If you'll be M-I-N-E mine, I'll be T-H-I-N-E thine, and I'll L-O-V-E love you all the T-I-M-E time. You are the B-E-S-T best of all the R-E-S-T rest—"

"What the heck are you singing?"

"Dad used to sing me all his old army songs." She laughed.

"That's an army song? And we still won the war? I think I'm going to go and just wait for my own call with him."

Now my father, on the screen, let out a howl of anguish and I could see him grimace with agony and sorrow. He tore at his cannula and his gown.

"Whoa," Livvy said. "What's going on here? I think he doesn't want you to go."

"That's not it. He hardly knows I'm here."

My father's face became a gash of pain. "*Bitte, bitte,*" he cried hoarsely. With one hand, he fiercely sliced the signal for "cut" at his throat.

"Speaking German. Still sharp," Livvy said.

"I don't think speaking one's college German right now is a sign of being sharp."

He was clearly hallucinating, agitated, imagining he was a prisoner of war; that was what it must have felt like to him—the cruel isolation, the medicine, the lights, the strange machines all around. Of course, during the war he had been in the Pacific theater. But hallucinations were not fussy about details like that.

He tugged at the tubes in his arms.

Terror flew from him in a kind of guttural howl like a whale song. "*Nein, nein, nein. Bitte. Nein.*" He thrashed around in the bed.

I texted Livvy: *I can't watch this. It's unbearable.* Did she no longer know what was bearable and what was unbearable? Well, no one knew anymore. *I will speak to him tomorrow. I'm going to give him his privacy.*

I got into bed. I turned off the phone ringer and just watched television. Every now and then, the numbers of telemarketers and scammers appeared in white on the screen. At night, my dreams often featured such alerts, scrolling like ticker tape across them, and I would spend much of the dream trying to figure out whose numbers they were.

The next evening—evening was better, Livvy said—I waited hours for the call from the hospital to come. I sat before my computer, waiting for the FaceTime icon to enliven itself. Livvy sent e-mails and texts: *Tell them to turn the lights down. They are too bright. I keep telling them to turn them down but they don't. Ask for Eileen or Carmen. One of them is usually on duty. Ask them if they got the pizza we ordered for them.* Livvy's patient advocacy, I feared, would get him killed. The overrun hospital would triage him, and the hospice staff would move in and put him down like a dog, thanks to his annoying daughters.

The call came in late. The face that filled the screen was a beekeeper's. Was it Eileen? Was it Carmen? I did not know. She seemed new. "Your very nice father is here, but he is asleep." She stepped away from the screen, and I saw him with his eyes closed, his head hanging off his neck in a tilted fashion, the oxygen cannula taped in place, his mouth a dark crescent. They had shaved him, so his face was now cleared of the patches of miniature birch forest that had sprung up there. His skin had a butterscotch tinge, and his neck was ropy against the blue cotton of his gown. The nurse stroked his forehead with a latex-covered finger. Gingerly, but several times. "He's asleep but he's hanging in there. He's a sweet man."

"Thank you for calling me. I'll try to connect with him tomorrow."

"Yes," she said. "I'll send you some pictures of him sleeping," she added, and began tapping the iPad. Then she looked up. "Good night!" she said brightly, performing the role of saintly nurse, her head filling the screen as she moved in to shut it off. Surely her loving-kindness would vanish as soon as the iPad went dark, and her demeanor would reveal an eagerness to be rid of this COVID-ic old guy with his bedsore and immobile hip, his catheter and oxygen tubing.

I called Delia of the camellias, lying on her chaise longue. "He's stranded there, like someone fallen on a battlefield," I said. "Everyone is just stepping around him. He's in the way." How could I speak the lonely, frantic improvisation of my inadequate self-reliance? She was well versed in her own.

"I told you. I did my crying last week. We had a good long talk just before his surgery. It contained dignity and charity for all. You'll have to call me when it's over." Her voice broke a little.

"Maybe he'll get out. Maybe he'll finally test negative and be released to rehab to get his hip working again." I could not imagine it. Not really. Even that would be hellish. Then I added, sounding still more insane, "Falconers return their old birds to the wild."

"That would be interesting, if Dad could test negative two times in a row," she said. "Perhaps he will take a long time to die, like a courteous Rasputin. That would be Dad's way. Don't get me wrong. Dad's a nice person. Just maybe a little on the spectrum."

"Not the Rasputin spectrum."

"Is that a spectrum?"

"I'm sure the hospital's hospice nurses think so."

"Is that who's tending to him now?"

"I suspect so. I'm not really sure."

"Well, you and I are a thousand miles away. All this is up to Livvy. She's always the boss, anyway."

"She doesn't complain."

"No, she instructs. Which creates rage."

"She's already antagonizing the nurses. I fear she's going to get him killed."

Delia, the baby, was beloved. Much more than Livvy or me. I was probably too mysterious to my father—no husband! no child!—for him to love me in more than an average way: a feeling he had in common with all the men I'd ever known. Still, like them, he seemed to enjoy talking to me. "What do you think of Biden?" he often asked. He was hoping to live until November, to cast his vote for the Democrats, and this was what he enjoyed talking about the most. As well as Brahms.

"Dad arranged to donate his body to the medical school," I said now, changing the subject only slightly, "but they can't possibly take it at this point. He would be like Typhoid Murray."

"Now you have made me laugh," Delia said, not laughing.

. . .

The next day, at Livvy's instructions, I waited the entire afternoon. When not watching for the FaceTime icon to jump up off the dashboard of my computer screen, I stared out the window at the haphazard latticework of trees against the sky, intersected with transformers and wires that had squirrels running along them like cursors. A satiny blue-black cowbird sat atop a phone pole, a cut-rate omen. The call was supposed to come in at three in the afternoon, but by nine p.m. nothing had come through except Livvy's texts: *Don't forget about the lights! Please ask about the music again! They keep playing that Sounds of the Seasons loop. Remind them that that pizza came from us!*

I called the nurses' station. "This is Dan Fordham's daughter—he's a patient on your wing? And I was supposed to get a call this afternoon but I've been waiting for hours and nothing has come through. I just want to make sure you have the right number?"

"Dan Fordham. Yes. Let me get back to you," the nurse said.

"I hope you got our pizza," I mumbled pathetically; she had already put me on hold.

And then we were disconnected and a dial tone buzzed in my ear, like a message from the universe. I called back and got the voice mail and so left my number and my e-mail. I waited several more hours. Even Livvy and her husband went to bed—*We're going to bed*—without waiting any longer for a report from me. And then it was midnight, and shortly thereafter the phone rang and I knew the message it contained. *The pipes, the pipes . . . From glen to glen.* I could not touch the phone. I would let the voice mail pick it up. My actual ear had not been readied. But then I grabbed the phone and said hello and received the news. I thanked the nurse. I added, "He wanted to make it until November so he could vote. Perhaps that was too much to hope for."

"I am very sorry," came the voice.

I went to bed. I wondered whether in the final moments a dying person said, "So this is death," or did they say, "So that was life"? Or did a nice man who had not planned to die so alone and isolated but in his own bed with family gathered around think anything at all? Perhaps at the end he was simply tired, in a condition of holy yet unenlightened bewilderment, all consciousness as fake as a skit. I missed him already and without comprehension.

I spent the next morning sending e-mails to those who needed them. By the afternoon, the sky had the slurry look it could have before a storm. Outside, things were starting to move and fly, with a heavy hand, a flat foot, and a hard rain: a derecho, four minutes of straight winds at hurricane strength. It tore up jungle gyms, knocked down power lines, uprooted trees.

Even this set was being struck. A transformer blew in the alley, and I cried out in fright.

The ensuing power outage darkened and enfeebled the town for almost a week. Traffic lights went dead in their various eyes. Neighbors in masks and nitrile gloves hauled thawed frozen food to the curb in black trash bags. Every evening, no phone or Wi-Fi, no communication of any sort, my cell uncharged, I ate a few apples with some peanut butter and went to bed at seven, when the sky lost all sun. With a flashlight, I read essays of zigzaggy piety and po-mo chic until I fell asleep. Could a thought become an idea without instruction? Could an emptiness of thought eradicate ideas? With my father gone, his body chilling in a Thermo King truck far away—did the workers, stacking him up in plastic wrap, talk to him, saying, "There you go, sir, there is nothing to worry about now. You are on your way, my man"?—I had lost all interest in myself and all conviction or belief in forms generally.

In the mornings, outside, chain saws dissected old red oaks, freeing them from tangled wire. After six days, unannounced, the lights came slyly, silently back on, as if a large cloud had discreetly shifted. Motors kicked in. Clocks flashed their incorrect times. All the little mice of my mind returned, found their corners, and began to set up shop.

Samanta Schweblin

Translated from the Spanish by Megan McDowell

An Unlucky Man

THE DAY I TURNED EIGHT, my sister—who absolutely always had to be the center of attention—swallowed an entire cup of bleach. Abi was three. First she smiled, maybe a little disgusted at the nasty taste; then her face crumpled in a frightened grimace of pain. When Mom saw the empty cup hanging from Abi's hand, she turned as white as my sister.

"Abi-my-god" was all Mom said. "Abi-my-god," and it took her a few seconds longer to spring into action.

She shook Abi by the shoulders, but my sister didn't respond. She yelled, but Abi still didn't react. She ran to the phone and called Dad, and when she came running back Abi was still standing there, the cup just dangling from her hand. Mom grabbed the cup and threw it into the sink. She opened the fridge, took out the milk, and poured a glass. She stood looking at the glass, then looked at Abi, then back at the glass, and finally dropped the glass into the sink as well. Dad worked very close by and got home quickly, but Mom still had time to do the whole show with the glass of milk again before he pulled up in the car and started honking the horn and yelling.

Mom lit out of the house like lightning with Abi clutched to her chest. The front door, the gate, and the car doors were all flung open. There was more horn honking and Mom, who was already sitting in the car, started to cry. Dad had to shout at me twice before I understood that I was the one who was supposed to close up.

We drove the first ten blocks in less time than it had taken me to close the car door and fasten my seat belt. But when we got to the main avenue, the traffic was practically stopped. Dad honked the horn and shouted out the window, "We have to get to the hospital! We have to get to the hospital!" The cars around us maneuvered and miraculously let us pass, but a couple cars ahead, we had to start the whole operation over again. Dad braked in the traffic, stopped honking, and pounded his head against the steering wheel. I had never seen him do such a thing. There was a moment of silence, and then he sat up and looked at me in the rearview mirror. He turned around and said to me:

"Take off your underpants."

I was wearing my school uniform. All my underwear was white, but I wasn't exactly thinking about that just then, and I couldn't understand Dad's request. I pressed my hands into the seat to support myself better. I looked at Mom and she shouted:

"Take off your damned underpants!"

I took them off. Dad grabbed them out of my hands. He rolled down the window, went back to honking, and started waving my underpants out the window. He raised them high while he yelled and kept honking, and it seemed like everyone on the avenue turned around to look at them. My underpants were small, but they were also very white. An ambulance a block behind us turned on its siren, caught up with us quickly, and started clearing a path. Dad kept on waving the underpants until we reached the hospital.

They parked the car by the ambulances and jumped out. Without waiting, Mom took Abi and ran straight into the hospital. I wasn't sure whether I should get out or not: I didn't have any underpants on and I looked around to see where Dad had left them, but they weren't on the seat or in his hand, which was already slamming his car door behind him.

"Come on, come on," said Dad.

He opened my door and helped me out. He gave my shoulder a few pats as we walked into the emergency room. Mom came through a doorway at the back and signaled to us. I was relieved to see she was talking again, giving explanations to the nurses.

"Stay here," said Dad, and he pointed to some orange chairs on the other side of the main waiting area.

I sat. Dad went into the consulting room with Mom and I waited for a while. I don't know how long, but it felt long. I pressed my knees together tightly and thought about everything that had happened so quickly, and about the possibility that any of the kids from school had seen the spectacle with my underpants. When I sat up straight, my jumper rode up and my bare bottom touched part of the plastic seat. Sometimes the nurse came in or out of the consulting room and I could hear my parents arguing. At one point I craned my neck and caught a glimpse of Abi moving restlessly on one of the cots, and I knew that, at least today, she wasn't going to die. And I still had to wait.

Then a man came and sat down next to me. I don't know where he came from; I hadn't noticed him before.

"How's it going?" he asked.

I thought about saying *very well,* which is what Mom always said if someone asked her that, even if she'd just told me and my sister that we were driving her insane.

"Okay," I said.

"Are you waiting for someone?"

I thought about it. I wasn't really waiting for anyone; at least, it wasn't what I wanted to be doing right then. So I shook my head, and he said:

"Why are you sitting in the waiting room, then?"

I understood it was a great contradiction. He opened a small bag he had on his lap and rummaged in it a bit, unhurried. Then he took a pink slip of paper from his wallet.

"Here it is. I knew I had it somewhere."

The paper was printed with the number ninety-two.

"It's good for an ice-cream cone. My treat," he said.

I told him no. You shouldn't accept things from strangers.

"But it's free. I won it."

"No." I looked straight ahead and we sat in silence.

"Suit yourself," he said, without getting angry.

He took a magazine from his bag and started to fill in a cross-word puzzle. The door to the consulting room opened again and I heard Dad say, "I will not condone such nonsense." That's Dad's clincher for ending almost any argument. The man sitting next to me didn't seem to hear it.

"It's my birthday," I said.

It's my birthday, I repeated to myself. What should I do?

The man held the pen to mark his place in a box on the puzzle and looked at me in surprise. I nodded without looking at him, aware I had his attention again.

"But . . . ," he said, and he closed the magazine. "Sometimes I just don't understand women. If it's your birthday, what are you doing in a hospital waiting room?"

He was an observant man. I straightened up again in my seat and I saw that, even then, I barely came up to his shoulders. He smiled and I smoothed my hair. And then I said:

"I'm not wearing any underpants."

I don't know why I said it. It's just that it was my birthday and I wasn't wearing underpants, and I couldn't stop thinking about those circumstances. He was still looking at me. Maybe he was startled or offended, and I understood that, although it hadn't been my intention, there was something vulgar about what I had just said.

"But it's your birthday," he said.

I nodded.

"It's not fair. A person can't just go around without underpants when it's their birthday."

"I know," I said emphatically, because now I understood just how Abi's whole display was a personal affront to me.

He sat for a moment without saying anything. Then he glanced toward the big windows that looked out onto the parking lot. "I know where to get you some underpants," he said.

"Where?"

"Problem solved." He stowed his things and stood up.

I hesitated. Precisely because I wasn't wearing underpants, but also because I didn't know if he was telling the truth. He looked toward the front desk and waved one hand at the attendants.

"We'll be right back," he said, and he pointed to me. "It's her birthday." And then I thought, Oh, please, Jesus, don't let him say anything about my underpants, but he didn't: he opened the door and winked at me, and then I knew I could trust him.

We went out to the parking lot. Standing, I came up to a little above his waist. Dad's car was still next to the ambulances, and a policeman was circling it, annoyed. I kept looking over at the policeman, and he watched us walk away. The breeze wrapped around my legs and rose, making a tent out of my uniform. I had to hold it down while I walked, keeping my legs awkwardly close together.

He turned around to see if I was following him, and he saw me fighting with my skirt.

"We'd better stick close to the wall."

"I want to know where we're going."

"Don't get persnickety with me now, darling."

We crossed the avenue and went into a shopping center. It was an uninviting place, and I was pretty sure Mom didn't go there. We walked to the back toward a big clothing store, a truly huge one that I don't think Mom had ever been to, either. Before we went in he said to me, "Don't get lost," and gave me his hand, which was cold and very soft. He waved to the cashiers the same way he'd waved to the desk attendants when we left the hospital, but no one responded. We walked down the aisles. In addition to dresses, pants, and shirts, there were work clothes: hard hats, yellow overalls like the ones trash collectors wear, smocks for cleaning ladies, plastic boots, and even some tools. I wondered if he bought his clothes there and if he would use any of those things in his job, and then I also wondered what his name was.

"Here we are," he said.

We were surrounded by tables of underwear for men and women. If I reached out, I could touch a large bin full of giant underpants, bigger than any I'd seen before, and they were only three pesos each. With one of those pairs of underpants, they could have made three for someone my size.

"Not those," he said. "Here." And he led me a little farther, to a section with smaller sizes. "Look at all the underpants they have. Which will you choose, my lady?"

I looked around a little. Almost all of them were white or pink. I pointed to a white pair, one of the few that didn't have a bow on them.

"These," I said. "But I can't pay for them."

He came a little closer and said into my ear: "That doesn't matter."

"Are you the owner?"

"No. It's your birthday."

I smiled.

"But we have to find better ones. We need to be sure."

"Okay, darling," I ventured.

"Don't say 'darling,'" he said. "I'll get persnickety." And he imitated me holding down my skirt in the parking lot.

He made me laugh. When he finished clowning around, he

held out two closed fists, and he stayed just like that until I understood; I touched the right one. He opened it: it was empty.

"You can still choose the other one."

I touched the other one. It took me a moment to realize it was a pair of underpants, because I had never seen black ones before. And they were for girls because they had white hearts on them, so small they looked like dots, and Hello Kitty's face was on the front, right where there was usually that bow that Mom and I don't like at all.

"You'll have to try them on," he said.

I held the underpants to my chest. He gave me his hand again and we went toward the changing rooms, which looked empty. We peered in. He said he didn't know if he could go in with me, because they were for women only. He said I would have to go alone. It was logical because, unless it's someone you know very well, it's not good for people to see you in your underpants. But I was afraid of going into the dressing room alone. Or something worse: coming out and not seeing him there.

"What's your name?" I asked.

"I can't tell you that."

"Why not?"

He knelt down. Then he was almost my height, or maybe I was a couple inches taller.

"Because I'm cursed."

"Cursed? What's cursed?"

"A woman who hates me said that the next time I say my name, I'm going to die."

I thought it might be another joke, but he said it very seriously.

"You could write it down for me."

"Write it down?"

"If you wrote it, you wouldn't say it: you'd be writing it. And if I know your name, I can call for you and I won't be so scared to go into the dressing room alone."

"But we can't be sure. What if this woman thinks writing my name is the same as saying it? What if by saying it, she meant letting someone else know, letting my name out into the world in any way?"

"But how would she know?"

"People don't trust me, and I'm the unluckiest man in the world."

"I don't believe you. There's no way she'd find out."

"I know what I'm talking about."

Together, we looked at the underpants in my hands. I thought my parents might be finished by now.

"But it's my birthday," I said.

And maybe I did it on purpose. At the time I felt like I did: my eyes filled with tears.

Then he hugged me. It was a very fast movement; he crossed his arms behind my back and squeezed me so tight my face pressed into his chest. Then he let me go, took out his magazine and pen, and wrote something on the right edge of the cover. Then he tore it off and folded it three times before handing it to me.

"Don't read it," he said, and he stood up and pushed me gently toward the dressing room.

I passed four empty cubicles. Before gathering my courage and entering the fifth, I put the paper into the pocket of my jumper and turned to look at him, and we smiled at each other.

I tried on the underpants. They were perfect. I lifted up my jumper so I could see just how good they looked. They were so, so very perfect. They fit incredibly well, and because they were black, Dad would never ask me for them so he could wave them out the window behind the ambulance. And even if he did, I wouldn't be so embarrassed if my classmates saw. *Just look at the underpants that girl has,* they'd all think. *Now, those are some perfect underpants.*

I realized I couldn't take them off now. And I realized something else: They didn't have a security tag. They had a little mark where the tag would usually go, but there was no alarm. I stood a moment longer looking at myself in the mirror, and then I couldn't stand it anymore and I took out the little paper, opened it, and read it.

I came out of the dressing room and he wasn't where I had left him, but then I saw him a little farther away, next to the bathing suits. He looked at me, and when he saw I wasn't carrying the underpants, he winked, and I was the one who took his hand. This time he held on to me tighter; we walked together toward the exit.

I trusted that he knew what he was doing, that a cursed man who had the world's worst luck knew how to do these things. We passed the line of registers at the main entrance. One of the security guards glanced at us and adjusted his belt. He would surely think the nameless man was my dad, and I felt proud.

We passed the sensors at the exit and went into the mall, and we kept walking in silence all the way back to the avenue. That was when I saw Abi, alone, in the middle of the hospital parking lot. And I saw Mom, on our side of the street, looking around frantically. Dad was also coming toward us from the parking lot. He was following fast behind the policeman who'd been looking at our car before, and who was now pointing at us. Everything happened very quickly. Dad saw us, yelled my name, and a few seconds later that policeman and two others who came out of nowhere were on top of us. The unlucky man let go of me, but I held my hand suspended toward him for a few seconds. They surrounded him and shoved him roughly. They asked what he was doing, they asked his name, but he didn't answer. Mom hugged me and checked me over from head to toe. She had my white underpants dangling from her right hand. Then, patting me all over, she noticed I was wearing a different pair. She lifted my jumper in a single movement: it was such a rude and vulgar thing to do, right there in front of everyone, that I jerked away and had to take a few steps backward to keep from falling down. The unlucky man looked at me and I looked at him. When Mom saw the black underpants, she screamed, "Son of a bitch, son of a bitch," and Dad lunged at him and tried to punch him. The cops moved to separate them.

I fished for the paper in my jumper pocket, put it in my mouth, and as I swallowed it I repeated his name in silence, several times, so I would never forget it.

The O. Henry Prize Winners 2022

The Writers on Their Work

Chimamanda Ngozi Adichie, "Zikora"
What inspired your story?

A friend had told me a story about an acquaintance who had been "ghosted" by a man she thought she was in a serious and near-perfect relationship with. It struck me as almost surreal, this idea of a person you think you know so well just disappearing, leaving you to question everything, including yourself. Also, since I had my daughter, I have longed to see in fiction the grittier and more realistic details of birthing a child. And so both ideas gradually coalesced to become "Zikora."

Chimamanda Ngozi Adichie is the author of award-winning and bestselling novels, including *Americanah* and *Half of a Yellow Sun*; the short story collection *The Thing Around Your Neck*; the essays "We Should All Be Feminists" and "Dear Ijeawele, or A Feminist Manifesto in Fifteen Suggestions"; and a memoir, *Notes on Grief*.

'Pemi Aguda, "Breastmilk"
What inspired your story?

"Breastmilk" was inspired by a lecture I attended in 2018 at the University of Michigan, given by Ruth Behar, poet and anthropologist. She told a story about a woman she'd met on her travels. She lost all her babies, this woman told Behar, because there was too much rage in her breastmilk. This image, and situation, stayed with me. That our bodies absorb and express mental unrest is true, yes, but to have this direct connection—this causality—stated so starkly was a jolt. Around me, there were also many conversations about what feminism looks like in the privacy of a home, inside a life, especially in a Nigerian context. What if a woman's grappling with these questions coincided with a similar psychosomatic breastmilk situation? What could an inability to breastfeed force her to confront? These questions led me to the story.

'Pemi Aguda is from Lagos, Nigeria. She has an MFA from the Helen Zell Writers' Program. Her work has been supported by a Bread Loaf writers' scholarship, an Octavia E. Butler Memorial Scholarship, and an Aspen Words emerging writer fellowship. Her novel-in-progress won the 2020 Deborah Rogers Foundation Writers Award. She is a 2021 fiction fellow with the Miami Book Fair and a 2022 MacDowell fellow. Her work has appeared in *Ploughshares, Zoetrope, Granta, ZYZZYVA,* Tor.com, *American Short Fiction,* and *One Story,* among others.

Tere Dávila, "Mercedes's Special Talent"
Did you know how your story would end at its inception?

I knew the story ended in death because it's what obsessed the real people who inspired it. Mercedes and George are the fictional names of my friend Robert Garni's parents, whom he described at length (accompanied by lots of eye-rolling) as we drank after work. As I wrote, I found myself speaking in my friend's voice—he finds irony and humor in every situation—and reacting to Mercedes's special brand of weirdness as if I were he. This is, after all, also Robert's story: when we first met, before knowing he was gay, I had a huge crush on him, and I imagine it must have been hard to come out to a woman like Mercedes back in the late 1970s.

When I was five years old my parents divorced, and I was sent to live with my maternal grandparents for a year. Some scenes in the story are drawn from memories of their relationship, which seemed to be fraught with conflict even though if anybody asked them to stop fighting (as people did) both would vehemently affirm they got along famously. Mercedes is also in part my own death-obsessed grandmother, a strong-headed woman who insisted, against everybody's advice, on running a tropical guest-house well into her nineties, and who once found Hollywood legend Eddie Fisher in her backyard (he strolled in during a visit to the island, in 1960, when he was performing in the nearby El San Juan Hotel), but instead of asking for an autograph scolded him for trespassing.

My own family has more than its share of quirky matriarchs. As one in a long line of driven women, I can relate to Mercedes and how her hypochondria became a mechanism (if not the most positive) of dealing with societal and personal expectations and with a sense of responsibility that overwhelmed her.

Tere Dávila is the recipient of two Puerto Rican National Literature Awards: for the novel *Nenísimas* and the short story collection *Aquí están las instrucciones,* both published in 2018. Her other short fiction books are *El verano de la carne de león* (2019), *Lego* (2013), and *El fondillo maravilloso* (2009). Her stories have been translated into English and featured in anthologies and literary magazines, including *The Offing, The Common, Hayden's Ferry Review,* and *World Literature Today.* In 2020, she won a Best of the Net Award for her story "Yellow Jaguar" and was a finalist in Puerto Rico's PEN Club literary awards. Her short story "El fondillo maravilloso" has been adapted into an award-winning short film.

Rebecca Hanssens-Reed is a translator and writer from Philadelphia. Her work has appeared in *World Literature Today, Conjunctions, The Offing, New England Review, Hayden's Ferry Review,* and elsewhere. Her translation of Tere Dávila's short story "Yellow Jaguar" was selected for the 2020 Best of the Net anthology. She has an MFA in literary translation from the University of Iowa, where she was also a Provost's Postgraduate Visiting Writer.

Yohanca Delgado, "The Little Widow from the Capital"
What inspired your story?

The initial spark for this story came from a Latin American children's rhyme, which was, for me growing up bilingual in New York and the Dominican Republic, the Spanish equivalent of "Eenie Meenie Miney Moe." It's called "Arroz con leche" and the gist of it is that arroz con leche, a delicious dessert—and apparently also a bachelor—is searching for a wife. According to the song, the perfect woman will be a little widow from the capital who knows how to sew, who knows how to embroider, and who puts the needle back in its place.

When I was working through this concept, of writing a story inspired by this nursery rhyme, one of my first convictions was the certainty that I wanted this woman's "ideal" qualities to be double-edged. So, the notion that she is a little unassuming widow, and therefore sort of sad and undemanding and grateful for any attention, is only a surface perception—it doesn't take into account that she possesses a fierce independence and that it has only been sharpened by experience. And in that same vein, when it came to the little widow's emblem of successful domesticity, her needle, I wanted it to reflect a very specific artistic mastery, and to also be a weapon, as sharp and dangerous as any sword.

That the story is set entirely in the domestic sphere is no accident. I wanted to celebrate how full of life and magic and imagination these domestic spaces are *because* they are the spaces that women have traditionally occupied. Ultimately, this is a story about women talking to each other at home, and about the power of our shared narratives.

Yohanca Delgado is a 2021–23 Wallace Stegner fellow at Stanford University and a recipient of a National Endowment for the Arts literature fellowship. Her recent writing appears in *The Paris Review, The New York Times Magazine, The Best American Science Fiction and Fantasy 2021, One Story, A Public Space,* and elsewhere. She holds an MFA in creative writing from American University.

Francisco González, "Clean Teen"
Is there anything you would like readers to know about your story?

"Clean Teen" went through several changes of narrative perspective over the course of two dozen drafts. The evolving story transitioned from third person to first and back again, with a few stints in second. Third person was most conducive to the outward zoom of the final passage, which confirms the protagonist's invisibility.

Francisco González's fiction appears in *Arts & Letters, Gulf Coast, The Southern Review, ZYZZYVA,* and elsewhere. He holds an MFA from Columbia University. He is a 2022–2024 Wallace Stegner fellow at Stanford University.

Christos Ikonomou, "Where They Always Meet"
Why was the short story format the best vehicle for your ideas?

I feel more at home with the short story format. In a good short story, there is always this sense of beauty, mystery, and rhythm—a sense of something that needs to be compact, exciting, both immediate and implicit, imminent, swift, urgent, vivid. There are no second chances in short story writing—you need to get it right down to the smallest detail, otherwise the whole thing will fall in pieces.

Christos Ikonomou was born in Athens in 1970. He is the author of numerous works of fiction. He has received several awards for his writing both at home and abroad. His work has appeared in many Greek and international anthologies and has been translated into fourteen languages.

Karen Emmerich is a translator of modern Greek literature and an associate professor of comparative literature at Princeton University, where she directs the Program in Translation and Intercultural Communication. Her translation awards include the National Translation Award in 2019 for Ersi Sotiropoulos's *What's Left of the Night,* the Best Translated Book Award in 2017 for Eleni Vakalo's *Before Lyricism,* and the PEN Award for Poetry in Translation in 2014 for Yannis Ritsos's *Diaries of Exile.*

Daniel Mason, "The Wolves of Circassia"
What inspired your story?

I began this story in April 2020, shortly after the first shelter-in-place orders in California. Beyond the medical questions we were asking during those early days, I found myself constantly thinking about how the sudden changes might affect our social and internal worlds as well. What would such "shelter" be like, and how would we endure the isolation? What would happen to relationships when people are brought together or pulled apart? How would the uneven burden of responsibility affect those who bear it? How would we make sacrifices between what we give to strangers and what we reserve for those we love? This story was a chance to explore these questions during a time of great uncertainty. Looking back now, it is strange to see how much has changed about the pandemic, and yet how so much of the story continues to unfold.

Daniel Mason is the author of the collection *A Registry of My Passage upon the Earth,* a finalist for the 2021 Pulitzer Prize and winner of a California Book Award, and three novels, including *The Winter Soldier* and *The Piano Tuner*. His work has been translated into twenty-eight languages and awarded a Guggenheim Fellowship, the Joyce Carol Oates Prize for fiction, and a fellowship from the National Endowment for the Arts. He is an assistant professor in the Stanford University Department of Psychiatry.

Amar Mitra, "The Old Man of Kusumpur"
What inspired your story?

In literature, one must have the guts to tread the untrodden path. And this connection let me recall my experience of visiting the river Subarnarekha. I was then staying at a mufassal gunge area ten miles from that river. During the time of "hut" (big rural bazaar two days in a week), I heard some traders and their clients coming across the river. Let me tell you that Subarnarekha is believed to have its sands mixed with gold particles. On the other bank of the river one can see the temple of Rameswaram Shiva and the vast area of jungle. I did not know how to negotiate this unknown path, how to reach the unknown villagers, to get to know the people I have never met. And there were those forests, the hills and the vast fields. One morning as I was walking alone toward the river I asked some passersby about the route I was supposed to take. The villagers were curious to know the village or the house I was going to visit. When they heard that I was going to see the river, they were visibly puzzled. Why should one take the trouble to see a river? That journey was actually my passage to the world of literature. I wished to reach the river, which was both real and imaginary. I feel that literature, like life, is a journey into the unknown, uncertain future. We write to reach to that unknown reality. While spending our days, we experience so many magical moments. These moments had been depicted in my short stories and novels. This is what inspired me to write this story, "The Old Man of Kusumpur." The myth of gold particles available at the riverbed allegorically creates the existence and nonexistence of the Big Man.

Amar Mitra, in 1947, at the time of India's partition, migrated with his family from East Pakistan (now Bangladesh). Brought up in the city of Kolkata, Amar Mitra has traveled extensively across West Bengal and studied the shades of rural Bengal, the land, its people. Having lived in Kolkata, he has also observed the nuances of urban living. The rural and the urban are present in equal measure in the body of his work. He has received numerous awards— the Sahitya Akademi Award (2006) for the novel *Dhruboputro,* the Bankim Puraskar (2001) for the novel *Ashwacharit,* the Katha Award (1998), the Sharat Puraskar (2018), and many others. He was also invited as a speaker at the First Forum of Asian Writers, held in 2019 in Nur-Sultan, Kazakhstan.

Anish Gupta is a senior journalist who has worked for leading Indian publications such as *Amrita Bazar Patrika, Sunday,* the *Hindustan Times,* and *The Bengal Post.* He also lent editorial support to English publications in Bangladesh. Currently, he works on writing and translation assignments. In 2019, Gupta translated Lal Bhatia's book, *Indicting Goliath,* into Bengali. It is an insider's account of an international money-laundering racket run with the connivance of some of the world's leading banks, and the U.S. Justice Department's refusal to clamp down. Gupta began his career as a documentary filmmaker, codirecting a prizewinning film on the Munda tribe inhabiting the present state of Jharkhand in eastern India. Gupta is well traveled in India, especially in the Himalayan region. The environment is among his many interests. He also publishes a Bengali paper on the subject for young people.

Lorrie Moore, "Face Time"
Did you know how your story would end at its inception?

Endings! The sound and meaning of the end must be a continuation of the sound and meaning throughout the story but also something of a surprise—not a twist but a small beam of differently tinged light. I knew the father character would die, as my father had, but what would be the words to describe it and its aftermath? I didn't know. A storm had indeed come through the day after his death, so I thought, *Why not go with what happened in real life?,* not always the best idea in storytelling. The final sentence I could not get right—I felt there was a beat missing. I showed it to three writer friends, one woman and two men. The two men said, "Whatever you do, don't touch the ending!" The woman writer friend said the ending needed more. I told her I agreed with her, that it needed one additional beat. But I couldn't find it. Couldn't find anything in service of that beat that suited, though I tried. Eventually I had to go with the advice from the guys. And sometimes I hear it the way they do, and other times I don't.

Lorrie Moore is the author of three novels and four collections of stories. She teaches at Vanderbilt University.

Eshkol Nevo, "Lemonade"
What inspired your story?

At the beginning of the first COVID lockdown in Israel, different people I know were repeating the same sentence (while collapsing, financially or mentally): "Let's try to make lemonade out of this lemon." I thought it was ridiculous. I thought it was heartbreaking. And I thought a story might be the best way to find out what happens if we take this attitude to the extreme.

As always, I started writing without knowing how it would end. As always, my own memories, fears, and passions osmosed into the story.

Eshkol Nevo was born in 1971 in Jerusalem. He is one of Israel's most critically and commercially acclaimed writers and also co-runs the biggest creative writing school in that country. All his books have been bestsellers in Israel, and his work has been translated into a dozen languages. His novels have sold over a million copies globally and won or been nominated for several literary prizes. *Homesick* (2004) was awarded the Reimond Vallier Prize in France (2008), shortlisted for the Sapir Prize in Israel (2005), and longlisted for the Independent Foreign Fiction Prize in the United Kingdom. *World Cup Wishes* (2007) won the Golden Book Prize in Israel and was awarded the ADEI-WIZO Prize in Italy. *Neuland* (2011) was awarded the Steimatzky Prize for Book of the Year and was included in *The Independent*'s books of the year for 2014. *Three Floors Up* (2015) won Israel's Platinum Book Prize, won the WIZO Prize in France, was a bestseller in Italy, and was described by *The New York Times* as "mesmerizing." It was also adapted for the big screen by Italian cult director Nanni Moretti and screened at the 2021 Cannes Film Festival. Nevo's last novel, *The Last Interview*, was published in 2018 and spent thirty weeks at the top of the Israeli bestseller lists. It was also a bestseller in Italy, voted one of the best books of the year for 2019 by the *Cor-*

riere della sera, and was on the short list for the Lattes Grinzane Prize. In France, *The Last Interview* was shortlisted for the Prix Femina Étranger in 2020. Nevo's most recent work, *Vocabolario dei desideri* (The Vocabulary of Desires), is a book based on his popular weekly column in *Vanity Fair* Italy. The book is a joint venture with the Italian artist Pax Paloscia. Eshkol Nevo lives in Ra'anana, Israel, with his wife and three daughters.

Sondra Silverston has translated the work of Israeli fiction writers such as Etgar Keret, Eshkol Nevo, Zeruya Shalev, and Ayelet Gundar-Goshen. Her translation of Amos Oz's *Between Friends* won the National Jewish Book Award for fiction in 2013. Born in the United States, she has lived in Israel since 1970.

Michel Nieva, "Dengue Boy"
Is there anything you would like readers to know about your story?

When the COVID-19 pandemic started, Argentina was suffering from an endemic dengue outbreak. This mosquito-borne disease is typical in tropical weather and had increased its geographical span due to climate change. Furthermore, agribusiness plays a key role in propagating this disease. The rapid advance of soy monoculture in the Southern Cone during the past twenty years produced a never-before-seen deforestation of jungles and uncontrolled pesticide spraying, phenomena that exterminate biodiversity, eradicate the ecosystems where mosquitoes live, and attract them to human populations, especially to suburban and impoverished areas.

The case of a friend who became seriously ill due to this disease during the COVID-19 pandemic inspired my interest in this major problem.

As I am a science fiction writer, it occurred to me to imagine a future where climate change and dengue would radically transform society. With the help of an illustrator, I designed a map of a future Argentina violently transformed by the melting of the Antarctic ice sheet, which turned Pampas and Patagonia into putrid and burning beaches.

The rest is the story you have in your hands.

Michel Nieva (1988) was born in Buenos Aires, Argentina. He is the author of the poetry collection *Papelera de reciclaje,* the novels *¿Sueñan los gauchoides con ñandúes eléctricos?* and *Ascenso y apogeo del imperio argentino,* and the essay collection *Tecnología y barbarie.* In 2021, he was chosen by *Granta* magazine as one of the best writers in Spanish under thirty-five.

Natasha Wimmer is the translator of nine books by Roberto Bolaño, including *The Savage Detectives* and *2666.* Her recent translations include novels by Nona Fernández and Álvaro Enrigue. She lives in New York City.

Joseph O'Neill, "Rainbows"
What inspired your story?

There are at least three stories here—the story of the mentor, the story of the Chinese immigrant family, and the story of the Irish narrator and her family—each separately inspired, and each the subject of separate entries in the file of story notes that I keep. It has become my method, I realize, to intuitively combine such apparently unconnected elements, and to trust my intuition in preference to more conscious, more mechanical processes. It's only after the story has been made into a single whole that the dream logic, or dream gravity, becomes more legible, and that I begin to see how the combination works, and to what effect. If the story feels rich and surprising to you, the writer, with luck it will have the same effect on the reader.

The Chinese family was directly inspired by the real-life family that operates the laundry my family uses, although I hasten to add that the somewhat scandalous events in which I fictionally embroil them are wholly concocted!

Joseph O'Neill is the author of four novels (including *Netherland,* which won the 2009 PEN/Faulkner Award) and a book of short stories, *Good Trouble.* His fiction has been published in *The New Yorker* and *Harper's Magazine.* O'Neill was born in Ireland, grew up in Europe, and now lives in New York. He teaches at Bard College.

Gunnhild Øyehaug, "Apples"
What inspired your story?

I'm often inspired by writing, or various forms of language in use, narration—it could be a sign, an article, a biography, a text written below a piece of art in an art exhibition, an official letter about vaccines, etc.—and I'm often fascinated with a certain tonality, or how a message is being performed. In this case it was an actor in a Norwegian television series; he was to me the embodiment of a certain dark, nearly pompous seriousness, which I find quite often is regarded as close to a sense of "truth," something "intimate, honest," as the narrator points out himself in the first part of the story. I borrowed that voice to write the first part, until reality kicked in with the metafictional shift. And that was the starting point, for how the story would move in and out of fiction and metafiction, and for how it would discuss the possibility of "freezing time," and reality, and narration, point of view. It had a very logical structure that presented itself almost in a flash, but at the same time, I didn't know Signe would have a daughter before she called out for her. And to me, that is really the core. I had a cousin who had Down syndrome, I grew up with her, and I loved her very much. When Sonja presented herself so unexpectedly in the story, I modeled her on my cousin, to remember and love her forever.

Gunnhild Øyehaug was born in Norway in 1975. She is an author and teacher at the Academy of Creative Writing in Vestland. She has an MA in comparative literature from the University of Bergen. She made her debut with the poetry collection *Slaven av blåbæret* (Slave of the Blueberry) in 1998. After a short story collection (*Knots,* 2004) and an essay collection (*Stol og ekstase* [Chair and Ecstasy], 2006), she had her great breakthrough with her first novel, *Wait, Blink,* in 2008. The novel was published by Farrar, Straus and Giroux in 2018 and was longlisted for the National Book Award. She has continued to write in different genres, as well as for film, and has received several awards, among them the Dobloug and Sult prizes in 2009. Her books have been translated into several languages. Her latest publication is the short story collection *Vonde blomar* (2020), which will be published by Farrar, Straus and Giroux in 2023, under the title *Evil Flowers.*

Kari Dickson is a literary translator from the Norwegian. Her work includes crime fiction, literary fiction, children's books, theater, and nonfiction. She is also an occasional tutor in Norwegian language, literature, and translation at the University of Edinburgh and has worked with the British Centre for Literary Translation and the National Centre for Writing.

Janika Oza, "Fish Stories"
What made you want to re-create this particular world/reality in fiction?

In this story, I wanted to occupy that ambiguous space between waking and dreaming. It's the space of hauntings: I'm interested in how we can be haunted by a memory, a place, an action we did or didn't take, and how these hauntings can manifest in very physical ways, like how we sleep or dream or digest. And I wanted to take it one step further and consider what it might mean if that haunting walked through the front door. For the mother in the story, this is absolutely real, and I was interested in how the daughter would respond to something she doesn't perceive but maybe wishes she could. It felt to me that the mother had opened her eyes to a better world, one in which her son had returned, but the whole time we're poised on the edge of this world, knowing that at any moment she might blink and see another reality. The important part for me was the idea of perception—both worlds are real, and in a way the mother's longing and grief are so strong that they materialize before her. The daughter may not see the world in the same way, but I also wanted her to occupy this space of possibility, where she chooses to accept rather than disrupt her mother's understanding of reality. It's an act of mercy or grace. I see it as a kind of love.

Janika Oza is a writer based in Toronto. She is the winner of the 2020 Kenyon Review Short Fiction Contest and has received support from the Millay Colony, the *Tin House* summer and winter workshops, Voices of Our Nations Arts Foundation, and the *One Story* Summer Writers Conference. Her stories and essays have appeared in publications such as *The Best Small Fictions* 2019, *Catapult, The Adroit Journal, Prairie Schooner,* and *The Cincinnati Review,* among others. Her debut novel, *A History of Burning,* is forthcoming in 2023 from Grand Central Publishing (United States) and McClelland & Stewart (Canada).

David Ryan, "Warp and Weft"
What inspired your story?

This story came out of this writing practice I'd started a couple of years ago—a generative method too convoluted and nerdy to get into here. But one branch of it involves freewriting as spontaneously as possible around the idea of a fugue and musical counterpoint: where there's an opening "statement," then subsequent freewriting plays around and counters that statement in different, often rather buried, ways. In this story, "Warp and Weft," I was interested in how one self-contained vignette might speak into the ear of a series of other short vignettes, each with their own narrative weave, their own beginning, middle, and end. Like a game of telephone in which very little might be recognized in the chain of whispers from one story to the next on the surface, and yet something like an X-ray of glancing elements is retained. The work gets laced up in the uncanny silence, the hidden impulsive glow of the bones.

But the much larger generative influence on this piece is much easier to name: my daughter. When she was born, I began to see the concept of time very differently than I had before. Or maybe it's better to say that I suddenly understood what "temporary" meant, how quickly life suddenly races along when you have a kid. And this sense of urgency bound up in time seems to have changed my understanding of love, too. A clock, a very different clock, is now ticking against every walk we go on, every book we read together, every good night I say. Because I can't fathom the idea of some next morning never arriving. The other thing is, having become a parent, I can only marvel at just how many ways I could screw up the time I still have. And, so, I seem these days to write a lot of stories that rehearse all our potential for failures of judgment. And then there's my love of the children's book author Leo Lionni—whose *Frederick* was my favorite book we'd read with our daughter. Though every bit of this story was a surprise as I wrote it, Lionni's *Frederick* dropping into the ending was the biggest surprise: as if the charged memory of reading it with my daughter had been the driving energy of this story all along.

· · · ·

David Ryan is the author of the story collection *Animals in Motion* (Roundabout Press). His work has appeared in *The Threepenny Review, Kenyon Review, Conjunctions, BOMB,* and elsewhere. A recent recipient of an Artistic Excellence fellowship from the Connecticut Office of the Arts and a past Elizabeth Yates McGreal writer-in-residence, he's currently at work on a novel.

Samanta Schweblin, "An Unlucky Man"
Do you consider your story to be personal or political?

It operates in both senses. It's personal, because it's autobiographical up until the waiting room scene. Also, as I've gained more distance over time, I've realized how much the character of the unlucky man could be based on my maternal grandfather and the mischief we used to get into when I was that age. But it's also political, because this story revolves around the idea of the perverse that we all harbor: in this story, the darkness happens above all in the reader's mind. Without the reader's fears and prejudices, this story wouldn't work. Without my own fears and prejudices, I never would have been able to write this story.

Samanta Schweblin was born and raised in Buenos Aires and is currently living in Berlin. She is the author of three multi-award-winning collections of short stories, some of which have appeared in many newspapers and magazines, such as *The New Yorker, Harper's Magazine, Granta,* and *McSweeney's.* Her two novels, *Fever Dream* and *Little Eyes,* were respectively shortlisted and longlisted for the International Booker Prize. Her works have been translated into more than thirty languages.

Megan McDowell has translated many of the most important Latin American writers working today, including Samanta Schweblin, Alejandro Zambra, Mariana Enriquez, and Lina Meruane. Her translations have won the English PEN award, the Premio Valle-Inclán, and the Shirley Jackson Award, and have been nominated four times for the International Booker Prize and once for the Kirkus Prize. In 2020, she won an award in literature from the American Academy of Arts and Letters. Her short story translations have been featured in *The New Yorker, Harper's Magazine, The Paris Review, Tin House, McSweeney's,* and *Granta,* among others. She is from Richmond, Kentucky, and lives in Santiago, Chile.

Shanteka Sigers, "A Way with Bea"
What made you want to re-create this particular world/reality in fiction?

I have a collection of stories that take place in my imagined version of Chicago. I'm never on the nose, block by block, but I hope it feels precise in spirit. I've lived a lot of my life there, so I suppose it naturally shows up as a comfortable setting for characters to roam about in. My mother and I both lived in Garfield Park and as I'd travel back and forth to her house, I would see so much to preserve and so much that needed to be rewritten.

Shanteka Sigers lives in Austin, Texas. She is a graduate of Northwestern University and New York University's MFA Writers Workshop in Paris. Her work has appeared in the *Chicago Reader*'s annual fiction issue, *The Paris Review,* and *The Best American Short Stories.*

Vladimir Sorokin, "Horse Soup"
What inspired your story?

In the fall of 1995, I was admitted to a Moscow hospital with an inflamed appendix, which was subsequently removed, necessitating a five-day stay in the hospital until the suture healed. I was sharing my room with another man. Somehow, we got to discussing the hospital's unpretentious lunch menu. This conversation caused him to remember an episode when he and his young wife had been on a train back to Moscow after their honeymoon in Crimea. A man joined them in the restaurant car. He also ordered something, ate, then said, "Thank you, young people, for being so beautiful and eating that beautiful food so beautifully" (they were eating steak and eggs). "I spent seven years in a camp, and for all those years, we ate the same food every day: pig's head soup and millet porridge. Around me were distinctly unbeautiful people, with whom I perpetually ate this disgusting slop. And these people ate very unbeautifully too. Might I just sit and watch the way you eat?" I never forgot this story. Five years later, I ended up in Japan, where I taught for two years at Keio University. There, I decided to write a book called *Feast* that would be dedicated to food. It consisted of various stories that were, in one way or another, connected to food, with the rituals of its preparation and consumption, with that archaic and, in many ways, mysterious process, occupied with which most people spend a good portion of their lives. It was then that my roommate from the hospital's story came back to me. It'd lain in wait for five years in my memory the way wild game is laid out in the cellar before being roasted. And I prepared my own literary dish using that story: "Horse Soup."

Vladimir Georgievich Sorokin is a writer of novels, short stories, theatrical works, and screenplays, and an artist. Born on August 7, 1955, in Podmoskovie, he studied at the Gubkin Russian State University of Oil and Gas and became a writer during the eighties in the Moscow underground. His first book, *The Queue*, was published in Paris in 1985. He has written twelve novels, as well as many short stories, theatrical works, and screenplays. His books have been translated into thirty languages.

. . .

Max Lawton is a translator, novelist, and musician. He received his BA in Russian literature and culture from Columbia University and his MPhil from the Queen's College, Oxford, where he wrote a dissertation comparing Céline and Dostoyevsky. He has translated many books by Vladimir Sorokin. Max is also the author of a novel currently awaiting publication and is writing his doctoral dissertation on phenomenology and the twentieth-century novel at Columbia University, where he teaches Russian.

Olga Tokarczuk, "Seams"
What inspired your story?

I believe that the short story is the most perfect and the most demanding form of prose. It requires focus and precision. The idea for this story came to me suddenly and right away in a finished form after visiting an elderly man who was trying to cope with life after the death of his wife. This visit touched me a lot and the only way to express my emotions was to find a literary form for them.

Olga Tokarczuk is the recipient of the 2018 Nobel Prize in Literature. She is one of Poland's most celebrated authors. She is the author of eight novels and three short story collections and has twice won the most prestigious Polish literary prize, the Nike Literary Award, for *Flights* (*Bieguni*) in 2008 and for *The Books of Jacob* (*Ksiegi Jakubowe*) in 2015. Her most famous novels include *Primeval* (*Prawiek i inne czazy*), published in 1996; *House of Day, House of Night* (*Dom dzienny, dom nocny*), published in 1998; *Flights,* published in 2007, which also won the 2018 International Booker Prize and was shortlisted for the 2018 National Book Award for Translated Literature; and *Drive Your Plow Over* the Bones of the Dead (*Prowadz swoj plug przez kosci umarlych*), which was published in 2009 and shortlisted for the 2019 International Booker Prize and longlisted for the National Book Award for Translated Literature, the Dublin Literary Award, and the Warwick Prize. *The Books of Jacob* was published in English by Fitzcarraldo, Riverhead, and Text Publishing in 2021 in a translation by Jennifer Croft. Her work has been translated into more than forty-five languages. Olga Tokarczuk lives in Wrocław in Poland, where she is setting up a foundation that will offer scholarships for writers and translators and educational programs on literature.

Jennifer Croft won the 2020 William Saroyan International Prize for Writing for her illustrated memoir *Homesick* and the 2018 International Booker Prize for her translation from Polish of Nobel laureate Olga Tokarczuk's *Flights*. She holds a PhD from Northwestern University and an MFA from the University of Iowa.

Alejandro Zambra, "Screen Time"
Did you know how your story would end at its inception?

Not at all. I just had this formless feeling and a few images I wanted to deal with. I was reluctant about writing about the pandemic. A part of me, like 62 percent, just wanted to play with my kid all day long. Maybe that is why I decided to write this in the third person. I felt that everything that was happening happened to me and to everybody in the third person.

Alejandro Zambra is the author of six works of fiction, including *Chilean Poet*, *Multiple Choice*, and *My Documents*. The recipient of numerous literary prizes and a New York Public Library

Cullman Center Fellowship, his stories have appeared in *The New Yorker, The New York Times Magazine, The Paris Review, Granta,* and *Harper's Magazine,* among others. He lives in Mexico City.

Megan McDowell has translated many of the most important Latin American writers working today, including Samanta Schweblin, Alejandro Zambra, Mariana Enriquez, and Lina Meruane. Her translations have won the English PEN award, the Premio Valle-Inclán, and the Shirley Jackson Award, and have been nominated four times for the International Booker Prize and once for the Kirkus Prize. In 2020, she won an award in literature from the American Academy of Arts and Letters. Her short story translations have been featured in *The New Yorker, Harper's Magazine, The Paris Review, Tin House, McSweeney's,* and *Granta,* among others. She is from Richmond, Kentucky, and lives in Santiago, Chile.

Publisher's Note

A Brief History of the O. Henry Prize

Many readers have come to love the short story through the simple characters, the humor and easy narrative voice, and the compelling plotting in the work of William Sydney Porter (1862–1910), best known as O. Henry. His surprise endings entertain readers, including those back for a second, third, or fourth look. Even now one can say "Gift of the Magi" in conversation about a friendship or marriage, and many people around the world will know they are referring to the generosity and selflessness of love.

O. Henry was a newspaperman, skilled at hiding from his editors at deadline. He spent his childhood in Greensboro, North Carolina, his adolescence in Texas, and his later years in New York City. In between Texas and New York, he was caught embezzling and hid from the law in Honduras, where he coined the phrase "banana republic." On learning his wife was dying, he returned home to her and to their daughter, and subsequently served a three-year prison sentence for bank fraud in Columbus, Ohio. Accounts of the origin of his pen name vary: one story dates from his days in Austin, where he was said to call to the wandering family cat, "Oh! Henry!"; another states that the name was inspired by the captain of the guard at the Ohio State Penitentiary, Orrin

Henry. In 1909, Porter told *The New York Times,* "[A friend] suggested that we get a newspaper and pick a name from the first list of notables that we found in it. In the society columns we found the account of a fashionable ball. . . . We looked down the list and my eye lighted on the name Henry, 'That'll do for a last name,' said I. 'Now for a first name. I want something short.' 'Why don't you use a plain initial letter, then?' asked my friend. 'Good,' said I, 'O is about the easiest letter written, and O it is.' "

Porter had devoted friends, and it's not hard to see why. He was charming and had an attractively gallant attitude. He drank too much and neglected his health, which caused his friends concern. He was often short of money; in a letter to a friend asking for a loan of $15 (his banker was out of town, he wrote), Porter added a postscript: "If it isn't convenient, I'll love you just the same." His banker was unavailable most of Porter's life. His sense of humor was always with him.

Reportedly, Porter's last words were from a popular song: "Turn up the light, for I don't want to go home in the dark."

After his death, O. Henry's stories continued to penetrate twentieth-century popular culture. Marilyn Monroe starred in a film adaptation of "The Cop and the Anthem." The popular western TV series *The Cisco Kid* grew out of "The Caballero's Way." Postage stamps were issued by the Soviets to commemorate O. Henry's one hundredth birthday in 1962 and by the United States in 2012 for his one hundred fiftieth. The most lasting legacy began just eight years after O. Henry's death, in April 1918, when the Twilight Club (founded in 1883 and later known as the Society of Arts and Sciences) held a dinner in his honor at the Hotel McAlpin in New York City. His friends remembered him so enthusiastically that a group of them met at the Biltmore Hotel in December of that year to establish some kind of memorial to him. They decided to award annual prizes in his name for short story writers, and they formed a committee to read the short stories published in a year and a smaller group to pick the winners.

In the words of the first series editor, Blanche Colton Williams (1879–1944), the memorial was intended to "strengthen the art of the short story and to stimulate younger authors."

Doubleday, Page & Company was chosen to publish the first volume, *O. Henry Memorial Award Prize Stories 1919*. In 1927, the society sold all rights to the annual collection to Doubleday, Doran & Company. Doubleday published *The O. Henry Prize Stories,* as it came to be known, in hardcover, and from 1984 to 1996 its subsidiary, Anchor Books, published it simultaneously in paperback. Since 1997, *The O. Henry Prize Stories* has been published as an original Anchor Books paperback. It is now published as *The Best Short Stories: The O. Henry Prize Winners.*

How the Stories Are Chosen

The guest editor chooses the twenty O. Henry Prize winners from a large pool of stories passed to her by the series editor. Stories published in magazines and online are eligible for inclusion in *The Best Short Stories: The O. Henry Prize Winners*. Stories may be written in English or translated into English. Sections of novels are not considered. Editors are asked to send all fiction they publish and not to nominate individual stories. Stories should not be submitted by agents or writers.

The goal of *The Best Short Stories: The O. Henry Prize Winners* remains to strengthen and add visibility to the art of the short story.

The stories selected were originally published between July 2020 and November 2021.

Acknowledgments

Thank you, Jacke Wilson, for the O. Henry Prize history, Joséphine de la Bruyère, Marion Minton, Jacqueline Cleary, Caroline Hall, Dan Quigley, Sam Quigley, Gus Quigley, Leo Quigley, Elizabeth Quigley, Heather Clay, Ashley Gengras, Lisa Stevenson, Gabe Hudson, Nicole Aragi, James Meador, Angie Venezia, Aja Pollock, Eddie Allen, Paige Smith, Linda Huang, Sal Ruggiero, Jen Marshall, LuAnn Walther, Diana Secker Tesdell for her inventiveness and kindness, and especially Valeria Luiselli for finding these stories.

—Jenny Minton Quigley

Publications Submitted

Stories published in magazines and online are eligible for inclusion.

For fiction published online, the publication's contact information and the date of the story's publication should accompany the submissions.

Stories will be considered from September 1 to August 31 the following year. Publications received after August 31 will automatically be considered for the next volume of *The Best Short Stories: The O. Henry Prize Winners*.

Please submit PDF files of submissions to jenny@ohenryprize winners.com or send hard copies to Jenny Minton Quigley, c/o The O. Henry Prize Winners, 70 Mohawk Drive, West Hartford, CT 06117.

Able Muse
www.ablemuse.com
submission@ablemuse.com
Editor: Alexander Pepple
Two or three times a year

AGNI
www.agnionline.bu.edu
agni@bu.edu
Editors: Sven Birkerts and William
    Pierce
Biannual (print)

Alaska Quarterly Review
www.aqreview.org
uaa_aqr@uaa.alaska.edu
Editor: Ronald Spatz
Biannual

Amazon Original Stories
www.amazon.com
Submission by invitation only
Editor: Julia Sommerfeld
Twelve annually

American Short Fiction
www.americanshortfiction.org
editors@americanshortfiction.org
Editors: Rebecca Markovits and
    Adeena Reitberger
Triannual

Antipodes
www.wsupress.wayne.edu/journals
    /detail/antipodes-0
antipodesfiction@gmail.com
Editor: Annie Martin
Biannual

Apalachee Review
www.apalacheereview.org
christopherpaulhayes@gmail.com
Editor: Christopher Hayes
Biannual

Apogee Journal
www.apogeejournal.org
editors@apogeejournal.org
Executive Editor: Alexandra
    Watson
Biannual

The Arkansas International
www.arkint.org
info@arkint.org
Editor in Chief: Geoffrey Block
Biannual

Arkansas Review
www.arkreview.org
mtribbet@astate.edu
Editor: Marcus Tribbett
Triannual

ArLiJo
www.arlijo.com
givalpress@yahoo.com
Editor in Chief: Robert L. Giron
Ten issues a year

Ascent
www.readthebestwriting.com
ascent@cord.edu
Editor: Vincent Reusch

**The Asian American Literary
    Review**
www.aalrmag.org
editors@aalrmag.org
Editors in Chief: Lawrence-Minh
    Bùi Davis and Gerald Maa
Biannual

Aster(ix)
www.asterixjournal.com
info@asterixjournal.com
Editor in Chief: Angie Cruz
Triannual

The Atlantic
www.theatlantic.com
fiction@theatlantic.com
Editor in Chief: Jeffrey Goldberg;
    Magazine Editor: Don Peck
Monthly

Baltimore Review
www.baltimorereview.org
editor@baltimorereview.org
Senior Editor: Barbara Westwood
    Diehl
Quarterly

The Bare Life Review
www.barelifereview.org
barelifereview.submittable.com
Editor: Nyuol Lueth Tong

Bat City Review
www.batcityreview.org
fiction@batcityreview.org
Editor: Sarah Matthes
Annual

Bellevue Literary Review
www.blreview.org
info@BLReview.org
Editor in Chief: Danielle Ofri
Biannual

Bennington Review
www.benningtonreview.org
BenningtonReview@Bennington
    .edu
Editor: Michael Dumanis
Biannual

Black Warrior Review
www.bwr.ua.edu
blackwarriorreview@gmail.com
Editor: Jackson Saul
Biannual

BOMB
www.bombmagazine.org
betsy@bombsite.com
Editor in Chief: Betsy Sussler
Quarterly

Booth
www.booth.butler.edu
booth@butler.edu
Editor: Robert Stapleton
Biannual

Boulevard
www.boulevardmagazine.org
editors@boulevardmagazine.org
Editor: Jessica Rogen
Triannual

The Briar Cliff Review
www.bcreview.org
3303 Rebecca Street
Sioux City, IA 51104
Editor: Tricia Currans-Sheehan
Annual

Cagibi
www.cagibilit.com
info@cagibilit@gmail.com
Editors: Sylvie Bertrand and
    Christopher X. Shade
Quarterly

CALYX
www.calyxpress.org
editor@calyxpress.org
Editors: C. Lill Ahrens, Rachel
  Barton, Marjorie Coffey, Judith
  Edelstein, Emily Elbom, Carole
  Kalk, and Christine Rhea
Biannual

The Carolina Quarterly
www.thecarolinaquarterly.com
carolina.quarterly@gmail.com
Editor in Chief: Kylan Rice
Biannual

Carve
www.carvezine.com
azumbahlen@carvezine.com
Editor in Chief: Anna Zumbahlen
Quarterly

Catamaran
www.catamaranliteraryreader.com
editor@catamaranliteraryreader
  .com
Editor in Chief: Catherine
  Sergurson
Quarterly

Catapult
www.catapult.co
catapult.submitable.com/submit
Editor in Chief: Nicole Chung

Cherry Tree
www.washcoll.edu/learn-by-doing
  /lit-house/cherry-tree/
lit_house@washcoll.edu
Editor in Chief: James Allen Hall
Annual

Chicago Quarterly Review
www.chicagoquarterlyreview.com
cqr@icogitate.com
Senior Editors: S. Afzal Haider and
  Elizabeth McKenzie
Quarterly

Chicago Review
www.chicagoreview.org
editors@chicagoreview.org
Editor: Gerónimo Sarmiento Cruz
Triannual

Cimarron Review
www.cimarronreview.com
cimarronreview@okstate.edu
Editor: Lisa Lewis
Quarterly

The Cincinnati Review
www.cincinnatireview.com
editors@cincinnatireview.com
Managing Editor: Lisa Ampleman
Biannual

Colorado Review
www.coloradoreview.colostate.edu
  /colorado-review
creview@colostate.edu
Editor: Stephanie G'Schwind
Triannual

The Common
www.thecommononline.org
info@thecommononline.org
Editor in chief: Jennifer Acker
Biannual

Confrontation
www.confrontationmagazine.org
confrontationmag@gmail.com
Editor in chief: Jonna G. Semeiks
Biannual

Conjunctions
www.conjunctions.com
conjunctions@bard.edu
Editor: Bradford Morrow
Biannual

Copper Nickel
www.copper-nickel.org
wayne.miller@ucdenver.edu
Editor: Wayne Miller
Biannual

Crab Orchard Review
www.craborchardreview.siu.edu
jtriblle@siu.edu
Editor: Allison Joseph
Biannual

Crazyhorse
www.crazyhorse.cofc.edu
crazyhorse@cofc.edu
Editor: Anthony Varallo
Biannual

Cream City Review
www.uwm.edu/creamcityreview
info@creamcityreview.org
Editor in Chief: Su Cho
Semiannual

CutBank
www.cutbankonline.org
editor.cutbank@gmail.com
Editor in Chief: Jake Bienvenue
Biannual

The Dalhousie Review
www.ojs.library.dal.ca
    /dalhousiereview
Dalhousie.Review@Dal.ca
Editor: Anthony Enns
Triannual

Dappled Things
www.dappledthings.org
dappledthings.ann@gmail.com
Editor in Chief: Katy Carl
Quarterly

december
www.decembermag.org
editor@decembermag.org
Editor: Gianna Jacobson
Biannual

Delmarva Review
www.delmarvareview.org
editor@delmarvareview.org
Editor: Wilson Wyatt Jr.
Annual

Denver Quarterly
www.du.edu/denverquarterly
denverquarterly@gmail.com
Editor: W. Scott Howard
Quarterly

Descant
www.descant.tcu.edu
descant@tcu.edu
Editor in Chief: Matt Pitt
Annual

The Drift
www.thedriftmag.com
editors@thedriftmag.com
Editors: Kiara Barrow and Rebecca
  Panovka
Quarterly

Driftwood Press
www.driftwoodpress.net
driftwoodlit@gmail.com
Editors: James McNulty and Jerrod
  Schwarz
Quarterly

Ecotone
www.ecotonemagazine.org
info@ecotonejournal.com
Editor in Chief: David Gessner
Biannual

Electric Literature
www.electricliterature.com
editors@electricliterature.com
Executive Director: Halimah
  Marcus; Editor in Chief: Jess
  Zimmerman
Weekly

Emrys Journal
www.emrys.org
info@emrys.org
Editor: Katie Burgess
Annual

Epiphany
www.epiphanyzine.com
epiphanymagazine.submittable
  .com
Editor in Chief: Rachel Lyon
Biannual

Epoch
www.english.cornell.edu/epoch
  -magazine-0
mk64@cornell.edu
Editor: Michael Koch
Triannual

Event
www.eventmagazine.ca
event@douglascollege.ca
Editor: Sashi Bhat
Triannual

Exile Quarterly
www.exilequarterly.com
competitions@exilequarterly.com
Editor in Chief: Barry Callaghan
Quarterly

The Fiddlehead
www.thefiddlehead.ca
fiddlehead@unb.ca
Editor: Sue Sinclaire
Quarterly

Fairy Tale Review
www.fairytalereview.com
ftreditorial@gmail.com
Editor: Kate Bernheimer
Annual

Five Points
www.fivepoints.gsu.edu
fivepoints.submittable.com/submit
Editor: Megan Sexton
Biannual

Fantasy & Science Fiction
www.sfsite.com/fsf/
fsfmag@fandsf.com
Editor: Gordon Van Gelder
Bimonthly

The Florida Review
www.floridareview.cah.ucf.edu
flreview@ucf.edu
Editor: Lisa Roney
Biannual

Fence
www.fenceportal.org
rebeccafence@gmail.com
Editor: Rebecca Wolff
Biannual

Foglifter
www.foglifterjournal.com
foglifter.journal@gmail.com
Editor: Chad Koch
Biannual

Fiction
www.fictioninc.com
fictionmageditors@gmail.com
Editor: Mark Jay Mirsky
Annual

Fourteen Hills: The SFSU Review
www.14hills.net
hills@sfsu.edu
Editor in Chief: Rachel Huefner
Biannual

Fiction River
www.fictionriver.com
wmgpublishingmail@mail.com
Editors: Kristine Kathryn Rusch
    and Dean Wesley Smith
Six times a year

Freeman's
www.freemansbiannual.com
eburns@groveatlantic.com
Editor: John Freeman
Biannual

f(r)iction
www.tetheredbyletters.com
/friction
leahscott@tetheredbyletters.com
Editor in Chief: Dani Hedlund
Triannual

Gemini Magazine
www.gemini-magazine.com
editor@gemini-magazine.com
Editor: David Bright
Four to six issues per year

The Georgia Review
www.thegeorgiareview.com
garev@uga.edu
Editor: Stephen Corey
Quarterly

The Gettysburg Review
www.gettysburgreview.com
mdrew@gettysburg.edu
Editor: Mark Drew
Quarterly

Gold Man Review
www.goldmanreview.org
heather.cuthbertson@
goldmanpublishing.com
Editor in Chief: Heather
Cuthbertson
Annual

Grain
www.grainmagazine.ca
grainmag@skwriter.com
Editor: Nicole Haldoupis
Quarterly

Granta
www.granta.com
editorial@granta.com
Editor: Sigrid Rausing
Quarterly (print)

The Greensboro Review
www.greensbororeview.org
greensbororeview.submittable.com
/submit
Editor: Terry L. Kennedy
Biannual

Guernica
www.guernicamag.com
editors@guernicamag.com
Editor in Chief: Ed Winstead

**Gulf Coast: A Journal of
Literature and Fine Arts**
www.gulfcoastmag.org
gulfcoastea@gmail.com
Editor: Nick Rattner
Biannual

Harper's Magazine
www.harpers.org
letters@harpers.org
Editor: Christopher Beha
Monthly

Harpur Palate
www.harpurpalate.binghamton
.edu
harpur.palate@gmail.com
Editor in Chief: Sarah Sassone

Harvard Review
www.harvardreview.org
info@harvardreview.org
Editor: Christina Thompson
Biannual

Hayden's Ferry Review
www.haydensferryreview.com
hfr@asu.edu
Editor: Erin Noehre
Semiannual

The Hopkins Review
www.hopkinsreview.jhu.edu
wmb@jhu.edu
Editor: David Yezzi
Quarterly

Hotel Amerika
www.hotelamerika.net
editors.hotelamerika@gmail.com
Editor: David Lazar
Annual

The Hudson Review
www.hudsonreview.com
info@hudsonreview.com
Editor: Paula Deitz
Quarterly

Hunger Mountain
www.hungermtn.org
hungermtn@vcfa.edu
Editor: Erin Stalcup
Annual (print)

The Idaho Review
www.idahoreview.org
mwieland@boisestate.edu
Editors: Mitch Wieland and Brady
    Udall
Annual

Image
www.imagejournal.org
image@imagejournal.org
Editor in Chief: James K. A. Smith
Quarterly

Indiana Review
www.indianareview.org
inreview@indiana.edu
Editor in Chief: Alberto Sveum
Biannual

Into the Void
www.intothevoidmagazine.com
info@intothevoidmagazine.com
Editor: Philip Elliot
Quarterly

The Iowa Review
www.iowareview.org
iowa-review@uiowa.edu
Acting Editor: Lynne Nugent
Triannual

Iron Horse Literary Review
www.ironhorsereview.com
ihlr.mail@gmail.com
Editor: Leslie Jill Patterson
Triannual

Jabberwock Review
www.jabberwock.org.msstate.edu
jabberwockreview@english.msstate
.edu
Editor: Michael Kardos
Semiannual

The Journal
www.thejournalmag.org
managingeditor@thejournalmag
.org
Managing Editor: Daniel Barnum
Biannual

Joyland
www.joylandmagazine.com
contact@joylandmagazine.com
Editor in Chief: Michelle Lyn
King
Annual

Kenyon Review
www.kenyonreview.org
kenyonreview@kenyon.edu
Editor: Nicole Terez Dutton;
Managing Editor: Abigail
Wadsworth Serfass
Six times a year

**Lady Churchill's Rosebud
Wristlet**
www.smallbeerpress.com/lcrw
info@smallbeerpress.com
Editors: Gavin J. Grant and Kelly
Link
Biannual

Lake Effect
www.behrend.psu.edu/school-of
-humanities-social-sciences
/lake-effect
gol1@psu.edu
Editors: George Looney and Aimee
Pogson
Annual

Lalitamba
www.lalitamba.com
lalitamba_magazine@yahoo.com
Editor: Shyam Mukanda
Annual

Literary Hub
www.lithub.com
info@lithub.com
Editor: Jonny Diamond

The Literary Review
www.theliteraryreview.org
info@theliteraryreview.org
Editor: Minna Zallman Proctor
Quarterly

LitMag
www.litmag.com
info@litmag.com
Editor: Marc Berley
Annual

Little Patuxent Review
www.littlepatuxentreview.org
editor@littlepatuxentreview.org
Editor: Chelsea Lemon Fetzer
Biannual

The Louisville Review
www.louisvillereview.org
managingeditor@louisvillereview
.org
Managing Editor: Amy Foos
Kapoor
Biannual

MAKE: A Literary Magazine
www.makemag.com
info@makemag.com
Editor: Chamandeep Bains
Annual

The Malahat Review
www.malahatreview.ca
malahat@uvic.ca
Editor: Iain Higgins
Quarterly

Manoa
www.manoa.hawaii.edu
/manoajournal
mjournal-l@lists.hawaii.edu
Editor: Frank Stewart
Biannual

The Massachusetts Review
www.massreview.org
massrev@external.umass.edu
Editor: Jim Hicks
Quarterly

The Masters Review
www.mastersreview.com
contact@mastersreview.com
Editor in Chief: Cole Meyer
Annual

McSweeney's Quarterly Concern
www.mcsweeneys.net
letters@mcsweeneys.net
Founding Editor: Dave Eggers
Editor: Claire Boyle
Quarterly

Meridian
www.readmeridian.org
meridianuva@gmail.com
Editor: Suzie Eckl
Semiannual

Michigan Quarterly Review
www.michiganquarterlyreview
.com
mqr@umich.edu
Editor: Khaled Mattawa
Quarterly

Mid-American Review
www.casit.bgsu.edu
/midamericanreview
mar@bgsu.edu
Editor in Chief: Abigail Cloud
Semiannual

Midwestern Gothic
www.midwestgothic.com
info@midwesterngothic.com
Fiction Editors: Jeff Pfaller and
Robert James Russell
Biannual

Mississippi Review
www.sites.usm.edu/mississippi
  -review/
msreview@usm.edu
Editor in Chief: Adam Clay
Biannual

The Missouri Review
www.missourireview.com
question@moreview.com
Editor: Speer Morgan
Quarterly

Mizna
www.mizna.org/articles/journal
mizna@mizna.org
Editor: Lana Barkawi
Biannual

Montana Quarterly
www.themontanaquarterly.com
editor@themontanaquarterly.com
Editor in Chief: Scott McMillion
Quarterly

Mount Hope
www.mounthopemagazine.com
mount.hope.magazine@gmail.com
Editor: Edward J. Delaney
Biannual

n+1
www.nplusonemag.com
editors@nplusonemag.com
Senior Editors: Chad Harbach and
  Charles Petersen
Triannual

Narrative
www.narrativemagazine.com
info@narrativemagazine.com
Editors: Carol Edgarian and Tom
  Jenks
Triannual

NELLE
www.uab.edu/cas
  /englishpublications/nelle
editors.nelle@gmail.com
Editor: Lauren Goodwin Slaughter
Annual

New England Review
www.nereview.com
nereview@middlebury.edu
Editor: Carolyn Kuebler
Quarterly

Newfound
www.newfound.org
info@newfound.org
Editor: Laura Eppinger
Annual

New Letters
www.newletters.org
newletters@umkc.edu
Editor in Chief: Christie Hodgen
Quarterly

New Madrid
www.newmadridjournal
  .submittable.com/submit
msu.newmadrid@murraystate.edu
Editor: Ann Neelon
Biannual

New Ohio Review
www.ohio.edu/nor
noreditors@ohio.edu
Editor: David Wanczyk
Biannual

New Orleans Review
www.neworleansreview.org
noreview@loyno.edu
Editor: Lindsay Sproul
Annual

New South
www.newsouthjournal.com
newsoutheditors@gmail.com
Editor: A. Prevett
Biannual

The New Yorker
www.newyorker.com
themail@newyorker.com
Editor: David Remnick
Weekly

Nimrod International Journal
www.nimrod.utulsa.edu
nimrod@utulsa.edu
Editor: Eilis O'Neal
Biannual

Ninth Letter
www.ninthletter.com
fiction@ninthletter.com
Editor: Jodee Stanley
Biannual

Noon
www.noonannual.com
1324 Lexington Ave, PMB 298
New York, NY 10128
Editor: Diane Williams
Annual

The Normal School
www.thenormalschool.com
normalschooleditors@gmail.com
Editor in Chief: Stephen Church

North American Review
www.northamericanreview.org
nar@uni.edu
Fiction Editor: Grant Tracey

North Carolina Literary Review
www.nclr.ecu.edu
BauerM@ecu.edu
Editor: Margaret D. Bauer
Annual

North Dakota Quarterly
www.ndquarterly.org
ndq@und.edu
Editor: William Caraher
Quarterly

Northern New England Review
www.nnereview.com
douaihym@franklinpierce.edu
Editor: Margot Douaihy
Annual

No Tokens Journal
www.notokensjournal.com
NoTokensJournal@gmail.com
Editor: T Kira Mahealani Madden
Biannual

Notre Dame Review
www.ndreview.nd.edu
notredamereview@gmail.com
Fiction Editor: Steve Tomasula
Biannual

The Ocean State Review
www.oceanstatereview.org
oceanstatereview@gmail.com
Senior Editors: Elizabeth Foulke
    and Charles Kell
Annual

The Offing
theoffingmag.com
info@theoffingmag.com
Editor in Chief: Mimi Wong

One Story
www.one-story.com
one-story.submittable.com
Executive Editor: Hannah Tinti;
    Editor: Patrick Ryan
Monthly

Orca
www.orcalit.com
orcaliteraryjournal.submittable
    .com
Senior Editors: Joe Ponepinto and
    Zachary Kellian
Quarterly

Orion
www.orionmagazine.org
questions@orionmagazine.org
Editor: Sumanth Prabhaker
Quarterly

Outlook Springs
www.outlooksprings.com
outlookspringsnh@gmail.com
Editor: Andrew R. Mitchell
Triannual

Overtime
www.workerswritejournal.com
    /overtime.htm
info@workerswritejournal.com
Editor: David LaBounty
Quarterly

Oxford American
www.oxfordamerican.org
info@oxfordamerican.org
Editor: Eliza Borné
Quarterly

Pakn Treger
www.yiddishbookcenter.org
    /language-literature-culture
    /pakn-treger
pt@yiddishbookcenter.org
Editor: Aaron Lansky
Quarterly

The Paris Review
www.theparisreview.org
queries@theparisreview.org
Editor: Emily Stokes
Quarterly

Passages North
www.passagesnorth.com
passages@nmu.edu
Editor in Chief: Jennifer Howard
Annual

Pembroke Magazine
www.pembrokemagazine.com
pembrokemagazine@gmail.com
Editor: Jessica Pitchford
Annual

The Pinch
www.pinchjournal.com
editor@pinchjournal.com
Editor in Chief: Courtney Miller
    Santo
Biannual

Pleiades
www.pleiadesmag.com
pleiadescnf@gmail.com
Editors: Erin Adair-Hodges and
    Jenny Molberg
Biannual

Ploughshares
www.pshares.org
pshares@pshares.org
Editor in Chief: Ladette Randolph
Triannual

Post Road
www.postroadmag.com
info@postroadmag.com
Managing Editor: Chris Boucher
Biannual

Potomac Review
www.mcblogs.montgomerycollege
    .edu/potomacreview/
potomacrevieweditor@
    montgomerycollege.edu
Editor: John Wei Han Wang
Quarterly

Prairie Fire
www.prairiefire.ca
prfire@prairiefire.ca
Editor: Andris Taskans
Quarterly

Prairie Schooner
www.prairieschooner.unl.edu
prairieschooner@unl.edu
Editor in Chief: Kwame Dawes
Quarterly

PRISM international
www.prismmagazine.ca
prose@prismmagazine.ca
Prose Editor: Kyla Jamieson
Quarterly

A Public Space
www.apublicspace.org
general@apublicspace.org
Editor: Brigid Hughes
Quarterly

PULP Literature
www.pulpliterature.com
info@pulpliterature.com
Managing Editor: Jennifer Landels
Quarterly

Raritan
www.raritanquarterly.rutgers.edu
rqr@sas.rutgers.edu
Editor in Chief: Jackson Lears
Quarterly

Redivider
www.redividerjournal.org
editor@redividerjournal.org
Editor in Chief: Bradley Babendir
Biannual

River Styx
www.riverstyx.org
BigRiver@riverstyx.org
Managing Editor: Christina Chady
Biannual

Room
www.roommagazine.com
contactus@roommagazine.com
Managing Editor: Chelene Knight
Quarterly

Ruminate
www.ruminatemagazine.com
info@ruminatemagazine.org
Editor in Chief: Brianna Van Dyke
Quarterly

Salamander
www.salamandermag.org
editors@salamandermag.org
Editor in Chief: Jennifer Barber
Biannual

Salmagundi
www.salmagundi.skidmore.edu
salmagun@skidmore.edu
Editor in Chief: Robert Boyers
Quarterly

Saranac Review
www.saranacreview.com
info@saranacreview.com
Editor: Aimée Baker
Annual

The Saturday Evening Post
www.saturdayeveningpost.com
editors@saturdayeveningpost.com
Editor: Steven Slon
Six times a year

Slice
www.slicemagazine.org
editors@slicemagazine.org
Editor in Chief: Beth Blachman
Biannual

Smith's Monthly
www.smithsmonthly.com
dean@deanwesleysmith.com
Editor: Dean Wesley Smith
Monthly

The Southampton Review
www.thesouthamptonreview.com
editors@thesouthamptonreview
.com
Editor: Emily Smith Gilbert
Biannual

The South Carolina Review
www.clemson.edu/caah/sites
    /south-carolina-review/index
    .html
screv@clemson.edu
Editor: Keith Lee Morris
Annual

South Dakota Review
www.southdakotareview.com
sdreview@usd.edu
Editor: Lee Ann Roripaugh
Quarterly

The Southeast Review
www.southeastreview.org
southeastreview@gmail.com
Editor: Zach Linge
Semiannual

Southern Humanities Review
www.southernhumanitiesreview
    .com
shr@auburn.edu
Editors: Anton DiSclafani and
    Rose McLarney
Quarterly

Southern Indiana Review
www.usi.edu/sir
sir@usi.edu
Editor: Ron Mitchell
Biannual

The Southern Review
www.thesouthernreview.org
southernreview@lsu.edu
Editors: Jessica Faust and Sacha
    Idell
Quarterly

Southwest Review
www.southwestreview.com
swr@smu.edu
Editor in Chief: Greg
    Brownderville
Quarterly

St. Anthony Messenger
www.info.franciscanmedia.org
    /st-anthony-messenger
samadmin@franciscanmedia.org
Editor: Christopher Heffron
Monthly

Story
www.storymagazine.org
contact@storymagazine.org
Editor: Michael Nye
Triannual

StoryQuarterly
www.storyquarterly.camden
    .rutgers.edu
storyquarterlyeditors@gmail.com
Editor: Paul Lisicky
Annual

subTerrain
www.subterrain.ca
subter@portal.ca
Editor: Brian Kaufman
Triannual

Subtropics
www.subtropics.english.ufl.edu
subtropics@english.ufl.edu
Editor: David Leavitt
Biannual

The Sun
www.thesunmagazine.org
thesunmagazine.submittable.com
Editor: Sy Safransky
Monthly

Sycamore Review
cla.purdue.edu/academic/english
    /publications/sycamore-review/
sycamore@purdue.edu
Editor in Chief: Anthony Sutton
Biannual

Tahoma Literary Review
www.tahomaliteraryreview.com
fiction@tahomaliteraryreview.com
Fiction Editor: Leanne Dunic
Triannual

Third Coast
www.thirdcoastmagazine.com
editors@thirdcoastmagazine.com
Editor in Chief: Kai Harris
Biannual

The Threepenny Review
www.threepennyreview.com
wlesser@threepennyreview.com
Editor: Wendy Lesser
Quarterly

upstreet
www.upstreet-mag.org
editor@upstreet-mag.org
Fiction Editor: Joyce A. Griffin
Annual

Virginia Quarterly Review
www.vqronline.org
editors@vqronline.org
Editor: Paul Reyes
Quarterly

Washington Square Review
www.washingtonsquarereview.com
washingtonsquarereview@gmail
    .com
Editor in Chief: Joanna Yas
Biannual

Water-Stone Review
www.waterstonereview.com
water-stone@hamline.edu
Editor: Meghan Maloney-Vinz
Annual

Weber
www.weber.edu/weberjournal
weberjournal@weber.edu
Editor: Michael Wutz
Biannual

West Branch
www.westbranch.blogs.bucknell
.edu
westbranch@bucknell.edu
Editor: G. C. Waldrep
Triannual

Western Humanities Review
www.westernhumanitiesreview
.com
ManagingEditor.WHR@gmail
.com
Editor: Michael Mejia
Triannual

Willow Springs
www.willowspringsmagazine.org
willowspringsewu@gmail.com
Editor: Polly Buckingham
Biannual

Witness
www.witness.blackmountain
institute.org
witness@unlv.edu
Editor in Chief: Maile Chapman
Triannual

The Worcester Review
www.theworcesterreview.org
editor.worcreview@gmail.com
Managing Editor: Kate McIntyre
Annual

Workers Write!
www.workerswritejournal.com
info@workerswritejournal.com
Editor: David LaBounty
Annual

World Literature Today
www.worldliteraturetoday.org
dsimon@ou.edu
Editor in Chief: Daniel Simon
Bimonthly

X-R-A-Y
www.xraylitmag.com
xraylitmag@gmail.com
Editor: Jennifer Greidus
Quarterly

The Yale Review
www.yalereview.org
theyalereview@yale.edu
Editor: Megan O'Rourke
Quarterly

Yellow Medicine Review
www.yellowmedicinereview.com
editor@yellowmedicinereview.com
Guest Editor: Terese Mailhot
Semiannual

Yemasee
www.yemasseejournal.com
editor@yemasseejournal.com
Senior Editors: Laura Irei, Charlie
Martin, and Joy Priest
Biannual

Zoetrope All-Story
www.all-story.com
info@all-story.com
Editor: Michael Ray
Quarterly

Zone 3
www.zone3press.com
zone3@apsu.edu
Fiction Editor: Barry Kitterman
Biannual

ZYZZYVA
www.zyzzyva.org
editor@zyzzyva.org
Editor: Laura Cogan
Triannual

Permissions